If Not For This

A novel of
joy and discovery

Nancy Moser

Mustard Seed Press
Overland Park, KS

If Not for This

ISBN 13: 978-1-7368108-7-3

Published by:
Mustard Seed Press
Overland Park, KS

Front cover design by Mustard Seed Press
Image by Victor Tongdee

Printed and bound in the United States of America

THE BOOKS OF NANCY MOSER

www.nancymoser.com

CONTEMPORARY BOOKS

If Not for This
An Undiscovered Life
Eyes of Our Heart
The Invitation (Book 1 Mustard Seed)
The Quest (Book 2 Mustard Seed)***The Temptation*** (Book 3 Mustard Seed)
Crossroads
The Seat Beside Me (Book 1 Steadfast)
A Steadfast Surrender (Book 2 Steadfast)
The Ultimatum (Book 3 Steadfast)
The Sister Circle (Book 1 Sister Circle)
Round the Corner (Book 2 Sister Circle)
An Undivided Heart (Book 3 Sister Circle)
A Place to Belong (Book 4 Sister Circle)
The Sister Circle Handbook (Book 5 Sister Circle)
Time Lottery **(**Book 1 Time Lottery)
Second Time Around (Book 2 Time Lottery)
John 3:16
The Good Nearby
Solemnly Swear
Save Me, God! I Fell in the Carpool (Inspirational humor)
100 Verses of Encouragement—Books 1&2 (illustrated gift books)
Maybe Later (picture book)
I Feel Amazing: the ABCs of Emotion (picture book)

HISTORICAL BOOKS

Where Time Will Take Me (Book 1 Past Times)
Where Life Will Lead Me **(**Book 2 Past Times)
Pin's Promise (novella prequel of Pattern Artist)
The Pattern Artist **(**Book 1 Pattern Artist)
The Fashion Designer (Book 2 Pattern Artist)
The Shop Keepers (Book 3 Pattern Artist)
Love of the Summerfields (Book 1 Manor House)
Bride of the Summerfields (Book 2 Manor House)
Rise of the Summerfields (Book 3 Manor House)
Mozart's Sister (biographical novel of Nannerl Mozart)
Just Jane (biographical novel of Jane Austen)
Washington's Lady (bio-novel of Martha Washington)
How Do I Love Thee? (bio-novel of Elizabeth Barrett Browning)
Masquerade (Book 1 Gilded Age)
An Unlikely Suitor (Book 2 Gilded Age)
The Bridal Quilt (Gilded Age novella)
The Journey of Josephine Cain
A Basket Brigade Christmas (novella collection)
When I Saw His Face (Regency novella)

Dedication

To my daughter Laurel, her husband Jake,
and children Hazel and Forrest.
Your strength and determination
are an inspiration.
May you enjoy God's richest blessings.
You *are* God's richest blessing.

**

How great is the goodness
you have stored up for those who fear you.
You lavish it on those who come to you for protection,
blessing them before the watching world.
Psalm 31:19

PROLOGUE

Wesley & Gracie

If you have faith and don't doubt,
you can do things like this and much more.
Matthew 21: 21

I waited outside the office for my new employee. My only employee.

I'd only met Gracie the one time and had hired her on the spot. It hadn't been an impulsive decision—I was never impulsive. But I was perceptive. I'd immediately known she was the one.

I believe she'd been more surprised to hear herself say yes to the offer than to me asking. Even as I told her the basics about the business, and made arrangements for today's meeting her eyes held onto a wariness, a caution as if she didn't trust me. Hopefully she'd warm up to me—and the work.

I saw her pull into the parking lot and waved her into one of the spaces right outside the door. I saw her give the office a good once-over. She did not look impressed.

With good reason.

"Welcome," I stepped forward as she got out of her car.

She shut the car door. "Thanks, Wesley. I'm not late, am I? You said eight and it's—" Her forehead was furrowed.

I'd appeared too eager. "No, no. You are not late."

Her face relaxed. She looked to the right, then to the left, taking in the strip mall. Our office was the center business. She cocked her head and looked again as though the slight change in visuals would make it better. "I thought the office would be . . . grander. More befitting of the important work you said we'd be doing."

"*Grand* is not for us to say, is it?"

"Apparently not."

I got the keys out of my pocket and handed her a spare.

She eyed it as if it were a foreign object. "You hired me yesterday. I haven't even started and you give me a key?"

"Don't you deserve a key?"

She shrugged and palmed it.

When she followed me inside I noticed once again how petite she was, almost pixie-like with pale blonde hair pulled back in a neat bun. Yet her brightly patterned blouse seemed a bit too large for her, like she was playing dress-up.

Once inside the office, Gracie turned in a circle. "This is it? A white room?"

"What would you prefer?"

She ignored my question. "It reminds me of one of those home improvement shows where everybody gets a white room to decorate."

"I assure you, that is not the case."

She drew in a deep breath. "Do you *have* something against color? I'm no decorator, but even an ivory or a pale green would make it more inviting."

"I'll take your suggestion into consideration." I was not going to question the details of the office—even though *I* wouldn't have minded a soft color on the walls. The point was and would always be: we were not in charge.

Gracie strode to the sleek glass desk that was centered in the middle of the room. She sat on the white rolling chair, touched a notepad with a single pen set next to it. The only other item on the desk was a phone. "Don't I get a computer?"

"There is no need."

She scooted back to better examine the desk. "There aren't any drawers either."

"Again, no need."

She picked up the phone's receiver. "At least there's a dial tone."

"As expected."

Gracie cocked her head. "So a working phone is expected, but a computer and drawers for supplies aren't needed?"

"You have paper and a pen. That will be sufficient."

"To do what?"

"Whatever is required."

She raised a hand between us. "Sorry, but I have to stop you. You hired me to help with your new business, but what can I possibly accomplish with just a pad of paper and a pen? Are you sure you've given me the right setup?"

"I am sure. But if you do find yourself in need of something, just ask."

She shook her head and looked at the phone. "Without a computer for emailing that means clients will call to make an appointment?"

I shook my head. "There will be no appointments."

"Then how do we know who's coming in and when?" Her

eyebrows rose in a challenging manner.

It was a valid question. "We don't," I said.

She expelled her breath with a puff. "Another non-answer."

I hoped she wouldn't be difficult. I stood at the guest side of the desk and peered down at her. "It is the only answer I have, Miss Sturgess. Would you rather I make up something more appealing?"

She shuffled her shoulders. "Actually . . ." She stood. "No offense, Wesley, but this office is a little *too* weird for me. I'm not sure this is going to work."

She couldn't quit. I had to keep her. "I'm sorry if the amenities are not as you hoped, but I do need you here."

"*Need* is a strong word."

I walked to the band of windows to the left of the door. A single guest chair backed against them. The view of the parking lot was uninspiring. As was the busy street and the graffitied bus stop. Trash blew by. The view *was* disappointing—though I would never tell Gracie that.

She stepped beside me, gazed outside, then spread her arms to encompass the breadth of it. "So this is how we rate?"

I turned to face her. "We do not *rate.* We serve."

She scoffed. "I'm used to that."

She was exasperating. I had no idea why we'd been paired together. Our assignment was serious and of the utmost importance. It wasn't to be taken lightly.

She pointed at the two interior doors. "So what's in there?"

"The door furthest back leads to a powder room."

"Noted and appreciated." She pointed at the other door. "I suppose that's *it.* That's the room you mentioned when you hired me?"

"That's not just the room, it is *the* Room, capital R."

She snickered. "Does that mean you are *the* Boss—capital B?"

I shook my head adamantly. "I am not the boss."

"What are you then?"

I thought of a better title. "I am the guide."

"*The* guide, capital G?"

She seemed to enjoy pushing my buttons, "As you wish."

She returned to her chair. "So what's my title?"

"Do you need one?"

"It would be nice."

Although I was instructed to hire her, I wasn't sure exactly how she was going to help. Was she my assistant, receptionist? Troublemaker? Whatever her title, she obviously *would* fill a need at some point. "You may choose your own title."

She grinned. "How about 'associate'? I've always wanted to be someone's associate."

"That sounds appropriate."

She chuckled. "I'm an appropriate associate. I like it." She pointed at the second door, near the front. "Can I see the Room now?"

I swept an arm wide, offering her the chance to open the door.

She hesitated. "Do I just go in?"

"That's generally how it's done."

Gracie pushed the door open tentatively, as if expecting something to jump out at her.

The walls lit up automatically with a soft glow. She stepped inside. "Wow. It's round."

"That, it is."

Gracie touched a wall, then raised an arm overhead without making contact. "Why is it round? It's like stepping into the inside of a sphere."

"Actually, it's a portion of a sphere," I said, for obviously we were standing on a flat floor. "As for why it is a sphere? Because it is necessary."

She gave me a disparaging look. "Sorry, Wesley, but your non-answers are getting old."

"Perhaps."

Gracie sat on the only piece of furniture, a padded, backless stool that was placed in the very center of the space. She spun around in a complete circle. "One lonely chair. Are people going to be interrogated?"

I was going to say "as needed" but found fresher words. "Interrogated is too harsh a word. But there will be interaction."

"Between you and them?"

I remembered the title I'd given myself. "Indeed. Remember, I am their guide."

"To what?"

"Knowledge."

She scoffed, then got off the stool and pushed the door shut from the inside, then opened it again to study it, then closed it again. "This door took some doing. It's shaped like a normal door on the office side, but on this side it's curved to fit into the sphere."

"It *is* ingenious," I said.

Suddenly the sphere was alive with a three-sixty image of outside the office.

Gracie backed up to the middle of the Room. "How did you . . . hey, that's us!" She pointed to a back view of the two of us standing next to Gracie's car. The floor looked like the parking lot.

A boy on a bike drove behind the cars.

"I remember that kid. Wow. We're *in* the movie." She turned in a circle. "It's like looking back in time."

The image faded and the walls were blank again.

"Hey! I want to see more."

"That will be everyone's goal."

"Everyone? You're going to show people movies of themselves?"

"Correct."

"What for?"

"Enlightenment."

She raised her shoulders then dropped them, looking skeptical. "Sorry, Wesley, I'm curious, but hardly enlightened."

I paused a moment, wanting to make sure I said enough, but not too much. "You did not get the full experience, Miss Sturgess. But if you'd like to see more . . ."

She cocked her head and studied me, then swept a stray strand of hair behind an ear. "No thanks. It's not real exciting to see myself walk in the building. I could've seen that much on a security camera. *Was* that from a security camera?"

"It was not. It . . ." I felt a nudge to *not* explain. "You'll have to trust me, but those who come into the Room will leave changed."

"And don't forget 'enlightened.'"

"I would never forget that." She was cheeky. But I liked her.

Gracie nodded toward the door. "Okay then. Why don't you tell me the gist of my duties."

We went back to the main office and I pulled the door of the Room shut behind us.

She sat in her chair. "How would you like me to answer the phone?"

"*Hello* will suffice."

Gracie gave me a slow blink. "Do I say the name of the business and the usual 'how may I help you?'"

"As of this moment there is no name to the business."

"You mentioned that when we first met. I'm pretty sure it's important to have a name. Or are we just going to call it the Room Store? Or . . . Weird Room, Inc. Or—"

I agreed with her. There should be a name.

"Without a name, how are you going to get customers?" Her eyes brightened. "Wait! I've got a tagline for you: *Go to your Room*. Though I'm pretty sure you wouldn't get many takers for that."

"I agree."

She took the pen and readied the notepad. "How much are you

going to charge people to be enlightened?"

"Nothing."

She tossed the pen down. "No name and no income. I hate to break it to you, Wesley, but this isn't a good business plan."

"It doesn't have to be. It is unique."

She scoffed. "Getting selfish here, but I, for one, need a paycheck. Plus, you have to pay rent, phone, utilities . . . Or do you have some rich—rather naive—investor who takes care of everything?"

"Something like that."

She leaned her forearms on the desk. "Good for you. Yet people do *not* make investments for no return. What do they hope to get out of all this—and please don't say 'enlightenment.'"

Although I found her questions annoying, they were giving me good practice. For others were sure to ask similar ones. "The investor is abundantly generous. He doesn't insist on results yet does offer the opportunity for clients to change."

"So this is a self-help company?"

An interesting question. "Not completely. Our clients—and they are clients, not customers—will come with a variety of attitudes."

"Such as?"

"Some will be eager, some reluctant, some dismissive, some fearful, and some may even be confrontational. All are welcome."

She sighed.

"Why the sigh?"

"I thought I was done dealing with difficult people."

I knew of her background and felt empathy for her. "You were chosen because—"

"Chosen?"

"Hired. You were hired because we believe in your ability to handle people in stressful situations."

She eyed me suspiciously. "How would you know that? You've asked me next to nothing about my past or my experience. You hired me blind. Actually . . . why did you do that?"

So many questions. "I am a great judge of character, Miss Sturgess. Some might even consider me intuitive. You are right for this job."

She held the stare a moment longer, then looked away. "I'll have to trust you on that."

I was relieved. "Where were we?"

"You were telling me that some people will be confrontational."

"A few."

"I don't like conflict. Been there, done that."

"I know you will do fine. When they arrive, greet them, and lead them into the Room. I will take it from there."

"I can do that." She looked toward the windows. "Back to our name . . . The Choice Store, Enlightenment Unlimited . . . discover something-or-other."

I appreciated her input. "I like the essence of the last name the best."

She gazed upward. Then her eyes brightened. "How about the Discovery Room?"

I let the idea simmer a moment. "I approve."

She beamed. "Do I get a bonus?"

"It will be considered." I cleared my throat. "From now on this office will be called the Discovery Room because every client will come out of the Room after discovering something important about their lives."

Gracie crossed her arms. "Not every client, Wesley. I didn't discover a thing. It appears you have a few kinks to work out."

"You did *not* experience the Room in its full glory."

She shook her head. "If this was a soft opening, it needs a lot of work."

"It does not. We are ready for our first client."

She leaned back in her chair and swept an arm toward the view. "Yeah, I see them lining up outside, clamoring to come in."

"They will be here at exactly the right time. It's a promise."

"Meanwhile . . . ?"

"Meanwhile we wait."

She nodded toward the Room. "Can I get HBO in there?"

"Sorry no. But feel free to bring a book to read."

Her eyebrows rose. "Actually I don't object to getting paid to do nothing, but . . ."

"It will not be nothing." I turned toward the door. "If you are settled I'll be off now."

"To do what exactly? Other than being the guide what's your part in this?"

"I need to contact some clients."

"Good luck with that."

Luck would not be involved.

****

A few minutes after Wesley left, I started to explore the place.

The office area didn't deserve a second look as there were only two chairs and my totally impractical glass desk. No matter how I looked at it, it was still just a dreary office in a dull strip mall—with no sign above the door or on the windows. And with no computer . . . I was pretty sure there wasn't a website either. Somebody needed a lesson in marketing. Thankfully, *that* wasn't my job.

The one thing that held any interest was the Room.

I strolled to the front door to make sure no one was about to come in, then went into the Room. I kept the door open. I ran my fingers along the walls but I couldn't feel or see any seams. The contractor who did the drywall deserved an excellent review.

Previously, the Room had been filled with a 360-movie. How had Wesley made that happen? He'd been standing right behind me . . .

I scoured the walls for a button of some kind. There was nothing. No light switch or electrical outlets either. There was one drawer that popped out, but it was nearly invisible and was empty.

"Maybe he had a remote that turned on a projector."

It was a logical assumption. Except . . .

I checked things out overhead. I didn't see any projector. With difficulty I stood on the swivel stool, trying to balance. My fingers skimmed the center ceiling where a light should be but I found nothing. No lens or opening of any kind. I was no techie, but shouldn't there be *something*?

"Hello?"

My heart rushed to my throat and I jumped down. "Just a minute."

I left the Room, pulling the door shut behind me. A man stood just inside the entrance. "May I help you?" I asked.

"I'm here to install a sign on the front window."

"A sign?" As of fifteen minutes ago we didn't have a name.

He unfolded a piece of paper that was in his pocket. "The Discovery Room. Is that right?"

"Well, yeah. I guess it is."

He folded the order into fourths, put it in his pocket, and pointed at the windows to the left of the door. "Here, I suppose?"

"That looks good."

"I'll get to work then." He went out to his van and returned with a large roll of vinyl.

"Can I see it first?"

"Of course." He unrolled the vinyl to reveal the words "The Discovery Room" written out in elegant font. "Do you approve?"

"It's really nice."

"We aim to please. Don't let me bother you, I'll be done in a jiff."

I sat on my chair, totally confused. How had Wesley arranged for a sign to be created, printed, and installed in mere minutes? Maybe he had the name already picked out and somehow he'd led me right to it? I tried to remember who'd come up with the final name.

Not ten minutes later the man was packing away his supplies. "Let's take a look outside. If it's acceptable I need you to sign off on it."

We stepped out. The sign looked real good. Professional. The letters were ivory with a royal blue outline. "It looks great."

He showed me where to sign. "Glad you like it. Have a good day."

He got in his van and left. Too late I realized I probably should have gotten a receipt. Or an invoice.

To put where? In my non-existent drawers?

I returned to my desk and just sat there, looking at the sign, waiting for our first client—who would *not* have an appointment and would not have to pay anything.

All indicators pointed to the Discovery Room folding sooner rather than later.

Chapter One

Tony

Backsliders get what they deserve;
good people receive their reward.
Proverbs 14: 14

I tried to sneak past my supervisor's office.

"Amato! Get in here!"

So much for sneaking. I backtracked and put on my most charming face. "Hey, boss. What's up?"

With a groan, Gus stood up from behind his messy desk and moved two boxes from the floor to the top of it. "Care to explain these?"

Not really. "Sorry. They were my last two deliveries yesterday, I was running late. I'll get them out first thing today. Promise."

"That's not the way it works, and you know it. People were promised delivery by end-of-day and now they're mad, which makes me mad, and you don't want me mad." He looked at me sideways. "Or do you?"

Gus was always mad about something. "Of course not. I got it." I went to pick up the boxes, but Gus motioned me back.

"Unfortunately, three strikes and you're out, Amato."

"Out?"

He stood, then hooked a thumb over his shoulder. "Gone."

He had to be kidding. "I'll deliver them first thing. Right now. And I'll work through lunch. It won't happen again."

Gus shook his head. "No can do. I've given you too many chances already."

He couldn't be serious. I'd made a little mistake. It was no big deal. I took a step toward his desk to plead my case.

Gus took a step back and put his hands in the air. Like I was threatening him.

In the six months I'd worked here, I *had* set myself up as a tough guy. But it was all for show – most of it anyway.

Being six-three and 280 could've made me come off as either a massive teddy bear or a brute. I chose the latter because there was power in intimidation. I'd known that since I was eleven, when Harry

Romano moved in next door. I was a hefty kid, but he was bigger and scared the pasta out of me. When I impressed him by landing a lucky hit on his chin he took me under his wing and taught me the advantages of being feared.

Gus flipped a hand at me. "Back off, Amato. And get outta here. We'll send your last paycheck."

"Come on, Gus. Give a guy a break. It was my kid's tenth birthday. Plus, you know I've had a hard year with the divorce."

His pudgy face softened, but he shook his head. "I couldn't do it even if I wanted to. I got bosses too." He sat down with an *oomph.* "Go on now. I wish you well."

No, he didn't.

But I left anyway.

In the parking lot I saw another driver walking toward his truck. I waved. When he didn't wave back, I saw a certain look on his face. He knew what had happened.

How many other guys knew I was going to be canned? Antonio Amato didn't appreciate looking like a chump.

Though I shoulda been used to it by now.

To show 'em how little I cared, I got in my car and peeled out of the parking lot.

I was lying about not caring *and* about me going to my kid's party. I couldn't even do that right. I *had* driven over to my ex's. I just couldn't handle being around Penny's family with their judgmental eyes and snide comments. They believed our broken family was all my fault. The fact they were ninety-percent right made seeing them impossible.

I'd pulled up to Penny's house—which used to be *our* house—and sat in my car. Over the fence I could see they were having the party in the backyard. Laughter. Balloons. A bounce house. The works. I'd even bought Zach a present - a football. But when a baseball came flying over the fence I realized I'd stupidly picked the wrong sport. I was the one who liked football. Zach played baseball. I wasn't sure how many games I'd already missed. There was no way I could go to the party.

I had no job and no family. I was definitely a two-time loser.

**

What was I supposed to do now?

Out of a job, I drove around for an hour, trying to enjoy my newfound free time. It was annoying to realize that when I had a job, I wanted more free time, but now that I had free time, I wanted a job.

Needed a job. I had rent to pay, a car payment, alimony, child-support. And—oh yeah—food. I was in a deep, slimy hole with no way out.

To distract myself I pulled into a Home Depot. There was something about this place that made me feel good. Maybe it was the memories of me and my dad buying stuff for projects. Or Penny and I buying a patio set back when we were happy. Whatever the reason, I tried to tap into any mood that was different from the mood I was in.

I strolled up and down the aisles, checked out the newest grills, sets of socket wrenches, and fancy tools. I didn't need any of them and couldn't spend money on them even if I did.

I noticed a steady stream of construction guys coming in for building supplies. They all had jobs, probably had the same job for ages. They didn't get fired three times in a year. At the end of the day they probably went home to happy families, coached their kids' ball games, and went on date nights with their wives.

They weren't losers like me.

I'd slipped down into that hole again. It was time to go home.

Home? What a joke. For the past year I hadn't had a real home. I lived in a crummy studio apartment with stained carpet and leaky faucets. Drip. Drip. Drop. A loser who didn't have a job, a family, or a home.

I turned to leave and nearly ran into a guy. He wore the usual orange apron so he must've worked there. "Sorry," I said.

"Can I help you find something, sir?"

I shook my head. "I ain't no 'sir', and no. I gotta go."

He took a half-step to the side to block me. "Before you go, I have something to give you."

Really, old man? He looked like a retiree who'd gotten a job to pass the time. "Whatever you're peddling I'm not interested."

"You should be."

I paused to look at him. His nametag said *Wesley*. "You got a lotta guts. Wesley is it?"

He smiled. "I will do whatever it takes to complete my assignment." He held out a white envelope. "For you."

"Listen, I don't want a credit card or vinyl siding or—" My name was written on the envelope. I grabbed it from him. "How do you know my name?"

He shrugged slightly. "You are specially invited."

I scoffed. I hadn't been specially invited to anything since my divorce papers were served. "To what?"

He waved an open hand toward the invitation. "Open it."

Inside was a white card: *Come to the Discovery Room at 316*

Crossway Road for special training. It sounded like a scam. "I just lost my job. I don't need special training."

"*Since* you lost your job, perhaps that's exactly what you need."

I handed the card back to him. "No thanks."

Wesley didn't take it. "Keep it. Perhaps you'll change your mind." He stepped out of the way. "Have a good day, Mr. Amato."

Fat chance.

**

I sat on the fold-out couch in my apartment and watched TikTok videos. Some made me smile, some were amazing, and some were cringeworthy, but it passed the time. And it helped drown out the volume of the TV coming from the next apartment. I'd never been home in the afternoon and had no idea that the old man who lived there watched game shows all day. Loudly. I'd tried banging on the wall but nothing changed.

I was going to go crazy.

My phone rang. It was Penny—who drove me another kind of crazy. She'd called a half-dozen times since yesterday's birthday party.

I figured I might as well take my lumps so I could move on. I closed TikTok and answered. "Yeah?"

"Where were you yesterday?"

"Sorry. I couldn't get off work."

"Really Tony? You should've called."

True. I should have. "I'm sure Zach didn't even miss me, what with your family there."

"How do you know my family came?"

Oops. "They always come. They were there, right?"

"*They* were. But Zach's father wasn't. What's wrong with that picture?"

Plenty. I knew it was wrong. My lack of Dad-skills was one of the reasons we'd broken up. In truth I didn't have many husband-skills either. Add that to the loser list. "Tell him I'm sorry." Yet maybe I could make amends. "Let me talk to him."

"You can't. He's at school."

Duh. It was probably for the best. I didn't do kid-speak well. "Like I said, tell him I'm sorry, okay?"

"Sure," Penny said with a loud sigh. "What's one more time covering for you?"

I didn't feel up to remembering more of my failures. "Anything else? I gotta get back to work."

"As if I don't?"

Round and round we'd go . . . "I gotta go, Pen. Bye."

"Whatever."

She hung up.

I felt a gnawing in the pit of my stomach. I was used to the going-no-where conversations and the ache that followed. From experience, I knew the best way to move on was to distract myself.

I turned back to Tik Tok and watched dancing dog videos while the sound of game-show applause and shouts echoed from next door.

I let myself drown in the absurdity of my life.

CHAPTER TWO

Minnie

The Lord directs the steps of the godly.
He delights in every detail of their lives.
Psalm 37: 23

I knew—without a doubt—that I would never use anything I learned in my Managerial Economics class. Taking notes was as boring as making a shopping list. Actually a shopping list was more interesting—times ten.

When the class ended—finally ended—I left the building and walked to my favorite patch of grass. I had an hour before I had to take a test in my next class--Business Policy and Strategy. Another barn-buster.

I sat with my back against my favorite tree—a huge oak that had to be over a hundred years old. In the fall it pelted me with orange leaves, and in the late spring it shaded me from the sun. We were friends.

I mentally shoved my classes aside and took out my sketchpad. Today I wanted to sketch people walking, specifically from the waist down. I had the most trouble with feet, trying to capture the view of the shoes coming and going. Sometimes I could see the top of the shoe, other times it was just a horizontal line, or a heel, or—

"Boo!"

My best friend, Ashley, dropped down beside me. She glanced at my drawings. "Legs and shoes?"

"In motion. It's hard."

She scooted to my right, finding a place to lean against the massive trunk. "If it's hard for you, I would find it impossible." She sighed deeply.

I remembered she'd had a test. "How did you do on your Russian history exam?" I asked.

"Aced it. I currently know everything there is to know about Ivan the Terrible—just in case you ever want to ask."

"*Was* he terrible?"

She nodded. "That he was. He liked to assassinate anybody who didn't agree with him—including his own son."

"How nice."

"Speaking of nice . . ." She swiveled to face me. "Tonight the Doorknobs are playing at the Union. A bunch of people from my dorm are going. Wanna come? You can crash in my dorm room after."

It was mildly tempting. "I'd better not. Mom was supposed to have a date tonight, but the guy canceled. She'll need me."

Ashley threw her hands in the air. "I need you, Min. In case you didn't know, college is more than just classes. It's being with friends, and you dear one, are noticeably absent most of the time."

I didn't have time for socializing. Right or wrong, my life revolved around my family. Since my parents' divorce I'd spent weekends at Dad's with my step-mom, Claudia, and their ten-month-old twins. They were ridiculously happy. During the week I lived forty-minutes from campus with Mom, who wasn't.

Mom was needy right now because she was between boyfriends. Although I hadn't liked any of her exes, I liked Mom better when she was dating someone she thought was special. She was happier. She smiled and was more easy going. Unfortunately, few of her boyfriends lasted more than a couple months. Sometimes she did the dumping, but most of the time, they dumped her. I always tried to build her up again—until the next one came along. Dad being happy and having a new family was like Mom getting dumped a zillion times.

"So will you come with us?"

"I'm sorry Ash, I just can't."

"You never say yes to hanging out with me anymore." Ashley stood and brushed off the back of her jeans. "This isn't how we planned it. "

"Sorry. But Mom's all alone."

Ashley shook her head. "So you're going to live at home forever? It's coming up on two years that I've been living here without you."

"I know. I'm trying to move out."

She made a *phht* sound. "Not hard enough." She pointed at my sketchbook. "You also promised *yourself* that you would get an art degree, not one in business."

"My dad really wants me to—"

"Stop, Min, just stop." She looked heavenward, her arms out. "What are we going to do with her?"

"Don't go calling God down on me. Even He says we're supposed to honor our parents."

"Honor them by becoming a full-fledged adult who makes her own choices."

"I am making choices. I'm choosing—"

"Yeah, yeah."

I hated when we argued.

But then, I heard a voice that might save me from the moment. "Hey Minnie."

I looked toward the sidewalk. "Hey, Gabe."

He walked across the grass, flashed me an amazing smile, then looked at Ashley. "Ashley, right?"

She smiled her cute-boy smile. "Hi, Gabe. Whatcha up to?"

"Class and more class. Winding up my college experience."

Ashley seemed confused, so I explained. "Gabe's graduating in May."

"That, I am," he said.

"In art, right?" Ashley asked, flashing a look in my direction.

I answered for him. "Gabe is a great painter."

His dark eyebrows lowered, making him look just like Mom's favorite singer, Josh Groban. "When have you seen my work?"

I looked down, embarrassed that I'd overstated. I'd seen one of his paintings. "There was an exhibition of student work at the union a while back, right?"

"Yeah. There was."

"Your piece was stunning." I wasn't lying.

"Glad you liked it." He dropped his backpack on the ground and sat. "How's *your* art going? I haven't seen you at the art store for a while."

Because I hadn't needed any supplies. "Actually it's not going much of anywhere. At all."

"That's not true," Ashley said. "Show him your legs."

I felt my cheeks grow hot. I opened my sketch pad. "She means *these* legs."

He took the pad to see better, and even flipped to other pages of heads and arms and trees.

"I'm just a beginner," I said.

"You're more than that." He handed the sketchbook back to me. "After seeing what you're doing there? I still think you're in the wrong major."

"That's what I keep telling her," Ashley said.

"If you ever want a tour of the art department, just ask." He got up. "Speaking of asking, my roommate and I are having a party at our place a week from tomorrow. You're both invited."

"Thanks," Ashley said. She took out her phone. "What's the address?"

I took out my phone too and typed it in, along with his phone number.

"I gotta get going," Ashley said. "Maybe I'll see you later, huh, Gabe?"

"Maybe."

"I need to get going too," I said. "I have a test in business strategies."

He took my hand and helped me up. "That sounds awful."

"Pretty much." We were heading in different directions. "I'll see you later."

"At my party, I hope."

"I'll do my best." I gave him a parting smile and walked to class.

And I *would* try my best, I really would. Gabe and I had met a year ago in Art's Art Shop where he worked. It was my go-to store whenever family got too much for me, which was often. I hadn't bought that much—mostly drawing supplies, but he was always fun to talk to. Once, I'd shown him a sketch of my mom—drawn from a photo because no way would Mom ever sit for me. He'd said I had talent. Plus, he'd been a TA in my art history class that I'd taken as an elective. He'd worked with my small group, and had asked me out for coffee more than once. I still didn't understand why I'd never accepted. Other than that, I rarely saw him around, seeings how the art and business departments were on opposite ends of campus.

But I was glad I'd seen him today. As far as going to his party? Unlike most social stuff, I really wanted to go. Just the way he'd smiled stirred something in me. Maybe I needed to pay more attention to him.

**

I drove home from college, blasting music all the way as I thought about Gabe and concerts and Mom and . . . life. It was weirdly ironic that one of the songs on the radio was by the Doorknobs.

I parked on the street since Mom got the garage. I walked toward the front door but pulled up short at the bottom of the porch steps. An older guy was standing in front of our door like he was ready to ring the bell. "Can I help you?"

He smiled then looked down at an envelope. "Perhaps. Are you Minerva McLaughlin?"

I squinted my eyes in momentary confusion. Nobody called me that. "I'm Minnie."

He came down the steps and handed me the envelope. "This is for you."

"What are you selling? Cuz we don't—"

"I'm not selling anything." He paused. "Forgive me for being rude. My name is Wesley, and this is an invitation especially for you."

"An invitation to what?"

"Open it and see."

I broke the seal, pulled out a card, and read it silently. "What's the Discovery Room?"

"It's a company that specializes in self-discovery. We offer insights that help people reach their full potential."

It sounded stupid, like some guru-psycho-babble-con. I handed the card back to him. "No thanks. I'm good."

He cocked his head. "So you *have* reached your potential?"

"Of course not. Have you?" Take that, mister.

"I have not." He handed me the invitation again. "I encourage you to think about it."

I looked at the card. "So what happens if I come?"

"We will help you pinpoint ways that you can pursue your dreams."

I shook my head. "I don't have time for dreams."

He cocked his head. "Everyone has dreams—or they should have." He nodded toward my sketch pad. "Are you an art major?"

I shook my head. "Business."

"But you are an artist too? You're interested in art?"

"I'm interested, sure. But my dad . . . he says a business degree is more practical."

"I see." He cocked a finger toward the house. "Are you visiting for the weekend?"

"Not visiting. I live here with my mom."

"Not on campus?"

"What can I say? She needs me."

He nodded once.

"Well, thanks, Wesley . . ."

"I encourage you to come see us, Miss McLaughlin—whenever it suits you. You don't need an appointment."

That was sketchy. "Okay."

"So we can expect you at your convenience?"

Man, he was persistent. "I don't know. But thanks for the invite."

"'Knock and the door will be opened,'" he said. "Have a nice evening."

He walked to the sidewalk and turned left. I waited to see if he went to the neighbor's front door, but he didn't. That could have made me feel special, but it mostly creeped me out because it meant he only came to my house. With a invitation. With my name on it. This was beyond weird.

My phone rang and I dug it out of my backpack. It was Mom.

"Hi." I unlocked the door and went inside. She wanted to know what I was making for dinner and to remind me to put a load of clothes in the washer. She'd be home in an hour.

A long time ago I'd accepted that *this* was my reality. Dreams were for everyone else.

**

The timer on the oven went off just as Mom got home. She came in carrying a huge sack of artificial flowers. Mom loved crafting, especially making wreaths. She dumped the sack on the couch then came into the kitchen. "Smells good. Is it what I think it is?"

"Spaghetti casserole." I took it out of the oven. The cheese on top was melted into gooey deliciousness. "I'm going to broil garlic bread. It'll be ready in a few."

"Give me a minute to change. You wouldn't believe the day I've had."

"Good or bad?"

She hesitated just a moment, as if she hadn't thought of it in those terms. She came up with, "Busy."

I knew I'd hear all about it. Mom worked at Hobby Lobby, her favorite place in the whole world. She'd worked there for years, ever since she stopped getting alimony from Dad.

I watched the butter on the French bread bubble and the edges brown. Perfection. I took the pan out of the oven, put two pieces on each plate, took up a hefty serving of casserole, and set them on the kitchen table. I got out the lettuce salad and sat down.

Where was she? "Mom? It's getting cold."

She walked into the room, slipping an arm into an old sweatshirt that said *I'm sorry. Did I roll my eyes out loud?* on the front. She fell onto her chair with an *oomph.* "Looks great, hon. Though I *was* looking forward to dinner with Jason." She sighed deeply. "I think he hates me."

It was her usual response to the smallest slight. "Jason doesn't hate you. Something came up. That happens."

"That happens all the time with me. No guy ever makes me his first priority. I'm going to be alone for the rest of my life."

"No, you aren't. You just need to wait for the right guy."

"It's been eight years. Your dad's remarried and has twins. When is it my turn?"

I didn't have an answer for her. I never had an answer for her.

It was best to change the subject. "So tell me about work."

She took a bite of salad and was off and running. "It got so busy that I only got fifteen for lunch. Fourth of July stuff came in today. Can you believe it? It's only April and . . ."

I stopped listening as she went through her day, step by step. Mom was a great conversationalist—as long as she was giving a monologue. I'd learned to go with the flow.

I tried interrupting a few times when she took a breath, but she jumped right back in. Even though I was used to it, tonight it was annoying. I'd given up the Doorknobs for her.

During one of her brief pauses I managed to say, "I was invited to go to a concert tonight. On campus."

Mom blinked, clearly flipping her thoughts from her work to me. "Why didn't you go? You should go."

She always said that, but I knew she didn't mean it. "I thought you'd be upset about your canceled dinner."

She squeezed my hand. "You're so sweet."

Yes, I was. I asked a question that would make me even sweeter. "Want to watch a movie tonight?"

"A Hallmark movie?"

Mom was obsessed with Hallmark movies. I liked them too, but once in a while I liked a story beyond boy-meets-girl. Yet it was easier to give in. "Sure," I said. "You can choose."

She clapped. "You are so good to me."

I'm glad she noticed.

CHAPTER THREE

Lydia

When troubles of any kind come your way,
consider it an opportunity for great joy.
For you know that when your faith is tested,
your endurance has a chance to grow.
So let it grow, for when your endurance is fully developed,
you will be perfect and complete, needing nothing.
James 1: 2-8

I hated my job.

I knew it wasn't fair to say that after only three hours, but it was the truth. Sitting in front of a computer forty hours a week might appease my husband's desire that I find something "satisfying" to do now that we were empty nesters. But sitting alone in a cubicle with no window in sight, entering data all day, was very *un*satisfying, and it wasn't going to fill any emotional, intellectual, or spiritual need.

My fingers typed as if they had a mind of their own—good thing, because my brain was somewhere else.

In my *before* life—before this job at the Department of Economic Security, aka the welfare office—I would have been at the city mission right now, helping in the kitchen, getting ready to serve lunch. I used to do that two days a week. On Monday, Wednesday, Friday I worked at our daughter's high school as a mentor. Helping kids who needed a little one-on-one attention made me appreciate JoJo. She excelled in every subject and had gotten through high-school unscathed. I liked to think I had something to do with that. Of course my husband being an amazing father didn't hurt either.

I finished entering a page of data and paused to rub my eyes. I already missed seeing the faces of the people I helped. Many of those at the mission who came through the chow line looked sad when they took up their plate. But after getting a good meal in their bellies and hearing a few kind words shared by me and the other volunteers, their pain eased. For the moment at least. Some even managed a smile.

The kids I helped at the high school were all very special to me. Though we sometimes started out rough, they grew to trust me, and I grew to love them as my own. We filled each other's empty places with smiles and a listening ear.

There were no smiles here. No eyes. No faces. Just the beige divider walls, the tap-tap-tapping of keyboards, and the hum of people on the phone. Disjointed words hopped over the partitions into my cubicle. My cell.

I was just starting another page when my boss, Mrs. Smith, stopped by. "How are you doing, Ms. Brogdon? Any questions about the position?"

How was I doing? I was frustrated, stifled, and miserable, and my only question was *why am I here?* But wanting to please, I said, "No questions yet. I'm doing okay."

"Good. Let me know if you need anything."

I thanked her, but inside I wanted to scream. *I want out!*

At least it would be lunch soon.

**

My plan was foiled.

I'd planned to go to the cafeteria to eat and meet people. If the actual work wasn't the reason God planted me at this welfare office, maybe it was the people.

I went through the line and got a sandwich and fruit cup, then scanned the room for somewhere to sit. Someone to sit with.

Most people were sitting alone, looking at their phones. It made me sad. How was it that the technology that opened up the world closed us off?

I spotted a young woman I'd seen in a cubicle near mine. I walked to her table. "May I sit here?"

She squinted when she looked up. "Sure."

I sat across from her, but to the side just a bit, to give her space. "Hi, I'm new." I held my hand across the table. "Lydia."

She wiped a hand on her leg, then shook the tips of my fingers. "Tammy." She went back to her salad, stabbing a cherry tomato. Her phone pinged.

She picked it up and started texting.

And . . . I lost her.

Even surrounded by people, I ate my lunch alone.

**

After being back in my cubicle an hour my mouse suddenly stopped working. I opened up the back, rolled the batteries to see if that would help. It didn't. I needed new ones.

I walked around my partition to the next cubicle that was inhabited by a balding, non-descript man. It was a rude assessment, but since I could only see his back . . . "Hi. Where do I get fresh batteries?"

He turned his head toward my voice the slightest bit as his fingers kept moving. "Supply room. Turn right at the corner, then left, then last door on the left."

"Thanks."

After only backtracking once, I found the room that had a SUPPLIES sign above it. There was a counter and stool in front of shelves and shelves of office supplies.

"Hello?"

A man with silver hair came out of the back and actually smiled at me. "How may I help you this fine afternoon?" he asked.

"I need two AA batteries. My mouse died."

"We can't have that, can we, Mrs. Brogdon?"

I was pleasantly surprised. "How do you know my name?"

He winked. "It is my job to know. "

"What's *your* name?"

"Wesley." He shook my hand. "Nice to meet you." He was a handsome older gentleman, probably near retirement age. But most importantly, he had a friendly face.

He turned a clipboard toward me. "Just sign here for what you're taking." He looked up and down the shelves as if he didn't know where batteries were located.

I could see them. "Over there. To the left."

"Thank you." He retrieved the right ones.

When I turned to leave he stopped me by saying, "I have something else for you."

He took a white envelope out of his shirt pocket. "For you."

It had my name on it. I assumed it was some kind of welcome letter. "You're the welcome wagon too?"

His smile made the corners of his eyes crinkle. "I guess I am."

I opened the card. Inside was an invitation to go to the Discovery Room for "special training"—at my convenience. I chuckled. "I'm not sure what special training I need to enter data, but if it gets me out of the building, I'm in."

Wesley cocked his head. "Weary already? It's only your first day."

I felt bad for disparaging the work. "Sorry about that. I appreciate the job. This is my first day working full time in ages. I've been at home raising my daughter for 18 of her 19 years. She's finishing out her freshman year at college."

"Good for her."

It felt wonderful to have a listening ear. "I decided to get a job, but being back in an office is . . . different. I'm sure I'll get used to it."

"If that's what you want to do."

What an odd thing to say. "Excuse me?"

Wesley ignored my question and pointed at the invitation. "Perhaps I will see you there."

"*You* need special training?"

He chuckled. "We all do."

**

I almost fell asleep driving home. Rush hour traffic in Kansas City was brutal. An accident up ahead slowed it down even more.

Once home, I was surprised to see Jeremy's car in the garage. When he was in town he usually didn't get home until at least six.

Then I noticed the time: 6:15. No way.

I hung my purse on a hook by the door to the garage. I braced myself for the "what's for dinner?" question and tried to squelch my initial reaction which would be some hearty cuss words—in mind, if not in speech.

"Sorry I'm so late," I said as I entered the kitchen. "There was an acci—"

Jeremy stood there beaming, holding a huge bouquet of flowers. "Happy first day!"

The cuss words scurried into hiding as he kissed my cheek. I took in the heady aroma of tulips and freesia. "Thank you, honey. They're beautiful."

As I turned to find a vase in a lower cabinet, I spotted an even better gift than flowers. Chinese food. I turned back to him. "You're my hero."

While I arranged the flowers, Jeremy took up the orange chicken and crab Rangoon. We sat at the island—a new habit since JoJo went off to college.

We ate a few bites in silence. "So," he finally said. "How was it?"

The full truth would sound whiny, so I tempered it. A bit. "My fingers hurt and my vision is blurry from looking at a screen."

"Did you meet some nice people?"

"I had a lovely conversation with a girl named Tammy." *Hi-bye.* "Then I met a nice older gentleman named Wesley. He actually smiled."

Jeremy gave me a pained look. "Hang in there. Working in a big government office should let you meet loads of people. Were you even trying?"

I didn't answer.

"Give it a chance, Lyd. *You* chose a data entry job because you thought it would give your mind a chance to wander, to think. To heal."

I remembered saying those words. "Unfortunately, I think I was wrong. I didn't have a single original thought the entire day. It's like my mind was on cruise control."

"Maybe cruise control is good for a while. You've been through so much."

He wasn't talking about JoJo moving out. I dipped a crab Rangoon in a plastic ramekin of sweet and sour sauce, took a bite, and tried to think of something positive to say. "I did get invited to some special training."

"Why is it special?"

"I don't know exactly. Wesley gave me a card with the info on it. I'm supposed to go to an office 'at my convenience.'" I took it out of my purse to show him.

"It says Discovery *Room?* That's odd."

I hadn't really thought about it, but yes it was. "Maybe they'll hook me up to a bunch of electrodes and zap my brain." I took a bite of chicken. I wanted to change the subject. "No more work talk. When we're done eating, do you want to binge watch something with me?"

"Like what?"

I shrugged. "I'm not picky. I know I'll fall asleep before the second episode."

He wrapped his arm around my shoulders. "How about one of your favorites: 'Downton Abbey'?"

"Ah, Jer. What did I ever do to deserve you?"

His answer was a smile and a wink.

Chapter Four

Gracie

Pay careful attention to your own work,
for then you will get the satisfaction of a job well done,
and you won't need to compare yourself to anyone else.
Galatians 6: 4

Although having a pud job sounded fun, it wasn't.

Since I had a key, Wesley told me to come in every day at eight—though I had no idea why, because so far no one had shown up. Not even Wesley.

On the third day I came into an office that had been painted a lovely sage green. It felt good to know that Wesley had listened to me.

Because of the paint, I grew bolder. I thought of a few items that would make the office more cheery. If Wesley had been around I would have asked him first, but since he wasn't . . .

I brought in a small table from home and set a Keurig on it, plus sweetener and a mismatched set of mugs. As a child I'd always given Mom a mug on Mother's Day. Might as well put a few of them to good use. Our clients needed to feel welcome, right? And I needed coffee. There was one mug that was mine alone: *Commas save lives: let's eat, Grandma. Let's eat Grandma.* Ha. It was perfect because I was a writer of sorts. I posted short essays on social media.

I also brought in a philodendron I'd had for years and set it on a plant stand by a window. And most recently, I hung a framed landscape that we'd had hanging in the hallway at home. The new paint complemented the green of the fields perfectly. It was a good start. I hoped Wesley wouldn't mind.

To pass the time I brought in my Kindle and had already read one-and-a-half books. Plus, my phone was getting a workout from solitaire and Wordscapes.

I was working on a particularly tricky game when I looked up and saw Wesley walking toward the door. My stomach flipped. I set my phone down. There was no reason to be nervous, yet the fact I hadn't seen him since that first day made his coming more important than it should have been.

I stood—which was a strange thing to do, but by the time I realized how strange, it was too late to take it back. "Hey there," I said when he came in.

"Good morning."

He appeared as trim and neat as he had before, like a silver-haired executive in a fancy car commercial.

I saw his eyes scan my office additions. I quickly said, "Thank you for having the walls painted. It's a nice color."

"Yes, it is." His gaze touched on the plant, the landscape, and finally came to rest on the coffee station. I rushed to my defense. "I thought it would be nice to offer clients coffee—plus, I need it to stay awake. This job is not exactly exhilarating."

"I realize it's been slow, but people *have* been invited."

I sat down and took up the singular pen and pad of paper. "Good. Finally, something to write down. What's the schedule?"

"As I said before, there are no appointments. There is no schedule."

"Then how do we know when people are coming?"

He checked his watch. "The first should arrive any minute now."

This didn't make sense. "If there isn't a schedule, then how do you know a client is about to show up?"

"When it's time for people to come, they will come."

I rolled my eyes. "I am never going to get a straight answer out of you, am I?"

"Truthful, yes. Straight?" He shrugged. "You know that patience is a virtue."

"Not my virtue. Is testing my patience your goal?"

"Not at all." He looked out the windows. "Since I expect our first client is coming today I'd like to tell you how it works."

Finally, some direction. "I'm all ears."

"I will not be here when people arrive."

"Why not?"

"I am not needed at first. Greet them, lead them into the Room, tell them to have a seat, and their experience will take over."

"Their *experience?*"

"Didn't you have an experience in the Room—short though it was?"

"I saw myself outside this building."

"The clients will see similar moments in time."

"They'll see *me* outside this building?" I put on a sarcastic face.

"Very amusing."

"Do I take their name and information?"

"No need. Just lead them to the Room. I will arrive at the right time and will periodically go in and converse with them. Any questions?"

"A few hundred."

He opened the door to leave. "You'll do just fine. I shall return."

I poured myself a second cup of coffee.

CHAPTER FIVE

Tony

Fear of the Lord
is the foundation of true wisdom.
Psalm 111: 10

I wanted to sleep late—meaning after eight—but the fact I could hear other tenants getting up to go to work made it impossible. Toilets flushed, people talked, kids ran, doors slammed, and a parade stomped down the stairs. And why did the majority of the cars driving by need new mufflers?

I burrowed into the pillow and closed my eyes for one more try at sleep.

I was almost there until someone dropped a pan in the apartment above me.

I whipped the covers off. "All right, all right. I'm up."

I went through my morning routine and grabbed a bowl of Frosted Flakes. I sat on the kitchen chair and looked for jobs on my phone. Since I never kept a job long, I was getting used to the process.

I opened the website of my usual job-placement company and logged on. I was just starting the search when my phone went dead. Completely dead.

Which didn't make sense. It had been plugged in all night. I fiddled with the cord and plugged it in again.

Until it had some juice in it I thought about places I could apply. So many of them had already turned me away or weren't hiring. I knew I could probably get a job at a fast food place. I'd never done food service but getting free food would help the budget—though not my weight. If I wasn't careful I'd succumb to the Flabby Forties.

To top off the annoyance-level of the morning, the neighbor's TV turned on. Another day, another game show.

If I stayed home, I'd break something. Or someone.

Fast food was worth a try.

I put my bowl in the sink to head out to the nearest McDonald's. Grabbing my car keys, I spotted the invitation from the Home Depot guy on the counter.

I read it again. Special training? That could mean almost anything.

I tossed it down, but immediately picked it up again. Maybe some training would help me find a job that was better than what I'd had before

It was worth a shot.

**

I parked in front of the Discovery Room. It sure didn't look like a place that delivered special training. I'd expected a snazzy corporate office, not a space in a strip mall.

Yet it couldn't be all bad. It was sandwiched between a Fan-tastic sports store and a liquor store. If all else failed I'd grab myself a new Chiefs shirt and a six-pack.

I hoped they had free coffee. I was all out at home.

I went inside and was greeted by a cute 30-something woman. She was on her phone and seemed shocked to see another human being.

I handed her the invitation. "A guy gave me this? It didn't have a time, so . . ."

She put her phone down. "This time is fine. Right now is fine." She sat up straighter in her chair. "I'm Gracie. And your name is?"

"Tony."

When she stood she only came up to my shoulders. With her white-blonde hair in a bun she looked like a fairy. Like Tinkerbell.

"Do you want coffee?" she asked.

"Sure. Black."

She put the Keurig to work and made me a cup. She handed me a pink "Happy Mother's Day" mug.

"Thanks."

"Sure." She wiped her hands against her hips. "I guess now . . . you should follow me."

"Don't I need to fill out something?"

She paused as if unsure. Then she shook her head. "Do you want to fill out something?"

I arched an eyebrow. She was confusing me. "Not really."

"Then we're good." She led me through a door into a room shaped like the inside of a soccer ball. "Wow. This is bizarre."

"Yeah, it is. But I assure you it's highly functional." She pointed at a lone swivel stool. "Have a seat, please."

"How long will I have to wait for the others?"

She smiled. "There are no others. You're it."

"It?"

She hesitated a short moment, then said, "Here at the Discovery Room we offer exclusive one-on-one attention."

I wasn't sure if that was a good or bad thing. "Cool," I said.

She glanced toward the door as if waiting for someone to come in. When they didn't she said, "Relax and enjoy."

I wasn't sure I could do either.

She studied my coffee. "Actually . . . I think it's better if you leave that with me."

I saw no reason why I couldn't keep it. I was seated. I wouldn't spill. But she was holding out her hand, so I gave her the mug before I'd even had a sip. She left me and closed the door.

I ran my hands up and down my thighs. Sitting on the only stool in a strange room made me want to run. Thanks but no thanks. "I predict this will be a huge waste of time."

Suddenly, the Room lit up. A scene covered the dome. I was looking toward a street corner near a school. But wait—

"Is that my high school?"

I didn't even have a moment to let the question settle when I noticed three teenage guys hanging out, smoking cigarettes, their baseball caps on backward. Their T-shirts were tucked into their jeans. I recognized the Nirvana T-shirt.

My favorite shirt ever.

I sat forward. "That's me! That *is* my high school." I stood and turned in a circle until the school was behind me. It was like I was seeing everything from twenty feet away. All sorts of '90s cars drove by, with kids hanging out the windows, honking at each other. Some girls walked by. Every single one had part of their hair pulled into a scrunchie—a term I only knew about because Penny still had some around. I remembered a few of their names: Jennifer, Amanda, Brandy…

"Wait!" I said to the Room. "How do you have this movie?" I turned in a circle a second time. "Anybody out there? Gracie? How do you have this?"

There was no answer.

It made no sense, yet it was mesmerizing. I sat down and watched. Man, I looked cheesy. It wasn't just the clothes. Jeans were jeans and T-shirts were T-shirts even after twenty-five years, but my hair was too long and sticking out under my backward Royals' cap. I was a baby pretending to be cool.

The other guys that were hanging with me—Matt and Jerry—*they* were cool. They were a year older and I'd wanted to be like them more than anything in my pathetic world. Even watching them now made my stomach gnaw with the old fear that I'd never belong. With any group.

I'd been one of the kids in the middle: not cool, not nerdy, not into band or sports. Just there.

Jerry handed me a cigarette. "Want one, Amato?"

I took it, but slipped it over my ear. "For later." I'd tried smoking after copping one from my dad. I'd coughed like crazy and hated the taste. I was glad I'd gotten all that out of the way, so I didn't make a fool of myself in front of the guys.

"So, dude," Matt said. "We know you want to hang out with us."

"And that's cool," Jerry said. "We're down with that. We always like hanging with new guys." He gave Matt a look and a grin. "But there's something you gotta do for us first."

The kid-me looked down at his high-tops, while the adult-me remembered what happened next.

Then Matt said the words that started everything. "We need some bills."

"Mega bills," Jerry added.

I pulled out my wallet, which had three dollars in it. "You can have what I got, but—"

They tipped their heads back and laughed. Matt swatted Jerry on the arm. "He's going to give us three bucks. He thinks that's enough. How lame is that?"

"Mega lame," Jerry said. He stopped laughing and glared at me. "Are you lame, Amato?"

Probably.

Absolutely.

I was a deer caught in the headlights. I felt now what I felt then. Every cell in my body wanted to run.

But then . . . something happened that I didn't remember.

Heather Greer walked by. She was gorgeous and looked like Tiffani-Amber Thiessen from *Saved by the Bell.* We'd sat next to each other in American History. I'd probably said less than ten words to her.

She looked in my direction but there was a weird yellow glow around her. What was that?

"Hey, Tony," she said with a smile.

"Hey . . ." I couldn't think of anything else to say—then or now.

"You got a minute?"

Matt spoke first. "He's busy."

"Yeah," Jerry said. "Move on, girl. Don't act like you're all fly."

She looked at the young me like she was waiting for me to say something, but I didn't.

When she moved on the glow faded away. As did the movie.

The walls were white again. Actually, it was a relief.

Then the old guy from Home Depot walked in the Room.

I stood up. "What *is* all this? What's going on?"

He held out his hand for me to shake. "Hello, Mr. Amato. Nice to see you again.."

I shook his hand then waved my arms at the sphere. "You have some explaining to do. This whole thing is nuts. Crazy. How did you get a video of that exact moment of *my* life? Was there a camera on a light pole somewhere? Was that technology even around back then?"

"The hows are not important, Mr. Amato. The moment is."

It *had* been an important moment. I knew that now, but back then…

I wasn't going to let him off so easy. "*This* moment is important and I need answers. Now. What is this place?"

"It's a place where you can discover your full potential."

I pointed at the white walls. "*That* moment had nothing to do with my potential. That moment ruined my potential."

He just stood there, totally erect and proper. He reminded me of a British butler, seeing everything, but not talking much.

"Explain what good it does to have me see . . . that."

"You need to see how you were given a way out."

"I didn't see any such thing."

"Actually, you did. Think about it."

The only moment that was unusual was seeing a glow around Heather. Of course there hadn't been a glow at the time, but . . . "You talking about Heather? Glowing?"

"You tell me."

Really? "Stop with the games and answer me."

He was silent a few moments, like he was thinking things through. "I *can* tell you that the glowing is a way to highlight the interventions that were offered to you."

"Interventions?"

"Opportunities to make a different choice."

"Says who?"

"Do you believe there have been missed chances in your life, Mr. Amato?"

"Well sure."

Wesley spread his hands as if that, was that.

I pressed my fingers against my temples, trying to fend off a headache. This had to be a reality TV stunt. I walked around the Room, looking for cameras in the walls and ceiling, but every surface was smooth as smooth could be. Nothing.

"You are not being recorded," Wesley said.

I pointed at the walls again. "Why should I believe you? You taped me back in the Nineties without me knowing, so why shouldn't

I think you're taping me now?" I looked upward and spread my arms. "Hey Mr. Cameraman! Here I am. Show yourself!"

Wesley sighed deeply. "No one else is here, Mr. Amato. We are here to help you."

"You said *we.*"

He blinked. "Pardon me. I am used to using the royal-we."

I rolled my eyes at him. "How can showing me one of the worst decisions of my life help me?"

"Would you like to see another scene?"

Wesley kept skipping over my questions. "There's another one?"

He nodded. "There are a few."

A few? "I'm not watching anything more until you explain how you taped the scenes in the first place."

"Then we are through."

I was shocked he didn't even try to explain it. "You can't tell me anything? Something?" I raked my fingers through my hair. "Lie to me if you want. But gimme some sort of explanation."

"I will never lie to you, Mr. Amato."

I couldn't do anything but stare at him. Here I was freaking out, yet he was completely calm and unflappable. I'd never met anyone like him. "Do you play poker, Wesley? Cuz you've got the face for it."

"I haven't had the pleasure." He just stood there, like he was waiting for me to say the next line.

"So . . . ?" I asked.

"So what have you decided about watching another scene?"

He *did* have my interest. The thing was, if I said no he'd think I was scared. Since that wasn't an option I said, "Sure. Why not? I love being humiliated."

"Humiliation is not our intent."

"You could've fooled me." I shook my head. "So what *are* you after?"

"Discovery."

He was talking in circles. "Reliving a mistake that I *know* was a mistake is hardly constructive, much less a discovery."

"It could be." Wesley left before I could argue.

As the door clicked shut, a new scene appeared. In spite of my nerves, I settled in to watch.

I was in an unfinished basement with low ceilings. Narrow stairs were behind me. There was junk everywhere. Within seconds I knew exactly where I was. And then I saw them. Papa and Nonna Esposito.

I gasped at how young they were. Nonna's hair was only partly gray and pulled into a tight bun. She wore her favorite apron with an apple on the pocket. Papa's reading glasses hung from a chain around his neck. He was wearing his daily uniform of khakis and a button down shirt.

I heard a sound from the corner. There I was, digging through a box.

"Can you find it, Antonio?" Papa asked.

The 15-year-old me stood up, holding two books. "Were these the ones you wanted?" I brought them close.

He put on his glasses, read the titles, and flipped through some pages. "Yes, yes. These are them." He turned them around so I could see the titles. "Two great books you have to read: *The Caine Mutiny* and *The Guns of Navarone."*

"Never heard of 'em," said my younger self.

Now, twenty-five years later, I *had* heard of them. However, I'd still never read them. After Papa died I hadn't wanted to remember—

Suddenly, I knew what we were doing in the basement. I remembered this exact day. First the street corner with Matt and Jerry, and now this?

Uh-uh. Enough was definitely enough.

I stood up and waved my hands at the scene being played out around me. "Stop! I don't want to see anymore. Stop!" When nothing happened I yelled again, "Wesley! Stop this! Now!"

The scene faded. I had to get out before it went any further. I walked toward the door.

Wesley intercepted me. "What seems to be the problem, Mr. Amato?"

"You know very well what the problem is. You've had your fun but I want it over. I gotta go." I tried stepping around him.

He stopped me with a gentle hand, easing me back. "Let's talk about this." He pointed toward the stool. "If you please."

Although I had three inches and a hundred pounds on him, and though I was thirty years younger, I didn't want to use that kind of force. Honestly, his calm unnerved me.

I stepped backward into the Room but didn't sit. "Listen, Wes, I gave it a shot. I don't know what your game is, but this is *my* life. You have no right."

"I'm sorry you feel that way. We don't mean to upset you."

"Then why else would you show me Matt and Jerry, and then the basement with my grandparents, just a day before . . ." I felt my heart beating in my throat which made it hard to get the words out. "I've put all that behind me. All of it."

Wesley clasped his hands in front of himself. "Have you?"

I held out my hands to stop him from coming any closer—bodily or with his words. "Whatever happened is ancient history and has nothing to do with now, and certainly has nothing to do with you or anybody else." I thought of the invitation. "I came for 'special training.' This is hardly—"

"This is exactly what was promised." He spread his arms wide. "It is very special training."

He was over-the-top weird. "Fine. Special training for what? And by whom? Who's behind all this?"

"That doesn't really matter unless you're willing to see what we have to show you."

"There's that 'we' again. You mean you and Tinkerbell out there? Who's the head honcho running this thing?"

"That bit of information will be revealed as we go along. Remember, our goal is discovery. We are, after all, the Discovery Room."

He had an answer for everything, yet an answer to nothing. "I want to know who's behind it now, *before* anything else happens."

Wesley shook his head slowly, giving the impression that nothing I said would push his buttons.

He certainly was pushing mine.

I returned to the stool and leaned forward, resting my arms on my legs. There were only two ways out of this: leave and never know how and why they—whoever they were—had movies of my past, or stick around and deal with it. Actually, nobody in the whole world knew the truth of what happened, so there was no way this stupid strip-mall company knew either.

Yet if they knew some of it, did they know all of it? Were they waiting for a full confession? Was Wesley working with the police?

And why now, after twenty-five years?

I was wiped out. I wanted to go home.

Wesley studied me a moment, then said, "Shall we continue, Mr. Amato?"

Chapter Six

Tony

The Lord is compassionate and merciful,
slow to get angry and filled with unfailing love.
He will not constantly accuse us,
nor remain angry forever.
Psalm 103: 8-9

Wesley waited for my answer. Did I want to see another scene?

Exhausted or not—creeped out or not—I knew I couldn't leave. I was the kind of guy who *had* to watch the end of a movie even if it wasn't very good. I had to see how everything fit together.

I had to see how my life fit together.

I thought of a compromise. "I'll see another one, but if I want to leave at any time I can. You won't stop me. Deal?"

He nodded. "I will not stop you. You came here of your own free will, and you will leave that way."

"Okay then." I took a cleansing breath. "Let's get it over with."

As soon as he left, I was back in the basement, seeing Papa paging through his war books.

Nonna called out to us. "Over here, men." She'd moved on to another corner stacked with boxes. I remembered why there were so many. They'd asked me to help them sort through the old junk in the basement because they were thinking of moving to a smaller house.

Nonna had one box sitting on top of another and had the lid off. "Look at all my pretties."

I saw a bunch of jewelry and jewelry boxes. It was like a treasure chest.

That's what I'd thought in that moment. It was treasure and treasure was valuable. And *that* had made me think of Matt and Jerry.

If only I hadn't thought of Matt and Jerry.

Nonna opened a box covered with black velvet. "These were my grandmother's. Look. They're real rubies."

"Those are worth something," Papa said. "Why are they down here in a box?"

"Because they're too fancy to wear. Nobody dresses up anymore." She closed the box and took up a red velvet bag. "Now these . . . these are the most precious of all—not monetarily, but because I wore them at our wedding."

She held up a short string of pearls. My stomach sank. If the eighty-something Nonna knew where they were now, she'd cry.

Papa kissed her cheek. "You're just as pretty now as you were forty years ago, *mia amata*."

She touched his face. "*Tesoro.*"

They'd always been lovey-dovey. It seemed cute now, but back then, it had made me cringe.

Nonna kept digging through the jewelry. "And look at this." She picked up a black leather box. "*You* wore this at our wedding."

Papa opened the hinged case. He turned it in my direction. "Oh yes. My Purple Heart."

Nonna beamed at him. "Your papa was so brave. He was wounded during the war."

I remembered at the time wondering which war she was talking about, but I hadn't asked. Since then I'd learned it was the Korean War, but back then I said, "How were you wounded?"

He put a hand to his side. "Shrapnel from a bomb. Missed my organs by this much." He squeezed two fingers together.

"Wow. Cool." I'd been impressed that Papa had been so close to death and had come out the other side. It was painful to watch and remember this conversation, knowing what I knew now.

"Enough war talk. It's lunch time," Nonna said. She put the jewelry back in the box and extended a hand toward Papa "Come on, soldier."

She took the stairs easily, so different from how she got around now.

"You coming, Antonio?" she asked.

"In a minute."

The grown me stood up from the stool. "Go!" I yelled at my young self. "Go eat lunch with them."

I knew it was stupid to yell like that or to expect something to turn out different. It was like watching *Titanic* hoping the ship didn't sink.

I saw myself walk slowly toward the basement window. My idea had been to unlock the window so the guys and I could come back later. I stood on the stool to reach it. But suddenly the legs broke and I fell. I scrambled away from the broken stool toward the stairs, afraid Nonna or Papa would hear.

With the stool broken, I'd had to forget the window idea. We had to find another way in.

But then the stool glowed.

"What? Why's it glowing?" I asked the Room.

The movie ended with me heading upstairs to lunch.

Wesley came in.

"I don't get it," I said. "Why did the stool glow? I didn't use it."

"You didn't use it because it splintered apart."

"The stool breaking was important?"

"Once again you were given a chance to stop the plan."

"But I didn't stop."

Wesley spread his hands. "Alas, no. But you *were* given a way out. An excuse to share with your so-called friends."

First Heather and now the stool. If only I'd taken the bait. "Maybe if I'd broken my leg when the stool broke that might have stopped us? Looking back I'd have gladly suffered a broken leg if I could take everything back."

"Your offer is commendable. But you will see that the process is sometimes more important than the outcome. Choices are stepping-stones to character."

"Are you saying I don't have character?"

"I did not say that at all."

He was making me mad again. I pointed at him. "You know how this turned out. You're showing me chances that would've made it different. What good does that do me now? If you want to make me feel worse than I feel every day of my life you're succeeding. I don't need any of this to discover what a loser I am."

"Don't you want it finished, Mr. Amato?"

"I am finished. Every day I feel finished."

Wesley shook his head. "You are far from finished."

Everything he said was so . . . neutral. Not hurting anything but not getting anywhere either. "Tell me exactly what I'm supposed to get out of this. Give it to me plain."

Wesley glanced up a moment. "James Joyce said, 'Mistakes are the portals of discovery.'"

The way he said the name suggested I was supposed to know who James Joyce was, but I didn't. "The mistakes I got. But I'm not seeing any portals of anything."

"They are there."

Now he was making me feel stupid. "I. Don't. See. Them. *Comprende*?"

When he just stood there I tried another approach.

"Look, Wesley. I'm not the kind of guy who thinks deep thoughts, who sees symbolism, who sits around and ponders life. I'm a facts guy. Give me a list of to-dos and I'll do them."

"Will you?"

Sheesh. Low blow. "I'll try to do them. But telling me to discover some vague something-or-other is like telling me to do calculus or fix a computer. I need more direction."

"We give you the tools, it's up to you to use them."

"But—"

"There is another moment to view. Are you willing to see it?"

I sighed heavily. Even though I felt like I was marching to the guillotine I said, "Sure. Why stop now?"

He nodded. "I'm proud of your choice, Tony."

I noticed that he'd used my first name. Since he knew all about me, he might as well call me Tony. And let him be proud. I was terrified.

The Room came alive. Me, Matt, and Jerry stood behind some bushes outside Nonna and Papa's house. We didn't need to come in a window because I'd remembered Mom had a key, so I'd pinched it from her. I left the guys long enough to peek in the garage. The car was gone. Mom had said they were going to a church dinner. How perfect could it get?

I used the key and we got inside. The house was quiet.

"Come on," Matt said. "Where's the stuff?"

I shushed him.

"No one's here."

"Still . . . shhh. Okay?"

"Whatever."

I needed to get this done. I led them down the basement stairs. I pointed to the box and started taking things out, but Jerry said, "Let's just take the whole thing."

I didn't want to argue with him.

Matt scoped it out. "There's tons of stuff down here. Anything else worth anything?"

I had no idea, but wanted out of there. "There's nothing else. Let's go."

Jerry carried the box upstairs.

But then, on the way out, I heard a noise. A thud.

"What's that?" Jerry asked.

More noise.

"You told us nobody was home," Matt said.

"They weren't supposed to be."

"Let's get outta here." Matt and Jerry ran out the door. "You coming?"

"Just—" I heard something else.

"Help . . ."

Hearing Papa's voice made me shudder.

I tiptoed into the living room and saw the hallway leading to the bedrooms. I walked closer.

"Suzanna? Are you there?" Papa called from the bathroom.

I froze. I couldn't answer him.

The entire door glowed.

Unfortunately, I knew why it was glowing.

"I need help! Suz, help me."

I remembered thinking that he probably needed help wiping his butt. No thank you.

So I ran out.

And Papa died.

And part of me died too.

The movie ended. I covered my face with my hands. If only I'd said no to the guys. If only I'd answered Papa. If only I'd opened the door and called 9-1-1. If only I hadn't been a thieving coward.

Wesley walked in. He stood next to me and touched my shoulder. "You didn't know he was going to die."

I brushed my hands across my face. "But he did. I killed him."

"You don't know that."

"Do *you*?" I glared at him. "Do you know differently? If so, tell me now."

Wesley blinked a few times. Had my question stumped him?

"Well?" I asked.

"There are a few more scenes."

I shot off the stool. "Where are your slick answers now, Wes? I talk about killing Papa and you just stand there like someone waiting for an elevator?"

"I'm sorry I have no definitive answer for you."

I scoffed. "Yeah. That's what I thought. You're silent for the one question that really needs an answer. Which means I *did* kill Papa." I returned to the stool. "Go ahead. Start 'er up. Add another log on the fire."

He left.

Before I could prepare myself, another movie started. Nonna and my mom were sitting on a couch in Nonna and Papa's living room. They were looking at a scrapbook. I was slouched in a chair nearby, wanting to be anywhere but there.

Mom pointed at a picture. "This would be a good one to have on the guestbook table."

Nonna looked at the photo and began to sniffle. She retrieved a handkerchief from the sleeve of her blouse. "Our wedding picture. He was such a handsome man."

"He was. And you were a beautiful bride," Mom said.

The wedding picture glowed. My stomach clenched as I

remembered what was coming.

Suddenly, Nonna touched the photo. "See there? He deserves to be buried with this medal.

"Really, Mom?" my mother asked. "That's such a special heirloom. Wouldn't it be better if you kept it for a member of the family?"

Nonna thought a moment, then said, "Maybe you're right. But *I* will wear my wedding pearls to the funeral."

Mom looked closer at the picture and nodded. "That would be lovely. I'll get them. Are they in your bedroom?"

Nonna shook her head, then looked directly at me. "They're in the basement. Antonio knows where they are. Come here and see what we're talking about, Antonio."

I reluctantly glanced at the wedding photo, even though I knew what she wanted: the pearls and the Purple Heart.

Which weren't there.

I hesitated, gazing between the photo and the basement door. "Go on, Tony. Go fetch them for Nonna," Mom said.

I watched myself go into the basement. All the turmoil I felt then, I felt now. I was doomed.

Once I got downstairs I remember having the brilliant idea to stage a robbery. I moved a sawhorse under the window, climbed up and opened it. I put the broken stool nearby. Then I messed up some other boxes like a thief searching through stuff. When I was done, I looked over the scene. It was believable. It looked like the thief had come in the window, stood on the stool, and broke it.

I ran upstairs and yelled. "They're gone! Somebody broke in. All your jewelry is gone!"

"What are you talking about?" Mom rushed toward the top of the stairs.

Nonna kept shaking her head. She held out a hand for me. "Help me up. I have to see."

We all went downstairs and looked around. Nonna began to cry. "Everything that was dear to me. Gone. Who would do such an evil thing?"

Me. It was me.

The scene ended. My shame and guilt from years past washed over me. I was the evil one.

This time when Wesley came in he didn't say anything. He just stood there, looking at me.

"If you wanted to make me feel worse than I already do, you succeeded."

"You saw the photo glow, yes?" he said.

"I did. So what was the choice? Telling Nonna I took them? She called the thief evil. I didn't want her to think of me as evil. Even though I was. I am."

"You are not evil."

I scoffed and wrapped my arms around myself, feeling cold. "What do you want from me?" I asked. "I've been punished my whole life for this mistake. These mistakes."

"You have not *been* punished, you have punished yourself."

"Are you saying I haven't wanted a good life?"

"I am saying you've locked a good life behind a door and secured it with a padlock."

"Cute."

"It is not cute at all. It is tragic."

"So what happens when I unlock the door? Is everything rainbows and butterflies? Does everything go my way?"

Wesley hesitated a moment, then said, "Sit. I have one last scene to show you."

He left immediately and I saw a movie of myself outside my family's church. People streamed in, all wearing black. It had to be Papa's funeral.

I stood across the street, my hands in the pockets of the suit Mom had bought me. The sleeves and the pants were too long.

I did *not* want to go in. I remembered planning how I'd wait for everyone to get inside, and then run off somewhere.

I saw myself look up at the sky—which was a brilliant blue. Papa was dead. Shouldn't it be a gloomy gray? I remembered seeing the cross on the steeple bright against the blue.

But now it glowed.

A middle-aged man walked by and looked up at it too. "A good reminder, that."

"What *that*?"

"The cross reminding us that Jesus died so all our sins are forgiven. That's life-changing."

He didn't know about Papa. I looked down, avoiding his eyes. "Not all sins."

The man walked on.

"I didn't go in," I whispered to the Room.

The scene ended and Wesley came back. I guessed what he was going to say so I beat him to the punch. "I didn't go to Papa's funeral. I'm a horrible person. I get it."

Wesley sighed—this time with disgust. "Doesn't this woe-is-me exhaust you?"

I was surprised by his change in tone. "That's rude."

"Haven't you learned anything from all this, Mr. Amato?"

I didn't know what to say.

Wesley paced halfway around the sphere, shaking his head like I was a complete failure

"Well, yeah. I suppose," I said.

He turned to face me. "No matter what you think you learned, I don't see it. All I see is a hurting man who wants to stay that way."

Had I pushed him too far? "I don't want to stay that way. I'd love to feel better."

Wesley put a hand to his chest. "It's not just about *feeling* better, it's about *being* better."

I felt desperation take hold. "I was sorry then and I'm sorry now. Is that what you're waiting for?"

Wesley clasped his hands in front of himself. He looked down like he'd had enough of me.

Somehow that scared me. *I* could say *enough,* but for him to say it?

"Show me something else."

He looked up. "There is nothing else, Mr. Amato. The show is over."

My breathing sped up. I felt panicked. "There has to be more. I'm not . . . I'm not good yet."

"That's your choice."

"But—"

Wesley raised a hand, stopping my words. "You came to this place and entered the Room. You have been given special training, special attention, and special knowledge. *You* were invited. What you do with this insight is up to you—as everything has been. You can continue on the same path you've been on, or you can apply what you've learned and change things."

The thought of my old life was painful, but it's the life I'd chosen and lived out for decades. How could I set it aside?

"I know I gave you a hard time," I said. "And I . . . I want to appreciate all this. I shouldn't because it's made me feel sick to my stomach, stupid, and evil. Plus, I hate reliving my mistakes, but . . ." I shrugged. "What am I supposed to do now? Fall to my knees and ask for forgiveness?"

Wesley's jaw tightened. "That is one choice."

"Really? That's not going to happen no matter how many flashbacks you show me."

He sighed and shook his head as if I was a lost cause. "Then our work here is done."

"Done? Just like that?"

"Your time is up, Mr. Amato. Thank you for coming." He took a step toward the door.

He couldn't leave! This couldn't be over.

I stood. "My time isn't up 'til I say it's up!" I grabbed the stool and hurled it across the room where it made a very satisfying dent in the perfect drywall. But what was even more satisfying was seeing Wesley take a step back.

Good. I'd scared him.

Yet a few seconds later Wesley calmly opened the door and motioned for me to exit. "If you please."

After throwing the stool there was nothing I could say in my defense. And nothing good had come out of the movies I'd seen. Why was I acting like I wanted more?

Wesley just stood there, waiting for me to leave.

I had no choice. I stepped into the office. Tinkerbell stared at me with wide blue eyes. Had she seen everything I'd seen? Did she know all the horrible things I'd done?

Wesley moved to the exterior door. "Take care, Mr. Amato."

I felt panic rise. This really was the end of it.

"If you will," Wesley opened the door wider. "Please."

I'd burned all my bridges. There was no other place to go. So I left. Wesley closed the door behind me and immediately flipped a CLOSED sign.

Seeing that sign hit me hard. It wasn't a friendly, CLOSED-COME AGAIN sign. But CLOSED. A you-had-your-chance kind of sign. A you-blew-it sign.

I got in my car and felt done-in, like all my energy had drained away. I was an empty shell.

I felt so weak I wasn't sure I could drive, yet I couldn't sit there while Wesley and Tinkerbell were inside, looking out at me.

I turned on the ignition and somehow managed to drive toward home. Maybe hearing the shouts of game shows would drown out the screaming in my head.

Chapter Seven

Gracie & Wesley

He will listen to the prayers of the destitute.
He will not reject their pleas.
Psalm 102: 17

I stared at the CLOSED sign that Wesley had flipped over, then watched as Tony got in his car and peeled away.

"What did you do to him?" I asked Wesley.

"I didn't do anything to him. He did it to himself."

I'd heard them arguing in the Room but hadn't been able to make out much of it. I'd also heard a big thud. "Is everybody going to be upset when they come out?"

"I expect he is in the minority." Wesley stood at the windows with his arms behind his back. "I hope so."

I'd never seen him concerned about anything. He was always positive and strong. I wanted to encourage him, even though I was rather shaken by what I'd witnessed. "I hope so too. Surely, the next one will be better."

Under his breath he said, "Indeed. Yet the first one was unfortunate." With a deep breath and a nod he faced me. "I will be gone for a while, Miss Sturgess, but I will be back for the next client."

"Which is when?"

"Whenever it happens."

I shook my head. "Now there's the Wesley I know."

He smiled, turned the CLOSED sign to OPEN, and left the office. I had the urge to get ahold of Tony, but I didn't have a number for him. Not that I could make anything better. I didn't even know what happened. Maybe it *was* Tony's fault. On first impression he'd seemed a little rough. Tough even. And it went beyond his size. There was a wariness about him, like he was daring people to cross him.

I understood wariness. I'd been out of the mainstream for so long that even a job as simple as this one made me want to run back home.

Above all, I was wary of angry men.

I went into the Room to see if there were any clues about what had happened. There was one big one: the stool was on its side against the wall, and three feet above it was a gash in the drywall.

The *thud* was explained.

I wished I could see what Tony had seen. On a whim, I clapped my hands, hoping the Room would turn on.

As expected, nothing happened.

I put the stool back where it belonged and returned to my desk. Should I call a drywall repair person? That idea didn't last long. Wesley was the kind of man who insisted on being in control. I needed to let him handle it.

I looked up when the front door opened. An older woman in her seventies came in. I introduced myself and got her name: Sandra. After a few pleasantries and offering her coffee—which she declined—I led her into the Room, ready to make apologies for the damaged wall.

I stood there blinking at it.

"Is something wrong?" she asked.

I stared at the place where the drywall had been damaged. There was no sign of wet paint. No powder of sanding dust on the floor. I touched it. The wall was perfect. "No, nothing's wrong," I said. "Nothing at all."

She didn't look convinced. I smiled, gave her the few directions I had to give, and left her. Within seconds, I heard sound coming from inside the Room.

How did it do that? When I'd been in the Room on my own no movie had started for me. And how did the Room repair itself? It was like it was a living . . . thing. I shook the crazy thought away.

Wesley arrived soon after and immediately headed in to join Sandra. I hurried to get a question in before he entered. "How does the Room know when someone's in there so it starts the movie?"

He gave me a patient smile. "How does 'the Room' know? The Room is just a room. It doesn't know anything."

I felt sheepish. "You know what I mean."

"I do."

"And the drywall is already repaired. I was here the whole time so how did it—?"

He just smiled at me. "Everything is as it should be, Miss Sturgess." With that he entered the Room, closing the door behind him.

Which was *so* frustrating.

And so I did something I wouldn't normally do: I pressed my ear to the door. I could only hear garbled voices. If only I could be a fly on the wall.

I went back to my book, but couldn't concentrate. I kept glancing at the door, waiting for it to open. Soon it did, and Wesley came out, just as he'd done multiple times while Tony was in there.

"Back to my questions?" I said. "There's the drywall repair, and the movie starting on its own, but also, I wondered how you know when to go in the Room?"

"You've heard the phrase 'the suspension of disbelief'?"

"Vaguely."

He pointed to my book on the desk. "When you're reading you are *in* the story and accept the world of fiction as real—even when you logically know it is not."

"I suppose that's true. But this," I waved an arm. "This *is* real. But it's also surreal. Things are happening that don't make sense."

He cocked his head. "How does your phone get pictures and videos on it?"

"I don't know . . . satellites or something?"

Wesley smiled. "Or something. Logic says it shouldn't be possible and yet it is. And do you really need—or want—to know exactly how it happens?"

He got me there. "Not really."

"You just want it to work."

"I do."

He pointed toward the Room. "So it is with the Room. The fact it works is all you need to know." He moved toward the door. "I am needed." He went back inside.

It was clear I had to accept that the Room was one strange place and Wesley was one strange guy. Even if it didn't make sense.

**

Ninety minutes after Sandra went into the Room, she came out. It was way different than how Tony had exited. She was smiling, almost giddy.

She pressed her hands to her chest. "I don't know how to thank you, Wesley. That was the most amazing experience of my life."

"You're welcome, Mrs. Lyons. Now follow through. Keep your eyes open."

"Oh, I will. I will." She gave me a little wave, then left.

Wesley took a deep breath, staring at the door as it closed. "Blessedly, that one was much better."

"So it seems. She was delighted."

"The difference is attitude. She offered an open mind and heart. There are rewards to that."

"What kind of rewards?"

"All kinds. Small to large."

I shouldn't have asked. "Helpful," I said sarcastically. "So what happens to her now?"

"That depends on her." He sat on the chair by the windows. "That answer applies to everyone, Miss Sturgess. Our present and our future are molded by our choices."

I let out a huff. "Not my choices. I didn't have any."

He shook his head. "I'm sure that's not true. Choices are impossible to avoid. Even making the choice not to make a choice, is a choice."

"Which makes my point." I thought of something else. "Are the clients in the Room dealing with good choices or bad ones?"

He cocked his head. "A mixture. But guidance is always available for the asking."

"People can call you?"

He scoffed. "Certainly not. Not me." He studied me a moment. "Do you believe in God, Miss Sturgess?"

God? It was something I didn't really think about. I shrugged. "My mom sure did."

"I'm not asking about your mother's faith, but your own."

"Then yeah. I believe there is a God." I didn't know much about religion but I liked to think He was there.

Wesley nodded once. "Do you pray?"

I shrugged. "Not often."

"May I ask why not?"

Good question. I offered the first excuse that came to mind. "Some of my prayers have definitely *not* been answered. For one thing my mom died."

"I am sorry for your loss. And your father also?"

How did he know about Dad? Yet I hadn't prayed for Dad to get well as fervently as I'd prayed for Mom. "Yes. Him too."

"All prayers are answered, Miss Sturgess. Sometimes the answer is *yes*, sometimes *no*, and sometimes *wait*."

"I hate waiting."

Wesley shrugged. "There is no escaping that either. Waiting is often necessary."

"Necessary for what?"

"Necessary in order to discover the right path." He sat back. "Can I give you a piece of advice, Miss Sturgess?"

"Sure." I was *sure* his advice would be anything but clear.

"You seem to approach life with a chip on your shoulder, full of skepticism. You're jaded. You're tough—or pretend to be."

He was partially wrong. "I am not tough. At all. As for the rest . . . if you'd gone through what I've gone through, you'd be jaded too."

He nodded. "I am sorry for your hard times, but rejoice that you are here, starting fresh."

I scoffed. "Sorry to burst your bubble, but I never aspired to work in a place like this."

"Then why did you take the job?"

I'd wondered that myself. "You caught me off guard. You asked and I accepted."

"I am grateful you did."

I gave him a sidelong look. "Because I'm so indispensable?"

He sat forward in the chair. "Your past experiences have melded together to create the unique journey of your life. A life which has led you here."

I was going to say something snarky, but didn't. Even if I didn't fully believe his words, *he* believed them. I did like the idea that my past might not have been random and meaningless.

Wesley stood. "Everyone who goes into the Room has gone through a lot. The Room opens their eyes to past choices that would have led them onto the best path. Some choices they took and some they ignored. Hopefully seeing what could-have-been changes them for the better so they don't miss such chances in the future." His eyes brightened. "If they open their eyes and *see* they will find joy, satisfaction, and peace."

"If they choose not to . . . see?"

He sat back. "They will find frustration and discouragement."

I snickered. "Some choice."

"Indeed. But you'd be surprised how many choose to remain blind. Old habits die very hard."

I'd lived the last fourteen years mired in habits, schedules, and lists. I hadn't been given choices, but duties. Wesley was talking about abstract mumbo-jumbo that had no place in my life.

"Would you like to go in the Room, Miss Sturgess?"

My mind said *yes* then *no* very quickly. "Isn't it invitation-only?"

He smiled. "I'm inviting you now."

I looked toward the door. Tony had come out angry. Sandra had come out elated. I'd have a 50/50 chance of having a good experience. "I don't know . . ."

Wesley stood. "The invitation is open. Just let me know."

I was shocked he didn't argue with me.

Then he said, "You may go home for today."

"No more clients?"

He shook his head. "Not today."

"How do you know?"

"I have my ways."
I bet he did.

****

As soon as Gracie left the office, I went into the Room, closed the door, and sat on the stool. Immediately a scene played out. I saw a college campus, bustling between classes. A cute girl cut across the grass. She had light brown hair parted down the middle, just like most of her peers. But she was definitely different.

She glowed.

I nodded. She would get the next invitation.

Chapter Eight

Minnie

You must each decide in your heart how much to give.
And don't give reluctantly or in response to pressure.
For God loves a person who gives cheerfully.
2 Corinthians 9: 7

Dad honked the horn.

"Bye, Mom. See you tomorrow night."

"Bye," she called from the kitchen. Mom had stopped hugging me goodbye at the door years ago because seeing Dad upset her. And if Claudia and the babies were in the car? She'd be a wreck all weekend.

Of course, I wasn't there when she was depressed, but she always let me know afterward how miserable she'd been. That's when I'd suggested hanging back and not seeing me off. Whatever worked.

Today Dad and Claudia had a family outing planned. When I went out to the van the side door magically slid open. "Hey," I said. I crushed past Bryn whose car seat was in one of the captain's chairs, pinged Benny on his nose as he sat in the other chair, and pressed myself back into the third row of seating. I sat in the middle of the bench because there was zero leg room for a twenty-year-old behind the seats.

"Seatbelt," Dad said—always said—even though I always put it on without thinking. He pulled away from the curb and headed in the opposite direction of their house.

"Where are we going?" I had to talk louder than usual because it was nearly impossible for those in the front seat to hear me from the third row.

Claudia looked back at me. "We're going to the mall to get me a fancy new dress."

I'd seen Claudia's closets. She didn't need to buy anything for a year and she still wouldn't wear anything twice. "What's the occasion?" I asked.

Dad looked at me in the rearview mirror. "Remember I told you I was up for a statewide award? Well, I won. They're having a banquet. For me."

I vaguely remembered him mentioning a sales award.

"Congratulations." I leaned forward and wiped snot off Bryn's nose with a wet wipe. She grimaced.

"Salesman of the year . . . all my hard work is paying off."

"That's cool, Dad."

He reached over and squeezed Claudia's hand. "That's why Mama needs a new dress."

She raised their clasped hands and kissed his. Even though I didn't want to be, I was touched by their displays of affection. They really did love each other.

I noticed Bryn staring at me, as if she knew what I was thinking. I wiggled one of her feet then did the same for Benny. They both giggled.

It was going to be a good day. I knew it.

**

Claudia tried on a dozen dresses, coming out of the dressing room to model for Dad and I. It wasn't surprising that she looked good in all of them. What was surprising is that Dad was involved. To my knowledge he'd never gone dress shopping with Mom. Of course I'd been twelve when they divorced, so maybe I'd forgotten. Either way, I'd seen Dad soften since remarrying. I often wondered if he would have been more involved with Mom, would they still be together?

Claudia came out wearing a pale blue dress with just the right amount of sequins to celebrate her spunk, and just the right amount of skirt length to look appropriate for a mother of twin babies. She always looked perfect.

"Oh my, oh my, that's the one," Dad said.

Claudia preened in a full-length mirror. "I think so too." She looked at me. "Do you like it, Minnie?"

I sat on the floor by another full-length mirror, letting both babies stand against it. Fingerprints and mouth-marks were everywhere.

"I do," I said. "You look very pretty." Claudia had an eye for good fashion. I admired her taste, but personally didn't pay much attention to styles. The college uniform of jeans and a top were all the fashion I needed.

Claudia turned around to face me. "Now that I'm done . . . would you like to try on dresses, Minnie?"

Me? I shook my head. "I can't remember the last time I wore a dress."

"At our wedding?" Claudia said.

She was probably right. I'd been a bridesmaid, wearing a royal blue strapless monstrosity that had made me tug at it all night.

"How about just trying some on anyway? For fun?"

It was nice of her to ask, but there truly was no reason to do it. Plus, I didn't want all of them watching. Judging. I was not a stunner like Claudia.

Dad said, "Go for it, Min."

I had to shut this down now. "Thanks, but no thanks. But if I ever need a fancy dress, you'll be the first person I call."

Claudia nodded but looked disappointed.

So be it.

**

On the way back to the car I walked next to Dad as he pushed the double stroller. Luckily both babies were sleeping. "I'll babysit for your banquet," I said.

"Oh. Good. I mean, I assumed . . . I mean, we were counting on you since you'd said you would when I first mentioned the award."

I'd forgotten about that. "When is it again?"

"Next Saturday."

I stopped walking. "*Next* Saturday?"

"Yup."

"Uh . . . I've been invited to a party. Ashley's going. All my friends are going." I didn't mention Gabe.

He stopped beside me. "What are the odds of that? I'm so sorry, Min."

It took me a moment to understand what he was saying. "I don't want to miss *this* party, Dad. I don't go to many. And I already gave up a concert last night."

"Did your mom make you do that?"

"No, but . . ." I didn't want to discuss Mom's dating issues with him. "I really need you to find another sitter."

Claudia joined the conversation, her dress bag draped over her arm. "What's this about another sitter?"

"Dad's banquet is on a night I have something planned. I can't babysit."

"Oh no."

Dad said, "You have to, Min. You promised."

I stepped back, needing room for my emotions. "I didn't know I'd get invited to something. I didn't know the banquet would be on the same night."

"That's unfortunate," Dad said, "but we're counting on you."

This couldn't be happening. "Hire someone."

Claudia shook her head. "You know we can't do that. The few

times we tried was a disaster. We don't trust anyone with our kiddos but you."

Usually I would enjoy the compliment, but not this time. "What about those neighbor girls down the street? Or maybe Mom could take care of them."

Dad's eyebrows rose. "The neighbor girls are way too young to handle twins. And your mother? Absolutely not. Number one, she'd never do it, and number two, I don't want her near our kids. She still can't have a civil phone call with me. No way I'd leave the babies with her."

Although he was painting Mom as a crazed ex, I couldn't really argue with him. Mom still carried a full-sized plank on her shoulder.

He put his hands on my shoulders. "This banquet is the culmination of twelve months of hard work to support you, your mom, Claudia, and the twins. It's *the* honor in my industry."

"I get it. But this is the biggest party of *my* school year." Pretty much the only party.

Dad checked out the sky a minute. Then he said, "How about I pay for you, Ashley, and a few of your friends to have your own private night out with a fancy dinner and maybe tickets to some music group that comes to town?"

It sounded fun, and the party *was* just a party—even if it Gabe's party.

"Please, Min. Please say you'll babysit. For me."

Duty called. When my parents first mentioned divorce I'd yelled a lot, pouted, stomped my feet, slammed doors. I'd quickly discovered none of it changed anything, and actually made things worse. Over the years I'd learned to adapt. Cope. And give in. Life was easier that way.

Dad and Claudia surrounded me, waiting for a yes. If I didn't give it to them, they'd hound me all weekend and we'd all be miserable.

"Whatever," I said. "I'll babysit."

Dad grabbed my face and kissed it. "You are a gem. A diamond."

Then why did I feel like a piece of gravel?

**

The good part of giving in was that Dad and Claudia treated me like a queen the rest of the day. They took me to my favorite Mexican place for lunch, and Claudia assured me that come evening I didn't have to give the babies their baths or get them to bed. She'd handle all of it.

As she should. Mom often told me, "You are not their maid."

Actually they never made me feel like one. I liked to help. I wanted to feel useful. I loved them all very much.

My least favorite role was being put in the middle as a peace negotiator. From the beginning Dad would gripe that Mom was the witchiest woman ever, and Mom complained that Dad was selfish and controlling. I'd only been twelve. The best way I could help was to be whoever they needed me to be. I laid low and didn't rock the boat because it was being rocked plenty without me adding to the waves.

I didn't mind spending time in both places. Mom and I had our routine down—until another boyfriend stepped in. And out.

And at Dad's I slipped into *their* routine that was determined by the twins' schedule. The babies were a nice distraction. If they were in the room I didn't need to make conversation. And when the kids were in bed, we were all too tired to talk so we watched a lot of movies—non-Hallmark movies. Fine by me.

But tonight I needed time alone. I excused myself and went up to my room. I had an important call to make.

Yet maybe I shouldn't make it. I'd never called Gabe before, and his invitation hadn't been formal—he'd made it to me *and* Ashley.

But I wanted him to know that I really wanted to come.

So I called.

Gabe didn't answer. Maybe it was better that way. I left a voice mail: "Hey, Gabe, Minnie here. I can't come to your party next Saturday. My dad needs me to babysit because of an award banquet. But thanks for inviting me." I stopped before I said, "I appreciate it." That would have sounded too desperate.

I hung up. Then I flipped open my tablet and did what I often did when I felt horrible—I watched an episode of "The Joy of Painting." Bob Ross always mesmerized me with his soft voice talking about "happy trees." He made it look so easy, but I knew it wasn't. Maybe someday I'd be able to paint like—

I closed my tablet, distraught. I was never going to be a painter like Bob Ross or Gabe or anyone else. I wasn't even in art school. And the way things were going, I was never going to live away from home. I was completely and utterly trapped.

I shoved my tablet across the bed and pulled a pillow to my chest.

It felt like there was a dome over my life. I was on display, a fly caught under a glass. And just like the fly I could buzz around all I wanted, but in the end I was destined to bang against the glass to the point of exhaustion.

And death.

Actually, there were two domes. One, when I lived with Mom,

and another when I lived with Dad. Some of the details under the dome were different, but I was still trapped.

I stared at nothing for a long while. But then I spotted the other invitation I had received, sticking out of my backpack. I took it out and read it again. The Discovery Room was an intriguing name, promising good things. And I was invited.

It was kind of impressive the invitation hadn't come from a mass-mailing. It had been hand-delivered by a handsome old guy named Wesley, who seemed kind and sincere, and was a good listener.

I reminded myself that con men were always kind and sincere and good listeners. That's how they tricked you.

Yet going to a place where they would help me figure out my future didn't sound like a con. Maybe I *could* accept the invitation.

But probably not. How would I ever explain it to Mom and Dad? What good would it do to pinpoint my dream when they wouldn't ever let me pursue it?

I was never going to escape the dome.

I shoved the invitation in the backpack and threw the whole thing off the side of my bed. The corner of it hit the lamp on my bedside table. It crashed to the floor.

Great.

Moments later Dad opened my door. "What's going on?" He saw the broken lamp. "How did that happen?"

I wanted to tell him it was all his fault. I wanted to gripe that it wasn't right for him to ask me to give up Gabe's party. I wanted to yell at him and tell him to just hire a babysitter, this one was busy.

"Min?"

With a fresh breath I pressed all the angry words into a corner where a thousand other angry words were stored. "It got knocked over. I'll pay for a new one."

He eyed me for a long moment. "You don't have to do that."

He bent down to clean the mess, but I beat him to the floor. "I got it." I grabbed my trash can and began filling it with broken pieces.

He didn't look convinced, but didn't ask again. I know he preferred times when the boat was steady and the waves were calm. When I was calm.

"Good night then," he said.

There was nothing good about it. I couldn't use the g-word, but managed, "'Night."

I cleaned up the mess and climbed under the covers. To fume. To cry. To feel sorry for myself.

My phone pinged. It was a text from Gabe: *Sorry you can't make it. Another time, okay?*

Another time? Really? I wrote back: *That would be great.*

He sent me a smiling emoji with a thumbs up.

I snuggled into my pillow, feeling better.

Until I checked Instagram and saw pictures of Ashley and her friends having fun together.

Everybody was having fun except me.

CHAPTER NINE

Lydia

For the Lord sees clearly what a man does,
examining every path he takes.
Proverbs 5: 21

I sat at the kitchen island and stared into my coffee. Jeremy poured milk into his cereal and sat beside me.

After two bites of Cinnamon Life he seemed to notice me for the first time. "What's wrong?"

"I'm done."

"With . . . ?"

"Work. I'm going to quit."

I felt his stare. "You've only been there a week."

"A wasted week."

"Why do you say that?"

I knew it would sound petty, but I told him anyway. "I haven't made a single friend."

"Sometimes it takes a while for people to accept a newbie."

"I've done my part. I've tried chatting in the elevator, the hall, at lunch, and even in the restroom, but all I've gotten was polite chit-chat. Not even that. More just a chit. No chat."

"That's strange because *you* can make conversation with a chair."

I swiveled on the stool to face him and threw my hands in the air. "I'd get more out of a chair. Is it because I'm older?"

"You're only fifty. How old are they?"

"Twenties and thirties mostly. From what I've overheard, they spend their free time at bars or exchanging info about who they've been matched with on some dating app."

"They *are* of that age . . ."

"A few have young kids. But *they* discuss potty training or what their kids won't eat. Anyone who looks over fifty is in management, so they're out of my league."

"I'm sorry, Lyd. That's tough."

It was nice to get his sympathy—not that it would do any good. *"What bugs me is that no one has asked me a single question about my life. Not even the usual 'Are you married?', 'Do you have kids?', or even 'What's your favorite Thai restaurant?'. Nothing."

"That is odd. Perhaps people who enjoy data entry don't have the same need for social interaction that you do."

"So they're all computer nerds?" I shook my head. "I'm doing the job and I'm not a computer nerd."

"You do it, but you don't enjoy it. "You were the one who wanted a change, away from people."

"Away from being responsible *for* people."

He finished his cereal and put his dish in the dishwasher. "You'll find your groove, Lyd. And remember, you don't have to work." He touched my shoulder. "I just want you to be happy."

"I know you do."

He put on his suit coat. When he dressed for work he looked like the king of the world.

Unfortunately, I was far from being the queen.

**

I went to work determined to have a real conversation with somebody.

I had no takers.

It was infuriating, which made me type in the data with extra gusto, pounding on the keys to deflect my anger. I knew I'd chosen this type of job thinking it would make me forget what had happened when I *had* been working with people, but this wasn't the answer. When they'd hired me I'd thought it was a God-thing because it came so quick and easy. Obviously, I'd been wrong to think it came from Him, and I'd been wrong to take it.

I heard sudden laughter coming from a few cubicles away. People connecting with people.

But not with me.

I sighed audibly but there was no one to hear it.

How pitiful was that?

It was the final straw. I was done. It was time to end the torture.

I stuffed my family picture into my purse, along with snacks and my favorite pens I'd brought from home. One hand carried my travel mug while the other carried an African violet. I took one last look to make sure I didn't leave anything behind. "Good riddance," I whispered to my cubicle.

I was about to walk out when the phone rang. It startled me. Nobody called me.

Curiosity won out and I set the plant down to answer. "Lydia Brogdon. How may I help you?"

"Hi, Mom. Wow. You sound so professional." It was JoJo. "I wanted to call you on your official office number."

The first and last call I'd get on this number. "That's so nice of you, sweetie. How are you?"

"I just finished a history test so my brain is fried."

"How do you think you did?"

"Good. I'm sure I aced it."

"Of course you did. You're so smart."

"I have my moments. How are *you?*"

I wondered if she'd talked to Jeremy. "I'm doing okay. But adjusting to a new job is hard."

"Of course it is," she said. "I'm really proud of you for putting yourself out there, for getting out of the house, and for . . . starting over."

But tomorrow I'd be starting over at home. Again. I didn't mention that, but said, "Thanks, sweetie."

"I have tomorrow free so I thought I'd pick you up for lunch. Noon okay?"

I sank into my chair. Lunch with my daughter—with *her* doing the asking? "That sounds wonderful. I'll meet you somewhere."

"No, no. I want to see your desk. I'll come up. If that's all right?"

I dug the family picture out of my purse and set it in place. "That sounds great. I'll see you then."

So much for quitting. Today.

**

My keyboard could thank JoJo for a reprieve from its abuse. After her call I flew through my work, fueled by the anticipation of lunch with my daughter.

Even though she went to a university less than an hour away, we didn't see her as much as I would have liked. Logic said—meaning Jeremy said--it was normal for college students to only come home occasionally. It had started off weekly, but eventually had slowed to once a month, which wasn't enough for me. Jeremy seemed to handle our empty-nest much better than I did.

Actually, seeing her tomorrow was perfect because tonight I'd decided to go to the Discovery Room to be trained in . . . whatever they wanted me to be trained in. Since I hadn't quit yet I needed to go before I lost the chance. Maybe it would help guide me in my next work endeavor.

I checked the clock. It was only three and I was out of coffee. I picked up my mug and headed to the breakroom.

The two guys who were there didn't look up as they played video games on their phones.

Hi, to you too.

I poured coffee in my mug, but as I was reaching for the sweetener, I tipped the mug over and it spilled all over the counter and floor. I reached for paper towels, but the dispenser was out. I checked in the cupboards but there were none there either.

"You can get towels in the supply room," one of the men said, glancing up from his phone.

"Thanks for your help." I wouldn't want to disturb your game.

It was obvious that chivalry—or common courtesy—was dead.

I went to the supply room. At least I'd see Mr. Wesley and could tell him I was going to the training.

I was met by a woman behind the counter. "What do you need?" she asked without a smile.

"The break room is out of paper towels."

She pointed to the clipboard and I filled it out.

"Is Mr. Wesley here?" I asked.

"Who?"

"Mr. Wesley? He helped me with batteries the other day."

"No Mr. Wesley here."

Hmm. That was odd. "Sorry, I must be mistaken. Thanks for the paper towels."

I took the towels and headed back to the break room. I passed by a string of caseworkers' desks to get there. Most had clients with them, people applying for help. Maybe that would be a better job for me. At least I'd have someone to talk to, to help.

Right after I passed the third office a young woman stepped into the aisle and said, "Mrs. Brogdon?"

I turned around and recognized her immediately. "Nova? Nova Wilson?"

She grinned. "Hi."

I hugged her. She'd gotten skinny. The last time I'd seen her was in high school. "It's so good to see you."

She let go and stepped back. She was wearing jeans and a man's shirt tied at the waist over a tank top. There was a rip in the sleeve and a stain on the tank. Her light brown hair was in a messy bun. That word described the gist of her look: messy.

"What are you doing here?" she asked me.

"I work here." I realized I had a thousand paper towels in my hand. "I spilled coffee in the break room. What are you doing here?"

"I uh . . . we uh . . ."

A caseworker appeared at the doorway of her office. "Can I help you?" she asked me.

"I work here," I said. "Nova and I have known each other since she was little."

"Hmm. Miss Wilson? Shall we continue with your financial aid application?"

Nova blushed, but nodded. "I gotta go. It was nice seeing you, Mrs. Brogdon. Say hi to JoJo for me."

"Will do." I thought about inviting her to our lunch, but didn't. Yet I was curious about what she'd been up to since high school. She was on public assistance?

Maybe JoJo would know.

**

That evening, I drove into the parking lot of the Discovery Room but chose not to park directly out front. The office looked . . . sketchy. I'd imagined that any special training used by a state agency would be handled by a big company, not a slot in a strip mall.

I shut off the car and called Jeremy. "I'm here."

"Good luck."

"I think I'm going to need it."

"Why do you say that?"

I didn't want to start out negative, but . . . "You know how people say first impressions are everything?"

"Of course."

"The Discovery Room needs to remember that. This place is a hole in the wall, with zero street appeal, set between a quilt shop and a beauty parlor."

"It can't be that bad," Jeremy said. "Think about who frequents quilt shops and beauty parlors: women. If it was surrounded by pawn shops or tattoo parlors, I'd be worried.

"I suppose."

"You'll be fine. Call if you need me."

I hung up and said a quick prayer that everything would go well. Then I collected a notepad and pen and got out. I hoped they had coffee.

Inside was a pretty young woman with light blonde hair pulled into a bun like a ballerina. "Welcome," she said.

I glanced around the office which was nicely done in a soft green. Yet there was something odd about it. Like it was half-done. I spotted one landscape picture on the wall, an out-of-control plant, and a coffee maker—which gave me hope of getting a cup. There were only two interior doors. I assumed one led into a conference room where I would receive my training. But where was everyone else?

"I'm Lydia Brogdon."

"Nice to meet you. I'm Gracie."

"Am I the first one here?" I asked.

"You're the only one here."

I took a half-step back. "I don't understand."

Gracie flipped a hand at my concern. "You will." She nodded at my floral blouse. "That's pretty. I've started to like bright prints too. This was my mother's." She pointed to her own shirt.

"I love pink and purple together," I said. And I did, though the sheer blouse over a tank was a style that was at least twenty years old.

Gracie took a step toward one of the doors. "Shall we get started?"

So much for coffee. I followed her into a room—one of the strangest rooms I'd ever seen. I did a full-circle scan. "It's like a planetarium."

She looked up at the domed ceiling. "I guess it is." She pointed at a single stool in the middle. "Have a seat, please."

I did as I was told. One stool? I'd expected a conference room with a speaker's podium, PowerPoint slides, and, most importantly, other people.

Gracie stepped forward. "You won't be needing your notepad. I'll take it and your purse and put it over here." She pushed on a portion of the wall and a drawer popped out. When the drawer closed, it blended back into the wall.

Oddly, I felt vulnerable without my purse to hug or the ability to take notes. Plus, being away from my phone was always disconcerting. *Now* who was the one obsessed with technology?

Sitting on the stool left me exposed. To what, I didn't know. Not knowing was a problem in itself. I was an organizer. A planner. This whole thing made me uncomfortable.

Gracie gave me a parting smile. "Don't worry. Everything will be fine. Enjoy." She left the Room.

Enjoy what?

The door clicked shut.

Suddenly the walls were covered with images.

I spun around on the stool and immediately recognized JoJo's elementary school. The street outside was teaming with parents picking up their kids after class. I couldn't count the number of times I'd been in that line, yet I hadn't minded a bit. It was my job.

And then . . .

There I was!

I put a hand to my mouth. I was walking out of the school with JoJo, helping her take home her solar system project. JoJo was wearing her blue Daisy Girl Scout vest. She'd been so proud of the badges she'd earned. All these clues meant she was six.

I spotted our Windstar minivan. I'd loved that van. I thought the emerald green color was the epitome of style. The young me opened up the back and got the project put away. JoJo climbed in and put her seatbelt on.

"Good girl," I said at the same time the younger me said the words.

I was just getting in the van when a dog started barking loud. Real loud. It made me turn to see it. Oddly, the dog had a yellow glow around it. What was that about?

But then I saw little Nova Wilson, standing alone by the curb. She kept looking right, then left. She seemed worried.

Memories flooded back and I realized this day was the beginning of our friendship. It was incredibly strange that I'd just seen the grown-Nova.

The young me stuck my head in the van and asked, "Who's that girl?"

JoJo sat up tall to see. "That's Nova."

"Is she in your class?"

"Uh-huh. But she's weird. What craft are we doing at Daisies today, Mom?"

I looked at Nova and she looked at me. I remembered that exact moment like it was yesterday. There was an instant connection between us. A little spark was lit. It was like someone nudged me.

I walked over to her and said, "Hey, Nova. I'm JoJo's mom. Is someone picking you up?"

"I . . . I think so, but sometimes Mom can't come because she's working. Then I walk home."

There weren't many kids left waiting. I hated the idea of this first-grader walking home alone. Plus, I didn't need to check my watch to know that *I* really needed to get home because other Daisy Scouts would be arriving for our meeting.

"Ask," I whispered to the Room, even though I knew what happened.

The young me said, "We're going to our house for Daisy Girl Scouts. We're going to have a snack and do a craft project. Want to come? You can call your mom and I'll take you home afterward."

Nova glanced toward the street one last time. "What kind of snack?"

"M&M cookies."

She smiled. "Those are my favorite."

We headed to the van.

But then the video faded and lights came on. "Hey!" I said. "I want to see more."

I was shocked to see Mr. Wesley come in the door. I stood. "*You're* here?"

"I am."

"I asked for you at the supply room. They'd never heard of you."

"Ah, to be so easily forgotten."

The impact of the video merged with the reality that I was inside a sphere watching home movies that couldn't be home movies because no one had been filming us, and . . ."What's going on here, Mr. Wesley?"

He held up a hand. "Just Wesley. I'm so glad you came, Mrs. Brogdon."

I shook my head. "What *is* all this?" I swept a hand to encompass the Room.

"Didn't you enjoy it?"

"I did. But I don't understand how you got such footage, or why you're showing it to me now when I'm supposed to be in a special training session."

He smiled the smallest smile. "Isn't *this* special?"

He was sharp but exasperating. "Yes, of course it's special. But what's this all about?"

He led me back to the stool. "You are a facts-person, am I correct?"

"Yes. I suppose I am."

"You like to be in control."

Now *that* sounded like a topic in a special training session. "I guess. I know I should ease up—my family is always telling me to back off." When he smiled broadly, I crossed my arms. "I think someone else likes to be in control. Am I right?"

"Touché, Mrs. Brogdon."

"Why was I shown this clip?"

He took two steps to the left, then back. Was he stalling?

"I asked, why—"

He faced me. "There was a moment, right before you got in the van. Something distracted you."

I thought back. "A dog barking."

He nodded. "Dogs bark every day, but this time . . . ?"

The image was fresh in my mind. "It made me see Nova." I

thought of something else. "The dog glowed. Why?"

"You could call it a marker of sorts."

Marker . . . "To show that it was important?"

"Very good." He touched the tip of his nose. "What happened after you saw little Nova?"

I was catching on. "I asked her to the Daisy meeting."

"You didn't have to do that," he said.

"I suppose not. I could have driven away."

"But you didn't."

"I did not." I gave a small smile. I felt like I'd earned a gold star.

"What happened then?" he asked.

"This first meeting was the beginning of our friendship. I took her under my wing."

"Because . . . ?"

He was playing twenty questions. "Because she needed another adult on her side. Even that first day I could tell something was wrong. At Scouts she wolfed down the snack in seconds. We were making Mother's Day cards but she just sat there while the other girls were cutting, pasting, and drawing."

"What did you do?"

I let my thoughts focus on the memory. "She and I had alone time in the kitchen because I'd asked her to help me put more cookies on the platter. It gave me a chance to ask about her mom and dad. She said her mom was mean, that she always yelled at her for nothing—like when Nova burned the mac and cheese. Gracious, she was only six! I wouldn't let JoJo use the stove at that age. Nova said she hadn't meant for it to burn."

"I'm sure she hadn't."

"Exactly. She shared a bit more and it was clear her mom had a mean streak."

"Such as?"

I'd tucked these memories away, yet once I started remembering one, another came back to me. "Her mom forgot her birthday. Nova had pouted, which made her mom demand to know why. When Nova reminded her it was her birthday, her mom had the gall to tell her, 'Don't be ridiculous. Nobody needs to celebrate when you were born.'"

"How did you feel after hearing that?" Wesley asked.

"It was a horribly cruel thing to say to a child. To anyone. I asked if she could talk to her dad about it, but he'd run off."

"Poor girl."

"She was such a sweet child. And yet . . . at that moment I thought about how hard it must be for her mom to be a single mother. I told Nova that at the end of the day her mom might be tired from work. I said moms get tired just like kids, and they can get grumpy, and even say things they don't mean."

"Did she agree?"

I shrugged. "She pretended to. I said maybe a card would brighten her day. So she made one. But unlike the other girls' cards that said, 'I love you, Mommy' she wanted me to help her write, 'Thank you for working hard.'"

"An appropriate sentiment," Wesley said. "Considering."

True.

"Did Nova join Scouts?" he asked.

I nodded. "Not officially, but she came every week. At the end of the school year we were having an awards ceremony and . . ." I smiled.

"Why are you smiling?"

"All the other girls had already earned badges that were sewn on their vests. But Nova didn't even have a vest. I'd given her a note to take to her mom with the information about where to buy one, but her mom said it was a waste of money."

"Perhaps she didn't have the money."

"Perhaps. But then another little girl was moving away and her mom asked if I knew of any girl who needed a vest. I said yes. It was a lucky break."

Wesley's eyebrows rose. "Lucky break?"

I blinked, unsure how much I should say. I didn't believe in luck.

"Go on, Mrs. Brogdon. Was it luck?"

My throat was dry. I swallowed. "No, it wasn't. It . . . I thought it was God."

I waited for his negative response, but he said, "Noted. Did she earn a badge?"

With his accepting response, I felt a weight lift. I was so used to watching my words while out in the world. To be able to speak freely about God was a relief. "Nova earned many badges. I didn't want her to go without at the awards ceremony, so I bought them and sewed them on her vest."

"That was nice of you."

"It all worked out. Nova was beaming when she got them. Unfortunately, her mom didn't make it to the ceremony."

"But you were there. You were a bright spot in her life."

"I guess I was." The praise felt good. In fact, I ate it up, which made me feel a bit needy.

"Would you like to see another scene?" Wesley asked.

I had a choice?

Before I answered I had an epiphany: I'd watched a nice scene—a time when I'd done the right thing. But I knew there were countless times I'd chosen wrongly. Odds were, any subsequent scenes could highlight the mistakes I'd made.

"Is something wrong?" Wesley asked.

"Not wrong, but . . . that scene was positive, but . . . will the new one be good too? Or bad?"

"You only want to see times you chose well?"

"Pretty much. If I have the choice."

"You do," he said. "You do have the choice."

I realized we might be talking about two different things. "I have a choice to see *only* the times when I did good, or I have a choice to see more scenes—however they play out?"

"The latter."

"Oh."

"Keep in mind that hard times garner strength."

"So do easy times," I said.

He shook his head slowly. "Very little strength is gained during easy times."

I had to think about that a moment.

"Do you agree, Mrs. Brogdon?"

Maybe. I plucked a thread from my pants. This conversation was difficult but it was probably best to be honest. "The truth is, I am the most non-confrontational person alive. I hate conflict. I don't like drama. I care—too much—what other people think. So seeing times when I blew it? That goes against who I am."

"So we're done here?"

I put up a hand. "Whoa! I'm not saying that. It's just that I'm hesitant to relive anything negative. I mean it's the past. It's not like I can change anything."

He sighed and looked to the floor.

I didn't want to disappoint him. *That* was against my nature too.

"Can I have a few minutes to think about it?" I asked.

He looked up. "If it is necessary, then yes, you can."

He left the Room. True to his word, another scene did *not* start.

What did I want to do?

CHAPTER TEN

Lydia

Don't be afraid, for I am with you.
Don't be discouraged, for I am your God.
I will strengthen you and help you.
I will hold you up with my victorious right hand.
Isaiah 41: 10

I paced around the circumference of the Room, my arms folded, my eyes down. Wesley was waiting in the main office for me to make a decision about seeing more scenes from my life—which would most surely include times when I'd made the wrong choice.

I stopped pacing and said under my breath, "I know I'm not perfect. Far from it."

So what was I afraid of? Seeing truth? It's not like anything would be a surprise. I was well aware of my bad choices.

I studied the amazing sphere that had somehow created scenes just for me. If God was behind all this then who was I to cut my time short? Did I trust Him or not?

I drew in a long breath and let it out. I bowed my head. "God? Show me what You've got."

Then I walked to the door and opened it.

"Yes, Mrs. Brogdon? Have you made a decision?"

"I want to see more. All of it."

"Very good." He came in the Room.

"I'm sorry to have caused problems."

He shook his head. "No problem at all. But we are glad you've decided to continue." He motioned toward the stool. "Return to your seat and the experience will resume."

"Thank you."

He left the Room. As the door clicked shut, I hoped I'd made the right decision. There was no turning back now.

Immediately, the Room was filled with a visual slice of time. It was a year after Nova came into our lives. The Husky Day Carnival was set up in the school gym with face-painting and games like corn hole, rubber ducky fishing, and ping-pong ball toss. There were tables selling homemade trinkets, Husky T-shirts, and caps. I was working at the bake sale table. I'd made my famous peanut brittle.

The doors were about to open when I saw Nova come in the gym. She was beaming and was pulling a woman along, a woman with long frizzy hair, a tiered hippie skirt, and sandals. I remembered thinking she looked like Janis Joplin.

It was Nova's mom.

I had a shocked look on my face, but I covered it quickly and greeted them. Nova took a plate of brownies from her mom. "Look, Mrs. Brogdon. Mom made brownies to sell."

The brownies glowed.

Why were they important?

The young me said, "That's wonderful, Nova." I moved to shake the mom's hand. "Hi, I'm Lydia."

She seemed squeamish, but shook my hand. "Meribelle."

I looked at the plastic covered treats on a paper plate. "Thanks for these. Everybody loves brownies."

I thought that would be the end of it but it seemed like she wanted to say more. Then Nova gazed up at her. "Tell her, Mom."

Meribelle's eyes skittered from side to side. She was clearly not comfortable being there. "I . . . I want to thank you for taking time with Nova. She likes going to your house, and the Scout-stuff."

It was the first indication she'd noticed. I touched Nova's shoulder. "We love having her. She's welcome anytime."

Meribelle nodded and patted Nova on the head. "I gotta get to work."

"Where do you work?" I'd always been curious.

"I'm a clerk at Sunshine Records," she said.

Her look suited the job. "Thanks for bringing the brownies. Do you want me to bring Nova home after the fair?"

I saw a look of utter relief on her face. "That would be great. Thanks." She walked away.

Jo-Jo and Nova checked out the baked goods, their eyes hungry. "Can we buy something, Mom?" JoJo asked.

"Let's let other customers go first," I said. The doors were opened and families streamed in.

I stepped back to stand with the two other mothers who were helping man the table. "It's nice Nova's mom brought brownies," I said to them.

One of the moms gave the plate a sideways glance, "They probably have pot in them."

The other mom chuckled. "Or worse. Once a pothead, always a pothead. And that name can't be real. Meribelle?" she snickered. "Really?"

I glanced at the girls. Nova was right *there,* not four feet away.

"Don't say such things," I whispered.

"Whatever. *I'm* not buying them and I'll steer—" A customer stepped up and began looking at Nova's brownies and another plate of brownies that had frosting.

"Hmm," the woman said. "How do I choose?"

The first mom pointed to the second plate. "These are better."

"Really?" the customer said. "If you say so."

The woman paid and left.

I watched Nova's face. She looked like she was going to cry.

In that moment I remember thinking: *buy her brownies.*

But I didn't. *I* didn't want pot brownies. And the thought that there *might* be pot in them . . . what if someone complained or got sick? That wouldn't help the school at all.

Thankfully, the girls moved on toward the games. While the other ladies were chatting, I placed Nova's plate in the back row.

The video faded and the lights came on.

Great timing because I didn't want to see more.

Wesley came in and I immediately hugged myself. "That scene made me feel awful."

"The truth can be tough to see."

"I felt horrible then and I feel horrible now, watching it. I should have bought the brownies to make Nova happy *and* to show those gossip queens that I didn't believe their lies."

"But you did."

There was no denying it. "I couldn't be sure. I mean . . . you saw her mom."

"So hippie skirts and long hair equal pot use?"

He was backing me into a corner. "Not necessarily, but stereotypes are stereotypes because they are based on reality." I tried to think of some way to defend myself. "I shook her hand. I talked to her."

"You were polite. One point for Lydia."

He was right. I'd done the minimum. "The other ladies were the ones saying the mean stuff about her."

"Which is on *them*."

I walked to the far side of the sphere, wishing there was a place to hide.

"Did someone buy the brownies?" Wesley asked.

Another layer of guilt dropped with a thud. "No. At the end of the evening there were only two unsold plates: Nova's and one other plate where a lot of the cookies were broken."

"How did Nova react when she saw that?"

"I still remember the pained look on her face when I gave the plate back to her." I pressed my hands against my temples. "That was another missed chance to buy them."

"What did Nova do with the brownies?"

I avoided Wesley's eyes, for this was the hardest memory. "On her way out of the gym she threw them in the trash." I pressed my hands against my chest. "Seeing that just killed me."

Wesley didn't say anything. His silence spoke volumes.

"I'm sorry I didn't make the right choice. Even if they were laced with pot I should've bought them to make Nova feel good about herself and her mom."

"Very true."

"Why didn't I do that? I didn't need the brownies to glow to know that was the right thing to do. I hurt her."

Wesley nodded. "It's good you acknowledge it. Yet missed chances happen to everyone."

I knew that. But I still felt bad.

"Shall I show another?"

"Is it better than this one?"

"That's for you to decide."

I nodded. "I think I need to see it."

Wesley tapped his temple. "Wise woman."

I got comfortable on the stool, Wesley left, and the video began.

The scene showed my kitchen. It had to be a couple years ago, as the wallpaper border that I'd originally had was gone and the walls had been painted a pale gray from their previous pale blue.

My hair was in my current shoulder length style, but I had bangs. Never again --turns out I hate the feel of hair on my forehead.

As if in response to the thought, I swept my hair behind my ears.

A cookbook was open to a chicken recipe. I still made that recipe. I saw a cherry pie on the counter. That was my father-in-law's favorite pie. They must have been coming for dinner.

I rummaged through the canned goods. "Drat," I said. "I need cream of chicken soup."

I saw a glow coming from the back of the cupboard. The soup was there?

But the younger me didn't see it. She checked her watch. I remembered weighing my options: I could make a different recipe or run to the store.

The family loved this chicken. I chose the store. I grabbed my purse and got in the car. No keys. I rummaged through my purse, then went back inside and checked on the kitchen desk and the counter. No keys. On a longshot I went to JoJo's bedroom. There they were, on her bedside table. They glowed.

They glowed?

I high-stepped over the messy floor, grabbed the keys, and hurried out. I'd just lost five minutes that I didn't have to spare.

I drove to the store, but had to slow down at the main intersection. There'd just been an accident—someone got T-boned. A woman was being helped to sitting on the curb, her hand to her head. A police car drove up and I heard an ambulance siren coming close.

The police officer directed traffic around the accident

I had to make up time. At the grocery store I rushed to the soup aisle and got two cans of cream of chicken. I was just turning to leave when I saw Nova turning into the same aisle.

She glowed.

Memories rushed back. Nova was seventeen and very pregnant. She and JoJo had gone different ways and I hadn't seen much of her since they'd both been in middle school.

I remembered getting an inner nudge to say hi, yet considering her situation . . . was she living at home? Was she keeping the baby? Was she even in school?

The sight of her brought up complicated issues, so I ignored her and quickly picked up a few other things I needed.

I went to check out, but only one lane was open.

And Nova was in it.

I could detour and roam around the store until she was gone, or just deal with it.

I got in line behind her. She looked up and saw me. "Oh, hi, Mrs. Brogdon."

"Hi, Nova. How are—?"

The clerk interrupted. "That'll be $32.98."

Nova got out her money, counting and recounting it. She obviously didn't have enough. She pointed to a few items "I need to put these back."

The clerk subtracted the items. Nova paid. "Bye," she said to me. "It was nice seeing you."

I felt like an idiot. A selfish idiot. I spoke aloud to the Room "I get it! Again I ignored what I should have done! I should have just paid the difference. I'm sorry."

The video faded and Wesley came back in.

"Well, that was fun," I said sarcastically.

"It wasn't meant to be fun," he said. "It was meant to be educational."

"Once again I feel horrible. I blew it. But I was in a hurry because of needing soup—"

"Which *was* in your cupboard."

I remembered seeing it glow. "Why did it glow?"

"You tell me."

An answer came to me, but it seemed a bit ridiculous. "God hid a can of soup?"

"What else happened?"

"I couldn't find my keys. There was a lot of hiding going on," I said.

"Why?" he asked.

"You're asking *me* why?"

"I am."

I stood. I hated when I felt clueless. I wanted to understand.

And then it was like the clouds parted to show me the light. I turned toward Wesley. "If not for the soup being hidden I wouldn't have gone to the store."

"Check."

"If not for the keys being missing I would have left five minutes earlier and . . . I might have been involved in the car accident."

"Check."

"Which led me to the store where I just happened to see Nova."

"Check. And yet . . . ?"

My stomach tightened with anger—at myself. "I avoided her, then I said hi but didn't give her whatever money she needed. She had to put things back in order to pay."

"That's an apt summary."

Too apt. "The truth is, I didn't want to be bothered with a girl who'd obviously gotten into trouble."

"But you're a mentor."

Ouch. "Yes, but I'd never been assigned a girl in that situation."

"Ah."

There were unspoken sentences in his "ah."

"Regardless, for whatever reason, I didn't do what I should have done."

"Your honesty is commendable."

"Even though my actions were not."

"Check."

I thought of Daisy Scouts, the bake sale, and the grocery store. "Why are all these videos about Nova?"

"Why do you think?"

The first-grade Nova, melded with the second-grade Nova, the junior-year Nova, and the grown up Nova . . . "I just saw her at work, at my new job."

"As arranged."

I gaped at him. As arranged by God? That gave everything more credibility. None of these things had been a coincidence. "Nova *was* a part of our lives and now she's back."

"That, she is."

"So what am I supposed to do next?"

"It's your choice."

Talk about complicated. "I'm supposed to help her? Now?"

"Do you want to help her now?"

Yes. No. Maybe.

I'd just complained to Jeremy that I missed interacting with people. But to contact Nova again, with all her problematic issues . . . I didn't even know if she'd kept the baby.

I thought of an excuse. "Although I *was* a mentor, I'm not necessarily good at dealing with teenagers and their problems. I tried with another kid. And failed."

Wesley nodded once. "Glen Freeman."

My initial thought of *they know about him?* was quickly discarded. Of course they knew about him. And me. And probably every detail of the entire, tragic situation.

"I failed Glen. I don't want to fail Nova."

"Sit," Wesley said. He headed for the door.

If this scene had anything to do with Glen . . . I felt sick to my stomach.

The Room filled with a movie. I was walking down the hall of the high school where I'd mentored. I turned into the office.

"Ready to get your next student, Lydia?" the secretary said.

"I am."

I whispered to myself. "It's the first week of school."

The woman opened one file, checked something, then opened another file. The second file glowed.

"Hmm," the secretary said. "It appears I have one student and one mentor out today."

"Sick?" I asked.

"It's that nasty flu going around. But . . . here's the rub. The sick student was supposed to be yours and the sick mentor was assigned to the well student." She looked at me and cocked her head. "You okay with trading? Who knows how long either of them are going to be out."

"I'm okay with that," I said.

The secretary seemed relieved. "Great. So here's yours. You can explain to him what's what."

The bell rang. "I'll do that."

The younger me hurried to the mentoring room. The older me shook my head. I didn't want to see more. I knew who was in that room. I knew . . . too much.

I watched myself walk inside and look stunned to see someone I knew. "Glen?"

He blinked when he saw me. "Mrs. Brogdon?"

We'd been friends with his family for years. "It appears we've been assigned to each other."

"Cool."

Seeing him now, knowing what would happen . . . he was such a cute kid but he looked too young to be a junior. His hair was a curly brown and he had dark soulful eyes. He was a kid who'd always been a tad strange, as if he was uncomfortable in his own skin. Plus, I knew he occasionally suffered from seizures—he'd suffered one during one of our sessions. I put a hand to my chest. It physically hurt to see him again.

I was shocked when the lights in the sphere came on.

I realized I was crying.

Wesley came in with a tissue. "Just seeing him is emotional, isn't it?"

"You could say that." I wiped my eyes and blew my nose. "He was such a good kid. And his grades improved so much second semester. He was shy at first, but later seemed happy. And he wasn't a stranger. Our families had known each other for years. We spent time together every few months. I still don't understand how he could've...." I shook my head.

"Overdosed?"

I couldn't hear those words and stay seated. I paced behind the stool. "If there were signs he was using, I missed them all. And his parents never hinted at anything. As far as I knew, things were good. He was the last kid you'd think would take drugs. They still don't know where he got the oxycontin."

Wesley nodded soberly. "If professionals and his own family missed the signs, you can't blame yourself."

I could and I did. "If I'd had any inkling, I could have saved him."

"That may not have been possible."

I didn't like the sound of that.

I had a big question for Wesley. "God obviously paired the two of us together—the glowing file. But why? I didn't stop him." I took a breath and said it another way. "If God can arrange our connection, then why couldn't He save Glen?"

Wesley glanced at the floor, then met my eyes. "Free will can have minor or major consequences."

I scoffed. "I consider a boy's life major."

"So would I. So does God."

I felt tears threaten again. "So why did He allow it?"

Wesley cocked his head. "'No one knows God's thoughts.' I'm sorry I don't have a better answer for you."

"Me too."

"In spite of what happened, you *did* help Glen."

"Better grades and a few more smiles seems inconsequential compared to his life."

"You have a history of helping children. Glen, the others you mentored, and years before that, Nova and all those Girl Scouts."

I thought back. "I like helping out."

"So why did you stop mentoring?"

I thought back to another time at the school when I'd been asked into the principal's office. "After Glen's death the school suggested I take time off from interacting with students."

"You have to know they didn't blame—"

"No, they didn't. But after he died, I lost it. I had huge mood swings and would go from crying uncontrollably to this deep explosive rage. I knew I was overreacting, but I couldn't seem to pull myself out of it." I took a fresh breath. "I was depressed."

"Did you get help?"

I shook my head and pointed at Wesley. "Don't you get on me too."

He lifted his hands in surrender. "So the school let you go. And you haven't been back."

"I have not."

"Would you like to go back to helping kids someday?"

I'd thought about it. "Maybe. I'm not sure."

" And yet a girl from your past has reappeared."

"Nova." And there it was. "So I *am* supposed to help her?"

"It is a choice." Wesley strolled in front of me, then stopped. "Looking at your life, it's clear you have a servant's heart. You are generous and willing."

An hour ago I would have soaked in the praise, but now that I'd seen the lesser side of my character . . . "I could do more."

"Everyone can say that."

I found that of little comfort.

"It's unfortunate that Glen's death sidetracked you, Mrs. Brogdon. Nearly, but not completely."

"It seems pretty complete to me. I've done nothing constructive since then."

"You've raised your daughter. She's a freshman at the university, correct?"

"She is, and she's amazing. But I'm not sure I had much to do with that. During my down times she and her dad helped me more than I helped them."

"But now you're all right again."

"I'm getting there."

"So . . . what might you do with that rightness?"

I blinked at him.

"Is it a coincidence that Nova has re-entered your life right now?"

I eyed him. "Of course not. I don't believe in coincidences."

"Meaning?"

There was only one answer. "I guess God placed both of us where we needed to be."

"Indeed."

I felt a sudden ray of hope. "So . . . that means that God arranged for me to get that job? I mean, I thought so at first, but then I hated it so much that I questioned—"

He grinned. "So the right path has to be easy and pleasurable?"

"It would be nice." I fidgeted with the buttons on my blouse. "But I get what you're saying."

"Would you like to see one more?" Wesley asked.

I was more sure now. "Absolutely."

As soon as he left, the Room filled with a scene of an office. It seemed familiar, yet not.

A woman I didn't know sat behind the desk. She had a nameplate in front of her: Belinda Thompson. Then I saw my boss, Mrs. Smith, come into the office and sit. She held a stack of papers.

"Can I help you, Mary?" Belinda asked.

"Here are the applications for data entry. I wondered if you wanted to choose who to hire."

Belinda flipped a hand. "I'm swamped. Choose the top one. If they can type and don't have an attitude, hire them."

Mrs. Smith stood, but fumbled the stack. The papers streamed to the floor and under the desk. One of them glowed. "I'm so sorry, so clumsy."

I watched as the stack was rearranged when she picked them up. The glowing application was now on top.

Belinda rolled her eyes. "As I said, top one. Hire them."

Mrs. Smith read the top one aloud. "Lydia Brogdon."

"Very good. Now move along."

As the lights came on, I laughed. "I was chosen because my application was on top?"

Wesley overheard me as he came in the Room. He raised a

finger. "Wasn't on top. Then was."

As odd as it was, it made me shiver. "My job—that I dislike—was one-hundred percent God's doing."

"So it appears."

"So what happens now?"

"That depends on you."

I chuckled. "I think it's best *not* to depend on me. My track record is inconsistent."

"Your track record is exemplary—it could be improved, but your eyes *are* open, Mrs. Brogdon. You are far more ready than most."

I liked the sounds of that. "Far more ready than most to . . . ?"

He smiled. "Keep looking for the choices God is giving you."

I loved the sounds of that—that there would be more. "I'll do my best."

Wesley opened the cabinet and handed me my purse and notepad.

Apparently my time was up. "Do you do this often, Wesley? I mean does everybody get to see snippets of their lives?"

"Everyone *can* see, everyone should see, but alas, everyone does not see." He opened the door for me. "You should feel honored, Mrs. Brogdon."

"I do. Honored and humbled." I walked into the office.

Gracie's raised eyebrows asked a question before she even said a word. "How did it go?"

"Very well," I said. "But I'm exhausted."

"Other people have said that too," she said.

"Have you used the Room?" I asked her.

"Uh-uh." She shook her head adamantly. "No thank you."

Wesley stepped toward her desk. "Gracie has been invited, but has yet to accept the invitation—which remains open."

"You should do it." I pressed a hand against my chest. "Truly. It was an eye-opening, wonderful experience."

She looked between me and Wesley. "Is that why Wesley took a tissue in for you?"

"Tears aren't necessarily a bad thing," I said.

She shook her head again. "I've shed enough tears in my life. I don't need to be reminded of them."

Wesley sighed, then turned his attention back to me. "Thank you for accepting the invitation, Mrs. Brogdon. May God be with you."

It was wonderful to know that He already was.

**

It was strange to walk into my kitchen like I did every day and see that nothing had changed.

Yet *I* had changed. I'd visited moments in my life spanning thirteen years. Yet it seemed like an entire lifetime. Intellectually, emotionally, and spiritually.

I was not the same woman I was when I went in the Room. But one question remained: what was I going to do about it?

I kicked off my shoes and sank into my favorite chair in the living room, stretching my feet out on the ottoman. I drew in the deepest breath I could manage. Then did it again.

I had just closed my eyes when I heard the garage door open. I sprang to my feet, ready to greet Jeremy. I rushed to the kitchen.

He came in from the garage. "Sorry I'm late."

"No problem." I kissed his cheek and gave him a big hug.

He snuggled into me. "I should be late more often. What's going on?"

I pulled out a stool for him at the island. "I have something to tell you. A lot of things."

He sat warily. "Good or bad?"

I waved his concern away. "Good. All good. But strange."

"You certainly have my attention." He did a double take. "Does this have to do with that Discovery Room place?"

I nodded. "I went for special training—and it was definitely special."

"How so?"

Now came the hard part. "Work didn't invite me there. God did."

He gave me his most skeptical look. "God did."

I nodded and rushed ahead with the proof. "I was shown videos of my life, my past."

"Home movies?"

"Not exactly." I told him about each one, pointing out the item that glowed, and the discussion I had with Wesley afterward. I could see he was suspicious at first—which went along with his pragmatic nature. But miracle of miracles, Jeremy listened. He didn't putter around the kitchen or tell me I was crazy. He didn't argue that God wouldn't do things like that. He didn't flip me off and ask what we were having for dinner.

Instead he said, "This makes me think about something else. You know how we've always marveled at the way we met?"

I changed gears and let the memory return. "I was riding with my mom when we had a flat tire in front of the bus-stop where you were waiting for a bus."

"I helped you fix it, and your mom introduced the two of you then asked if my mother was Agnes Brogdon, and I said yes, she was."

"It turned out they were on a committee together."

He nodded. "As thanks for changing the tire, she asked me to come for dinner."

I smiled at the memory. "Where you charmed her, and charmed my father because you knew a lot about the Civil War—which is his passion."

Jeremy spread his hands. "And I charmed you if I'm not mistaken. The rest, as they say, is history." He flattened his hands on the island. "I've always thought if not for your car breaking down right in front of me, if not for your mom knowing my mom . . ."

"If not for the Civil War, we never would have fallen in love and married?"

He laughed. "That's a stretch, but yeah. Your 'if not for this' stories today? They're like that. I believe every word."

My throat tightened. "You do?"

"They were strange and definitely out-there, but you don't lie. If you tell me it happened like that, I believe you."

Oh. My. Goodness. I needed to hug him. I pulled him up into my arms. "I'm so lucky to have you," I said against his chest.

"Luck had nothing to do with it," he said.

Touché.

Chapter Eleven

Lydia

Teach me to do your will,
for you are my God;
may your good Spirit lead me on level ground.
Psalm 143: 10

I needed to find Nova.

The day after my time in the Room, I stopped at the desk of a caseworker, the woman who'd been helping Nova. It was a long shot, but I had to try.

I introduced myself, calling her by the nameplate on her desk. "Hi, Sylvia. We met yesterday? I'm Lydia, in data entry." I pointed over my shoulder. "I work just over—"

"Is there something you need?"

Skip the pleasantries. Got it. "You had a young woman in here yesterday, Nova Wilson? She's an old friend of the family and I was wondering if you could tell me what kind of services she's applying for. I mean, if *I* could help her, I'd like—"

She turned back to her computer. "No can do. All personal information is confidential."

Stupid privacy laws.

"Anything else?" Sylvia asked.

Apparently not. "Thanks anyway."

I went to my desk, but before I started to work, I looked up Nova Wilson on my phone. Nothing. No social media. No address. No phone number. I tried to look up her childhood address in a city directory. . . I remembered her mother's name: Meribelle.

Nope. No Meribelle Wilson.

I tried other online places for Meribelle but there was no Meribelle Wilson anywhere. Such a dead end wasn't unheard of, and it didn't mean Nova and her mom weren't in touch, but the possibility Nova was alone made me sad.

I started work. Hopefully, JoJo would know something at lunch.

**

I met JoJo at my desk and showed her around. My attitude

toward my job had changed since my time in the Room but the place was still pretty mundane. "There's not much to see," I said softly. "Just a field of cubicles."

"I didn't expect you to have a corner office," JoJo said. "I'm proud of you anyway."

I was so lucky to have her. And Jeremy. Our bond and support for each other was a huge contrast to Nova's isolation.

We went to our favorite Mexican restaurant and ordered lunch. I got right to the point. "I saw Nova Wilson yesterday."

JoJo blinked. "Wow. What a coincidence."

"What do you mean?"

"I ran into her too."

My stomach did a flip. "Where?"

"I was at the downtown library getting a book that they didn't have at the university and she was checking out some books. She had her baby with her."

I hadn't seen a baby. "Boy or girl?"

"Boy. Theo." She dipped her chip in salsa. "Really cute."

"How old is the baby now?"

"She told me he was twenty-one-months. So specific. Why can't people just say almost two?"

"Is she married? Where does she live?"

"She didn't mention either and I didn't ask."

"Why didn't you ask?"

JoJo gave me an impatient look. "Gee, Mom. I didn't know I was supposed to grill her. It's the first time I've seen her since high school. She dropped out our junior year."

Seeing Nova in the office was the first time I'd seen her since the grocery store—where I'd tried to ignore her and hadn't helped her.

"What was she doing at your office?" JoJo asked.

"They wouldn't tell me, but we're there to offer food stamps and other assistance, so I assume she's in need."

"Why are you so focused on Nova all of a sudden?"

I braced myself to answer her. "Don't make fun, but . . . God brought us together."

Her eyebrows rose. "Really."

"Really." I hurried forward with the conversation before she could put a damper on it. "He just brought Nova and you together too. That has to mean something, right?"

She considered this a minute. "I never once considered God was involved."

"An oversight, I'm sure."

She stirred sugar into her iced tea. "I suppose it could mean something. There's no way to know."

At least she didn't completely shut me down. "But maybe there *is* a way to find out. Maybe it *is* something. I want to follow through and see what happens."

"Mom." She stretched out my name like I was in trouble. "What does 'follow through' entail?"

"I'm not sure yet. But it won't do any harm to seek her out and see how she's doing."

"I suppose not." JoJo double-dipped a chip "Actually . . . Nova did say she liked to bring the baby to the library because it was a short walk from where she lived."

I clapped my hands together. "It's a clue. She lives downtown. "

JoJo laughed. "Ok, sure. She lives downtown along with thousands of other people."

True. And yet . . . "If she's in assisted housing, I could try there first."

"Go for it, Mom. What do you have to lose?"

Nothing. And I had so much to gain.

**

In my quest for information about Nova I side-stepped the never-helpful Sylvia and went to my supervisor's office.

Mrs. Smith looked up from the stacks of paperwork on her desk. Computerized or no, the department still generated loads of paper. "Hi, Ms. Brogdon. What can I do for you?"

At least she smiled. "I have a friend—" Too late I realized I'd jumped into a stereotypical phrase. "I really do have a friend who might be in need of housing assistance and food stamps. Is there a list somewhere of buildings or complexes and their locations?"

"There is." She started writing on a sticky-note. "Go to this site and click on *Housing*." She ripped the note off the pad and handed it to me.

"Thanks so much."

"Any time. Let me know if she wants an appointment."

"Will do."

I went back to my desk and immediately brought up the web page on my computer. There was even a handy map so I could choose the complexes that were downtown. I felt hopeful until I saw that one building had 54 units, and the other had 36. How would I ever find Nova without going door to door? But if that's what it took I was determined to find her.

I noticed the time. I was on the clock again. I took the pile of papers out of my inbox and began to enter the data.

I was in the groove, entering names, dates, and addresses when I found myself typing *Nova C. Wilson*.

I looked at the paper and my screen again. "What?"

It was her application for additional assistance. It was filled with everything I needed. Phone. Address. Birthday. Child's name and birthday. It had everything.

I was suddenly overcome with this very obvious intercession from God. He *did* want me to do this. He was giving me everything I needed to do this.

Nova already had housing assistance, but needed more food stamps. And . . .

She needed me.

I felt a deep shiver course up and down my spine like a *You got it* response from the Almighty. A heavenly confirmation.

I'd take it. I longed for it.

This was my destiny.

**

During my afternoon break I did two things. I texted Jeremy and JoJo to say I'd found Nova's information. And I called Nova.

When she picked up I heard a baby fussing in the background. She was out of breath. "Hello?"

"Nova, this is Mrs. Brogdon, JoJo's mom?"

I heard her shush her son. "Oh, hi. How are you?"

"I'm doing just great." I decided to focus on the baby. "JoJo said she'd seen you at the library. She said your baby is adorable."

"He is that. And he's cranky right now."

I needed to talk fast. "No worries. I was wondering if you'd like to come over for lunch some day to catch up? We live in the same house as always. You remember it?."

There was a pause. "I do but I don't think there's a bus stop near you."

I made a mental note: she didn't have a car. "I could pick you up. Would that work?"

"Well, yeah. I suppose it would. When?"

"Saturday? I'll pick up the two of you at eleven?"

"Well . . . yeah. I think that would work." She gave me her address.

I didn't tell her I knew it because I didn't want to freak her out. "See you then." I hung up and did a little upper-body dance in celebration.

Chapter Twelve

Tony & Gracie

People who conceal their sins will not prosper,
but if they confess and turn from them,
they will receive mercy.
Proverbs 28: 13

I opened one eye and saw it was morning. I closed it again. I had no reason to get up.

I was a mess.

It had been four days since my session in the Room. What a disaster. I'd hid out in my apartment ever since—from what, I wasn't sure. Nobody was coming to check on me. My family didn't know I'd gone to the Discovery Room, and I wouldn't be able to explain what it was even if they did. I didn't have co-workers to talk to anymore. And friends . . . what friends?

And I was completely sure Wesley would never come knocking on my door to see how I was, or to ask me to come back for more . . . discoveries. I'd burned that bridge for good.

It was my usual MO. If someone got too close, I'd lock myself away in that emotional hideaway room Wesley had talked about—and double lock it. Or was it the other way around? Come to think of it, I think he said I locked a *good life* behind a door and I was on the outside. That sounded more like it.

Whichever way it was, it wasn't good.

I knew there were a lot more scenes they could've shown me where I'd had a chance to do the right thing, but didn't. I could've been there for days. Although I'd given Wesley a hard time about the experience, in a sick way I'd enjoyed it. I'd enjoyed having someone truly see *me* without having to cover anything up. I'd always wanted to be a what-you-see-is-what-you-get kind of guy, but I'd spent my life disguising *me*. People saw the tough me, the arrogant me, the fake me. Nobody knew the real me, because the real me was that loser in the Room, doing secret stuff that I hid from everybody.

Except Me.

My eyes popped open.

Me? Me who?

I held my breath, waiting for some kind of answer.

I got nothing.

Which was a relief. I didn't need an inner voice arguing against myself. I was confused enough.

I heard the shouts and applause of "Price is Right" playing next door. It was almost eleven.

I got up and stretched in front of the window of my ground-floor apartment. Ground floor. The worst floor because everybody outside walked by my windows. I had no privacy at all. I checked out my crummy neighborhood. A tree had a plastic bag hooked on a branch. Somebody's car was propped up on a jack, missing a tire—whether from a flat or a thief was a toss-up. A lady across the way shook a rug out her window. Dust flew everywhere.

This was a grand old life I had going here.

My stomach growled. I'd missed breakfast so I heated up a pepperoni Hot Pocket and sat at the kitchen table with a bag of Fritos and a Coke. A bachelor's menu, that's for sure.

I scrolled through my phone watching videos of people singing, and others of people falling off their skateboards, but they didn't hold my interest long.

I changed to Facebook to see what great things everybody else was doing that I wasn't.

Somebody had posted an inspirational quotation: *Twenty years from now you will be more disappointed by the things you didn't do than by the ones you did do—Mark Twain.*

That was kinda cool. If I'd seen it in the Room, would it have glowed?

I read it again. As much as I liked the idea of it, Twain's wisdom didn't hold true for me. I was where I was now because of the things I *did* do. That's what I regretted.

I stopped mid-chew. Or was it? All those scenes in the Room had showed me chances to do the right thing—or avoid the wrong thing. Chances I hadn't taken.

I hadn't said no to Matt and Jerry.

I hadn't talked to Heather.

I hadn't let the broken stool stop me.

I hadn't helped Papa.

I hadn't admitted the theft when Nonna asked me to get her pearls.

I hadn't gone into the church for Papa's funeral.

I blinked and realized I was sitting with a half-eaten Hot Pocket in my hand. It was cold. I tossed it aside and scrolled through more nothingness on my phone. Every time I stopped to watch something there'd be an ad. So annoying. By the tenth one, I noticed the ads were always Home Depot. What was going on?

The last time I'd been at Home Depot, Wesley had given me the invitation. Wesley, the man who'd given up on me when I'd been a putz in the Room, not to mention me throwing the stool, damaging the wall. I was such a class act.

I thought of Twain's quote again. Maybe instead of regretting the things I did, I needed to do the things I should?

Suddenly I got an idea. I stood up and let it settle. I wasn't going to be able to do much of anything until I made amends. Wesley might not want to hear it, but I had to tell him I was sorry.

****

I watered the philodendron I'd brought into the office and wound the long vines around the legs of the plant stand. I'd never seen a plant grow so fast. Pretty soon I'd have to clip it around the window frame.

I looked up when I heard the sound of a car pull out front. Tony got out. What was he doing here?

I met him at the door. "Hi there."

"Hi." He scanned the office. "Is Wesley here?"

"Not at the moment."

"I need to talk to him. Apologize."

Yeah, he needed to. No one else had thrown the stool or made Wesley kick them out. But I was pretty sure Wesley didn't want to see him.

I finished with the plant as I talked. "I'll let him know you stopped by."

Tony considered this a moment. "Can you have him call me?"

"I could, but honestly, I've never seen Wesley with a phone. He's pretty old-fashioned."

Tony pointed to my desk. "You have a phone on your desk."

"It doesn't ring."

"It's not connected?"

"It just doesn't ring." I shrugged. "I think it's for show."

Tony ran his hand through his dark, combed-back hair. He looked pure Italian, like a beefed up Milo Ventimiglia from *This is Us.*

I must have looked at him too long, for he said, "Is something wrong?"

"No. Not a thing." I held a candy jar toward him because I didn't know what else to do.

"No thanks. Why were you looking at me like that?"

I set the jar down by the phone. "I was just thinking you look

Italian. Are you?"

When he smiled his face softened from a tough guy into somebody I might like.

"Yeah, I'm Italian. Amato? Antonio Amato?"

"I love the sounds of your name. It sings. Not like mine."

"Gracie is a pretty name."

"Not coupled with Sturgess."

He put my names together. "Gracie Sturgess." Then he shook his head and chuckled. "Yeah. I guess I win the name game." He smiled. "Your last name does *not* suit you, Gracie. It's not near pretty enough."

I felt myself blush. I hadn't flirted in years—but I liked it.

Tony picked up a few fallen leaves and palmed them. "Now that we've been formally introduced can you find a way to fit me into the schedule?" he asked. "To see Wesley?"

I returned to my desk chair and rolled into place. "Actually, we don't have a schedule. I never know who's coming or when." That wasn't quite accurate. "*I* don't know, but Wesley does. He always shows up at just the right time."

Tony looked toward the door. "Which isn't now."

He seemed so disappointed. "But Wesley *could* be in soon. Do you want to wait? You won't bother me because I have no responsibilities whatsoever." I held up my Kindle. "I've read six books since I started this job."

"I'm impressed. I haven't read six books in . . . forever. Or ever. I like movies. Do you like movies?"

Was he asking me for a date? My stomach did a little flip. "I do, though I haven't been to one in . . . forever." Since high school.

"Maybe we can go sometime."

He *was* asking. "That would be nice."

He glanced over his shoulder, out the windows. "But I really want to get this done first."

"I understand." No one had ever come back after visiting the Room.

"If it's okay, I'll wait."

"Want some coffee?" I asked.

"Nah, I'm okay."

It was a little awkward to have him sitting in front of me, yet I realized it gave me a chance to ask some questions. "What exactly went on in the Room?"

"Don't you know?"

"Wesley's invited me to try it, but I don't think it's for me."

"Why not?"

A good question. "If the Room is all about choices made or not made—I've gotten that much out of Wesley—then it wouldn't do me any good. I haven't had choices in my life. All the choices were made *for* me."

"I doubt that."

"It's true. My mom died when I was eighteen so I had to take over all her house duties—actually I started a year before while she was sick. Then Dad needed me, especially after *he* got sick. I've been pretty tied up taking care of my parents for most of my adult life."

"That's a bummer."

I didn't mind him feeling sorry for me. "Yeah, it is. Or was."

Suddenly Wesley came in the door, surprising us. We both stood up.

"Mr. Amato. To what do I owe this pleasure?"

Tony repeatedly fisted then unfisted his hands like he was having second thoughts. "I'm afraid there's no pleasure in it, sir. It's just that I've been thinking and feeling real bad about how we left things."

"It was not your best moment. Or mine."

Since this was a conversation for the two of them I motioned toward the door. "If you'd like me to step out . . ."

Tony was quick to press his hands downward. "No, no. Please stay. This won't take long." He added "I hope" under his breath.

Wesley clasped his hands in front of himself. Waiting.

Tony took a deep breath. Let it out. Then took another one. "I'm really sorry for being such an . . ."

I could tell he changed the word he was going to use.

"Such a difficult person," he said. "The whole Room-thing shocked me, and the movies brought back bad memories, but that doesn't mean I should've thrown the stool or taken my temper out on you. I'll pay for the damage."

"No need. It is fixed."

"Good, but . . . I also feel bad for being uncooperative and talking back to you."

"It isn't talking back to me you should be worried about."

Tony looked down. "I get it. That choice-stuff."

"Exactly."

"That stuff's hard for me to comprehend, Mr. Wesley."

"Just Wesley."

Tony nodded. "I'm not a deep guy. I'm not used to looking for choices beyond the obvious. When I get going in a direction, I keep going."

He sounded stubborn but I admired his honesty.

Tony added, "Maybe I shouldn't be that way, but that's the truth of it."

"You not seeing alternate choices doesn't mean they aren't there."

"Maybe so, but I'm not used to looking for 'em, seeing 'em."

Wesley's eyebrows rose. "So that's that, is it?"

Tony looked like a kid who'd told the teacher a wrong answer. "I'd like to do things differently, but I . . ."

He looked at me. I gave him a reassuring smile.

"I don't know how."

I was impressed by his candor. I was used to my father, who never admitted he didn't know anything about anything.

Wesley nodded. "Open your eyes and be enlightened, Mr. Amato."

Tony laughed. "I can honestly say I have never had the word 'enlightened' apply to any part of my life."

"Then you have something to aspire to."

Tony rubbed his hands over his face, clearly flustered. I felt sorry for him. Wesley wasn't making it easy.

He finally let out a deep sigh. "Anyway, I'm sorry. All right?"

Wesley hesitated, but nodded. "All right. And I am not without fault. I pushed you too hard."

Tony's face lightened. "You *did* push me—off the cliff of my comfort zone. So we're good?"

Wesley held out his right hand. "We're good."

The two men shook hands.

"Thanks, Wesley. I feel better now."

"As do I."

Tony looked at me. "Nice talking to you, Gracie. I'll be in touch."

I nodded.

After he left, Wesley stood at the windows, watching him go.

"It was nice he apologized," I said.

"It was."

"What kind of things did he see in the Room? It must've been pretty bad for him to get so mad."

Wesley turned to face me. "His experience is private."

"Confidentiality? That kind of thing?"

"Exactly." He smiled at me. "There is only one way for you to discover what goes on in the Room . . ."

"Once again, I will have to decline your invitation."

He shrugged, then noticed the candy jar. "What kind?"

"Butterscotch" I held the jar out for him.

He unwrapped one and popped it in his mouth. Then suddenly his face perked up. "I must leave. Make yourself ready."

Someone else was coming. I unwrapped a candy for myself.

Moments later, a car pulled up.

As I readied myself for the client I realized I'd done exactly what Wesley had previously asked me to do. I'd permanently suspended my disbelief.

Whatever this was, it was real. Really amazing.

Chapter Thirteen

Tony

Lord, you know the hopes of the helpless.
Surely you will hear their cries and comfort them.
Psalm 10: 17

I was living in limbo land.

I didn't have a job, I'd had a super weird experience in a room that was right out of a sci-fi movie, I'd lost my temper with a guy while discussing *my* life, I'd apologized to said-guy, and I'd met a really nice woman named Gracie.

At the moment the latter couldn't overshadow the former. I was still lost.

I sat at the kitchen table, scanning my phone for job openings. Again. There were a lot. Then why couldn't I focus on any of them?

One reason was because the cheers of happy people on a game show interrupted my thoughts. Overpowered my thoughts. Made my nerves scream.

There was constant noise here. I'd never thought of myself as an introvert—I could party with the best of them—but I'd recently discovered that I hated second-hand noise, which in my building was constant. The footsteps, the television, the toilets flushing, the people talking, and dogs barking. It was too much.

I wanted to move, but I couldn't even begin to look until I got a regular paycheck, which I wouldn't get until I got a new job, which I couldn't get until I could concentrate and—

The cycle was exhausting.

Suddenly I heard something fall in the next apartment. A big thud. More noise.

Then I heard a groan.

The old man?

I held my breath, waiting to hear more. I'd never met the guy, had only seen him in the hall. We both kept to ourselves.

I put my ear to the wall, but it was hard to hear anything above the game show garbage.

Then I heard it. The faintest *Help . . .*

I sucked in a breath as the memories of another call for help flooded my brain.

My heart beat double-time. I would *not* make the same mistake twice.

I rushed out of my apartment over to his. I thought about knocking, but if he'd fallen . . . I knocked once quickly and tried the knob. The door was unlocked. I went in.

There he was on the floor in the kitchen, his walker tipped over on top of him.

"Help!"

I lifted the walker aside and knelt beside him. "Is anything broken? Are you hurt?"

He lay on his side and pointed to his arm. "I landed on my arm."

I looked it over, but didn't notice any obvious broken bones or blood.

"I need to get you up," I said. "I'll be careful. We'll take it slow."

For once in my life, my beefy size paid off. I could almost lift him to standing. I maneuvered the walker so he could grab hold, but his left hand couldn't grip it.

"Here, take my arm and I'll get you to a chair."

There were only two places to sit in the living room. One was a recliner. The remote was on the arm. That must be *his* place.

I eased him to sitting. He held his elbow with his good arm. "Oww."

"Can you bend it?"

"What?"

I turned off the TV but spoke louder. "Can you bend it?"

He could. But he moaned as he did it.

I kept my voice loud. "You need to have that looked at. Want me to call 9-1-1?"

He shook his head. "There's an ER a few blocks away. I can still drive."

"Nonsense. I'll take you there." Though I didn't want to get that involved, I didn't have a choice.

I helped him change from slippers to shoes, and got his wallet and apartment key. I rushed across the hall and got my wallet and keys too.

Though I complained that my apartment was on the ground floor, right now I was glad for it. I couldn't imagine trying to manage the old man going down stairs.

At the curb I left him standing awkwardly with his walker. I pulled my car up front, helped him in, got his seatbelt buckled, and put the walker in the back. I headed out.

"You'll be okay, Mister . . . ?"

"Billings. Harvey Billings," he said. "And who are you?"

It was a bigger question than he realized.

"I'm your neighbor, Tony."

**

The ER took hours. Though I thought of leaving Harvey there alone, I couldn't. And more than that, I didn't want to.

What was up with that?

Harvey was a good old guy. Beyond involuntary moans and groans, he didn't complain. In fact, he kidded with the nurses and doctor and everyone seemed to love him. When they wheeled him away to get an x-ray I heard him tell the orderly, "Take a pretty picture now. My left side's my best side."

It was way different from how I'd handled my ER visit after I broke a finger at work. I'd complained about how long it took, the pain, the x-ray, pretty much everything. No one could stand to be in the same room as me.

It was odd sitting in the ER exam room, waiting for a man I'd known for three hours, a man I'd complained about more than once. Why was I being so . . . nice?

Wesley's voice came in my head: *Choices are stepping-stones to character.*

Choices. I could've ignored Harvey's cry for help.

But I didn't.

I could've called 9-1-1 and let them handle it.

But I didn't.

I could've gotten him settled into the ER room and left.

But I didn't.

"Wow."

A nurse who was restocking a drawer said, "Wow what?"

I hadn't meant to say it out loud. "I'm just thinking about what would've happened if I hadn't heard Harvey call for help."

"You're not family?"

"I live next door. We'd never even met."

She pointed to the ceiling. "Sounds like a God-thing." She shut the drawer. "I hope he's okay."

A God-thing.

I drew in a breath and knew she was right.

God did it. God arranged it.

For me.

And for Harvey.

Suddenly a slew of choices came back to me. If not for me losing my job I wouldn't have been home. If not for me *not* finding a new job, I wouldn't have been home. If not for my apartment being next to Harvey's. If not for it being on the ground floor so I could get him to my car.

The phrase *just a coincidence* came into my head but I pushed it away. Maybe I would've called it that before, but now . . .

I thought of Wesley and the scenes of my life and the fact I'd been invited to the Room at all.

I had to say it again. "Wow."

At that moment, Harvey was wheeled back into his ER room. I stood up. "How'd it go?" I asked.

"My pictures didn't break the machine."

"Okay . . ."

"And my arm's not broken either," he said.

"I'm glad."

The orderly left him in the wheelchair. "The doctor will be in shortly, Harvey. I hope you feel better soon."

"Thanks, Davey."

While we waited, Harvey stared at me. "I didn't know if you'd still be here."

Me either. "We're in this together," I said. I surprised myself by saying such a thing. It was so . . . encouraging. So not like me.

"Eh?" he asked, with a hand behind his ear.

I was forced to repeat it louder. "We're in this together."

He nodded. "You're a good man, Tony."

Maybe. Maybe I could be.

**

While driving home I came upon road construction that blocked our route with cones and signs. "They weren't working here when we came by earlier."

Harvey didn't answer. He had his eyes closed. Poor guy. Going to an ER was draining for anybody, much less to somebody really old.

I turned onto a side-street for a detour. It shouldn't take us more than a few extra –

I spotted Gracie up ahead. She was pushing a big, unwieldy box toward the street. I pulled up to the curb. "Hey. Need some help?"

She blinked. "Tony? Hi. Yeah, I guess I do."

I put a hand on Harvey's leg. "I'll just be a minute." I got out and picked up the huge box of newspapers and set it by the curb. "Impressive. You must read a lot."

"They're not mine. They're from my dad. He was kind of a hoarder. Recycling comes tomorrow."

I caught one of her words. "He *was?*"

"He died three months ago."

"I'm so sorry."

"Thanks."

I didn't want our conversation to end there. "Are you cleaning out his house?"

She glanced toward the front of the 1960s ranch. "My house now. It's never-ending. I try to work on it a little every day but I'm not sure what I'm doing."

"It's a big job."

"Humongous." She looked toward the car. "Is that *your* dad?"

Harvey? I moved so they could see each other. "No, this is my neighbor, Harvey. Harvey, this is Gracie."

Harvey nodded at her. "Nice to meet you."

"You too."

"We're on our way back from the ER. Harvey fell and hurt his arm."

Her expression was kind. "I'm so sorry about that. I shouldn't keep you. Thanks for stopping to help, Tony. You're a lifesaver."

"Anytime. Just say the word and I'll be here." I emphasized the word again. "Anytime."

She cocked her head and smiled. "I might just take you up on that."

I liked the sounds of *that*. A lot.

**

Back in Harvey's apartment, I helped him to his recliner.

"Home again," I said.

"Home again." His arm was wrapped in an Ace bandage for support. He'd been told he could use the walker, but to take it easy.

I was glad for that. I didn't know what Harvey would do if he couldn't use his walker.

His eyes were pale and tired. "Do you want to lay down?"

He used his right hand to make the chair recline. "I sleep here as much as in bed. I'll be okay."

I glanced toward the kitchen, where he'd fallen. "You want me to get you something to eat before I go?"

"Don't worry about it. You've already done so much."

I was starving. He had to be hungry. I went to the kitchen and opened the fridge. Cold cuts and fruit. "How about a sandwich?"

"You're too kind, Tony."

I'd been called a lifesaver, good, and kind.

Would wonders never cease?

As I prepared the food, Harvey insisted I have a sandwich and apple with him. We even watched a bit of "Jeopardy" before he drifted off.

I turned off the TV, put our phone numbers in each other's phones and made sure his was next to the recliner along with a glass of water and a couple of Oreos I'd found in the cupboard. Then I went back to my apartment, needing my own nap.

Being a good guy was exhausting.

CHAPTER FOURTEEN

Minnie

But I, the Lord, search all hearts
and examine secret motives.
I give all people their due rewards,
according to what their actions deserve.
Jeremiah 17: 10

I watched as Claudia straightened Dad's tie. They were all dressed up, ready to leave for the awards banquet.

"You look pretty," I told Claudia. I meant it. She was a knockout.

"Don't I look pretty too?" Dad asked.

I rolled my eyes. "Pretty handsome."

He turned serious and put a hand under my chin, looking me in the eyes. "I know what you gave up, Min. Don't think I don't appreciate it."

"I know." But it was good to hear him say it.

Dad got out his billfold. "Here's money to grab something to eat. You can go out or order delivery."

"Out?" Claudia said. "I'm not so sure—"

Dad flashed her a look. "We talked about this Claudie."

She sighed. "Fine. If you go out, you can take my car since it has the car-seats. But be careful," she added. "Extra careful."

I said thanks, but taking two babies to a restaurant was not in my top 100 wanna-dos. They were a handful to feed at home, much less in public.

"We won't be too late," Dad said.

"I'll be here." Of course.

He gave me a wistful look. Playing the martyr gave me some satisfaction. Benny crawled toward us from the family room. I scooped him up. "Have a good time," I said.

Dad ruffled his hair and Claudia gave him a kiss. "Be a good boy for your big sister."

And then they were gone.

"Well then, Benny-boy. Let's find your other sister."

The three of us played until it was time for them to eat. As usual it was a messy affair. Though I could have ordered take out, I just didn't feel like it. Instead I ate leftovers from the fridge.

I gave the babies their baths and tried to put them to bed by seven, but neither one of them cooperated. I must've gone in and out of the room six times. It was after eight before they actually fell asleep.

Finally, I had the house to myself. I got out a carton of cookie dough ice cream, grabbed a spoon, and dove in. I flipped through channels, trying to choose something to get my mind off Gabe's party. I ended up watching the original Avengers movie for the thousandth time. Ten minutes in, I went back to the fridge and doused the ice cream with chocolate syrup, Heath bits, and six maraschino cherries. I saw a can of Reddi-wip and shot some directly into my mouth before creating a mountain on top of the ice cream.

I settled in on the couch and watched the movie. Iron Man was my favorite hero, and of course Thor was gorgeous.

I almost—but not quite—finished off the carton. Sugar overload. I put the carton back in the freezer as it was—Claudia would understand. I downed a huge glass of water.

I sat on the couch and scrolled through social media. I spotted an Instagram update from Ashley. She'd posted a selfie of herself and a bunch of friends. I spotted Gabe in the background. *BEST TIME EVER!* she wrote.

"Great." I slumped down in the cushions.

Although I knew it would make me feel bad, I kept scrolling and saw Gabe in another group pic—not including Ashley.

Everyone looked like they were having a blast.

Everyone except me.

I silenced my phone, muted the movie, curled up on the couch, and cried.

**

"Min?"

I opened my eyes to see Dad standing over me. I had an afghan pulled up to my chin. The TV was still on.

I sat up and turned the TV off. "How was it?" Claudia gave a little wave as she climbed the stairs to the bedrooms, carrying her fancy heels.

Dad sat beside me and undid his tie and top shirt button. "It was really good."

It better have been good. "What did you get as your award?"

He pointed toward the table in the entryway. "It's over there."

He didn't move to get it, so I did. It was made of heavy glass in the shape of a star. It was engraved with the honor, his name, and the year. "This is pretty cool, Dad. Impressive."

He shrugged. "How were the kids?"

"They were good." I didn't mention the problems getting them to sleep.

"Where did you eat?" he asked.

"We ate in. Your money's in the kitchen."

He waved away my words. "Keep it. A pittance for giving up your evening." He patted my knee. "I'm really sorry about that. It was a lot to ask."

Yes, it was, and I was very happy to witness his guilt.

He stood. "Next Saturday you are officially off baby-duty. You can go shopping or do something fun."

The last two weekends I'd missed a concert and a party. I wasn't sure I knew how to have fun.

Chapter Fifteen

Gracie

The Lord is close to the brokenhearted
and saves those who are crushed in spirit.
Psalm 34: 18

I was worried about Wesley. He'd come in this morning to work with a client in the Room, but instead of leaving when it was done like he usually did, he'd stayed and was peering out the windows.

"Waiting for someone?" I asked.

"Always."

I'd been thinking about something for a while. "How many invitations have you given out so far?"

"Two hundred and thirty-two."

I blinked. "Two hundred and thirty-two? That's a ton! But in the few weeks since we opened we've only had like ten clients."

"Fourteen."

"Your ROI isn't very good."

"ROI?"

"Return on investment."

He looked over his shoulder and smiled. "I like that term, but no, unfortunately, my ROI is not good – though it is as expected."

"You expected only a few to come out of that many?"

"'The gateway to life is very narrow and the road is difficult, and only a few ever find it.'"

"That's discouraging."

"Not really. In the long run, attaining something easily doesn't mean as much as conquering something hard. Correct?"

Probably. But I shrugged. "If so few come, then why do you keep inviting people? When do you just call it a bust?"

His eyes widened and he shook his head somberly. "It will never be considered a bust."

I wasn't so sure.

It was rare for me to have him in the office so long, so I kept asking the questions that had been on my mind. "This next question might be considered confidential and none of my business, but . . . out of those who haven't come yet, is there someone you're looking forward to having in the Room? If you can name names maybe I can be on the lookout for them."

He thought about this for a minute, then said, "There are so many, but I keep thinking about one specifically. Minerva McLaughlin."

"Gracious. That's a mouthful."

"I believe she's called Minnie." He stroked a leaf on my crazy-growing philodendron. "She may not need the Room more than anyone else, yet I feel a soft spot for her."

"Why her especially?"

He smiled. "Now *that* is none of your business." His smile widened. "Actually, the person I'm most looking forward to having in the Room is you."

I didn't like the pressure. "I really appreciate your interest, but I'm still not ready."

His smile faded. "What if your readiness doesn't coincide with your chance?"

I had never thought of that. "Are you saying I can lose my chance?

Wesley swept a hand toward the Room. "I'm saying it is waiting for you."

"You make *it* sound like a living, breathing thing."

"Wisdom breathes. Ignorance suffocates."

His witty catch phrases were sometimes too much for my brain. "Are you calling me ignorant?"

"Don't goad me, Miss Sturgess. It doesn't become you."

I knew I was being testy. "I don't mean to act ignorant or scared or whatever else I'm feeling about that stupid Room, but—"

His right eyebrow rose.

"But I'm just not ready yet."

With a sigh he looked outside again. Then he suddenly said, "A client is coming. I'll be back."

Before I could let it register, he was out the door. I never knew where he went because I'd never seen his car. The pet store and vitamin shop on either side of us were always closed so he didn't go there. He had to have a lookout who somehow alerted him at just the right moment, because he always hit his cue perfectly.

Ten seconds later, a car pulled up.

How did he know?

**

After work, I hung my keys on the Home Sweet Home hooks by the door to the garage. The cutesy plaque had been my mother's doing. It had been there my entire life, yet I also remembered many a time in the fourteen years since she'd died, that I'd purposely *not* hung up my keys in protest, choosing to toss them with a clatter on the mauve Formica counters.

I sloughed off my shoes and hung my purse from a coatrack. For the umpteenth time I noticed Dad's jackets, still hanging there, and for the umpteenth time I thought about taking them down.

But I hadn't done it. I wasn't sure if that made me weak, pitiful, or lazy. Maybe all three. At least there was no one around to condemn me for it. The last thing I needed were labels. Right now the whole of my life was about survival. One day at a time and all that nonsense.

I opened the fridge to figure out what I wanted to eat—*really* wanted to eat, not *had* to eat because of Dad's special diet. Due to his condition, Dad had needed low-sugar, high-protein foods. In the years before the cancer appeared I'd been able to get away with more normal foods. But it still meant cooking a full meal every night. I much preferred to graze.

Once, during the years he was home because of a work injury, I'd gone wild and had Chinese delivered. You would have thought it was a mortal sin. "So I'm not worthy of you spending time in the kitchen?" he'd said.

I'd given my excuses that I was tired and pointed out that he loved rice and chicken, and a little variety was a good thing. He'd pushed the plate away. "You think *I'm* not tired of being stuck in this house?"

He was an expert conversation flipper. He'd even said, "There's only one person to please in this house, and that's me."

Even the memory made me sigh deeply, taking a breath from a place deep in my lungs where my resentment had built a sturdy home.

I closed the fridge and got out two slices of bread. I spread them with peanut butter, then laid the slices on a cookie sheet and slid them under the oven broiler.

The doorbell rang. When Dad was sick we'd have the occasional visitor checking on him, sometimes praying over him—which *really* ticked him off. He said that God was responsible for him being unable to work, and then, on top of that, giving him cancer. He wasn't about to spend one minute of his leftover life praying to Him. I hadn't minded their prayers, and had even privately prayed a few of my own.

I peeked out the side window by the door and saw Tony. I ran my fingers across my pulled-back hair, hooking a few stragglers behind my ears. I opened the door.

"Surprise!" he said.

"Hi there."

There was an awkward pause, then he said, "Can I come in?"

I stepped aside and closed the door behind him. "What brings you to my corner of the world?"

He put his hands in the pockets of his jeans. "You."

My insides jumped with pleasure, even as my way-too-logical mind forced me to say, "Why me?" Which had to be *the* dumbest reply in all creation.

Tony laughed. "I never thought of you as a woman who lacked confidence. Not with that smile of yours."

"Thanks." I wasn't used to compliments.

"You'd said you might want help?" He looked at the boxes strewn about the living room.

He *had* offered. "I do, I will, but I still don't have a clear plan about what—"I smelled burning bread. "Ack!" I ran into the kitchen. Smoke was coming out of the oven. I grabbed an oven mitt and pulled the baking sheet out.

Tony coughed. "What *was* that?"

"Broiled peanut butter."

"Char-broiled, I'd say."

I slid the burnt bread into the sink and poured water on it. "Not my best execution but usually it's delicious. I'll start over. Want some?"

"Maybe. I do like peanut butter."

"Doesn't everyone? Have a seat." I gestured toward the cluttered kitchen table.

He picked up a copy of *Sports Illustrated.* "You like sports?"

I began to spread peanut butter on four more slices. "Dad did. Football mostly. He liked the Chiefs."

"And you?"

"I didn't pay much attention." I slid the bread under the broiler and stood watch. "When he was into a game it gave me time to do other things."

"Like what?"

I'd never discussed my writing with anyone. "I write a little."

His eyebrows rose. "Are you writing a book?"

I shook my head. "I write short things. Online posts mostly."

He got out his phone. "Are you on Facebook?"

"No, no. Don't look me up. What I post is not for you."

"Me personally, or me in general?"

I cracked open the oven door to check on the bread. "In general. I speak to caregivers. I have a page for people to connect."

"That sounds nice."

I didn't want to go into it. Reading about my frustrations with caring for Dad would not impress him. "You want to pour us glasses of milk?"

"Sure."

I pointed to the glass-cupboard and he poured. I checked the bread. The peanut butter was bubbling. I counted to ten out loud. "One, two…"

"What are you doing?"

"Nine, ten." I took the pan out. "Mom always said to count to ten after the peanut butter started bubbling. That gives it time for the edges to be just a little crispy." I held the pan toward him. "See?"

He eyed my work. "Well done."

I pushed the slices onto plates and sat down. "Give it a second because it can burn your mouth."

"Should we count to ten?"

"Cute." We took a bite. "Good, yeah?"

"Very," he said. "Even I could make this."

As we ate, something felt . . . off. I looked around the kitchen, noticing a picture of the Lord's Prayer on the wall, and the cow cookie jar on the counter. "Huh. I've never seen the kitchen from this angle. This was my dad's chair. I always sit there." I pointed to his seat.

"Want to switch?"

Yes. But no. That would be dumb. I shook my head. "I didn't realize what a creature of habit I was. He's been gone a few months yet I still sit in *my* chair."

"Which chair did your mom sit in?"

"That one. I've never sat in her chair either and she's been gone fourteen years." I sat back, incredulous. "I have no idea where the time went."

"Have you lived in this house all your life?"

"Every non-exciting, tedious moment."

"It sounds like you've been through a lot."

"Yeah. But I'm sorry to blast it out like this. My bitterness gets the best of me sometimes."

"We'll have to see if we can create some exciting, non-tedious moments, yes?"

He was so sweet. "That would be nice."

Tony drank the last of his milk and wiped his mouth. "I bet it was hard to see them sick."

"Very. Mom got sick when I was in high school. I did most of the caring for her because Dad ranked zero on the compassion scale. She died a few weeks before I graduated."

"Bad timing." He shook his head. "Sorry. That was insensitive."

I liked his honesty. "It's ok, and you're right. It was bad timing." There was more to it that I didn't want to share. "Dad was a wreck after she died. I tried going to college, but had to stay home and . . . take care of life."

"That doesn't sound very fair. You were grieving too."

Exactly. "Even though Dad wasn't great about showing affection, he really loved Mom and he grieved hard and long. I had no choice but to stick around. Plus, he was helpless around the house. Mom had a servant's heart and he was used to being served."

Tony got an *aha* look on his face. "Then *he* got sick?"

"You're two for two. But actually there was a work accident in between that kept him at home on disability. *Then* he got sick and had six years of fighting cancer. The last two he was bedridden."

"At home?"

"Right here."

"Wow. I'm so sorry. Did you have help come in?"

I shook my head long and slow. "He wouldn't have strangers touching him."

"Doesn't that make it a little hard for the doctors?"

"Somehow doctors were okay—as long as they were male doctors." Memories of him refusing help from a day nurse crept back. He'd screamed at her to leave. "I had to learn how to handle all the to-dos of nursing care."

I must have made a face because he said, "Yuck."

"Yeah. That pegs it."

He pushed his plate away and leaned on the table. "What did you want to do before all this happened? What were you going to get your degree in?"

I snickered. "I have no idea. History? Basket-weaving? It was easier for me to forgo college because I didn't have a goal. I probably would have wasted four years trying to find myself." I gazed at the ancient kitchen. "And here I am, still looking for Gracie, living in my parents' house. Alone."

He reached across the table and put a hand on mine. "You're not alone anymore. Got it?"

I wanted to cry. "Got it. Thanks for listening."

"Any time." He looked around the tiny kitchen. "By the way, this is way better than where I live. I sleep on a foldout, I don't have a job, and I'm alone too. Divorced."

Because of the interest he was showing me I'd assumed he was single but I'd never asked. "Do you have any kids?"

"A boy. Zach just turned ten." His eyes turned down and he pressed a crumb on his plate with his finger and licked it.

I made a curlicue near his face. "Your expression changed when you mentioned him. You look sad."

"Really?" His eyes were wistful.

"What's the story behind that look?"

He shook his head, but smiled. "I did not come over to tell you my life story."

I cocked my head. "I told you mine. Fair is fair."

He sighed deeply, then traced the edge of his plate. "I haven't been that great a dad."

I wondered about the details, but didn't ask. "I can tell that you *want* to be."

"How, how can you tell?"

Yikes. He'd put me on the spot. "I guess I haven't had the greatest role-model of a father figure, but I like to believe that everybody who has kids wants to be a good parent."

"Wanting and making it happen can sometimes be very far apart." He moved his milk glass an inch to the right, then back again. "Have you ever been married?"

"I thought about it, always wanted it. I even met a really great guy, but whatever we felt for each other didn't have a chance. Taking care of Dad took so much of my time that I had to break it off. He's married now and has a couple kids."

"I had that happen with a girlfriend too. She broke my heart and now she's married and happy."

I scoffed, then smiled. "We are the leftovers of love."

He laughed. "The question is whether we're past our expiration date."

"Ouch!" I really hoped he was wrong. "I do want to find love. Don't you?"

"Sure. Yet I think I'd better get my life figured out first. My time in the Room kinda threw me for a loop."

"It's nice you apologized to Wesley."

"Yeah. Well. When I'm cornered, I tend to fight."

"How did he corner you?"

Tony wiped the palms of his hands on his jeans. "He showed me times in my past when I was stupid, times when I messed everything up." He shook his head and snickered. "Times that helped me become the upstanding, successful man I am today."

I appreciated his self-deprecating nature yet wondered about the whole truth. He was hurting, yet I had no clue how to help. "The Room is supposed to enlighten people."

"That's definitely a Wesley-word. He reminds me of a stern school master in a black and white movie."

I nodded. "Or the head butler at a fancy manor house in England who insists on things being spit-spot."

"I thought that too. He doesn't mince words, that's for sure."

I slipped my plate on top of his. "What happened in the Room -- if you want to share."

Tony brushed a crumb off the table and shook his head. "Maybe someday. Right now I've got a lot of thinking to do."

"Not a bad thing, thinking. That's where I'm at too."

He nodded and hooked a thumb toward the living room. "I saw boxes. You said you were cleaning out stuff? Are you moving out?"

"It's too soon to say. Right now I'm just trying to wrap my head around the whole thing."

"You want help?"

I did, but I didn't. "I'd let you help if I knew what I was doing, but I seem to be packing up boxes without knowing if I'm selling things, moving things, or just want them out of sight."

"Since your dad left you the house you don't *have* to move. You can stay."

I noticed the picture of Monet's sunflowers above the table. It was a paint-by-number kit I'd done when I was ten. "I'm torn. Do I stay because it's a good old house and it's full of family history, or do I sell it for the same reason and start fresh?"

"You do have some thinking to do."

I felt overwhelmed every time I thought of it. "The truth is, I don't know how to be on my own. I've always had at least one of my parents around. They determined my life. Their needs came before my own."

Tony nodded. "Like you said at the office, you don't feel like you've ever had any choices."

It was nice he remembered. "Now all I have is choices and I'm out of practice."

"Then take a break. Don't choose anything. Chill."

I chuckled. "I haven't heard anyone say that in years."

He sat back in the chair, looking pleased with himself. "Take a chill-pill, Gracie Sturgess."

I laughed. But as my laughter faded I realized how long it had been since I'd really laughed.

He pointed at me face. "You're laughing but your eyes look worried."

Tony Amato was not an ordinary man. "You sir, are very observant."

"So?"

"I just realized it's been ages since I laughed."

He nodded once. "I suppose there's not much to laugh about when you're dealing with cancer."

"You got that right."

He sat forward again. "The thing you gotta remember is you're not dealing with cancer anymore. It's done and gone. It's outta here." He waved. "Bye bye, cancer. Don't come again another day."

I really liked how he got me to think beyond my problems. "I'm so glad you stopped by. I needed this."

"And I needed a broiled peanut butter sandwich." He stood. "Last chance: you want help packing—or not packing?"

"I think I'll hold off on both. For now."

"There you go. You made your first choice. May it be one of many to come."

He headed to the door. When he stepped out on the stoop he turned to me with a sheepish grin, "Do you want to go out for Italian with me on Saturday? I know a great little hole-in-the-wall that has alfredo to die for."

"I usually work until five but that sounds lovely."

"I'll pick you up at six."

He gave me a wink and left me feeling something I hadn't felt in ages.

Hope.

CHAPTER SIXTEEN

Tony

So let's not get tired of doing what is good.
At just the right time
we will reap a harvest of blessing if we don't give up.
Galatians 6: 9

I was late to Zach's softball game because I realized I'd never given him his birthday present. I stopped on the way to the game and returned the football I'd bought him, and got him two other gifts along with a big gift bag. Better late than never?

I had a hard time finding a parking place at the softball fields. I grabbed a water and started to jog toward field four, but quickly changed to a fast walk. A man as big as me—jogging—was a lumbering bear. Best to be a few *more* seconds late than draw that kind of attention to myself. As I passed, the roar of the fans sitting on bleachers and in lawn chairs rose and fell. I sidestepped little brothers and sisters who were playing tag while their parents watched their big brothers and sisters play ball.

I spotted Penny's straw hat in the stands and braced myself. She'd give me a hard time about being late. Although we'd been divorced a year, the chances of a normal, friendly conversation were slim to none. I snaked my way around other people to step up to the seat beside her.

"Hey," I said.

"You're late. Really late."

"I know. Sorry. What's the score?"

"Eight-seven, we're losing. It's the last inning. They have two outs, then we're up."

I searched the field for Zach and found him in centerfield. He was messing with his glove instead of getting ready to field a hit. At least he wasn't squatting down looking for bugs like he did when he was little.

"How's work?" Penny asked.

I hadn't told her I'd been fired, yet she'd find out soon enough when I was late with my child support. "I'm done with them. I'm looking for a better job."

"Again?" She angled to look at me, but I couldn't see her eyes behind the hat's brim and her sunglasses. I didn't need to see them. I knew that look. "This is getting old, Tony. Two jobs in a year?"

Actually three . . . "I'm looking, okay?"

"You couldn't keep that job while you're looking?"

The crowd shouted. The other team had three outs. It was our turn to bat. "How's he batted so far?"

"Pretty good. Got to first once."

"Good for him." I cracked open my bottle of water. "I'd like to take him overnight some weekend," I said.

"Are you still in that studio apartment?"

I wanted to remind her that it was all I could afford because of alimony and child support, but didn't. "I'm still there. It's not fancy, but it's clean. We can have a campout on the floor and watch a superhero movie."

"That might be doable. But Tony, watching TV and playing video games is all you do with him. It's nice outside. I know he'd like to go to the zoo or a park. Or to a Royals' game."

I couldn't afford two out of three. "Why don't you take him?" I asked her. "I'm pretty tapped out."

"You wouldn't be if you kept a job for more than a minute."

Penny made decent money -- more than me For the last six years she'd been a food instructor at a community college. Zach and I had always loved the leftovers she'd bring home.

As if reading my thoughts, she opened a small cooler by her feet. "Want a lemon bar?"

"Always." She made the best lemon bars.

She suddenly stood up, "Go, Zach!"

He was coming up to bat. I stood beside her. "Get a hit, Zach!"

He looked in our direction and smiled. I waved. He waved back.

That smile . . . I needed to come to his games more often. Even though I'd missed most of them, there was no reason I should ever miss one again. He was worth it.

I remembered something Wesley had told me: Choices are stepping-stones to character.

Why did I usually choose wrong?

Zach swung and missed, tipped one, and finally hit one toward third, which let him get on base. Penny and I shouted like he'd got a home run. Zach beamed at us as he settled in at the base.

We sat down. "How are your parents?" Penny asked. "Zach misses seeing them."

"They miss him too. They love their new place down in Florida."

"Does your dad miss working?"

Who would miss working? "I don't think so. They're really busy with friends. I swear they eat out almost every night."

"Good for them. How about Nonna? I invited her to the party but she had a cold. Is she feeling better?"

I didn't want to admit I hadn't talked to her in months. "She's doing okay."

"I don't like the idea of her still living in the same old house. That must be lonely at her age. I mean she's eighty-eight. She should think about going into one of those retirement communities."

I *certainly* didn't have money to help her with that.

"I sent her a birthday card." She looked at me. "Did you?"

I never paid attention to birthdays.

"Did you?"

"No. I always counted on you to handle stuff like that."

"That's not my job anymore, Tony."

I remembered something Wesley had said. Something about not just feeling better but being better.

Fat chance. So far my life was tied zero-zero.

**

Penny and I waited for Zach after the game. He came running toward us. There was that smile again.

Penny engulfed him in a hug. "Good game, hon."

I gave him a high-five. "Congrats on the win."

"Thanks." His cheeks were red and his dark hair was a matted mess from the ball cap.

We began walking toward the car when I remembered his gift. "Hey. Stop at my car. I've got a birthday present for you."

"You do?"

"I do. It's not everyday my favorite kid turns ten."

"Thanks, Dad." Zach said.

A few of Zach's teammates interrupted and he went to talk to them, holding up a finger to tell us he'd be back in a second.

"The gift's a little late, isn't it?" Penny said.

"The truth is, I bought him a football and was going to give it to him that day, but—"

"He doesn't like football. *You* like football."

"Yeah. I remembered that. So I got him something else."

Zach ran back to us. "Where's your car, Dad?"

I waved a hand to the right. "Way at the back."

He ran ahead. Penny and I walked the rest of the way in silence—which was a relief.

When we got to my car, Zach had his eyes cupped to the

window, trying to see in.

"It's in the trunk, bud." I unlocked the car and made the trunk open.

He took a slime-making set out of the gift bag. "Wow. Cool. I love slime." He turned the box over, checking out what came with the kit.

"There's more in the bag," I said.

He took out the other box but looked confused.

"It's a dinosaur dig set. You have to excavate in the sand and stone to find bones."

"I love dinosaurs! That's cool, Dad." He gave me a side hug. "Thanks."

"You're welcome."

Penny crossed her arms. "Two toys that make a mess? Really, Tony?"

Zach's smile faded a bit. "We can do them at your house, right Dad?"

"We can. Sometime soon?"

"When?" Zach asked.

"Next weekend?" I looked to Penny.

She shook her head. "We're going to see my parents."

"But Mom, I want to go to Dad's house."

Zach and I not seeing each other much wasn't just my problem. Penny often had a reason to shut me down.

"Soon, bud," I said. "I promise."

Zach nodded, but his smile had left him.

He knew like *I* knew that my promises didn't mean much.

I needed to add "see more of Zach" to my list of to-dos in my better person column.

Chapter Seventeen

Lydia

Those who oppress the poor insult their Maker,
but helping the poor honors him.
Proverbs 14: 31

I prayed a lot on the way to pick up Nova and Theo for our Saturday lunch. I wanted to do things right, which meant I wanted my plans to match up with God's. Knowing that He'd brought Nova and me together was like adding buttercream frosting to a cake: there was an extra element of deliciousness in our relationship.

Plus, I loved babies. I'd wanted more of my own, but it wasn't meant to be. I was already looking forward to JoJo giving me grandbabies, but that would—and should—be far in the future.

For now, there was Theo. Even before meeting him I had fun shopping for clothes, books, and one of those dolls that toddlers use to learn how to button and zip and tie.

And—miracle of miracles—I'd also found a highchair and a porta-crib at a garage sale. Talk about a God-thing. I was totally prepared for our luncheon *and* prepared to have a place for Theo to nap if everything went great. If not, I could sell them at my own garage sale—or wait for JoJo's babies.

There were no parking places in front of Nova's building, so I parked a block away. Even if Nova had a car, the lack of downtown parking would be a pain. Especially hauling a toddler and kid paraphernalia around.

She'd told me to meet them at the curb, but since my car wasn't at the curb, I backtracked to her building. It was old and the elevator was out of order. She was on the fourth floor. Looking up the stairwell, I thought about calling her down to meet me, but curiosity won out. I wanted to see how she lived.

On the way up the stairs I was careful to avoid the handrail. From the myriad of fingerprints on the wall it seemed best. As I went by each floor I heard the bass beat of music, babies crying, and a few loud conversations. Nothing to cause alarm, just people living their lives.

The four flights winded me and I paused to catch my breath

before finding her apartment. Once there, I heard Theo fussing inside. I knocked and Nova opened the door. She was obviously surprised to see me. "Hi. I thought we were going to meet outside."

"We were, but I had to park a block away." I felt guilty for being nosy. "I can wait downstairs if you'd like."

"No, no. You're here. Come in." Her voice was resigned.

As she stepped back, she made a quick sweep of toys and clutter. "Sorry. I didn't expect company."

"Nothing to be sorry for." Theo walked up to me and I was glad for the distraction. I bent down to his level. "You must be Theo. Hello! How are you?"

He gave me a toothy grin. "Grrr."

He was holding a stuffed tiger. "Ti-grrr?" I said. I took the animal and stroked its back. "Nice tiger." I gave it back.

"It's his favorite," Nova said.

While she finished packing a diaper bag I looked around. A tiny kitchen was at one end of the main room, with a highchair set at a two-person dinette table. I could see a hallway with doors to one bedroom and a bath. The furniture was used, but there were pictures on the wall, and a few bright-colored throw pillows on the couch. Theo was decidedly king of the house as his toys overflowed from a plastic football toy chest. She'd made a nice place for them. Simple, but nice.

"It's not much," Nova said, looking around the room and zipping up the bag.

"It's very nice. It reminds me of the first apartment Jeremy and I lived in. I could vacuum the entire place from one outlet."

Her shoulders relaxed a bit. "Yeah. Pretty much."

I glanced at the refrigerator. "Your fridge is large compared to the one we had. The freezer section in ours was so small, I had to choose between meat or ice cream."

"Which food won?"

"Guess." I winked at her.

It was nice to share a chuckle. She picked up a small, hooded sweatshirt. I held out my hand for it. "I'll put it on him—if that's okay."

"Sure."

I sat on the edge of the couch and beckoned him closer. "Shall we go bye-bye, Theo?"

He came to me willingly—which filled my heart. I zipped up the jacket with a sound effect. "Ziiiipppp." He smiled.

Nova put the diaper bag on her shoulder and picked him up. She pointed to the car seat. "Can you grab that? It will save me a trip."

I took the bulky seat and we headed down. She didn't even try the elevator. I couldn't imagine climbing four flights of stairs day after day with a toddler. "You've probably worked up some mighty muscles doing this," I said.

She held Theo on one hip. "That, I have. The elevator works when it wants to, which isn't often. I can't wait until Theo's old enough to handle the stairs himself."

"Those days are coming, quicker than you think," I said.

We walked to my car and she expertly installed the car seat in seconds. I had no idea there were already metal hooks for it in the backseat. I hadn't needed to know.

Until now.

I had a thousand questions, but didn't want to bombard her, so I was glad when she asked how JoJo was doing. I talked about her college classes--as much as I knew.

"I always wanted to go to college." Nova glanced in the backseat, at Theo. "But I messed that one up. Never even graduated high school."

"You could get your GED then take a few college classes."

"Could. But why?"

By her tone she was implying she had few options, but I took her words in a different direction. "What are your interests? What are you good at? When you were dreaming about college, what were you going to go into?"

Nova scoffed. "*None* of that matters now."

"Of course it matters. You're only nineteen. You could live another seventy years. Are you going to give up on life before you get started?"

She crooked a thumb toward the backseat. "I *have* started. *I* didn't give up on life, it gave up on me."

I had to be positive. "That's not true. You still have lots of--"

She angled toward me in her seat. "Let me make something really plain: I've got lots of nothin' and I'm going nowhere fast."

I had no idea what to say. And yet I did. I'd been a mentor. I'd heard students be pessimistic before. "You *are* going somewhere, Nova. You've got a decent place to stay. You're getting financial help, and--"

"I'm getting charity! I'm so down and out, I'm getting charity. And my place isn't decent. The toilet runs constantly, I've got roaches in the cupboards, water spots on the ceilings, and most of the time the whole building reeks from people cooking with spices that smell gross."

Father, Father, help me . . . But before I could figure out how to respond, she waved a hand. "Turn around. Take me home. This was a dumb idea."

"Nova, wait." What just happened?

Theo broke through the moment. "Mama!"

When I glanced at Nova her entire face changed as she turned her attention to her baby, reaching in the backseat to touch him. "It's okay, tiger." Her voice was light. "Mama's right here."

And I was right here too. I couldn't give up so easily. I also changed my tone. "I've got a yummy lunch for you, Theo. Are you hungry?"

"Hun-gee."

Nova faced forward again.

"I really do have a yummy lunch for us," I told her. "Does that sound okay?"

She sighed. "Yeah. Sure. I suppose we gotta eat."

**

As soon as Nova came in the house, she stopped. She looked around. She walked to the dining room table and touched it as if it was sacred. "I remember sitting here in Daisy Scouts." She moved to a certain chair and fingered the back of it. "I sat right here."

In my mind's eye, I saw a skinny little girl, sweet and eager. And needy. "I'm so glad you joined. You girls had fun."

She nodded. Her eyes were foggy like she was seeing memories. "There were lots of juice boxes and cookies eaten here. Lots of craft projects."

"Too many to count."

I let her mind linger, not wanting to break the moment—for they were good memories.

Nova did the breaking. "Mom threw away almost every project I made. Even the card I made her."

I'd talked about the card in the Room. "Why did she do that? It was a nice card."

Nova blinked. "Turns out she'd just lost her job so having a card that thanked her for working hard made her mad."

"You couldn't have known that."

She shrugged. "I *shouldn't* have known a lot of things. But I did."

Yes, her mom was different from most moms, but this sounded ominous. "What kind of things?"

"It doesn't matter now." Nova helped Theo out of his jacket and set it on the back of one of the chairs. He walked right into the kitchen and pointed to the fridge. "Hun-gee."

I'd thought a lot about what to serve for lunch. I'd even checked online for what 21-month-olds liked to eat. I had mac and cheese and apple slices ready. Nova and I would eat grilled chicken salad and fresh muffins. Within minutes everything was ready to serve.

To make it more casual, we ate at the kitchen table. I set the freshly cleaned highchair from the garage sale close by. The porta-crib was set up in the guest room. I'd fulfilled the Scout motto to "Be prepared."

Once we settled in, Nova said, "This is nice. Thanks."

"Glad to do it." I passed her the muffins.

"Dat!" Theo said, pointing.

Nova chuckled. "It's his latest thing. He wants 'that' all the time."

I removed the muffin paper and cut one in half. "You want *dat,* then you shall have dat."

He set down an apple slice and ate the muffin greedily.

"I bet your mom loves having a grandson around," I said.

"Not really."

"Why not? He's adorable."

"She's off doing her own thing. Last I heard she lives in Alaska."

"Why Alaska?"

"Long story, but she met a guy online and that's where he lives. Seward, I think."

I perked up. "We've been to Seward! Jeremy and I kayaked there. It was amazing because a bald eagle flew right over us."

She ate a bite of chicken and I realized now was not the time to relive vacation moments. "I'm sure her moving was hard on both of you."

"Not for her."

"I hoped that wasn't true. "JoJo being away at college this past year was really hard for me. I'm sure it's hard for your mom to be away from you and Theo."

"I wouldn't be so sure." Nova tried to help Theo use his kid's fork on the mac and cheese, but he gave up and used his fingers. "Mom left before Theo was even born. Actually, I've never told her about him."

I couldn't believe what I was hearing. "That's crazy. She deserves to know she's a grandma."

Nova's eyes widened. "She *deserves* to know? *She* left me when I needed her most. I was a lost, pregnant, junior in high school who needed her mom. And she left."

"She left while you were still in school?"

"She did." Nova held a glass of iced tea with both hands, as if the cold of it was soothing.

"That must have been awful," I said.

Nova shrugged. "The whole thing came down on Christmas Day, which was really ironic, because that's the same day my dad left when I was five."

"Oh Nova, that was hardly a merry Christmas."

Nova nodded, but went on. "Mom made eggs and toast for Christmas breakfast. It was really nice. So nice that I decided I was going to tell her about the pregnancy. But she beat me to it by announcing that she'd met the love of her life and was moving to Alaska."

"I didn't realize you've lived in Alaska."

Nova put a hand to her chest. "*I* never moved there. Mom moved in January. She pretended she was going to send for me later, but she never did."

It was hard to wrap my head around. "She left you alone, in your house."

Nova shrugged. "Yeah."

I was taken aback. "Is that even legal?"

"Mom didn't care about legal. She said I could handle it. She said it was okay."

"It was not okay." I remembered what she'd said in the car. "You were still in high school. You had three semesters left. Did you ever consider asking me or a teacher to help?"

She shook her head. "I didn't want to get authorities involved." Her fork played with the lettuce in her salad. "And for the most part, it worked out because Mom paid the bills. But she never did send for me. When we talked on the phone she didn't ask much about how I was doing. It was all about her and Fred, her dream guy. That's why I didn't tell her I was pregnant. I didn't want her to be mad at me *or* happy about it." Her jaw tightened.

"I'm so sorry."

"Yeah. Me too. It was a really hard semester."

"I'm sure it was." I couldn't even think of leaving JoJo like that. "When was Theo born?"

"June fifteenth."

I smiled at the precious little boy and gave him the other half of the muffin.

Nova ran her fingers over the condensation on her glass of tea. "After he was born I just didn't have it in me to stick with school. Mom acted like it was no big deal when she found out I didn't finish." She sighed deeply.

I kept my angry feelings about Meribelle to myself. "I'm so sorry," I said again. Then I remembered where Nova lived now. "But your family's house, why aren't you still living there? "

"Mom needed to sell it to fund her new life. She and Fred needed money to buy a fishing boat." Nova sipped her tea. "Actually, she was behind on house payments and utilities, so it was going to be foreclosed on anyway."

"Was this before or after Theo was born?"

"After. He was six months old when we had to move out. That's when I got our lovely apartment."

She amazed me. "What a strong girl you are. Who was with you when he was born?"

Nova wiped milk from Theo's chin. "Since I was only seventeen I was afraid social services would take him away, so I had a friend of mine come to the hospital for the birth and say she was my sister." She shrugged. "It worked. I got to take him home with me."

"What about the baby's father?"

Her forehead furrowed. "He died."

I gasped. "What? How?"

She shook her head, fighting tears. "How doesn't matter. Dead is dead. I'd just told him about the baby and he was happy about it, but then he died. Yeah, except for Theo, that whole year was a disaster."

I couldn't imagine. I reached across the table and put a hand on hers. "I'm so sorry, Nova. You're a brave girl to endure so much."

She pulled her hand away. "Brave? How am I brave? I didn't do a single thing that's brave. All I did was survive—and not very well when you get down to it."

"Don't say that. You're doing everything you can." I thought of a way I could help. "You mentioned your job? If you need help with babysitting, I'm here."

Nova cocked her head and studied me. "*Here* is a long ways away from where we live."

She was right. Plus, there was the question of my job. "When I can, I'd love to help."

Nova nodded. "I'm a waitress downtown. Luckily, I usually have the breakfast and lunch shift. A lady in my building takes care of Theo for me."

I felt bad for feeling relieved. "That's a good arrangement. But if you ever need a sitter in the evenings, I'd be happy to help."

"Thanks." I could tell by her body language she was feeling more comfortable with me. And I with her. "Where's Mr. Brogdon today? Does he work Saturdays?"

"He's helping a friend put in landscaping. He won't be back until this evening."

"I only met him a few times but he was nice. He made me laugh."

That was Jeremy. "More tea?" I asked.

She nodded. When I got up to get the pitcher she asked, "How long you been working at the welfare office?"

"A few weeks."

"Not long at all. Do you like it?"

I thought about saying yes, but that wouldn't do anyone any good. "Not really."

"Then why did you take the job?"

I filled our glasses. "I took the job because God wanted me to run into you." From the look on Nova's face, I wanted to take it back.

"That's a crazy thing to say."

"Crazy but true."

"Why did you say that?" She finished buttering a muffin. "How can you say that?"

I wasn't sure how to explain. I didn't want to tell her about the Room experience, but I wanted her to understand how God worked. *Words, Lord. Words!* To buy time I took a sip of tea, but splattered it when I set the drink down.

This spilled drink made me remember another spilled drink. I dabbed at the spill with a napkin. "The morning you and I ran into each other I was ready to quit. I was primed to go into my boss's office—"

"You'd just started to work there. Why is it so bad?"

"It isn't bad, it just isn't for me. Being in data entry means I don't get to interact with people. I can't help them. That's what I'm good at."

"I know."

Her compliment felt good. "Anyway, I didn't quit because I got a phone call from JoJo."

"And she told you not to quit?"

"No, but her call delayed me at my desk so I could see you. But it was spilled coffee that really set it up. God did that."

She looked at me like I was bonkers. "How do God and coffee mix together?"

I sat forward, counting off on my fingers. "Because of the spilled coffee I needed paper towels, but there weren't any in the break room. So I went to the supply room, which led me down the aisle where you were talking to your caseworker." I spread my hands. "To go back further, if not for me giving up mentoring and being an empty nester I wouldn't have applied for any job. And if not for the data entry job I wouldn't be working where I met you. If not for JoJo's phone call, I would have quit that very day. And if not for the spilled coffee—"

"We wouldn't have seen each other."

I was pleased she'd followed my if-not list. "Exactly!"

"That's a lot of coincidences, I'll give you that."

I shook my head. "Coincidences? There's no such thing."

"Sure there is."

I kept my head shaking. "Coincidence is a word the world uses to explain away God's interventions."

She looked skeptical. "Sounds like something a grandma would cross-stitch and hang above the toilet."

It kind of did. "Do you ever notice coincidences in your life?"

"Not really."

I took a shot. "Think back to how you came to be at the office that morning, talking to your caseworker."

"She's not my usual lady. I usually see Mrs. Hopkins, but she was out sick."

"Bingo. And Mrs. Hopkins's cubicle. Where is it?"

"It's on the other side of the floor. Actually, they wanted me to reschedule, but I'd already gotten off work, and my boss wasn't keen on me messing up his schedule again, so they told me to talk to another lady."

Theo tipped over his sippy cup but I righted it. "If not for your boss saying you couldn't take off at another time, if not for Mrs. Hopkins being sick, if not for the powers-that-be assigning you to Sylvia . . ."

Nova blinked a few times, taking it in. "Which put me where I could see you as you walked by."

"Which led to us sitting here today."

She sat back and sighed audibly. "Wow."

I was so relieved she saw it. I thought of something else. "Do you know how I got your address and phone number?"

"You work for the government, so I figured you have full access to everything about everybody."

"Actually, no. But out of all of the information that I input, yours happened to be in the pile of applications that I was entering into the computer that day. Right when I needed it."

"That *is* pretty cool."

"It's more than cool," I said. "It's God at work."

She paused a minute, speared a piece of chicken, and ate it as she thought. I wanted to say more, but I got a nudge to be quiet. Let Nova say the next words.

She dabbed her mouth with a napkin, then said, "I have one problem. Why would the God of the entire universe be bothered with a coffee spill and my schedule? Doesn't He have better things to do?"

I chuckled. "I hear you. It's a mystery why God would be so involved in the tiniest details of our lives, but He is, all the time—whether we see it, acknowledge it, or not." I thought of the main point. "He loves us that much."

Nova pushed her salad toward the center of the table. "If He loves me that much, then why did He let me get pregnant when I was in high school? Why did He let my mother abandon me? Why did He let Theo's father die?"

She'd hit me with the hard ones. It was my turn to stall while eating a bite to give my thoughts time to marinate. *God? This is important. Help me here!* I shared the only thing I could think of. "We all have free will to choose, which sometimes leads to mistakes, and—"

Nova set her fork down with a clatter. "I did not *choose* to get pregnant. I did not *choose* to be abandoned, and Theo did not *choose* to lose his dad—a dad he never even got to meet."

I felt a wave of panic.

"You're not answering me."

I took a cleansing breath, deep, from my toes. "That's because I don't have a good answer."

"Ha. You got nothing." Nova seemed pleased by my defeat.

"That's not true. I have *something,* but I don't have everything."

She crossed her arms. "So? What's your something?"

I started with the response I'd heard many times in my life. "God uses hard times to make our lives better."

She scoffed. "Oh, yeah. Me and Theo's lives are proof of that."

"God's has plans for those trials. We all suffer. We all go through bad times."

"What was your bad time? Not getting a dinner reservation when you wanted?" She rolled her eyes.

I was hurt. "That was mean, Nova. You know it was."

She shrugged.

I didn't usually talk about my suffering because it was private. But now was not the time to hold it in. "I lost two babies after JoJo. We tried for years but finally I was told I couldn't have any more kids. It was devastating to me, and to Jeremy."

Her face softened. "Sorry. I didn't mean for it to be a contest of who's hurt the most."

I gave her a wistful smile. "There is no contest, yet it is true that some people suffer more than others. But the thing is, God uses every hurt and every moment of pain to bring us closer to Him. *That's* the ultimate goal."

"What if I don't want to get closer to Him?"

"That's another hard question. But He might just keep adding to your pile of pain until you do."

Her head jerked back. "I don't like the sounds of that. He's saying pray to Me or I'll make you pay?"

"His goal is to have you pray, not pay. Pray to Me because I love you unconditionally and want to have a relationship with you. That's God's goal." I thought of a quote I'd heard ages ago. "'If you only pray when you're in trouble, you're in trouble.'"

"Meaning?"

"We're supposed to 'pray without ceasing.'"

She waved a hand between us. "With my job and Theo and surviving I barely have time to think two original thoughts all day. Much less take time out to pray all the time." She shook her head, wiped Theo's hands and mouth, and took him out of the highchair, setting him on her lap. "Praying like that is *not* going to happen. I have too much on my plate as it is. If that's a requirement then God is asking too much."

"Praying doesn't have to take long," I said. "I've prayed multiple times during lunch."

Her eyebrows rose. "You did not. I didn't see you."

"You don't have to kneel or clasp your hands or even bow your head. God appreciates short snippets of prayer too."

"What did you pray?"

"I prayed for the right words to tell you about God."

She gave me a slight smile. "And He told you what to say?"

"Not exactly but . . ."

Nova's phone pinged and she glanced at a text.

I got an idea. "I like getting texts," I said. "Don't you?"

She peered at her phone then back to me. "I guess."

"I like them because they're short and let me know someone is thinking about me."

"I suppose. I don't get that many."

"Yet if I want to really interact, I like Facetime or phone calls better because I can say more."

She shook her head. "I have never Facetimed. Wouldn't even know how to do it—or who to do it with."

I was losing her. "The point is, God would prefer talking with us at length but he'll take a prayer-text too."

Nova nodded and smiled. "I guess that makes sense."

I smiled. "Then *I* guess God answered my prayers."

Nova set Theo on the floor and stood. "Actually, that was a text from work. It *was* my day off, but they want me to come in cuz Barry called in sick. I gotta go."

I stood too. "I could keep Theo while you're working and bring him home later."

"I won't get off 'til nine."

I thought about my day, which now would be a different day than I'd planned. "That'd be fine."

I could see her mind thinking it over. "I guess that'd work." She dug through his diaper bag. "There's plenty of diapers in here, and wipes. His blankie and tiger. He'll take a nap pretty soon and usually goes to bed at seven. I'll try to get off early."

"We'll get along fine," I said.

She looked to the door, then stopped. "How am I going to get to work?"

I hadn't thought of that. "We'll all get in the car, I'll drop you off, then Theo and I will come back here."

"I guess that works." She picked up Theo. "I'll get him a new diaper so he's fresh."

And so we all got in the car, I dropped Nova off, and I came home with a baby.

I hoped I remembered how to do this.

**

It was almost seven-thirty, past Theo's bedtime. I stood in JoJo's bedroom, near the porta-crib.

Theo was sleeping. Finally. But I didn't dare move or even breathe. I'd spent the last hour in the room, trying to escape. But every time I moved he raised his head. The first two times I told him to lay down and even rubbed his back, but quickly learned that when I stopped, he'd raise his head again. I'd transitioned from having my hand lay still on his back, to just standing beside the bed. I'd see him open an eye to check if I was there. But in the last minute I'd made three steps toward the door—which I'd wisely left ajar. A few of these tricks had come back to me, as well as the memory of how exhausting it was.

I took in a deep but silent breath and held it as I made the final spring into the hall. I carefully pulled the door shut, but not latched, then tiptoed downstairs to the living room.

I'd just collapsed into a chair when I heard the garage door open. I bolted to my feet and met Jeremy at the kitchen door, a finger to my lips in *shush* mode.

"Don't make a sound," I whispered.

He looked around the kitchen. "Why?" he whispered back.

"Nova's baby is sleeping upstairs."

"Nova's baby? I thought you were having them for lunch. How did—?"

"Long story."

He glanced upward. "I worked hard in Bill's yard. I need a shower."

"We can't risk the noise. I just got him to sleep."

He cocked his head. "How long is he staying?"

I don't know wasn't going to fly. "Nova usually works until nine, but will try to get off early. She's going to call."

"And come here?"

I shook my head. "She doesn't have a car. I'll bring Theo to her place." Which was four flights up. I knew I couldn't carry him, the car seat, and the diaper bag. I'd have to call Nova to come down and get him. It would be complicated.

Jeremy checked out the pot of spaghetti on the stove.

"Theo likes pasta."

"I do too." He began to take out a plate for himself, then asked, "There's still a lot here. Have you eaten?"

"Not really. Just a few bites when I fed him."

He took up two servings. We sat at the island.

"How does Bill's yard look?" I asked.

"It looks great, but every bone in my body hurts. I'm not used to manual labor."

We ate a few bites in silence. Then Jeremy set down his fork. "What have you gotten yourself into, Lyd? Lunch is one thing, but babysitting all day? Putting him to bed here?" He thought of something. "Is he old enough to sleep in a bed?"

"Almost. But I found a porta-crib at a garage sale."

He nodded toward the highchair. "Another garage sale find?"

I shrugged. "God wanted me to be prepared."

He studied me a moment, then moved a lock of my hair behind my ear. "You look as beat as I am."

"Completely and utterly. He's a great little boy, but I'd forgotten how much energy it takes."

"Yet another reason why people have kids when they're young."

I poked around at my dinner. If I closed my eyes I'd find myself face-down in the pasta.

My phone rang, startling me. It was Nova. She was off work early. "Sounds super," I said. "I'll bring him home. See you soon."

Jeremy glanced up from his plate. "Do you want me to come along?"

I shook my head. "You've worked hard enough today." I put my plate by the sink and headed toward the stairs.

Jeremy reached out and touched my arm. "Watch yourself, Lyd. We both know from experience that your heart of gold can get broken."

"I know. But Nova is different. I've known her for thirteen years."

"You've known *of* her for most of those years. She's not a kid anymore. She's grown up, has a life of her own, and is a mom herself."

He was right. "I'll be careful."

But I knew it would be hard.

Chapter Eighteen

Minnie

You guide me with your counsel,
leading me to a glorious destiny.
Whom have I in heaven but you?
I desire you more than anything on earth.
My health may fail, and my spirit may grow weak,
but God remains the strength of my heart; he is mine forever.
Psalm 73: 24-26

I had the Saturday after Gabe's party planned. Dad had given me $100 and told me to go shopping. No babies in the back, no errands to run, no schoolwork to finish, just free time to use as I wanted to use it.

I wasn't used to shopping solo. I usually went with Mom or Claudia, and sometimes Ashley. I was a passenger on their shopping trains.

Truth be told, I didn't mind being a follower. But today I was in charge. After shopping—if I felt up to it and felt brave—I might even stop at that Discover place. I had the invitation in my purse, just in case. Money, free time, *and* discovering my potential? The afternoon might be a home run.

Or a bust.

One step at a time. My first stop was the art store to see Gabe. We'd texted off and on all week. It was like that chance meeting at the tree had sparked something in both of us. We went from once-in-a-while friends, to being close and getting closer. But I was wary. I'd never had a real boyfriend and had always figured that kind of romantic connection didn't happen to girls like me. I had no real reason for thinking that way. And I hoped I was wrong.

Art's Art Shop was in an older part of town, in the bottom half of a two-story brick building with a stone pediment on the front that had "1912" carved into it. The building was on a corner and had a faded mural painted on its side: *Drink Coca-Cola. Relieves Fatigue.* The store was dripping with character.

I parked in front and was getting out when Gabe startled me. He walked toward me.

I put a hand to my chest to stop its pounding. "You scared me."

"Didn't mean to do that." He held up a cup of coffee emblazoned with the name of the shop next door. "Just got a cup. Want me to get you one?"

"No, thanks. I'm good."

We headed toward the door of Art's. "Nice to finally see you," he said, smiling.

"You too." I smiled shyly and walked in as held the door for me. What a gentleman.

The owner called out from his stool. "You pulling customers out of cars now, Gabriel?" Then he lowered his glasses and peered at me. "Oh, it's you. You've been in here before, haven't you?"

"Yes, sir. But not recently."

"I never forget a face." He pointed at a jar of candy. "Have a peppermint."

He always said that. I took one.

Gabe and I moved toward the pencil and sketch pad area. "So," he said. "Did you come in for supplies, or . . ." He grinned. "For another reason?"

I tossed it back to him. "What do you think?"

"I'm open to any reason that gets you here."

I felt myself blush. "Actually, I think I would like to give watercolors a try."

"Good for you. How much have you done?"

"Very little. I've thought about setting up an easel at my mom's, but . . ." I fidgeted with a few brushes before getting to the point. "I know I've told you this before, but I was really sad to miss your party."

"It missed you too." He strolled to the paint section. "Don't worry though. I'll have others. I'm sticking around after graduation."

That was wonderful news. "Super. What are you going to do?"

"I'm going to keep working on my art."

"Of course," I said.

He smiled. "Plus, I'm going to work here full time." He looked past me, toward the owner, then spoke softly. "Art has mentioned retiring. I know it would be a big step, but I was thinking of buying him out."

"That's huge."

"Enormous. And it may not work out. It's just an idea."

"It's a good one." When I set my purse on the counter so I could look at paint it tipped over, spilling its contents to the floor.

"Sorry," I said. "Clumsy me."

As we picked things up, our hands touched. My breath caught and my heart started racing. We both pulled our hands back and looked at each other—which reminded me of something I'd seen a hundred times in a Hallmark movie.

Calm down, Minnie.

When Gabe stood he was holding the invitation. "Sorry. I shouldn't have read this but I did. "You're invited . . . ?" He handed it to me. "Sorry, it's none of my business."

"It's okay. The invitation is from a company that's supposed to help me 'discover my potential,'" I said, using air quotes. "Or some such rot."

"That doesn't sound like rot to me. Everybody wants that."

I shrugged.

"Is it through school?"

"Not at all. In fact, an older guy came to my house and delivered the invitation in person."

"That's special, but also a tiny bit creepy. Isn't it?"

I shrugged. "A little. But he seemed harmless. He was nice."

"Sorry. I didn't mean to rain on your parade. It does sounds special. Are you going?"

"I don't know." Though I *was* a little more inclined to go now that Gabe thought it was special. How pitiful was that? "I mean, what can strangers tell me about *my* potential? They don't know me."

"Maybe they'll give you a personality or aptitude test and guide you from there."

"Maybe."

"When are you supposed to go?"

"Whenever. There's no date and time." I held the invitation so he could see.

"That's kind of odd."

"I know. But Wesley—that's the man's name—said I could come anytime."

"They are definitely accommodating. You should go."

"I'm not so sure . . ."

"Won't you regret it if you don't? Years from now when you're at a crossroads, you don't want to look back and say, 'If only I'd gone to the Discovery Room and discovered my full potential.'"

His eyes danced in amusement, clearly joking, but what he said could be true. "When you put it that way . . ."

He nodded. "Okay then. Go do it and let me know what happens. Then maybe I'll go too."

I smiled a teasing smile. "But *you* didn't get an invitation."

He waggled his eyebrows back at me. "Maybe you can get me one."

Art cleared his throat. We looked in his direction. "Less gabbing, more selling, Gabriel."

"Yes, sir."

I put the invitation away. "I'd better buy something." I whispered.

He shook his head and lowered his voice. "Don't worry about it. Besides, that means you'll have to come back." He smiled. "You'd better get going."

"Now?"

"Why not now? Come by afterward and tell me all about it."

I felt a stirring in my gut. Was I nervous about the connection I felt with Gabe or about following through with the invitation?

He walked me to the door. "This could be exciting."

"I doubt it," I said.

He shooed me out the door and waved.

I went to my car and took a moment to reset. I'd thought about using my invitation today and now I was on my way. I plugged the address into my phone. It was five minutes away.

There were no more excuses.

Chapter Nineteen

Minnie

Be on guard. Stand firm in the faith.
Be courageous. Be strong.
1 Corinthians 16: 13

The store front for the Discovery Room was far from impressive. It was in a strip mall between a used bookstore and a craft store called Bead-It. But the company name *was* on the window, which made them at least look legit.

I parked directly out front and went in. The office was minimal. There was a single desk and chair, with one guest chair by the windows. A massive plant curled its way around the windows and door.

A receptionist smiled. She had her hair pulled tightly back like a dancer. She wore an orange and pink flowered blouse like I'd seen in a vintage thrift store I'd gone to with Ashley.

"Hi there. What brings you to the Discovery Room on this fine day?"

I flashed her the invitation. She nodded as if that explained everything. "Your name is?"

"Minnie McLaughlin."

"Oh." She paused. "You wouldn't be Minerva by any chance?"

"How do you know my given name?"

She pointed to the card.

Dumb. I was acting like I was guilty of something. "I liked to be called Minnie."

She smiled like she was truly pleased I was there. "We've been waiting for you, Minnie." She stood. "I'm Gracie. If you'll follow me?"

No waiting. That was nice. I followed her into a room—a very weird room, like being inside a smooth igloo. Everything was white and there was a single backless stool in the middle.

"Have a seat."

I followed directions, but felt panicked when she started to leave. "Excuse me? Gracie? Who am I waiting for? What happens now?"

She smiled. "You'll see. Relax and enjoy it." She left, pulling the door shut behind her.

I turned in a complete circle on the swivel stool. I felt like a specimen on display for a scientific study.

Suddenly, the Room was alive with a scene, only as I swiveled around a second time it was like I was *in* it, like it was some kind of virtual reality. I saw Ashley and me on the university campus. Our moms were with us. "What in the world?"

I tried to place the moment . . . then pegged it. "This is orientation, the summer before our freshman year."

Ashley and I had been so excited for college because we were going to room together. We'd been planning it since we were little. Ashley was going into education. I was going into business.

About three dozen newbies and their parents were gathered at the student union. Mom was half-heartedly talking to Ashley's mom. She looked wrecked—with good reason. Her boyfriend had broken up with her the day before. I'd had to beg her to come to the orientation. I remembered hoping she wouldn't start crying in front of everybody.

A dozen older college kids, wearing matching school T-shirts, began dividing us into smaller groups.

The older me gasped when I saw Gabe walk toward us.

"Gabe? I don't remember Gabe being our guide." Why didn't I remember that?

He introduced himself then went around my group of six and asked everybody what their major was. He had a kind comment and a specific brochure to match each answer. When it was my turn I said, "My major is business. But I really like art."

He cocked his head. "My major is art. If you decide to go in that direction perhaps we'll see each other." He handed me two brochures, one for each college. "Just in case."

The brochure for the art college glowed.

The scene ended and the lights came on. A man came in the Room and I recognized him as Wesley, the man who'd delivered my invitation.

"It's nice to see you, Miss McLaughlin. I was beginning to worry you wouldn't show up."

"What just happened?" I asked. "I saw myself two years ago, like I was in a movie."

"Was there anything special about it?"

"Other than it's impossible? Were there cameras at the university that day?" I shook my head. "There had to be, otherwise how could you have gotten this scene."

He shrugged. "Was there anything special beyond that."

That was a pretty big point.

"What else was special about the scene?" he asked again. "Did you see anything that stood out?"

A few hundred things.

He was waiting for an answer, so I picked something that might appease him. "One of the brochures glowed."

Wesley smiled. "It was not a coincidence it glowed at just that moment."

I didn't get it. "What about it glowing at all? Things don't glow."

"That you've noticed."

I huffed. "Tell me one thing that's glowed outside this Room."

He took a deep breath and let it out. "Miss McLaughlin, if you are going to benefit from anything you see today, you need to suspend your disbelief." He explained. "It's a matter of believing something is true, even though it is implausible. Can you do that?"

"I don't know."

"Do you enjoy superhero movies or movies set in outer space?"

"Sure."

"Can you explain how people fly or how we can interact with space aliens?"

Ok. I was getting it. "No, I can't." I waved him off. "Fine. I will suspend my disbelief as far as this . . . totally impossible movie goes."

"It is much appreciated." He took a fresh breath. "Now, back to my question. The brochure glowed. It was not a coincidence. Which means there is a rea—"

"Reason it glowed."

"Very good. What do you think that might be?"

I shrugged.

He kept looking at me patiently, like he had all the time in the world. Then he asked, "Which brochure glowed?"

That, I could answer. "The one for the art college."

"Which college was the other brochure for?"

He knew very well what college it was for. "The business college."

"Which college are you currently enrolled in?"

This had to be a joke. Were Ashley and Gabe in on it? "Business."

"You told the guide you loved art. Actually, you shared that with me when I gave you the invitation. You mentioned your father wanted you to be in business and your mother wanted you to live at home."

"That's the gist of it."

He took two steps to his right. "Your mother seemed very sad that day. Was something wrong?"

"Boyfriend problems. She tried to act excited for me, but what she feels always shows on her face. That night I found her crying in her room."

"About the boyfriend?"

"And about the thought of me moving away from her. She said she was afraid of being alone and didn't know what she would do without me around."

"Those are normal concerns for parents of students starting college."

"Maybe so, but it didn't help that Dad had remarried the month before. At the time of the orientation, he and Claudia were still on their Caribbean honeymoon. I was a bridesmaid at their wedding. Obviously, *that* hadn't gone over well."

"Explain again why you chose—you choose—to live at home?"

"I just told you. Mom was torn up about everything. I just wanted her to be happy, so I told her I'd go to college but live with her. She hugged me so tight."

"How about you? Now it is two years later. Do you still like living at home?"

I let out a breath. "Do we have to talk about this right now? I mean, look where we are." I swept a hand to showcase the dome. "This is a real room in the here and now, which suddenly turns into another place in another time. Since I'm supposed to accept that this impossible is possible, I don't want to waste my time talking about me living at home. It's not that big a deal."

"Hmm. Why don't we visit your parents again." He gestured toward the stool. "Have a seat." He left me alone.

My heart fluttered. Whatever this was—however this was—it was really happening. To me.

But why?

Another scene started and it took me a moment to figure out where I was. But then I recognized the red leather couch and knew I was at my dad's first apartment after the divorce. I'd loved staying in a high-rise in downtown Kansas City because it was completely different from the suburbs. The building had a doorman, a pool, and an exercise room. I remember loving that it was clean and modern, not like Mom's house that had clutter on every surface, and flowery wallpaper everywhere. Yuck.

And there I was, twelve years old, rolling a pink Hello-Kitty suitcase out to the foyer.

"We're going to Florida," I said to the Room. I remembered it all. The divorce had just been finalized. Dad wanted to celebrate with a trip and had asked me to go with him. I'd wanted to go to the mountains, but Dad insisted on the beach. I didn't like sitting in the sun because I burned easily, but he said I'd have fun. There was no arguing with Dad. What he wanted, he got.

The young me went back to a bedroom and grabbed my backpack. I was ready to go.

The phone rang in the kitchen. I glanced at the caller ID. It was Mom. I took a step back. I shook my head.

I remembered not wanting to talk to her because she'd been furious about the trip. Dad was taking me out of town on a grand vacation to celebrate him being free—of her. I couldn't blame Mom. Looking back the trip was clearly a way to hurt her

I let the answering machine take the call. Then the phone suddenly glowed. I heard Mom's voice, leaving a message. "Ben, if you're hearing this, stop listening. This message is for our daughter so try to find *some* integrity and let her hear it alone." She paused a moment, then continued. "Hey, Min. Please call me back. I'm really hurting here. It's so unfair and I'll miss you so much. Please, sweetie." I heard Roberto's voice in the background. He was Mom's live-in boyfriend. "Stay here with me and Robby. I need you. And I really need to talk to you about something. Call me back." She hung up.

I immediately erased the message.

The scene faded and Wesley came in the Room.

I put up a hand, stopping whatever words he was going to say. "I know I shouldn't have erased the message. And if Roberto hadn't been around, I might have returned her call. But hearing his voice in the background . . . he was such a sleaze with his greasy hair and smarmy way of touching Mom all the time. Plus, he called me Min-Min." I shuddered even now.

"Just because you erased the message doesn't negate the fact that hearing that message offered you a choice."

"But I didn't like the choice. If I'd talked to Mom she would've wanted me to give up the vacation with Dad. To do what? Hang around with her and sleaze-ball?"

"You have mentioned several times that your mom needs you. Didn't she need you then? Especially then?"

"She *always* needs me." The words had come out rude. "Sorry about that, and I do love her. I want her to be happy."

"What happened to your mom while you were at the beach?"

I inwardly fought against the truth. "That's not fair. Having me around wouldn't have changed the two of them running off to get married."

"Wouldn't it?"

It was a question I'd often asked myself. "I don't know, okay? Maybe I could've talked her out of it, but I was just a kid, and when Mom thought she was in love, she didn't think straight. If I had my way, she wouldn't have had any boyfriends. Wouldn't *have* any boyfriends now. She seems incapable of choosing good, stable guys."

"In your expert opinion."

I held up a hand. "I getcha. I don't have a lot of guy experience, but I do know that none of the boyfriends stuck around. Sometimes I wondered if they broke up with Mom because she was *too* needy. Desperation isn't sexy."

"You speak of other boyfriends, which means the marriage with Roberto didn't last?"

I scoffed. "It was over in six weeks. Actually, his is the only relationship where Mom instigated the breakup. Turns out he lied about his great job and his finances, plus he never told her he'd already been married three times. He was broke, and right from the start he sponged off her. A real loser. I had to pick up the pieces for her. Again."

"Does she really rely on your influence that much?"

I thought of the eight years between then and now. "Definitely. Mom needs a confidante. She's too easily swayed by hunky guys saying pretty words. Someone needs to keep her grounded."

"And that someone was you? Is you?"

I suddenly felt exhausted. "My parents' divorce made me grow up fast. I just wanted them to get along and for everybody to be happy."

"Big goals for a young person. Is that still your goal?"

"Of course." I thought back to the glowing phone. "Now I know that call was important, but how could I have known that back then?"

Wesley thought about this a few moments. "There *is* no way of knowing whether anything is important other than to make sure your intuition is turned on during all interventions in your life."

I huffed. "Interventions?"

"Special choices."

"You mentioned intuition. Isn't intuition a feeling? Everybody says feelings aren't reliable."

"Discernment and intuition take practice." He put a fist in front of his gut. "It's learning to listen to that inner, small voice that spurs you to answer that phone call—or not answer."

"That doesn't sound very scientific."

"Intellect plus emotion equals intuition. Hopefully it leads to knowledge and then wisdom."

This was deep stuff, and I wanted to understand. "The phone rang. I saw it was Mom. Logically, I should have answered it."

"Very true."

"But my emotions back then were up and down. I just wanted to stop thinking about the divorce and go on vacation. I didn't want to be bothered by Mom's whining."

"Perhaps the next time you feel a nudge you'll pause just a moment, consider the consequences of your choice, and tap into your intuition."

"So that's what you're trying to teach me? To look for choices? To think them through better?"

He nodded. "Bravo, Miss McLaughlin."

"Thanks. I guess. But is there another scene—maybe a happier one? I'm two for two making the wrong choice."

"Happy or not, they all serve a purpose." He nodded, as if making a decision. "We've seen a few choices you've made regarding your family. How about revisiting the roots of your gift?"

"What gift are we talking about?"

He just stood there, half-smiling.

"My art?"

He nodded. "I'll be back soon."

CHAPTER TWENTY

Minnie

In his grace, God has given us different gifts
for doing certain things well.
Romans 12: 6

After Wesley left the Room. I sat on the stool and waited, praying this time he'd show me a flashback where I made the right choice.

A moment later a scene appeared. It was an old-time drug store with checkered floors and narrow aisles. But not just any drug store. "It's Ben Franklin's in Dawson!" I said aloud. I always went there when I stayed with Grandpa and Grandma McLaughlin.

I gasped when I saw Grandma come down an aisle. She was so young! Her hair was more brown than gray.

A little girl walked behind her.

"That's me!" I couldn't stop looking at myself. I was only six or seven. I remembered the pink polka dot sundress as one Grandma had made for me. I'd loved twirling to make the skirt poof out.

I was so innocent. Not a care in the world.

My parents and I visited Grandpa and Grandma for most holidays, but one time I'd stayed with them for a whole week when Mom and Dad went to Hawaii. This had to be then.

The child Minnie stopped in front of the toys.

"All right, Minerva," Grandma said. "We're here because I promised to get you something special to play with this week. You can buy anything you want—within reason, of course."

The grown me was mesmerized by seeing her. Grandma moved differently, not like she did now with her bad knees. If I was six . . . this was fourteen years ago.

I watched myself look through the toys. I picked up a Barbie. I remember doing just that, and even remembered thinking that I already had a Barbie at home. There were boy toys, stuffed animals, sticker books, and puzzles. I'd always been good at puzzles. I was reaching for one when a set of colored pencils fell to the floor.

They glowed. The light pulsated a few times before it faded.

"There's that glow again!" I called out. Last time Wesley had said a glow pointed out a choice. How were pencils important?

"Colored pencils," Grandma said, picking up the box. "Did you know your grandpa is a very good artist?"

"Huh-uh."

"He'd love to show you how to draw." She checked out the shelves and found a big art kit in a wooden box with a handle. "Look at this set: you get paper, markers, crayons, and . . ." She checked the price tags. "We could buy these pencils too. What do you think?"

I saw myself nodding. I'd loved that set. I'd used the pencils down to their nub.

I watched as Grandma and I went to the checkout. The scene faded and the lights came on. "No! Don't go! I want to see more."

Wesley came in. "A good memory, yes?"

"Very. And buying the pencils was a good choice, right?"

"Correct. What happened with the drawing set your grandmother bought for you?"

"I used it. I remember Grandpa and I sitting with our sketch pads, drawing pictures of a vase in the kitchen and the bird feeder outside. He taught me how to draw. We had so much fun together."

"You enjoyed being with him."

"Very much. Even during that first time he pointed out how the vase I drew looked flat. He showed me the technique of chiaroscuro to shade the side." I shook my head. "It was a big concept for a six-year-old, but I never forgot about it."

"It was a special time. Perhaps more special than you realize?"

"How so?"

"Think on it a minute."

Little by little my thoughts came into focus until I experienced an aha-moment like I felt when I figured out the mystery in a movie. "It was the first time I thought about being an artist."

Wesley spread his hands. "If not for pencils falling to the floor at your feet, would you have learned how to draw?"

I shrugged. "Maybe. But I doubt it. Mom and Dad have always said drawing was a waste of time. Being an only child they wanted me to play sports so I'd get involved with other kids."

"Did you?"

"Reluctantly. I played soccer for a while. I was horrible at it. And all that running and sweating. Ugh."

"Did you continue to draw?"

"I did. When I was with Grandpa *and* on my own—as I could."

"As you could?" His eyebrows rose. "In secret?"

"Partially. I think Mom and Dad knew about it, but I didn't show them what I was working on and they didn't ask. And after the divorce they didn't really care."

"That is regrettable. You said your Grandpa continued to teach you?"

I smiled at the memories. "He still does. And Grandma has always posted my art on their refrigerator. For fourteen years I've sent them drawings, and Grandpa has sent some of his to me. He taught me a little about chalk and charcoal, but I don't like those much. Too messy. Every birthday they'd give me new art supplies."

"It's good to have people who believe in you."

"Without them I'd have nobody in my corner."

"Do you still enjoy creating?"

I shrugged. "I do. But my life is pretty busy with school and family. There's not much time for it."

"Time is fleeting . . ." Then he said, "Would you like to see another scene?"

"Of course."

As soon as he left, a new scene surrounded me. It was the art room in my high school—my junior year by the looks of it. The teacher, Mrs. Minor, was telling everybody about an art contest. "The winner gets to go to Italy for two weeks to see the great art of the ages."

There were murmurs of excitement all around

I was looking at the room from the back, so I didn't see my younger self at first, but then I spotted me, slumped down in my chair.

Ashley shared the front table with me and leaned close. "Are you going to enter something?"

I shook my head. "It wouldn't do any good."

The bell rang and we all headed to the door. But Mrs. Minor called out to me. "Minnie? A moment?"

I went to her desk.

"Doesn't that contest sound exciting?"

"Yeah. Sure."

She handed me a color brochure of Italy. It glowed. "I think you have the perfect entry already. I'd like you to enter your sketch of the lake."

"Really?"

"Really. It's very well done. I believe you'd have a good chance to win."

It didn't matter if I had a chance, there was *no* chance my parents would let me go.

"Why are you shaking your head?" Mrs. Minor asked.

"Mom and Dad want me to focus on more 'practical pursuits.'" I said the last two words how Dad said them. I continued with another of his quotes. "Dad says that ninety-nine percent of all artists are starving. Art is not a reasonable career choice."

Mrs. Minor's eyebrows dipped. "I'm not asking you to make a career in drawing—though that is an option. I'm offering you a chance to use one of your gifts to try to win some extraordinary experiences."

It sounded good, but still meant little. "They only let me take this art class because the speech class was full. It's not gonna happen, Mrs. Minor, no matter how good you think I am." I glanced toward the hall. "I gotta get to my next class."

She waved me away. The lights came on.

The pain of regret still stung.

"I should've entered," I said, when Wesley came in. "Later on, even Dad told me that."

"Your father said that?"

I nodded. "A month or so later he went to teacher conferences and Mrs. Minor told him about the contest that I'd missed. He was so disappointed I hadn't entered, to at least try." I shook my head. "It blew my mind that he cared. I'd never even considered talking to them about it."

"'You do not receive because you do not ask.'"

"Apparently." I remembered the brochure. "It glowed. Does that mean I would've won?"

"I don't know. But no risk, no reward."

"I know that now."

"Do you?"

"Of course." Every question made me second guess myself.

"Where is the risk in your life right now?" Wesley asked.

I ran a hand over my forehead. "I have no idea. Risk involves mistakes and having to do things over, which takes time. I don't have time for any of that. I'm in survival mode right now. Both of my parents need me."

"Do they?"

I got off the stool and took a step away from him. "They need my help all the time. At Dad's, and especially with Mom. Who babysits whenever they ask? Who buys groceries and cooks most of the time? Who does the laundry and cleans and makes sure the garbage and recycling are out on the right day?"

"You are definitely a hard worker."

"I am."

"And no one else can do these things?"

"Sure. I suppose. But I like to help. And they appreciate me. Plus, I'm Mom's protector."

"That's a serious job."

"Very."

He nodded once. "How would you rate your mother's confidence level?"

"What do you mean?"

"Is she a confident woman?"

I had no idea what he was talking about. "She works full time at Hobby Lobby. She likes her job."

"Does she have many non-work activities?"

"Not really."

"Does she have friends?"

"She says I'm her best friend."

"What about women her own age?"

Sheesh. Twenty questions. "She has me." I thought of something. "She did go out with her coworkers once for someone's birthday."

"Once."

He was making me mad. "We've been doing fine."

"Ah. Fine. In the later years of life, when a person is asked to describe the tenor of their days, I don't think a single one will say, 'It was fine.' Don't *you* want an exceptional life, Miss McLaughlin?"

"Exceptional? That sounds too lofty. I don't think many people have an exceptional life."

"I don't believe you can speak for everyone, but do *you* want an exceptional life?"

He'd backed me into a corner. "How can I say no?"

"*Is* the answer no?"

"No," I said. "I mean, yes, I want an exceptional life!" I paced behind the stool. "I don't mean to talk back, but who are you to judge my life, whether it's good or bad? Whether I'm a risk-taker or not? Or exceptional?"

He lowered his voice to a calming tone. "I am not judging, I am asking questions."

I was done. "I'm not sure I can take any more of this."

"You can. I know you can. Sit. Draw in some deep breaths."

I was embarrassed. It's like he'd purposely pushed all my buttons.

Yet I also knew his advice was good. So I did as I was told. I sat. My breathing calmed.

"Better?"

"I think so."

He nodded. "Where do you see yourself in ten years?"

I truly hadn't thought about it. "I suppose I'll be working in some business."

"What kind of business?"

"Probably real estate. Dad has always talked about me joining his team."

"So you see yourself working forty to fifty hours a week and most weekends? With little time for family, friends, and hobbies?"

That *was* Dad's life. "When you put it that way? Not really."

"What if working for your father was off the table. Ten years from now, how would you like to spend your days if the sky was the limit? No restrictions."

I thought about it for a long moment. "I guess I'd be married and have a couple kids, a house with big trees in the back where I could set up an easel. Or maybe we'd have an out-building where I could have a studio."

"That sounds lovely."

The images kept coming. "My husband and I would travel to Europe so I could study the masters. And I'd help beautify the community somehow. I'd give art lessons and get my work in a gallery. Or maybe we'd travel around to be in those art shows where you rent a booth and meet lots of people and other artists."

Wesley's smile was large. "Now *that* sounds like an exceptional life."

I put a hand to my chest. "It does. It sounds like a dream."

"What do you have to do to achieve that life? That dream?"

I stood again and pressed a hand to my forehead to keep my thoughts from bursting out of my brain. I knew what he wanted me to say. I knew what *I* wanted to say. "I need to become an artist. I need to change my major to art."

"An excellent start." He cocked his head. "Do you think your father's life is exceptional?"

"That's an easy one. Yes. He's very happy. He makes a good living and wins awards. He's fulfilled."

"Do you think your mother is living an exceptional life?"

"That's also an easy one, but with the opposite answer: No."

"Why not?"

"Because she's needy and lonely." I returned to the stool "And she's dependent on me."

"Her being dependent . . . is that a positive aspect of her life?"

"Kind of, maybe, I don't know. I don't do chores because she forces me to, I just like to help. I love her."

He nodded. "Yet loving someone often involves letting them go."

"Go? I'm not letting her go. My mother needs me at home."

"Does she?"

I popped up from the stool. "Stop it! You're tossing my entire life in a blender. You want me to change my major and move away from Mom. Those are huge changes."

"They are. You will need to think about them, and decide what's the right choice for everyone."

"But I . . . I don't know!"

"Of course you do." He took a step toward me. "To summarize your discoveries: up until now you have given up the chance to be an exceptional artist by deferring to your father's wishes."

I sighed. "I guess that's true."

"And in kind, your mother has given up the chance to be an exceptional woman by deferring to *your* wishes to remain at home."

I made a time-out T with my hands. "She wanted me to stay. She wants me to stay."

"Have you asked her? Have you offered to leave, or told her you would like to live on campus?"

Surprisingly, I'd never thought of doing that. "No. I haven't."

"Perhaps you should give *her* the choice. What do you think would happen if she lived alone? Would she eat, clean, wash the clothes?"

"I suppose so."

"Would she continue to date?"

"Sure."

"I asked you where you see yourself in ten years. How do you think your mother would answer that question?"

He was shooting from all sides. "I'm not sure."

"Does she see herself alone? After all, by that time you will be thirty. You'll probably be married and have your own family."

The thought of Mom being alone—truly alone—made me sad. "I hope she has someone by then. A permanent, good man who loves her."

"Can she get that without you living in the house?"

"Probably. Maybe. But she does like my opinion."

"Which I'm sure she will ask for when the time comes, whether you live in-house or not. The bottom line is that she's a grown woman who's gone through hard times. And she's searching for better times, which might include a soul mate."

"Are you saying I'm in the way?"

"Are you?"

The truth hurt and the challenges were scary. "I don't know how to make these changes without hurting my parents."

"Hurt might be inevitable." Wesley took a step closer. "You, standing up for yourself and not being a doormat might also help your parents find a deeper fulfillment. There are always growing pains while discovering your full potential." He smiled at a thought. "And, there are no doormats in heaven."

"Clever." I sat up straight. "So the only way for all of us to reach our potential is to say no to my parents?"

"Not all the time, but yes, in situations that are important."

"How do I know which situations are important?"

Wesley pondered this a minute. "Important situations require courage. They evolve from intuition."

"Courage?" I scoffed. "Me?"

"Absolutely you. You are not a child anymore, Miss McLaughlin. It's time to learn that giving into everyone else's requests is not always the right thing to do."

I sighed. "I'm a pro at giving in. I feel like a broken record, but I just want everyone to be happy."

"You were a pro. And happiness needs to includes yourself. Isn't it time to change?"

I shook my head. "I've had enough change. I just want things to carry on smoothly. No hiccups."

"Isn't that rather boring?"

I thought of my life: being home every night and weekends, not going to school activities. "So what if it is boring?"

"Isn't your life also rather safe?" he asked.

That was easy to answer. "Absolutely. I like safe. Safe means everyone is content and in their corners."

Wesley slowly shook his head back and forth like he was disappointed in me.

"You want me to be something I'm not," I said.

"By staying the same you will miss changing into someone amazing."

"Promise?"

He surprised me by nodding. "It is a promise."

"I'm happy enough."

"To be blunt, no, Miss McLaughlin, you are not, and you certainly are not exceptional. Yet. No person can be truly happy if they're not on the right road."

"What road is that?"

"The road that leads to your destiny."

I waved my hands at him. "First 'courage', and now the word 'destiny'? That's too high and mighty for me. And who chooses that road and determines my destiny?"

"Who do you think?"

"I do."

"I hate to break it to you, but you are not actually the creator of your destiny. So I ask again, Miss McLaughlin, who do you think determines this road?"

I let his words sink in and a realization rushed over me.

"God?"

He smiled broadly. "Exactly."

I was not one to think about God, except in passing. And yet this idea made sense. "Actually, bringing Him into the mix makes things fall into place. When you talk about my destiny it makes sense that it involves something . . . supernatural. It's a relief that it isn't all on me."

Wesley smoothed the sleeves of his white shirt. "Young lady, you are wise beyond your years."

No one had ever called me wise.

Wesley held up a finger, ready to make another point. "It comes down to this: "We can make our plans, but the Lord determines our steps."

"Steps, as in choices? All those choices?"

"Those and ten thousand more."

My mind was spinning. "It's hard to believe God is t*hat* involved in my life."

"Do you believe in Him?"

"Sure. But I don't pray much. When I was little I used to go to church with Mom and Dad: Sunday school, Christmas pageants, the whole package. But since the divorce none of us go. We're hardly on God's top-10 'most faithful' list."

"'Healthy people don't need a doctor—sick people do.'"

"Sick people?"

"Those who are hurting. They're the ones who need Him."

"Like me?"

"It's time to stop living a mediocre life, Miss McLaughlin."

"*That* pep talk needs work."

"I say mediocre in that you are presently lukewarm. God says, 'I know all the things you do, that you are neither hot nor cold. I wish that you were one or the other! But since you are like lukewarm water, neither hot nor cold, I will spit you out of my mouth!'"

"That's harsh. God said that?"

"He did. Revelation three, verses fifteen to sixteen."

I might not be close to God, but I didn't want Him to be disgusted with me. "I've tried really hard to keep the peace in my family. Isn't that a good thing? Even a God thing?"

"Of course. But at what expense?"

I fidgeted, feeling the answer poke at me. "Mine?"

He nodded. "You are complacent—neither happy or sad. Where is the joy, Miss McLaughlin? You *can* be more than you are right now. There is an exceptional path, just for you."

I shivered. "That sounds so . . . grand. I've never felt like a grand person."

"Finding your purpose is a grand journey. Noble even."

I scoffed. "Me? Noble?"

He smiled. "You, noble. If you choose to be."

It was beyond comprehension. "What does God have in mind? Will I like it? Will God make me do the right thing?"

Wesley made a face. "To answer the third question, absolutely not. He has given free will to all people. For doesn't it mean more if people willingly choose His way?"

"I suppose."

Wesley's eyes lit up with a thought. "As the Knight Templar told Indiana Jones, 'Choose wisely.'"

"You're quoting movies now?"

"Is that not allowed?"

"Sure, but . . ." I took a deep breath. I was overwhelmed. Important concepts had been discussed: being exceptional, courageous, noble, joyful, and wise. All while living out my destiny?

"Talk with your parents. Find ways to be exceptional. And open your eyes and watch for the ways God is working in your life."

It sounded easier than it was. "If only things glowed."

Wesley smiled. "Maybe they do and you just haven't noticed."

He had to be kidding. "I think I would've noticed that."

He shrugged. "Watch for Him. Seek Him. Seek His guidance and ask Him to show you His plan. Be courageous and exceptional."

I rubbed my hands over my face. "I have never talked about God as much as I've talked about Him these past few minutes. This is deep stuff."

"God doesn't deal with fluff."

"But He dealt with colored pencils, phone calls, and brochures?"

"Important details are not fluff."

I'd take his word for it. I shifted on the stool. I had one more thing to ask him. "So, Wesley . . . since you are so good at deciphering all these events, I was—"

"I have not deciphered them, Miss McLaughlin. I have merely asked questions and helped you organize your thoughts. Any discoveries have come out of your own insight and your desire to understand."

"Have they? I'll have to think about that one, but there's one thing I don't understand."

Wesley smiled. "Only one?"

"When I was shown the scene at college orientation our tour guide was Gabe. I know Gabe from an art store in town, and once in awhile we run into each other on campus. In fact, we've crossed paths a lot in the last week or so. But I never remembered him from orientation. I don't think he's made the connection between then and now either."

He smiled his usual all-knowing, ever-patient smile. "There are no coincidences, Miss McLaughlin. The inter-weavings that make up a life are intricate and infinite." He laced his fingers together. "Everything fits."

I shivered. "So Gabe showing up in my life then and now . . . it fits?"

"Doesn't it?"

"I'd very much like to think so." I smiled. It felt good and right and I was eager to tell Gabe about everything I'd seen.

Wesley took a deep breath. "If there is nothing else, I believe we are finished here."

I felt finished. My heart and mind overflowed with inspiration. I stood and shuffled my shoulders to ease the tension there. "I don't completely understand what's happened, but I thank you. It's been amazing."

"You're quite welcome."

"Can I come back and see more?"

He shook his head no.

"No? But doesn't God want me to notice everything He's done and is doing and . . . and will do?"

"He does. So see it. 'Keep on asking, and you will receive what you ask for. Keep on seeking, and you will find. Keep on knocking, and the door will be opened to you.'"

"You make it sound so simple."

"It *will* get easier."

I looked at him incredulously. "Who *are* you, Wesley?"

"A spokesman."

"For God?"

He leaned forward confidentially, his eyebrows raised. "You could be a spokesman too."

I shook my head. "I don't think so."

"Anyone can. All you need to do is share what you know."

I snickered. "All I know right now is that I've got some hard thinking to do—and some hard conversations to have."

"That, you do."

He opened the door of the Room for me. "Go out into the world, Miss McLaughlin. Be exceptional and see what happens next."

Impulsively I hugged him. "Thank you. I'll never forget any of this."

"*That* is the plan."

Chapter Twenty-One

Minnie

Come and listen to my counsel.
I'll share my heart with you and make you wise.
Proverbs 1: 23

After my time in the Discovery Room, I started driving back to Dad's house to help make dinner. But when I hesitated about which way to turn, I knew I needed a moment to figure things out. I pulled into the parking lot of a grocery store.

If I went to Dad's I'd get swallowed up in the usual domestic busyness: dinner, dishes, diapers, and small talk. I'd just gone through a life-changing experience. I couldn't reenter the real world just yet.

And so I called Dad and did something I rarely did. I lied: "I've been invited out to dinner with friends. Is that all right?"

"Uh, sure, Min. Claudia was making pork chops because she knows it's your favorite, but . . ."

Guilt trip #8302. I almost gave in. But then I remembered what Wesley had said about courage.

I held my ground. "I won't be late."

"Okay. Sure. See you then."

I was a bit surprised that Dad gave in. How many times could I have done what I wanted if only I'd asked and been . . . courageous.

The small victory added to my new sense of anticipation, like it was the day before a big trip where nerves and excitement intertwined.

My heart beat ridiculously fast as though I'd just run ten laps. I pressed a hand against it and took deep breaths. Standing up for myself shouldn't take my breath away. Maybe with practice, it wouldn't.

I needed to talk with someone about the Room and immediately thought of Gabe.

I texted him: *I have a lot to tell you. When are you free?*

Seconds later he texted back: *I get off in ten minutes. Want to grab some food?*

Perfect. I'll come by the art store.

Turns out I wasn't lying to Dad after all.

**

Apparently, the parking space in front of Art's had my name on it, for once again, it was open. I was nearly at the door when Gabe came out.

"Good timing. Want to go for a walk?" He pointed to the left. "Half a block down is a great Italian place. You like pizza?"

"Of course." We turned in that direction. I had so much to tell him but I didn't want to pounce and overwhelm him. One step at a time. "Were you busy today?" I asked.

"We're always busy on Saturdays. The store is open until eight, but Art lets me go at five. He says I'm only young once."

"He seems really nice."

"He is."

"How long have you worked there?"

"Off and on since I was fifteen. Every summer and on breaks."

"You are definitely loyal. It's exciting that you're thinking about buying him out."

"*Exciting* is not exactly the word I would use."

"Why not?"

He picked up a candy wrapper from the ground and put it in a trashcan. "It's a decision that will determine my future for a lot of years. And Art hasn't even agreed, even though he does keep talking about retiring."

"One plus one equals . . . ?"

"A *big* decision.

We reached Angelo's Ristorante. It had a small dining room with loads of cozy charm. We got a table by a window.

"Do you like pepperoni and sausage?" he asked.

I wasn't keen on sausage, but I said yes. So much for standing up for myself.

When the waiter came, Gabe ordered. He got a Coke so I did too.

As we waited for our food, the conversation flowed easily. We talked about our favorite meals—mine was pork chops and his was an avocado bacon burger. We talked about which TV series we'd been streaming. We both liked complicated plots and hated horror movies. He asked about my family and I gave him a condensed version. His older sister was married with two kids, and lived in Minnesota. His parents lived there too and had been married for thirty years. His mom taught high school history and his Dad was an engineer. Both were supportive of his art.

If only . . .

I loved watching him talk. His eyebrows were his most expressive feature, raising up when he was happy, and dipping down when he talked about something serious.

I also loved that Gabe listened when I talked, like he truly wanted to hear it. The few guys I'd gone out with should take a lesson. And when he smiled? It was like turning on a light.

The best part was that I sensed I didn't need to impress him. I could relax and just *be*.

Eventually the conversation turned back to Art's. "If you're still torn about the store, my dad says it's good to write down the pros and cons."

"I've done that."

"Which side won?"

"It's pretty even."

"So how will you decide?"

He wrapped a straw wrapper around his finger. "This will sound dumb. And very unscientific."

"You have my interest."

"I'm waiting for a gut feeling. "

My eyebrows shot up in surprise.

He took my silence as disapproval. "You don't believe in intuition?"

The timing of this conversation could *not* be a coincidence, and that knowledge emboldened me. "Last week I might have flipped away your talk of gut feelings. But today, after what I've seen . . . I get it."

"Because of that Discover place?"

I nodded. "The head guy, Wesley, said that intellect plus emotion equals intuition, which is supposed to lead to wisdom. And courage. Something like that."

He pulled the straw wrapper off his finger and tossed it aside. "He sounds pretty wise himself."

"Very. It's like he knows everything and was trying to find a way to get me to understand."

"I'd love to have a mentor like that. I'm waiting for the intuition to kick in, where I just know it's the right choice. I'm trying to be wise. Like you said."

"It'll come. Then you'll be doing the right thing."

"I hope so." He cocked his head and studied me a moment. "Enough about me. Something big clearly happened in that place."

Discovery. Wisdom. And God.

I readjusted the napkin in my lap. "What I'm going to tell you is really 'out there' strange. Cool but strange."

His eyebrows rose. "You certainly know how to pique my interest."

I looked around the restaurant which was filled with normal people doing normal things, and talking about normal things. What I had to share wasn't normal at all.

"It all started when I was led into a round room where I saw scenes from my past, times when I was given certain choices that were important, but I didn't know they were important, and sometimes—but not always—I chose—"

"Back up. You went where and saw what?"

I did a mental rewind. I needed to slow down. "I went into a round, white room with only one single stool in the middle. And when I sat down, movies of my life came on, covering the inside of the dome. They were short scenes, but they were important because of the choices I made—or didn't make." I fiddled with my straw and took a sip of my drink.

"That's clear as mud."

I sighed. I'd made a mess of it. "It made more sense when I was there."

"Can you give me an example of one of these choices?"

It was hard to put into words an experience that was beyond words. Beyond logic. Yet Gabe was looking for a sign in his own life. Maybe something I said would be useful to him.

"First off, I saw a movie of school orientation two years ago. Me and Ashley and our moms were there." I paused. "You were there too."

"What? Excuse me?"

"You were our guide. Don't you remember me?" I wiggled my eyebrows at him.

His forehead furrowed. "I did give tours a few years back. I'm sorry, Minnie, I don't."

"I'm just kidding you. I'm sure you saw hundreds of incoming freshmen. Plus, I didn't remember seeing you either. Anyway, right off the bat, you asked everybody in our group about their major. I said I was going into business but loved art."

His eyes lit up. "I do remember a girl saying that. I gave you both brochures."

"You did. But I chose to stick with business. Or rather, *Dad* chose."

"Just think of how much we would have seen each other if you'd chosen art."

"Right? Beyond you being a teacher's assistant in art history, my only art class."

"If *not* for art history we might not have connected."

"If not for you helping my small group with our report on Da Vinci we might never have talked."

He smiled. "*Grazie*, Leonardo!" He turned serious. "Why didn't you ever accept my invitation to go for a coffee after class?"

"I honestly don't know." I turned it back on him. "Why did you stop inviting me?"

His eyes met mine. "We missed a lot of chances to get to know each other."

I sighed loudly. "It seems so."

He put his hand on mine. "But we're here now."

"We're getting a second chance to . . ."

"Get to know each other. And maybe become . . . ?" He gazed into my eyes, waiting for me to finish the sentence.

I squeezed his hand, feeling fluttery inside. "And maybe become really, really good friends." Friends? Why did I say friends?

"Well I guess that's a start." He shook his head and smiled. "I already know I'd like more."

My stomach fluttered again. "That'd be okay with me too."

He raised my hand toward his mouth and kissed it. With that one gesture I felt our connection deepen and I knew that a part of me would always remember this moment.

The waiter came and refilled our Cokes.

Gabe squeezed my hand then let it go. "Continue your story about the orientation. You--we--were at orientation and I gave you two brochures."

It was hard to move from thoughts of our relationship back to the Room. "One of the brochures wasn't normal. The one for the art department glowed."

He blinked. "What do you mean it glowed?"

"As in, it shined with a yellow light."

"How did it do that?"

I shrugged. "That's what happened in all the clips. Whenever God gave me an important choice, something glowed so I could spot it."

He sat back in his chair. "God?"

Oops. I held my breath. I had no idea what Gabe believed--or if he believed in any higher power. But I couldn't lie. "Yes, God," I said.

"Okay then," he said. "I'm good with that. You just surprised me."

I let out a sigh and smiled with relief. "It surprised me too. Yet you wanting your intuition to kick in so you'll know buying the store is the right choice? That's God-stuff. My moments were God-stuff too."

The pizza came. We both dove in. After a few minutes we were on our second slice.

Gabe's eyes darted back and forth like he was really thinking about what I'd said. He sat forward. "Let's say—for the sake of your story—that the glowing brochure was something God used. How did He use it? And why?"

"Actually, it wasn't just the brochure. There were other things that glowed in each scene that I watched." I told Gabe how the pencils led me to get an art set, which led me to begin learning how to draw with Grandpa, which got me interested in being an artist.

"Back up a minute," he said. "I need to talk about the elephant in the room: how did they have recordings of these specific times in *your* life when there weren't cameras around?"

"Who knows? I asked Wesley that and he told me to suspend my disbelief like we do all the time in movies." I shrugged. "I had to just go with it. It wasn't scary or anything—it was amazing—but I have no idea how they did it."

"You accepted it. On faith?"

I liked that explanation. "I did."

Gabe took another bite and pondered this a moment. "Then that's what I need to do. Ok. Moving on . . . so these things that glowed changed your life?"

Wow. He was amazing.

I told him how me ignoring the phone intervention had enabled Mom to marry a bad guy.

"I made the wrong choice on that one. I will always wonder if I'd taken the call and stayed home . . . could I have stopped her?"

"She got through it okay, didn't she?"

"She did, but not without suffering."

"Which must've been hard on both of you. What else did you see?"

I took a large swig of Coke to fuel myself. I told him about the art contest that I didn't enter in high school and the trip to Italy that never was. "Turns out I held *myself* back. Later Dad told me that I should've tried. It was a huge, missed opportunity."

"That's a tough one."

"Thinking back, I put so many barriers around myself, and added new ones to what was already there. It kills me that I might have won a trip to Italy."

"Everybody has coulda-shoulda moments."

"I've had too many."

"Are there any more scenes to tell me about?"

I shook my head. "That's it."

"That's quite a lot. But what now?"

That was the burning question, yet my answer was clear. "I need to talk to Dad about changing my major to art."

"Really?"

I nodded. "Really."

He leaned over to kiss my cheek. "That's amazing Min. You'll love it."

I nodded. My cheek felt warm where he'd kissed it. "I also need to talk to Mom."

"Does she care about your major?"

"Not really. But she and I have another issue. I need to move out of the house—for my sake *and* hers. We're holding each other back from opportunities that could make our lives more exceptional."

He chuckled. "Exceptional. That's a grand goal."

Courage rushed through me. "It is. But I'm ready for it."

"How do you get an exceptional life?" he asked.

I thought back to all Wesley had told me. It came down to one thing. "I'm supposed to look for ways God is working in my life. Keep my eyes open. Use my intuition."

"Intellect plus emotions gets you intuition and wisdom, right?"

I remembered how this conversation had started, with him looking for direction. "I know it's not going to be easy, but we should all be looking for ways to move forward wisely. I mean, you want to make the right choice about buying the store and—"

"Or *not* buying it." He tossed his napkin on the pizza round. "I'll keep my eyes open. But I sure wish things would glow."

"Me too." I chuckled. "Wesley said maybe they do and we don't notice."

"*That,* I'd notice." He looked out to the street, at people walking by. "Do you need to get back to your Dad's?"

I didn't want to go. I felt such contentment with Gabe. "Not yet. Tell me more about your day, your art projects." I took a breath. "I just want to hear more about you. Anything at all."

He grinned. As he talked I felt full inside—full far beyond the pizza.

Chapter Twenty-Two

Gracie & Minnie

O God, listen to my cry! Hear my prayer!
From the ends of the earth,
I cry to you for help when my heart is overwhelmed.
Psalm 61: 1-2

Was I really going on a date with Tony?

The very thought of it gave me butterflies. He was a great guy—as far as I knew—but I hadn't had much practice with guys of any sort, great or not.

My stomach flipped when the doorbell rang. I tugged at my long sweater, took a deep breath, and opened the door.

Tony grinned. "Hi."

"Hi yourself."

His rust-colored Henley shirt brought out the brown of his eyes. He pulled a vase of flowers from behind his back. "Ta da!"

"Thank you." There were pink carnations, daisies, and baby's breath. I was relieved they weren't roses, for I was pretty sure roses were associated with a full-blown romance. I didn't think I was ready for that.

I asked him to step inside. I held the flowers to my nose and drank in the fragrance. "Mmm. Delicious."

"Glad you like them. And I can see you like flowers." He pointed toward my sweater which was emblazoned with a bright floral print.

"I do like flowers, though this was my mom's, probably from the seventies. I've been raiding her closet as mine is on the comfy-but-ugly side."

"You look very pretty."

I bobbed a little curtsy. "Thank you. You look nice too."

"Thank *you.*" He mimicked the curtsy, making me laugh.

I took one last whiff and put them on the coffee table. He had his hands in his pockets as he scanned the room—which was still full of boxes. "I like what you've done to the place."

"Don't make me feel more guilty than I already feel."

He raised his hands in surrender. "I meant no offense. Truly.

And as I said before, I'm willing to help anytime."

I believed him. I got my purse and phone. "All ready."

He held the door open for me. "And away we go . . ."

"I've been looking forward to Italian food. I'm starving."

"Then let's get you fed."

I liked that he opened the car door for me. Chivalry wasn't dead.

We exchanged small talk in the car. Clearly, I wasn't the only one who was a bit nervous.

Ten minutes later we walked into Angelo's Ristorante. As Tony said, it really was a hole-in-the-wall place. It only sat ten tables, and had dozens of black and white family pictures on the walls. Tony pointed to one. "That's my Aunt Rosa and Uncle Angelo. They own the place." He looked past me. "Speaking of . . ."

A silver-haired man waved from behind a counter. "Antonio!"

Tony rushed toward him and they embraced with slaps to the back. "It's been too long, *il mio ragazzo.*"

"I'm not a boy anymore, Uncle Angelo. Not for a long, long time."

The man laughed. "To me, always." He glanced in my direction. "And who is this beauty?"

Tony motioned me close. "This is Gracie Sturgess. Gracie, meet Uncle Angelo."

His two hands engulfed mine. "*Benvenuta, bella signorina,*" he said.

I didn't know the literal translation, but I guessed how to respond. "*Grazie?*" That was the extent of my Italian.

Angelo was impressed. "Oooh. A keeper, this one, Antonio."

I found Tony's blush charming. "Did you save a table for us?" he asked.

"Of course. The best one, by the window."

There were only two tables with a view, bisected by the entrance. But as I glanced at the other window-table, I recognized a girl with long brown hair. I paused. "Minnie?"

She blinked. "Gracie?"

I detoured to their table. She was sitting with a handsome guy who was a little older than she was. They were just finishing a pizza. She and I introduced Gabe and Tony.

"What's the occasion?" I asked. "Are you out celebrating your visit to the Room?"

Minnie seemed a bit embarrassed. "I guess I am."

Gabe nodded. "She told me all about it. It's pretty amazing."

I nodded as if I knew. "I'm glad you enjoyed it."

"What do you do there?" Gabe asked.

"I'm the receptionist."

Tony stepped closer. "I had a session there too."

Minnie's eyes lit up. "Wasn't it remarkable?"

"You could say that," Tony said.

"So, Gracie . . . how do I get an invitation?" Gabe asked. "It seems I'm the odd one out."

I shook my head. "Not to worry, I haven't done it either." I suddenly realized how dumb that sounded. "I've been invited, but I haven't gone through with it."

"Yet," Tony said.

To answer Gabe's other question I said, "I have no idea how the invitation list is created. But I'll put in a good word for you with my boss."

"I'd appreciate that," he said.

Out of the corner of my eye I saw a waiter place waters and menus on our table. "It was nice seeing you," I said to Minnie. "And nice meeting you, Gabe."

Tony and I sat down, and a few minutes later Minnie and Gabe gave us a wave as they left.

I nodded toward them. "That was a bit awkward."

"Not really," Tony said. "We have a lot in common."

"To be honest, I'm not sure I should be fraternizing with you."

Tony put his hand to his chest. "Is there a rule against going to dinner with a strikingly handsome man?" He handed me a menu.

He made me smile. "A man who is also a client."

"Previous client. It's not like I can come back. And what's this about you still not taking a turn in the Room? You need to go."

"Why do you say that? You didn't have a great experience."

"That's me." He set his menu down and leaned forward. "You need to do it, Gracie, because the Room is all about showing us that nothing is a coincidence. It's all a part of some mysterious plan." He waved his hands by his head.

"You're making fun of that plan."

"Not really." He shrugged. "And what can I say? I'm a rebel."

"Nobody should dare tell you what to do?"

"You got it." He straightened his silverware. "But one thing I do believe is that you and I were supposed to meet."

I scoffed. "That sounds like a pickup line if I've ever heard one." Which I hadn't. "So us meeting is destiny?"

He waggled his eyebrows. "Maybe."

"How about dumb luck?"

His face grew serious. "I used to think like that—and still do most of the time, but I'm thinking about thinking differently."

"It's good you're so committed."

"Yeah, well. You've heard about people with commitment issues. That's me."

"Me too. I know how hard it is to change gears," I said. "You get in a groove—right or wrong—and it's hard to jump out of it."

"I'm with you there." He glanced at Minnie and Gabe's table. "Minnie was in the Room this afternoon?"

"A few hours ago. She was our last client of the day."

"Did it go good for her?"

"It seemed to. She hugged Wesley when she left and told him thank you."

"Oh."

"You sound disappointed."

"You know how I left." He stared out the window. "No hugging, just yelling."

I remembered it well. Although everyone didn't exit the Room glowing with happiness, no one had come out angry like Tony had. "Wesley did not yell at you. And you apologized. Leave it. It's resolved."

He picked up the menu, then set it down again. He probably knew exactly what he wanted to order. "I recommend the Alfredo. It's what I get every time—with a Caesar salad." His demeanor lightened with the change in subject.

"I'll get that too."

A waiter came and took our order.

I leaned my arms on the table. "How many times have you had this meal?"

He looked at the ceiling. "Two thousand twenty-three—give or take."

I glanced at his uncle, chatting with other customers. "Your uncle is a natural with people. He's so at ease. I envy him."

Tony seemed taken aback. "You're at ease too."

I lowered my voice and leaned close. "I'm going to let you in on a little secret. I'm a good faker."

"You must be. I never would've guessed."

I smoothed the napkin against my legs. "I'm so used to being cooped up that I'm nervous being *out.*"

"This is but one a many outings for you and I."

"That would be nice."

He slapped the table. "It's a deal then."

"Since we were talking about Wesley . . . you said you'd tell me what happens in the Room?"

"Why don't you ask Minnie?"

I shook my head. "You're the first client I've gotten to know past hi-bye."

"There's not a little peep-hole where you can spy on us?"

"I wish there were."

"You can't put your ear to the door?"

I raised my hand. "I tried that. The words are too muffled. But from what people have said afterward, I know you see scenes from your past. Right?"

"Right. Like home movies when there couldn't have been home movies."

"Did Wesley explain how that happens?"

He scoffed. "Are you kidding? Wesley, explain? You work there. Has Wesley explained anything to you? I was hoping you could give *me* inside information."

It *was* odd that the clients knew more about the Room than I did. "Sorry. No can do. On my first day on the job, the company didn't even have a name, much less a sign until I pointed it out to Wesley. I was the one who suggested he paint the walls, and it was me who brought in the plant and put together the coffee station. Did you notice I don't even have a computer?"

Tony blinked. "I did notice your desk was pretty bare."

"My desk doesn't even have drawers. We don't have files on anyone either."

"I liked not having to fill out forms."

"True. But I never know who's coming next, or when."

Tony looked incredulous. "Then what do you do all day? Sorry, that sounds really rude."

"Why am I there?"

He nodded.

"I haven't a clue. I greet people and lead them into the Room. Wesley does the rest."

"Which leads to another question. The movie starts, then ends, then he immediately walks in. He has to be able to see it from a projection room."

"You would think. I hunted for that kind of room, but there isn't any. There's only a restroom—which no one but myself has ever used. Maybe he's bugged the place and that's how he knows." I flipped the notion away. "However he does it, the whole place has mysterious vibes. It could be on an episode of that old show, *The X-Files*."

The salads came. I loved the shaved parmesan on top. A small loaf of crusty bread came too, and the waiter drizzled olive oil and balsamic on a plate for dipping. We began to eat.

"Yum," I said, sopping up the oil with the warm bread. "I'm in absolute heaven because of the food, and because of that." I pointed out the window. The sunset had made the sky radiate pink and purple.

"I know, right? I never get tired of it."

"Sunsets or the food?" I teased.

"Both." He waved a fork at Angelo, then gave him a thumbs up, complimenting the food from afar.

It was nice to see Tony relaxed around family. "I wish I had a family like yours. One set of my grandparents passed away when I was little and the other lived in Canada and were too far away to visit. Both of my parents were only children."

"No aunts and uncles?"

"Or cousins."

"That's sad. Beyond my ex and our son . . ." He nodded toward the kitchen. "Uncle Angelo has five kids, and there are even more cousins on my mom's side. My parents retired in Florida, and I still have one grandmother living nearby."

"You're very lucky."

"I never thought of it that way, but yeah. I guess I am."

"Did any of your family show up in your scenes in the Room? "

"You're not giving up on that, are you?"

"I don't mean to grill you, but . . . I'm truly interested."

Unfortunately, the moment was interrupted when the pasta came.

Luckily, after a few bites of the most delicious Alfredo I'd ever had, Tony answered. "Will you be satisfied if I tell you about one episode in the Room?"

"I'm listening . . ."

He swirled a fork in his fettuccine. "One of the scenes was from twenty-five years ago, when I was a punk kid who stole from my grandparents. I didn't think anyone was home, but my grandpa was in the bathroom." A cloud came over his face. "As we were making our getaway I heard him fall and call for help, but I was too chicken and ran out."

"Was he okay?"

"He died."

I sucked in a breath. "Oh Tony, how awful. That must have been horrible to experience the first time, much less seeing it again."

"It was more than awful, and good ol' Wesley didn't spare me. Over and over he showed me that I'd had choices right in front of me. Choices that might have saved Papa. But I ignored them all and did what I wanted to do." He paused, holding a piece of bread in his hand. "As you can tell, I can be rather pig-headed. I'm also stupid and blind and arrogant and . . ." He shrugged. "You name a flaw, I've lived it."

"I'm sure that's not true. I hate to see you so hard on yourself. Did Wesley show you times when you made the right choice?"

He scoffed. "Nope. Though he didn't have many to choose from."

Tony was a man in desperate need of encouragement. Unfortunately, giving atta-boys was not my forte.

I spun my fork in the pasta. "Maybe you just need to find a way to move on?"

"Piece of cake."

"Everybody has regrets, Tony."

"Not like mine."

I felt so sorry for him. "It sounds like Wesley put you through the wringer. No wonder you came out mad."

"Mad at myself, mostly. But yeah, I was not a happy camper and took it out on him."

"I will say, Wesley has never put the closed sign up since—" I put a hand on my mouth. "Sorry. That wasn't necessary."

Tony snickered. "Leave it to me to be the one and only problem child."

"You are not a problem. Wesley was upset because he thought he'd failed you."

Tony's face softened. "He said that?"

"He did."

Tony looked out the window, though now it was dark and all we could see were our own reflections. "He kept harping about self-discovery and non-coincidences and what not."

"So, what are you supposed to do with what you saw?"

"What can I do? It was twenty-five years ago."

I shook my head. "Can you make things right somehow?"

He smiled a wistful smile. "I'm not sure. But I am thinking about thinking about it." He held a forkful of pasta in the air. "Never do today what you can put off until tomorrow."

I didn't like his attitude, yet who was I to talk? "If there's anything *I* can do . . ."

"I appreciate the offer." He stopped, then started again. "There might be one thing."

"What's that?"

"Take your turn in the Room."

I shook my head vigorously. "And see scenes from my life? There's not much to pick from. Mom died. Dad fell apart and I took care of him. Then he got sick and died." I clapped my hands together once and lifted them on either side of my head. "Game over. In many ways the last fourteen years have been wasted since I've been stuck at home. And my next fourteen don't look much better. The highlight of my day is falling asleep watching 'Columbo' reruns."

"And going out to dinner with me." He winked.

I expelled a breath and willed my bitterness to flow away. Tony was a hurting man, yet also a charmer. Maybe we would be good for each other. I reached out and put a hand on his. "Together we have a trunk full of baggage, don't we?"

"A pickup load." He ran his thumb over my fingers. "You're easy to talk to, Gracie."

"So are you."

"I really would like to see you again."

I didn't hesitate. "I'd like that."

He raised his water glass for a toast. "To good company."

"And new discoveries."

We clinked our glasses together.

****

After dinner, Gabe and I strolled around the block. I felt so at ease with him, like we were two magnets that had found each other. I felt grounded with him, stable, yet excited.

We walked back to my car in front of the art store and stood at the curb. "Thanks for dinner," I said. "And for listening to me ramble on about the Room and intellect leading to intuition and all that nonsense."

"Not nonsense, I enjoyed it. You inspired me." I must have looked surprised because he added, "Don't look so shocked."

"I'm more of a listener than . . ."

"A motivator?"

I chuckled. "Definitely not that."

His face got serious. "Don't sell yourself short, Minnie. You've got an important place in this world. You were invited to see amazing things in the Room. That means something."

I felt my confidence grow just a little. "Thanks for the compliment. I'm not used to hearing stuff like that."

Gabe shook his head. "Then shame on the world."

Suddenly I felt tears threaten. I looked down, willing them away. I didn't want to end our lovely evening with tears. And what was I crying about anyway?

He touched my shoulder. "You've had a long day. Go home and

get some sleep. You're about to make some big changes. Give yourself a little grace."

I put my hand on his. "You're so good to me. For me."

"To *me* and for *me*, too, Minnie." He touched my cheek. "Want to meet for lunch Monday?"

"I have class until two."

He nodded. "We'll work it out. I can't wait to see you again."

"Me too." I got in the car and waved before I pulled away.

My entire body was trembling inside. I'd been flooded with information overload. Emotional overload too. I'd never met anyone like Gabe. Or Wesley.

These two men had unexpectedly stepped into the forefront of my life. If Wesley was right, God had put them there. That's the reason I wanted whatever came next to be right.

Thankfully, I hit every stoplight so I had time to collect my thoughts before I got to Dad's. Even so, I took a moment for a few deep breaths before I went inside.

I found Dad in the living room. Claudia was just coming downstairs. She put a finger to her lips. "I just got them to sleep."

I nodded and we joined Dad. I sat in my usual place on the couch. I wasn't sure what to say. They knew nothing about the Discovery Room or Gabe. I'd never kept this much from them.

Dad asked his usual question. "Did you have fun shopping?"

"What did you buy?" Claudia asked. "I don't see any sacks."

"I didn't buy anything." I held my hands up. "But that's okay." I added quickly.

Claudia tucked her feet beneath her. "So what did you do instead?"

There were two reasons I couldn't explain the Room to them. Number one, they'd think it was strange and crazy, and get after me for accepting the invitation of a stranger. And number two, I wasn't up to it. As Gabe said, it had been a long day.

I gave them the condensed version. "I went to a training session that helps people discover their potential."

"For school?" Dad asked.

"Outside of school, but yes, it will help me *in* school." Sort of.

"You should've told us," Dad said. "I don't like you telling us you're going one place and then you go another."

I was going to defend myself, but didn't have the energy, "Sorry."

Claudia came to my rescue. "Ben, stop it. Minnie is twenty years old. She doesn't have to check in like that."

I flashed her a smile of thanks.

"Whatever," he said. "What friend did you see for dinner?"

"A friend from Art's Art Store. His name is Gabe. We went for pizza."

Claudia's eyebrows rose. "Is he the cute guy who works there? Isn't he older?"

"How old?" Dad muted the TV.

"He's only twenty-two," I said. Surely they couldn't object to his age.

"He's a clerk in a store?" Dad asked. "Did he ever go to college?"

I hated his quick judgment. "Yes, he did. He's graduating next month. He might even *buy* the store."

Suddenly, we heard Bryn crying on the baby monitor. Benny chimed in.

Claudia started to stand but I waved her off. "I'll take care of it."

"But we want to hear more about your training," Dad said.

"And Gabe," Claudia said.

I knew I couldn't handle more. "Another time. I'm really tired."

I calmed the babies and went to my bedroom. As the adrenaline of the day wore off I crashed. The mere thought of telling Dad I was changing majors seemed impossible.

Wesley had talked about being lukewarm? That was me. I felt weak, sad, and frustrated.

And completely unexceptional.

Chapter Twenty-Three

Tony

He has given us his very great
and precious promises.
2 Peter 1: 4

The days after going out to dinner with Gracie were a blur. I wanted to go out again, but all we'd managed were a few phone calls.

Surprisingly, my time had been taken up by Harvey. He loved playing Gin Rummy—for money. I owed him forty-three cents. He was an interesting guy too. He was a Vietnam vet and had great—if you could call them that—war stories to share.

He reminded me of Papa.

Yesterday during a game I learned that in addition to being a veteran, he'd worked at a box factory for forty-five years.

That was beyond strange to me. "A box factory? Sorry, but that sounds incredibly boring, plus nobody stays in one job that long."

"Why not?"

I'd never really thought about the whys of it. Or considered such a thing for myself.

Harvey put a wrinkled hand on the discard pile, stopping the play. "I'll tell you *why* people nowadays move from job to job. It's because they live their lives in thirty-second snippets. They can't concentrate on one thing for more than a blink, plus they think the grass is always greener on the other side."

I saw truth in everything he said.

"You ever thought about the pioneers much?" he asked.

I chuckled at the awkward transition. "Can't say as I have."

"Think about 'em. Think about those brave men and women who left everything behind out East and headed West to find a new life. They had no way of knowing if it was going to better, or whether they'd even make it there."

I remembered what I'd learned in school. "They were looking for land, freedom, something new. All that greener grass stuff."

"They were, *but* . . . At some point, they came over a hill and saw a stretch of land that poked at their dreams, filled their mind with possibilities, and ignited their innards. They made the very hard choice to say, 'This is it. This is enough.'" He paused and tapped the table. "If they hadn't done that, if they'd kept going, always thinking there was something better ahead, then something better'n *that,* we'd have no people in the middle of the country at all. They had to stop and appreciate what they saw right *there.* They had to embrace it and make it grow beneath their feet, and not worry about what they couldn't see beyond the horizon."

He was pretty eloquent for an old coot. "So it sounds like they. . . settled."

He adjusted his wire-rim glasses. "It might sound that way, just like you think I settled for *my* job all those years. It's a matter of perspective. I didn't think of it as settling at all. I got to really know the people there. I knew about their families, asked about their weekends, and they asked about mine. Plus, I became an expert at whatever position they put me in. I did my best where I was planted."

"Like that saying, 'Bloom where you're planted.'"

He nodded. "Exactly. Good one."

"But wasn't it boring?"

"Of course," he said. "Every job has boring parts. Every job has hard parts and easy parts and good and bad days. It's the same whether you haul garbage or run a tech company."

"That isn't the same at all. The person running the tech company makes a ton more money."

"I'll give you that. And I'm not saying me and Dorothy couldn't have used a bit more money over the years. It's all about choices."

He sounded like Wesley. "The right choices," I said semi-sarcastically.

Harvey raised a finger. "The right choices for me. And my family."

"But didn't you long for variety?"

He leaned forward on the table and leveled me with a look. "You're not one of those men who always want something new are you?"

It sounded like a trick question. "Not new," I said. "But different. I'm not good enough to be—"

"It's not about being good. It's about choosing good. I was married fifty-four years to Dorothy. Should I have left her for someone new? For a bit of variety?"

That one hit home. "Wow. That's a long time."

"How long were you and Penny married?"

"Over ten years."

"That's a good start. What happened to ruin it?"

"It was my fault. I just couldn't . . . It's not like I was unfaithful or anything like that. It's not because I needed *that* kind of variety."

He sat back, still looking at me. Studying me. "How many jobs have you had during the last year?"

It would sound as bad as it was. "Three."

"Why did you bounce around like that?"

"I told you, I needed something different." If I told him I'd been fired two of those times, he wouldn't think much of me.

"Sounds like a man wanting variety to me. But let me tell you, Tony, after living seventy-nine years I've learned a thing or two about life. The things I've learned may or may not apply to your life, but they're worth knowing just the same." He chuckled. "At least I like to pretend they're worth knowing."

"I'm sure they are. Tell me." I was surprised that I really wanted to know.

Harvey set his cards face down. The card game was over for now. "Number one: people matter. You can have all the money in the world and if you don't have people you care about and who care about you, it's all for nothing."

I fiddled with my cards. I didn't really have anybody. Except maybe Gracie. Being around her gave me a spark of hope.

He reached over the discard pile and touched my hand. "Even having just one somebody can be enough. Someone to know you as you are."

"What if what I am isn't worth knowing?"

He swatted my hand and pulled his back. "Nonsense. You're living and breathing, aren't you? You've been given a *life*. If you've made mistakes? Join the club. Those you can fix, fix. Those you can't, learn from and walk away."

I scoffed. "Easier said than done."

He shook his head. "For fifty-four years my person was Dorothy—until she died two years ago. We have two kids and four grandkids—one family on each coast. They don't make it back here often, but we stay in touch." He swept a hand around the apartment. "Not that there's much *back* to come home to now. With Dorothy's medical bills I had to sell the house and move here. Life isn't easy and it rarely turns out like we plan. But that's okay."

"It doesn't sound okay to me."

Harvey tossed his hands in the air. "Whatcha going to do about it? Sleep all day? Get mad at everybody because they're not suffering like you are?"

I shrugged. Pretty much.

"What's that getcha?" He didn't give me time to answer. "Which leads to number two on my list of life lessons: every single person on this earth has been created with God-given gifts. The trick is to find out what yours is."

"Gifts? I don't have any gifts."

"That you know of. Yet," he said. "You haven't a clue to your gifts, *yet*. You need to open your eyes and see the clues all around you."

"Clues?"

His pale eyes sparkled. "The little things that happen, like doors opening, or things that get your attention and lead you over to the right road."

A Wesley word came to me. "Interventions?"

He considered this a moment. "That's a good word for it. The point is, God didn't go to all the trouble of creating you and *then* try to think of something for you to do, or *then* think of a gift He might give you. Those things were in you before you cried your first cry." He put a hand flat against his chest. "Want to hear a good one?"

I wasn't sure what *one* he meant, but I said, "Sure."

"'Before I formed you in the womb I knew you, before you were born I set you apart.'" Harvey smiled like he'd just been given the keys to a kingdom. "If that doesn't get your heart pumping, you're dead." Then he eyed me. "You dead, Tony?"

My heart was beating faster. "No. I'm not."

He flung his hands in the air. "Then be alive! You can keep going on the same road you've been on, or you can use what you've learned and change things."

Wesley had said something like that too.

"You want to change things, Tony?"

"Yeah. I do."

"Good, because that brings me to number three: time goes by *fast*. It seems like a blink ago I was sixty, and two blinks ago I was holding my firstborn in my arms." He teared up. "Now look at me. I'm a weak old man who's making you shout so I can hear you. I live alone and keep the TV on for company."

He shook his head. "I'm not complaining—actually, I guess I am—but it's more of a holy-shamoley kind of thinking that comes to everybody at different times. I didn't really get it until I retired. But then . . . to realize that I didn't have all the time in the world in front of me, that most of my time was in the past? Gone? It makes a person get mad for wasting so much of it, for not appreciating it when you have it. And now that time is short and I know I probably don't have ten more years, might not even have five . . ." He waggled a finger at me. "Learn it now, son. Live now! Don't put off living the best life you have while you wait for some other time! You might not get it."

A tear escaped down his cheek. I'd never been good at dealing with other people's tears. I got up and snatched a tissue from the bathroom. "Here."

"Thanks." He wiped his eyes and cleaned his glasses. "I get emotional about it but Dorothy would tell me there's nothing wrong with a few tears. I got worked up because it's just real important you get what I'm saying."

"I get it. I do."

He took a cleansing breath. "There's one more lesson, and it's probably the most important one there is."

"Like the other three haven't been important? I can't imagine what—"

"God." He paused like that one word clearly explained the last lesson.

I shook my head. "I don't think about God much."

"That's your loss. I'm betting He's been trying to get your attention since you were born. The sooner you stop what you're doing and ask, 'Yes, Lord?' the sooner you'll find the core of who you are and who you're meant to be."

"What if there is no God?"

Harvey tapped his cards into a nice stack. "Here's the way I figure: if you believe God and Jesus are who they say they are, your faith gets you into heaven. If you don't believe, the deal's off."

"Meaning you go to hell?"

"You got it. The point is, you've got nothing to lose by believing in Him. If you reject God when He *does* exist, you lose everything. If you reject Him and He doesn't exist, you lose everything. The only winning hand involves believing God *is.*"

I fanned my cards, then closed them again. "You're sounding like a wise old man, Harvey."

"Hope so," he said. "As is anybody who realizes they're not *all that,* and God is."

I chuckled. "Not 'all that', huh?"

"Pretty much." He leaned toward me. "I'm sure you've heard Jesus-stuff all your life—most people have—but the kicker is when you start thinking it doesn't apply to you. You start thinking you've got it handled." He shook his head back and forth. "That's dangerous territory, son."

I felt an uncomfortable tug in my gut. "I'm fully aware I don't have it handled. I do believe in Him."

He clapped his hands together once. "Hoo-ya! Then you're on your way." He pointed upward. "Praise the Lord!"

I wasn't sure exactly what I'd done to make him say that, but I liked that I'd made him happy.

He winked at me. "Now *you* say those three words."

I had *never* said those words.

"Come on. You can do it."

How could I refuse him? "Fine. For you, I will."

"No! For *you* you will."

I found myself taking a deep breath as if it took effort. It was kind of embarrassing that it *did* take effort. But I said it. "Praise. The. Lord."

"Thata boy."

His praise meant the world to me. "Now what?"

Harvey took up his cards. "Now you open your eyes and see what God's doing. Then you join Him."

"Yeah, but—"

He shook his head like a dad who'd already said something a million times. He pointed at my eyes. "Open your eyes, boy!" He pointed at my heart. "Open your heart!" He pointed at my head. "And open that very closed-up mind of yours and fully *see* what He has to show you!"

I shivered.

He slapped a hand on the table and chuckled. "Man oh man, I like seeing that shiver. God sometimes talks to me in shivers when I'm on the same page as He is."

"Really?"

He nodded once. "Guaranteed."

I shivered again.

Chapter Twenty-Four

Tony

To those who use well what they are given,
even more will be given, and they will have an abundance.
But from those who do nothing,
even what little they have will be taken away.
Matthew 25: 29

After Harvey dropped his life lessons on me, I didn't sleep well. Would I ever have half the wisdom he had? And just because I heard it once didn't mean I'd remember it. Or use it. I knew myself too well.

When I got up, my thoughts were like a pinball banging against the bumpers, being whapped by the flippers, trying to win the prize for the most points—or at the very least a free game. Another chance.

Which made me think of the missed chances I'd seen in the Room with Wesley. All my life I kept putting a quarter in to play another game but I rarely won. Most of the time my play yielded a "Better luck next time."

Honestly, I didn't want to play anymore. I was supposed to change but I didn't know where to start.

I thought of Gracie.

She'd encouraged me to move on from my mistakes and make things right with my family. As in confessing to Nonna? I'd told Gracie I was thinking about it. And I was. Kinda. Sorta.

Remembering our dinner date last Saturday made me smile. Gracie intrigued me. She definitely was a Tinkerbell: sassy, smart, wary, and adorable. She wasn't an obvious beauty in that she didn't exude—or over exude—sexuality like so many single women did. She showed a tough innocence. She'd lived a hard life, but I saw in her traces of a huge heart capable of deep love—once a person earned her trust.

I hoped I could do that. We were both outcasts, each in our own way. We didn't expect anything to come easily, and were surprised when good things happened to us. Where I tended toward the tough side, there was something delicate about Gracie. She was vulnerable yet gutsy when she felt the need. Bottom line? She'd melted my heart—which wasn't an easy thing to do.

I was able to open up to her easier than I'd opened up to any woman in . . . maybe ever. I'd never told Penny about stealing or my part in Papa's death—and we'd been married.

Until the Room I'd kept it all hidden away. Yet one dinner with Gracie and I'd let her see my dirty laundry?

She'd been kind about it. Helpful even.

But had I said too much? If all she knew about me was the worst of me, then how could she ever truly like me?

And what did I have to offer? I was divorced, lived in a studio apartment, and was out of work. Getting involved with me would lead to nowhere. And above everything else, I didn't want to hurt her.

She'd called yesterday—just checking in. Hearing her voice made my insides flutter. We'd talked for hours about everything and nothing. She finally had to go when someone showed up at the Discover office.

Which led to another area of my life I was ignoring: a job. Oddly, I didn't feel any urgency to get one. I knew that was stupid and irresponsible and a dozen other negative words, but I didn't care.

Why didn't I care?

That question led to the one thing that *was* going right: Harvey. Turns out I loved spending time with the old guy. There was no one more shocked about that than me. Since Papa died I'd pretty much stayed away from old people. When Penny and I were married I saw Nonna occasionally, mostly when Penny invited her over for dinner. But since the divorce? Nonna called me every so often, but I never called her. Or saw her. In general I avoided anyone who dared to be old. It's not that I couldn't relate to them, but I didn't want to get close to anyone who might die on me.

Then why had I latched onto Harvey, who had literally fallen into my life? It was completely weird.

Also weird, was how he brought out the nice in me. In the past few days I'd taken him out to buy groceries and get his prescriptions. We'd even stopped at a park, where we'd sat on a bench and watched parents help their kids swing and go down the slide.

I loved listening to his stories about where he was when Kennedy was shot, the first time man walked on the moon, and when the Challenger blew up. We shared stories about 9/11. It's like I saw history—that I'd mainly ignored—in a new light through his eyes.

I'd also fixed a few things in his apartment. He'd asked the landlord to do repairs but nothing ever happened. So I fixed the icemaker in his fridge, secured a cabinet door, and pried open a window that wouldn't open. When a few of the other tenants heard about me fixing things, they asked for help with a jammed door, a garbage disposal; that sort of thing. No biggie. I liked using my hands.

What I found the most amazing about Harvey was that he didn't complain. Not ever. Yet the one thing I knew bothered him was his hearing. He'd ask questions about me and my life, but I could tell he was frustrated by how many times he had to ask me to repeat things. It was easier for both of us if he did most of the talking.

Today I was going to do something about it.

I knocked on his door, bringing over four blueberry muffins I'd bought at a bakery down the street.

His eyes lit up. He'd made coffee so I got him settled at the tiny table in the kitchen and served them up.

"Yum," he said after taking the first bite. "Almost as good as Dorothy used to make."

"High praise." He talked about Dorothy's cooking a lot.

He ate half of it, then sat back. "You said you had a surprise for me today? Beyond muffins?"

My stomach stirred. "Yes, definitely beyond muffins." I tried to sit back but couldn't. I was too excited. "We've talked about how you need hearing aids."

He put a hand to his ear. "Aye? What?"

I smiled. "Very funny."

"I thought so."

"I know you think you can't afford them, but you can if they're free."

"What?"

I sat forward, repeating myself. "Free hearing aids. I did some checking around and found a way."

"I tried getting 'em when Dorothy was alive, but they weren't covered."

"Now, they are." I got a slip of paper out of my pocket. "I found an audiologist close by. I got you an appointment."

His eyebrows rose. "That's mighty nice of you, Tony. When is it?"

The biggest surprise. "This morning."

"How did you manage one so soon?"

"Luck, I guess. When I first called they said their first opening was two months from now but they called yesterday and told me they had a cancellation."

"God be praised."

I couldn't argue with him.

**

Harvey got his hearing tested, and miracle of miracles, the right hearing aids were in stock. He had them fitted as well, which made for a long morning. When we got back home he thanked me profusely, then said he *had* to take a nap. I got him to turn off the TV for a while so I could take my own nap to make up for my fitful night.

I'd only been back in my apartment a few minutes when there was a knock at the door. No way could Harvey move that fast. And no one else visited me.

I looked through the peep hole, but didn't recognize the stranger. I answered the door anyway. "Yes?"

A tall man dressed in a yellow golf shirt smiled. "Are you Tony Amato?"

"Who wants to know?"

"Sorry." He handed me a business card. "I'm Abe Caruthers. I just bought this apartment building and the one next door."

I raised my eyebrows. "Congratulations on becoming a slum lord."

His face reddened. "Funny. Can I come in for a few minutes and talk?"

I glanced over my shoulder. I had clothes draped over furniture, dishes all over the kitchen, and a lot of take-out boxes. But whatever.

I opened the door wide and he followed me inside. "What do you want to talk about?" I asked.

"I want to offer you a job."

I was taken aback. "Doing what?"

"Maintenance work. I've heard you're good at fixing things."

Word had gotten around? "I can fix a few things. But hardly everything."

He shook his head. "The big fixes like HVAC can be subbed out. But everyday fixes like you've been handling . . ."

I could do that. I would love to do that. "It's possible. What does it pay?"

He said a number that was lower than what I'd been making. But then he added, "You'd get free rent."

Ding ding ding! We have a winner!

"I would also like you to mow what little grass there is, and keep the bushes trimmed. Equipment's in the shed."

"I could do that."

He scanned my apartment. "I plan on making some minor improvements too."

I was skeptical. From my experience landlords didn't like to spend money. "People would appreciate that, but . . ."

"Yes?"

"Make things nice, but not so nice that you raise the rent and force people to move." Because I didn't want to move or have Harvey move.

He considered this a minute. "I'll keep that in mind. So . . . are you interested?"

It was a no brainer. "Count me in."

"Excellent. I'll be in touch about specifics and how you should go about buying materials and supplies." He held out his hand for me to shake. "Glad to have you on board, Tony."

"Thank you," I said as I walked him out.

The first thing I wanted to do after he left was tell Harvey that I'd be around all day—permanently.

But he needed his nap.

And as much as I needed one too, I was too excited to even try.

**

As soon as I heard Harvey's TV come on, I went next door. With a knock I let myself in.

He was heading to his chair from the bathroom.

"Have a good rest?" I asked.

"I did."

I helped him transition from walker to chair. "Where's your hearing aids?" I asked him.

"Over there."

I helped him get them on. "Remember they'll take getting used to."

"I know." He pointed at the TV. "Turn that thing down!"

I did.

"I didn't realize I had it on so loud. Has it been bothering you?"

"It's all good now."

I sat on the edge of the loveseat.

He got settled, looked at me, then did a double take. "What's up with you? You look like a kid who just got an A on a test."

"That's exactly how I feel. I got a job."

"Good for you! I didn't realize you'd been applying. Where at?"

"Here."

"Here, where?"

"Here in this building. You are looking at the building's new maintenance man."

He blinked, then chuckled as he put everything together. "Well I'll be. Congratulations."

"Thanks. I never expected that fixing a few things would lead to something."

He sat back nodding. "I love set ups."

"Huh?"

"God set you up for the job. He set up opportunities to help me, and then the other tenants. People talk. And the powers-that-be noticed." He clapped his hands once. "Voila! You have a job."

I shivered.

"Ha! There you go again!" Harvey said. "Shivering."

I shrugged.

"A shrug? Really?" He cocked his head and looked at me. "You can deny it all you want, but that doesn't stop the connection from being a connection to the Almighty."

Because I shivered? That was a stretch.

Harvey's expression turned thoughtful. "Over cards the other day you mentioned accepting an invitation to a special room. You wouldn't tell me more then, but now that I can hear, I want to know all about it."

I shook my head. I'd told Gracie too much. I couldn't imagine telling anyone else.

Harvey saw my hesitation and was having none of it. "I've told you hours of my life stories so it's definitely your turn." He pointed over his shoulder at the kitchen. "Grab a kitchen chair and set it close. I want to be able to see your eyes during the telling."

It was tough figuring out how to explain the Room so I decided to only hit a few highlights. "Gracie led me into an empty room except for one stool in the middle."

"A strange arrangement for special training."

I scoffed. "That was only the beginning of *strange*. Suddenly—with no introduction or anything—a movie appeared all around me, three-sixty."

"I went to an I-Max once, but it wasn't all around. Just huge. Larger than life."

I shook my head. "This wasn't larger than life, it *was* life. My life. In the past. It was like I was right there, seeing *me* being *me*. I was an observer. Watching."

"So what did you see?"

I was just about to tell him about stealing but I couldn't.

"What's wrong?" he asked.

"What I saw wasn't good. The scenes were bad. Really bad."

"They couldn't have been that bad. How many scenes were there?"

I mentally counted through them. "Five."

"That's a lot of bad."

I nodded.

He sat back a minute, thinking. Then he said, "Why were you shown these particular moments?"

"They were times I was given an out, but ignored it."

"Ah," Harvey said. "The dratted free will."

"That's what the guy who was running everything said. Wesley said we all have choices. I went there by choice and I could leave by choice."

"But you stayed."

"It was like watching a train wreck, I couldn't look away."

Harvey shook his head. "You stayed because deep down you want to know the truth."

"Knowing the truth is the problem."

"Knowing the truth and facing the truth are two different things. Have you faced it, Tony?"

"Probably not."

"There's no *probably* to it. If you had, you'd know because 'the truth will set you free.'"

I certainly wasn't free.

"Give me details about what you saw in this room."

Details no. But I could summarize it. "I saw a dumb kid who messed up his life by trying to impress other dumb kids."

He chuckled. "You're not the first one of those and won't be the last."

Sad but true. "Bottom line? I stole some jewelry from my grandparents when I was fifteen."

Harvey scratched his scruffy chin. "What did you do with it?"

"My friends pawned their haul, but I . . . I kept the two things that meant a lot to Nonna."

"That's nice. I'm sure she was glad to get some of it back."

More confessions. "She doesn't have it back and she doesn't know it was me. I hid the stuff in the woods. As far as I know it's still there."

Harvey drew in a deep breath. "Well now. How many years ago was this?"

"Twenty-five."

"That's a mighty long time to be held prisoner."

"Prisoner?"

"Those hidden things in the woods have kept you captive to the truth *and* from putting it all behind you." He leveled me with a look. "Am I right?"

I sat back in the chair with an *oomph.* "I never thought of it like that."

"What did Wesley want you to do about it?"

I remembered how frustrated he'd been with me at the end. "We didn't get that far. He told me to leave."

Harvey's eyebrows rose. "Why would he do that?"

I *had* faced the truth of *that.* "I was a jerk. I argued and complained and didn't want to listen. My temper got the best of me. He gave up on me and said I'd had my chance."

"That was harsh."

I focused on a stray thread on the carpet. "I deserved it." I looked up. "Later, I went back and apologized to him."

"Good, good," Harvey said. "Did he let you have another go?"

"Nope. He accepted my apology but said he couldn't do more."

Harvey rocked up and back in his recliner. "Remember me saying time goes by fast and you just never know when—or if—there will be another chance?"

I nodded. Being out of chances was so final. Irreversible. Irrevocable. Game over.

I stood and stepped away, needing to get away from such thoughts.

"Hard to hear that, isn't it?" Harvey said.

I pressed a hand to my forehead, trying not to get emotional. "I don't want to be out of chances."

"Of course you don't. But think about this: though your chances in that Room may be over, God doesn't give up on you. But you need to exercise due-diligence and get the most out of the chance you did get in there."

I took a deep breath and ran my hands through my hair.

"Come on, Tony. Isn't it possible that the movies were God's way of getting you to change direction?"

"I guess that could be true."

"No *guessing* about it. Who else but God would go to the trouble? He's all about second chances—and third and beyond. It has to be His doing. You think a business would care about something that happened twenty-five years ago? Invite you to rehash it all by watching impossible movies? For what purpose?" Harvey shook his head. "Come on, Tony. It has to be God's doing."

I knew he was right, but it was still hard to admit that God would do something so personal—for me.

Harvey cocked his head. "Don't go doubting things because they don't fit into the box you've built around yourself. There's more to Tony Amato than you let yourself see—and let other people see." Harvey patted the chair in front of him. "Come back here. Let's finish this."

I returned to the chair and welcomed its strength to hold me.

Harvey sat forward and put his hands on my knees. "I see you, Tony. I see past the character you play. You were invited to that Room by God Himself. Do you believe that?"

Despite wanting to argue, there was only one answer. "I . . . I do."

"Good for you, boy! Admitting it is the first step. The angels in heaven are singing alleluia."

"What am I supposed to do now?"

"God helped you face the truth. Wesley talked about getting on the right road. What choice will get you there?"

All the bits of knowledge I'd been given from Wesley, Harvey, and Gracie converged: *Open your eyes and be enlightened, face the truth, make things right.*

Which shoved me toward one thing . . .

"I need to tell Nonna."

Harvey clapped his hands together. "Atta boy!" Then he said, "What else?"

"Isn't that enough?"

"With confession comes restitution."

"Bring her the jewelry?"

"Absolutely. Go out to those woods first thing in the morning and find what you stole. Then bring them to your grandma, confess, and make things right."

My whole body cringed at the thought. "I'd rather get my teeth pulled."

"A little pain will lead to big relief. In the end it'll feel good. I promise."

"What'll you give me if you're wrong?"

He winked at me. "My condolences."

Great.

**

As soon as I got back to my apartment I dug out the box that held my childhood mementos. I set it on the kitchen table and took the lid off.

A flood of memories flowed out.

I immediately grabbed my old baseball glove and ball. It made me think of playing catch with Dad. I set it aside for Zach.

I picked up the Skeletor and He-Man figurines. Masters of the Universe was the best.

There was an eyeball Madball that had broken one of Mom's vases, some Garbage Pail Kids trading cards, two Transformers, a Rubik's Cube, and a bunch of loose rocks that I'd collected on a family vacation in the Rocky Mountains.

Next were three Teenage Mutant Ninja Turtles comic books. And under them . . .

"Got it!"

I took out *the* piece of paper I was looking for. It was folded into fourths so I flattened it against the table. Except for the occasional glance I hadn't really looked at it since I was fifteen.

It was a map to Nonna's jewelry.

My first thought was how childish it looked. I definitely had zero artistic ability and my handwriting was horrible. But it showed the names of the crossroads, and called out a few landmarks in the woods.

It was a complete longshot, but it was all I had.

Chapter Twenty-Five

Lydia

Seek the Kingdom of God above all else, and live righteously,
and he will give you everything you need.
Matthew 6: 33

I didn't want to be pushy regarding Nova and Theo. Though I longed to help and be involved in their lives, I didn't want to annoy her by trying too hard. I'd done that with JoJo for a while.

When JoJo was in high school and didn't want to spend as much time with me, I tried to be her buddy even when her friends were over. So much so, that at one sleep-over she pulled me aside and said, "Mom, I got it. Leave us alone, okay?" I cried that night, but thankfully I'd learned something.

I didn't want Nova to say, "Leave me alone."

So I was taking things slow.

One good after-effect of reconnecting with her was that I was praying more. Not just the rote prayers I said every morning, but heartfelt prayers that reflected a real longing to do the right thing. And since the Room, I'd been praying to *see* what God was doing. It would take practice. I had a tendency to zone in on my to-do list so much that I didn't see anything else. But since God *had* gotten my attention I began to slow down and look at my life with expectancy: what was He going to show me today?

The anticipation was exciting. And He *was* showing me stuff, or at least was making me wonder about the reasons behind everyday happenings.

Like when I was stuck in traffic. Was it because He was protecting me from an accident? Or when the woman in the grocery store in front of me was short $4, was it a Divine opportunity to make up the difference?

None of this God-stuff was quantifiable, and if skeptics asked me to prove it, I would have to admit I couldn't. But as the instances became more frequent, I discovered I didn't really care if others believed me. I believed. And maybe that's what God was after all along.

Maybe it's like the time when I made chocolate-chip cookies because *I* was hungry for chocolate-chip cookies and JoJo bopped in and thanked me profusely, saying how great it was that I'd remembered she needed to bring snacks to her study group. I hadn't remembered at all. Even then, I knew my nudge to bake could have come from above.

I also knew there were probably times I gave God credit for some cool moments when He had nothing to do with them. But why not err on the side of being overly aware and lavishly thankful?

Today I planned to dig around in the flower bed, pulling out dead annuals to make room for new ones. I was just heading out to the garden center when Nova called. Her babysitter was sick. Could I keep Theo for the day?

Absolutely! She suggested I call when I was close by and she'd meet me at the curb. The transfer went smoothly and Theo and I were off.

He whimpered a bit and said Mama a hundred times as we drove away, but luckily he didn't full-on cry.

To distract him I babbled on about where we were going and how we were going to spend the day planting flowers. He repeated a few random sounds I thought I recognized: he said "Owsigh" when I said "outside", "fowr" when I said "flowers", and "tuck" when a loud truck went by. Every shared word was a victory.

At the garden store, I put him in the shopping cart. He took it all in, pointing at the fountains and some fluttering birds that had flown into the massive greenhouse. When I passed the garden gear I saw a kids' brimmed hat and put it on his head. Surprisingly, he didn't take it off. "You look so handsome."

He grinned.

Sold.

I chose pink begonias, white impatiens, and was choosing red geraniums when someone said my name.

"Lydia?"

I looked up and saw Glen's parents. I hadn't seen them since his funeral, which was a few years ago.

"Bob, Betty, hi." We hugged. "So nice to see you again. It's been too long."

"It has." Betty smiled at Theo. "And who's this?"

"This is Theo, the baby of a friend. We're going to plant flowers today."

Bob winked at him. "Our granddaughter is coming over this weekend to help us outside too."

Since they lost Glen it made me feel better that they had a married daughter, Mandy, and a grandchild. I hated to think of anyone alone. "How old is Ellie now?"

"Four."

"Four and feisty," Betty said. She looked at her husband, then back to Lydia. "Though this is long overdue we really wanted to thank you again for your kind notes and for what you did for Glen. I think your mentoring helped him in his studies and to be more at ease in his life."

"I'm not sure about that but you're welcome. How are you two doing?"

They shared some highs and lows with me, and seemed to have found ways to move forward.

"I admire your strength," I said.

They shared a look and Betty nodded. "We don't know what we would have done without our faith."

Theo pointed at bunny decorations for Easter. "Bun, bun!"

When a thought came to me I mentally said, *Yes, Lord.*

"How would you and your daughter's family like to come over for Easter dinner?" I hadn't asked Theo and Nova, but I would. "I could have an egg hunt for Theo and Ellie."

"It *would* be nice to reconnect. Mandy asked after you the other day."

Another God thing.

"Sure," Betty said with a nod. "That would be lovely. What can I bring?"

**

I only lost one geranium to Theo during the backyard planting. When I wasn't looking he decided to pluck off all the petals.

His attention span in digging in the dirt was not only destructive but short—which was probably for the best when I considered the mess of it. So I created an alternative play area. I gathered a pail of water, a paint brush, and measuring cups, and set him on the edge of the patio to play with the water. He started painting the legs of a lawn chair and water went everywhere. He looked so adorable in his sun hat.

The planting was eventually accomplished, as was lunch. When he took a nap, I took a nap—something I remembered doing from my young mother days. For dinner, I called Jeremy and he brought home McDonald's. Theo snarfed up the nuggets and apple slices.

When Nova called that evening, I drove him home and she met me at the curb for the hand-off.

"Thanks so much for taking him on short notice. The babysitter called and said she was better, so you're off the hook for tomorrow."

"Call whenever you need. We had a good time. Since we were planting flowers I bought him a sun hat. I hope you don't mind."

"Hath!" Theo said.

I got it out of the bag to show her. He wanted it on, which made her smile. I hoped my invitation would make her smile too. "I was thinking about Easter coming up. Jeremy and I would love for you and Theo to come church with us and then join us for a ham dinner and an Easter egg hunt. JoJo will be there, and some friends who have a four-year-old girl." I took a breath. "Please come."

She adjusted Theo on her hip. "I don't know. The last time I went to church on Easter my mom said the cross with the white cloth draped over it gave her the creeps. She pulled me out of the service and we never went again."

I held in my shock. "Then it's high time you give it another try. We'll pick you up at eight-thirty."

"I—"

God nudged me into action and I quickly moved to the driver's side to escape before she could say no. "We'll see you then. Bye-bye, Theo."

I left Nova at the curb looking uncertain as Theo waved bye-bye.

Chapter Twenty-Six

Minnie

Let us strip off every weight that slows us down,
especially the sin that so easily trips us up.
And let us run with endurance the race God has set before us.
We do this by keeping our eyes on Jesus.
Hebrews 12: 1-2

My weekend had been full of significant events: the Discovery Room, Gabe, dinner, and *not* talking to Dad and Claudia about my major.

I hadn't slept well since. On the third day I slipped out of Mom's before she was up, and drove to campus earlier than usual. I grabbed a campus newspaper and found a comfy chair in the student union.

I skimmed the articles about upcoming activities, school elections, opinion pieces about world events, and sports scores. Even if I'd been interested in any of those things, I didn't feel up to reading them.

I saw a coupon for a nearby coffee shop and scanned the code. Then I skimmed over ads for sporting goods, a bookstore, a pizza place . . .

And twenty-percent off all supplies at Art's Art Shop. Good for them. Everybody loved a sale.

I turned the page and my gaze landed on another sort of ad: *Need to change your major? It's not a major deal! Come to Room 230 in the Admin building.*

I looked out the window and noticed that the administration building was right across the square.

I might not be ready to tell the world about switching majors but the least I could do was get information about it.

**

Since it was so early, there wasn't a line at the admin office.

"From business to art?" the clerk typed on her keyboard.

"Yes. I'm just wondering how many credits would carry over."

"I've got your file here." I watched her eyes read the lines on the screen. "It looks like you have 57 credits so far—under sixty makes it more doable."

"How doable?"

She looked back to her computer. "It's possible. I see you already took an art history class as an elective."

"I did. I loved it." I squirmed in the chair. "I made a mistake going into business. My heart is in art."

She looked at me. "Let me guess. Your parents chose business."

"You've heard this before?"

She smiled. "Happens all the time." She pointed at the screen. "You've got a good foundation of courses here, but not all will transfer. You may have to take summer school, take more than 15 hours in your remaining semesters, and possibly even add a semester."

I'd expected as much. "But it is possible?"

"Anything is possible. Would you like to proceed?"

If only I could. "I still need to talk to my dad. He's the one who pays."

"Understood. Give me your contact info and I'll email you the requirements and a class catalog."

I left the office exhilarated. The mere thought of immersing myself in art tapped into my creative juices. And courage.

I had to do this.

**

I texted Gabe and he agreed to meet me on campus.

He invited me to come to his neck of the woods—the art building. "Come to Carlson Hall and check out the painting lab. You can see what I've been working on."

My heartbeat doubled at the idea of being surrounded by art again and seeing artists in their element.

The buildings for the art college were on the other side of campus from the business buildings. It was like leaving one country for another.

I knew I was just imagining it, but the students seemed happier over here. Lighter. Free-er. Was that because they were tapping into their creativity every day?

And not just as a hobby.

I spotted Gabe sitting on the steps of the building. He greeted me with a hug. "Welcome to Oz," he said.

I smiled back at him. "Will I see the wizard?"

"Probably not, but you'll see a lot of fantastical things." He led me inside, into an enormous open room. Easels were scattered all around, with canvases small to large, to ones so big they were propped up against the walls. A few people were painting, immersed in the creative experience.

My throat felt tight. I turned in a slow circle "This *is* Oz."

He laughed, put an arm around my shoulders, and whispered, "Click your heels together and say, 'There's no place like home.'"

I was suddenly overwhelmed and my eyes started to tear up.

"Hey, hey," Gabe said, pulling me into his arms. "Don't be sad."

I shook my head against his chest. "These aren't tears of sadness." I smiled as the warm emotions swam over me. "You're right. This is home."

We stood there a long time—though not long enough. Being among artists, being held by Gabe . . . it felt so right. So completely complete.

Someone cleared their throat. An older man with Bob Ross hair stood nearby. "I should tell you to take it outside, Morton."

Gabe pulled back, but kept an arm around me. "Professor Hobbs, I'd like to introduce you to Minnie McLaughlin. She's thinking about joining the art department."

"Well then. I welcome you. Are you currently enrolled?"

I nodded. "But not here. In the business college. Two years there. But I want to change to art." I looked around the room and took a deep breath. "This is where I belong."

"Excellent. You should talk to Dean Weaver." He smiled mischievously. "He'll help you come over to the dark side."

I shook my head. "This is definitely the light side."

"The right side," Gabe said as he gave my shoulders a squeeze.

When the professor left, Gabe looked down at me with sparkling eyes, "Want to see my latest painting?"

"Absolutely."

He led me to an abstract painting of a girl's face. She was wearing sunglasses, and in the lens was the reflection of what she was seeing.

I reached out to touch it, then pulled my hand back. "Is it wet?"

"Nope. Go ahead."

I wanted to touch it because it was three-dimensional. "How did you create the texture?"

"It's oil paint, applied with a palette knife."

"Not a brush?"

"That too. A mixture."

I stood back to look at the painting as a whole. "It's amazing."

"Thanks."

"You have amazing talent, Gabe."

"Thank you. I still have a long way to go." Once again he pulled me into his arms. "We both have a long way to go."

I loved hearing the beat of his heart. Feeling it. "I could get used to this," I said.

"Me too." We lingered a few moments. Then he asked. "So, seeing my work wasn't the only reason you wanted to meet up. What did you want to talk about?"

I shook my head and swept an arm to encompass the room. "This room, the art-in-progress, the canvases, your painting . . . they did the talking. It's decided. I'm going to change my major."

He let out a loud "Woo-hoo!" as he picked me up and spun me around. His joy echoed in the room.

And up to the heavens.

**

The rest of the day was a blur. I went to my business classes, but if my motivation was lacking before, it was non-existent now. It was hard to concentrate knowing that next semester I would be on the other side of campus, igniting my talent, letting my creativity soar.

Driving home, I called Dad to see if he had time for me to stop over tonight. Mom was working a rare evening shift, so I was free.

"Of course, Min. We'll be here. Anything wrong?"

"Not a thing."

"Want to come for dinner?"

"Thanks, but I was thinking around seven?"

"See you then."

I had a sudden thought that God had arranged the day just for me. As soon as I hung up my stomach tightened. This was really going to happen. I was really going to be brave and make choices for my own good.

It was time to start being exceptional.

**

Dad and Claudia were just settling into the family room to watch TV when I arrived. Hugs were exchanged, and I joined Claudia on the couch.

A cop show was playing on the TV. Dad turned it off.

"What's up, Min?" he asked.

I nearly panicked when I felt my resolve wanning before I'd even started. Then I remembered Wesley telling me that I was not a child anymore. I had to be courageous and strong.

I sat forward on the edge of the cushion. "Last Saturday I went to a place where they help people discover their potential."

"You mentioned it. Was it good? "

"Very. They encouraged me to pursue my dreams."

"That's good advice," Claudia said. "So what *are* your dreams?"

And there it was. A door had been opened. "I want to be an artist."

Dad shook his head. "Min, we've talked about this. You want to be an artist doing what exactly?"

"Creating something out of nothing. I'm not sure whether I'll be good at painting or drawing or even sculpture, but I want to find out."

"I get that you've always loved art. But why don't you take evening art classes with the extension office?"

I hated that idea. "No. No, Dad. That's not enough. I need to immerse myself in all mediums, the people, the places, the experiences. I need to see where it will lead."

He tossed the remote on the side table. "I can tell you that right now. Art might be something fun to dabble in, but practically? It will lead you nowhere."

"You don't know that."

He pushed the ottoman away and sat up straighter. "Neither do you."

My throat was dry. "In the Discovery Room, they asked me where I saw myself in ten years."

"What did you say?" Claudia asked.

"I said I wanted to be married, have a couple kids, and a house with big trees in the back where I could set up an easel, or have a studio."

Claudia looked between me and my dad. "That sounds lovely."

Her words were the same as Wesley's—they gave me courage. "But even more than that, I can see us traveling around Europe so I could study the masters. And I'd use my art in the community too. Maybe I'd give lessons, or show in a gallery, or travel around to be in those art shows where you rent a booth."

"I love those shows," Claudia said. "Your dad and I went to one last month."

I wanted to hug her.

Dad was not impressed. "All that takes money. You can't earn money as an artist."

"Money isn't everything, Dad, and I don't want to earn money selling real estate." I clapped a hand over my mouth. "Sorry, but it's true."

"So this is about not wanting to work with me?"

I could see pain in his eyes. "It's not that. Not at all." A good example came to mind. "What if I told you that *you* needed to become an accountant."

He waved a hand at the idea. "Min, this is not the same thing."

"Indulge me."

"Fine. I would hate it. I'm not good at math and honestly can't think of anything more boring. I like working with people."

"Exactly!" I felt a glimmer of hope. "You wouldn't be good at it because it doesn't allow you to use one of your greatest gifts—helping people." I put a hand to my chest. "I am not a people-person like you. I'm not exactly sure what my gift is, but I get excited about being creative."

"I can see that in you," Claudia said.

Dad flashed her a dirty look. I hoped that wouldn't silence her.

He leaned forward and rested his arms on his legs. "I'm not asking you to never draw or paint, Min. Just don't bet your future on it."

One of the scenes in the Room came to mind. "Remember when my high school art teacher wanted me to enter a drawing in a contest where I could have won a trip to Italy?"

"Vaguely."

"I told her no because I knew you wouldn't approve."

"I wouldn't."

"But you did. Afterward—when it was too late—you told her that I should have entered the contest, to at least try. You said I'd missed an opportunity."

"You said that?" Claudia asked him.

He scowled. "I don't remember. Maybe."

His admission was a small victory, but I jumped on it. "I want to get an art degree. I don't want to look back years from now and wonder what could have come from it. I want to try."

Claudia gave me a small, approving smile.

Dad sat back, rubbing his hands on the arms of his leather chair. I got a nudge to be quiet. Let him think.

I prayed and prayed . . .

He sighed and rubbed his face. "What would changing to an art degree entail?"

I wanted to jump off the couch and pump a fist in the air. But I remained calm because I knew Dad responded better to logic rather than emotion. "I stopped at the admin office today and they said it would involve some summer classes and might take one semester more."

"That's not too bad," Claudia said.

"Maybe, but it also means more money," Dad said.

I drew in a breath. I'd never once thought about the cost of it. How clueless was that?

"You're right," I said. "I'll pay for any extra classes I have to take. I'll get a part-time job. I usually work for you in the summer, but maybe I can find something else that—no offense—pays more." Dad paid me minimum wage which I used for gas, car insurance, and a few other expenses. To actually *need* to make good money was daunting. But that couldn't stop me. "What do you think?"

He sighed deeply. "I suppose. You can—"

This time I did jump off the couch. I rushed toward him and enveloped him in an awkward hug. "Thank you, thank you! I promise I'll do my very best and make you proud."

When I straightened up he took my hand. "What I was saying was that you can try it for a semester. If you don't feel it's the right road, you can go back to the business college. *That* scenario, I'll pay for."

I squeezed his hand. "Time will tell. But I know that being on the right road is the only way to be exceptional."

"Exceptional?"

"That's my goal."

Dad nodded. "You've always been exceptional to me, Min."

I pulled him to standing. "I need a real hug."

He wrapped his arms around me as only dads can. It felt so good I wanted to cry.

He let go and turned toward Claudia. "Look at this, Claudie, our daughter is all grown up."

Claudia joined us. When she hugged me, I whispered to her, "Thanks for backing me."

She whispered back, "Any time."

**

I went home to an empty house. Mom wouldn't be home until after nine, which gave me the liberty of celebrating. I let out a big *whoop!* and jumped around in an awkward happy dance. I was going to major in art!

I fell onto the couch and called Gabe. When he didn't answer I realized he was at work. Unable to contain my joy, I texted him:

I wrote: *Call me tomorrow. Good news!*

A moment later he texted me back: *An art degree?*

Yes!

Congratulations!

It just feels so surreal.

I bet. To celebrate, want to go to an Impressionist exhibit at the museum Saturday?

Yes!

I'll call you tomorrow.

It was perfect. Now, I had a strong reason to go to art exhibits because *I* was going to be an artist too.

I was excited to share the news with Mom. To celebrate I made a pan of brownies. There was nothing like walking into a house where brownies were baking. I also made a pitcher of iced tea and put it in the fridge.

She got home right when I expected her.

"Do I smell brownies?"

"You do." I got out plates. "I made tea too. Have a seat."

She sat at the kitchen table. "Wow, Min. This is great." She smiled. "Are you buttering me up for something, or are we celebrating something?"

I served the brownies and drink. "We are celebrating because . . ." I did a drum roll on the table. "I am changing my major to art."

Her head jerked back. "I thought you'd let that go."

"I never let it go. Not fully. And then I got excited about it again."

"What brought that on?"

I realized I'd never shared anything about the Room with her. I remembered thinking she wouldn't understand and would think it was weird and a dozen other reactions. But it wasn't fair that I expected her to treat me like an adult when I'd held things back like a child.

"I think I told you about an invitation I got to a place that would help me discover my potential?"

"Maybe . . ."

Her wishy-washy answer spurred me to pare down my explanation. "They helped me see that art has been an important part of my entire life—since Grandma McLaughlin bought me an art set when I was six."

"I remember that set. You would put it on this table and work so hard drawing and coloring things in."

"Grandpa taught me a lot about drawing."

"They were always giving you art supplies."

"They believed in my talent." Unlike you and Dad . . .

"I always thought you had a flair for it, but your father—"

"You did?"

She finished chewing her brownie. "Sure. Nobody could draw a vase like you could. You even used shading."

"Grandpa taught me that."

"I know." She looked toward the counter by the garage door. "I've seen all the drawings you two send each other. It's real nice. I never had that kind of relationship with my grandparents."

"We *are* close. Very close." I needed to call them and tell them the news. They'd be thrilled.

Mom sat back in her chair. "Art makes sense for you, Min. When you were in high school you liked to work in the theatre department, painting sets and backdrops. That was a kind of art."

"It was."

"Your father's to blame for making you go into business. You and I have a need to create—me with my flower arrangements and you with your drawing. All Ben cares about is status and money."

She wasn't completely wrong. Yet Dad *was* a good family man with me and the twins —though I couldn't tell her that.

Mom slapped her hands against her thighs. "I say go for it. But your father will be the hard cookie to crack."

"He already approved."

She cocked her head. "No way."

I told her about my conversation with Dad and Claudia, and about the admissions office. "Dad said it will cost more for the extra classes, but I'm going to get a better-paying job this summer to help with the expenses."

Mom stood and pulled me into a hug. "I am so proud of you, Min. I'm glad you're following *your* dreams and not relying on your father's." She kissed me on the forehead. "Way to go, sweetie."

She brought her dishes to the counter, then turned back to face me. "Plus, it's good you live here, so that expense isn't added to the tab."

Shoot. I hadn't thought about that. She was one hundred percent right.

I had a lot more to think about.

But tonight, I was happy to take one victory at a time.

**

I was just about to turn out the light when I realized I hadn't called Grandpa and Grandma yet.

It was after ten. Too late to call. So I texted the news.

Hi, Grandpa. Good news. I'm changing my major to art next year! We'll talk tomorrow.

I set my phone on the bedside table and was about to turn out the light when it rang.

I was surprised it was him. "Hi, Grandpa. You're up late."

"Hi, yourself. Tell me about this good news of yours. I'm putting you on speaker so Grandma can hear too."

I heard Grandma chime in, "Hi, honey."

I told them my story, how both Dad and Mom gave in.

"It's all come together. I have you to thank for a big part of it. If not for Grandma buying me that first art set; if not for you teaching me how to draw; if not for all those gifts of art supplies, I wouldn't be doing this." I put a hand to my heart even though they couldn't see me. "I *know* this is what I'm supposed to do."

"Oh, honey," Grandpa said. "We're proud of you for not giving up on the gift God planted in you. I know it was hard and you had lots of obstacles."

They understood me—they always had. "Thanks for encouraging me—no matter what."

"You're most certainly welcome," Grandpa said. "And we'll continue to be here as long as God allows."

"God's got you right where He wants you," Grandma said.

I couldn't have said it better myself.

Chapter Twenty-Seven

Tony

Truly, O God of Israel, our Savior,
you work in mysterious ways.
Isaiah 45: 15

Not surprisingly the woods had changed since I'd last been here. What used to be off dirt roads at the edge of town, was now surrounded by civilization. Suburbs had spread across the land, gobbling up open fields, leaving the occasional meandering band of trees and bushes to mark what used to be.

Surely my hiding place was long gone. I imagined a backhoe digging a basement, and a construction guy stopping to see what was in the cookie tin that had been unearthed.

If that was the case, all was lost. I was lost. Without the jewelry there would be no chance at redemption. No chance to return to Nonna what I'd taken from her. I could go empty-handed and confess, but reminding her of her loss might make things worse.

I reached the right cross streets and was shocked to see that a portion of the woods was still there—miraculously still there. I sat at the intersection and stared at the forest. Neighborhoods had been built up on all four sides, yet here was a patch of woods about a half-mile square. A small parking lot and some playground equipment had been added, but otherwise it looked untouched. Why hadn't this land been developed? Why was it still here?

Honk!

A car had pulled up behind me. I lifted a hand to wave sorry, then drove through the intersection and turned into the lot and parked. My whole body hummed with energy and I could hear myself breathe. I needed to calm down. Everything pointed to one big fact: I was supposed to be here.

I needed to do what I'd come to do. I took the map out of my pocket and smoothed it against the steering wheel. The few landmarks I'd noted were vague: *tall pine, three big rocks* and *yellow flowers.* Two out of the three could easily be gone. My best bet was finding the rocks.

I noticed a mom with a toddler on the swings, and a grandmother-type sitting on a bench while her dog sniffed around. When I got out of the car they both gave me a wary look. I suppose it *was* strange that a forty-something guy would stop at such a park. Alone. In the middle of the day. If I'd been wearing jogging clothes I could have swung it, but wearing jeans and a faded Bruce Springsteen T-shirt probably made me look iffy. I glanced back at the car and realized I needed my hand spade. I couldn't just carry it into the woods without looking even more suspicious, so I put on a jacket and slipped it up a sleeve.

"Hi," I said as I passed the mom. She said hi back. Then I passed the grandma. Her dog—some kind of terrier—ran up to me and I leaned down to pet it.

"Now, now, Marvin," she said. "Leave the man alone."

"It's okay," I said. And it was. I missed having a dog. I reached down with my non-spade hand and scratched behind Marvin's ears. He licked my hand.

Grandma slapped her knee. "Come here, boy." Surprisingly, Marvin obeyed.

I turned toward the woods. "Have a nice day."

"You too."

I felt her watching me. There wasn't a real walking trail, more of a deer path. It made me feel like I was a baseball player in *Field of Dreams,* walking mysteriously into a cornfield where I would fade away. I walked quickly out of their sightline. There was a lot of leafy ground cover, though it wasn't as dense as it would be in a few months.

I kept walking until I couldn't see the parking lot anymore. I paused to look up. Twenty-five years of tree growth had made the woods more shadow than sun. The temperature was a good ten degrees cooler. It was real pretty and reminded me of camping trips I'd taken with my parents as a kid. We'd camped from Missouri to Colorado to Arkansas. Wherever we were, Dad and I would look for long sticks to use to roast marshmallows for s'mores. I'd climb a tree and pretend to be on the lookout for pirates, never once acknowledging that the nearest sea was thousands of miles away.

I heard a noise and saw a squirrel scamper through the undergrowth and up a tree. He stopped to look at me and chittered, accusing me of trespassing.

I turned my eyes forward. I needed to focus on finding the jewelry. I wandered around, looking for three large rocks, but didn't see anything. Surely someone hadn't moved rocks? There'd be no reason to—

"Marvin! Get back here!"

I looked toward the parking lot. It was the grandma's voice.

"Marvin? You come back here right this minute!"

I heard a faint rustling in the fallen leaves, and then the swishing of feet walking through the ground cover. Grandma was coming in.

I saw the dog run past. "Marvin!" I called. "Stop!" I ran after him, but that only spooked him.

"You found him?" Grandma called from the right.

"He's over this way." I waved my hands over my head.

She spotted me and called out, "I'm coming."

She high-stepped her way over the undergrowth while I went after Marvin. He was a wily thing, darting around, making the plants rustle and bend.

We both spotted him, and Grandma went to the left while I went to the right to surround him. We slowed, hoping he'd calm down.

"Come on, boy," Grandma said in her best doggy-mama voice.

I watched him glance at her. Then at me. Then he started digging, making dirt and leaves fly. It gave us a chance to close in. Grandma stealthily slipped in behind him and grabbed him. "Gotcha!"

I was out of breath. "Good catch."

She pulled him into her arms, then held him at arm's length as his muddy paws had messed up her shirt. "He's never done that before. Ever. Thanks for your help." She walked back toward the parking lot, scolding the dog.

I leaned forward, resting my hands on my thighs, trying to get my heartrate back to normal.

But then I saw the place where Marvin had been digging. It was right next to three rocks and a huge pine tree.

No way.

Way. Even before I started digging I knew my tin would be there. I pulled the spade out of my sleeve and dug. A foot down I heard metal hit metal.

And there it was. I brushed dirt off the cookie tin I'd nabbed from Mom's kitchen. The embossed poinsettias were rusty, but still showed red and green.

This was it. This was the box connecting the now-me to the kid-me.

I started to open it, but hesitated and looked around.

What was I afraid of? Someone stealing from *me?* A cop appearing to arrest me for the crime?

Get a grip.

I sat on one of the rocks and took the lid off. Inside was a big plastic baggie. I was surprised I'd had the foresight to think about protecting the jewelry, but the baggie had done its job. I wiped my hands on my jeans. I took out the purple velvet bag and could feel the outline of Nonna's pearls inside.

I loosened the drawstring, feeling the weight of the pearls mix with the weight of my bad choices. The necklace tipped out of the bag onto my lap. The pearls looked perfect, a creamy white against my jeans. I remembered the photo of their wedding day that I'd discounted as unimportant because it was before my time. Ignorant kid.

I carefully dropped the pearls back in the velvet bag. Next I took out a navy, hinged case. I ran my fingers along its edges, remembering the time Papa had shown me this treasure. I opened it carefully, afraid of what the years of decay might have done.

Yet inside, hanging from an unscathed purple ribbon, was Papa's medal, the size of a silver dollar. It was a purple heart surrounded by gold, and on top of the heart was a profile of George Washington. My throat tightened just looking at it. It had meant little to the 15-year-old me, but now that *I* had friends who'd been wounded or even killed in Afghanistan and the Middle East . . . and Harvey had served in Vietnam. No wonder Papa wore the medal at their wedding. It was a badge of honor. And service.

What service had I ever performed? For anyone, much less my country.

None. Nada. Zilch. Zero.

Suddenly I began to cry.

No! Stop it!

Me, Tony Amato, cry?

Yes. Me. Cry.

Cry because I'd stolen more than mementos. I'd robbed Papa of his reward for bravery and sacrifice by taking his medal. I'd robbed Nonna of the comfort of wearing her wedding pearls to his funeral, and holding them dear for the many years after.

My cry wasn't just a sniffle. I don't know where it came from but I began to sob with tears and moans and gasps for air. It was like my insides were being torn apart, pulling me inward.

And downward.

I slid off the rock to my knees. But I went further and fell forward with my head resting on my hands. "I'm so sorry," I whispered to the ground. "I've done so many things wrong, hurt so many people. I've been such a screw up."

Then suddenly in my head I heard Wesley's voice: *You can continue on the same path you've been on, or you can use what you've learned and change things.*

I sat back on my heels, shaking my head. "I want to change things."

Then I remembered my initial reaction to his words: *What am I supposed to do now? Fall to my knees?*

Wesley had said it was an option—one that I'd laughed off, saying it was never going to happen.

Yet here I was, on my knees in the woods. Saying I was sorry. Seeing the awful truth about my wasted life. Wanting to change.

I looked up through the trees and saw blue sky. And something else. Two jet trails had left their marks in the blue, one going north-south, one going east-west, their jet-trails forming a perfect cross.

I shivered.

Then I said the words I should've said twenty-five years ago and a thousand times since. "Please forgive me."

I hung my head.

But then I felt a lightening, as though the weight of my guilt had fallen away.

A breeze swept through the branches, then swept through me, making me suck in a breath. Not just any breath, a new one. A fresh one, free of my past.

I smiled.

I was cleansed.

I was free.

**

When I got back to the parking lot, I saw Grandma over by the mom and her toddler. The little kid was playing with Marvin.

And I swear—I would honestly swear—that Marvin glowed.

**

Although I wanted to talk to Harvey as soon as I got home, my body insisted I rest.

Actually, my mind too, for my mental muscles had endured more than my bodily ones. And my spiritual muscles had definitely broken any previous Tony-record.

I sprawled out on the couch and was asleep in seconds. I woke an hour later, feeling more refreshed than I usually felt after a full-night's sleep. *Now* I could visit Harvey.

I knocked and entered—as I usually did—and found him heating chicken noodle soup on the stove. "Hey, you're back. How did it go? How did your grandma react?"

He'd skipped too far ahead. "I haven't seen her yet, but I did find the jewelry in the woods."

"Good for you." He got out two bowls and spooned out the soup without asking. I liked that.

"Some strange things happened."

He blew on a spoonful. "How so?"

"Loads of houses and neighborhoods have been built in that area, but miraculously, the woods were intact."

He pointed his spoon at me. "Like God was keeping it safe for you."

It was such a relief to hear him say that. "I thought that too, but why would He do that for me?"

I expected him to say something cheesy like, "because you're special to Him." Instead he said, "This isn't about you—or not just about you—it's about your grandma."

It took me a second to take that in. "So she *needs* to get her stuff back? Even now, after all this time?"

Harvey shrugged. "Again, I don't know the mind of God. But it's something to consider."

I ate some soup, thinking about it. Somehow having the whole thing be important to Nonna made it more important to me.

"What else was strange?" Harvey asked. "Did you have a hard time finding the jewelry?"

"I was overwhelmed at first, seeing as my only landmark to go off of was finding three rocks. But then a dog, Marvin, escaped from his owner and led me right to it."

He nodded thoughtfully. "So if not for Marvin running into the woods . . ."

"I might not have found the spot."

"See? God even works through man's best friend."

Dogs were amazing, so that didn't surprise me. "There's something else."

"Go on."

I set my spoon down. "I had a moment out there. A special moment. Kinda spiritual."

His gray eyebrows rose and he also set down his spoon. "A God moment?"

I nodded again.

"Good for you."

"Yeah, it was good for me. I mean . . ." I didn't know how to explain it—or if I even should. "Somehow I ended up on my knees in the dirt, bowing my forehead to the ground."

Harvey's eyebrows met in the middle. "Been there a few times myself. It can get pretty intense."

"Yeah, it was."

He held out his hand, like he wanted me to shake it. Which I did. "What's that for?" I asked.

"Congratulations on you finally letting God get your attention."

"He certainly did that."

Harvey picked up his spoon and pointed it at me. "Now that you're aware of Him, don't lose it. Keep your eyes open. I have the feeling this is just the beginning of a beautiful relationship."

I liked the sounds of that. Even if it terrified me.

Chapter Twenty-Eight

Gracie

Work willingly at whatever you do,
as though you were working for the Lord
rather than for people.
Remember that the Lord will give you
an inheritance as your reward,
and that the Master you are serving is Christ.
Colossians 3: 23-24

I awakened before my alarm went off—which was unusual. I tried to sleep a few more minutes, but my brain wouldn't turn off.

I gave in, and sat up in bed. I opened my laptop and checked my social media accounts. I had barely posted anything about my job—other than I'd got one. I hadn't mentioned where, because if I mentioned the Discovery Room to my readers they'd ask what kind of discoveries happened there. What kind of room was it? Wesley had told me to keep whatever happened in the Room confidential. Clients could share as much as they wanted to share, but as an employee, I needed to keep mum about it.

Actually, there wasn't much I *could* say. Tony had urged me to go for it, and of course Wesley had invited me many times. And he'd even told me not to wait too long or I might miss my chance. It's like an unseen clock was ticking down the minutes.

It was heady stuff.

I didn't feel up to writing anything new, so I read new comments for my old posts. Nothing pleased me more than when people interacted with each other. I joined in when I could add something new, but most of the time they did fine without me. In fact, more than once I'd learned something from *them*. We were a family—the only one I had.

I read the newest comments connected to the post I'd written a month after Dad's death. I'd spilled my guts on that one, writing about my grief, my guilt, and my anger toward Dad—and toward the total waste of the last fourteen years. This particular post had over 300 comments—my most ever.

I read a comment posted by a woman named Jess:

It's been so healing to move past the death of my parents who died within a year of each other. The only way I could do it was by facing the tension I was still holding against them and God for letting it happen. I was so full of anger that I couldn't function. I found a great therapist and she helped me revisit some of the key moments of my past. I saw the truth of my mistakes – and some successes – with new eyes. If not for doing that, I wouldn't have been able to release the anger and forgive. And nearly forget. And now, for the first time in ages, I feel renewed! I heartily advise everybody to do whatever it takes to move on.

I swiped away a tear.

I looked at the replies to her comment: thank yous, questions, and congratulations. Her problem was not uncommon.

Her problem was mine.

I read her words a second time. A few stood out: healing, tension, anger, mistakes, truth, release, forgive, forget, renewed.

Oh, to forget and move on, to face the truth of my past so I could live differently *now*.

I closed my laptop and sat in silence. What *was* the truth of my past? I'd been a daughter, a caregiver, a housekeeper, a nurse, a prisoner . . .

Finally the most important truth stepped forward: I'd been alone.

But before I let myself wallow in the pain of my loneliness, I thought of something positive. I *had* been alone. But I wasn't alone anymore.

I set the laptop aside and dangled my legs off the side of the bed.

Getting the job at the Discovery Room had been a huge step toward releasing me from my isolation. I hadn't applied for the job. I hadn't sought it out. But when Wesley offered, I'd said yes to him, *and* to letting other people in. Getting to know him and meeting the clients, made me breathe deeper, like our interactions filled an empty cavern inside.

I smiled when I thought of Tony. He was the biggest blessing of all. Tony made me feel whole. He made me feel real.

I was not alone anymore. I had people.

I looked upward to where God lived and repeated my revelation: "Hey, God. I have people now. Thank you. But what next?"

I startled when my clock radio came on. Which meant it was time to get up to go to work.

I climbed out of bed and stretched, but then . . .

The lyrics of the Mamas and the Papas' music made me stop with my arms in the air:

You've gotta make your own kind of music.
Sing your own special song.
Make your own kind of music.
Even if nobody else sings along.

Could I do that—make my own kind of music? Live my own kind of life?

Special. Tony made me feel special. He and Wesley were trying to help me deal with the past so I could move forward. Yet I couldn't depend on them to make me feel or do anything.

I had to do it myself.

Another line of lyrics seemed to be sung just for me: *To do your thing's the hardest thing to do.*

I closed my eyes and let the rest of the song whirl around me. I sang along with the chorus. I felt a stirring inside.

I had to honor Wesley and Tony's effort by doing my part.

I had to act. Which meant . . .

I opened my eyes and said the words out loud. "I have to accept the invitation."

**

I went to work knowing I was going to visit the Room.

But from the moment I got to the office we had a steady stream of clients. There wasn't a big enough break where I could even tell Wesley about my decision, much less take my turn. Which made me question myself. Was I supposed to say yes?

Or was my morning epiphany because of the Mamas and Papas' lyrics nothing more than a clueless whim?

It was nearly closing time and my stomach was in knots from waiting. Finally, the last client walked out. Wesley stood at the door and waved after them.

"Well then," he said. "We've had a very busy day."

My stomach threatened to do something nasty. "I don't think we've ever had that many clients in one day." I hesitated, clicking and reclicking a pen. "I . . . uh . . . do . . ." My words caught in my throat. I knew once I said them there would be no going back. I forced them out. "Do you think we have time for one more?"

Wesley looked outside, as if watching for someone to drive in. "I don't believe . . ."

"How about me?"

He turned toward me, clapped his hands together once, and beamed—the most emotion I'd ever seen from him. "Thank You, God Almighty! Gracie accepts the invitation!"

I blushed. "It's not that big a deal."

Wesley pointed at me. "*Au contraire,* Miss Sturgess. It is an enormously big deal. We've been waiting a long time."

"We?"

"The Almighty and I."

I rolled my eyes. "Stop it."

"I absolutely will not." He strode to the door of the Room and opened it. "After you."

I had waited so long, but now it was happening so fast.

I stepped into the Room. My heart was beating so loud I was sure Wesley would hear it. It was beyond strange to walk in as a client—or "victim" as Tony called them. I sat on the stool.

"I'm nervous, but I don't know why," I said. "I know what's going to happen."

Wesley cocked his head. "Do you? Do you *really?"*

My throat was dry. "Can we just get started?"

He chuckled softly. "I suppose you've waited long enough. And so, we shall begin." He left the Room.

The Room lit up immediately with a scene—a familiar one. I was in the kitchen of my house, making Dad soup and a sandwich. How many times had I done that? How many lunches? Dinners? Breakfasts? The kitchen looked exactly the same as it did now, yet I knew by my teenaged attire of double tank tops and long straight hair that it was soon after Mom died.

I didn't have time to marvel at the existence of the movie because a bell rang. I inadvertently found my grown self cringe at the too-familiar sound of Dad's summoning call.

"Coming." I poured an enormous glass of homemade sweet tea and went into Mom and Dad's bedroom—now just Dad's. He was propped up in bed, flipping channels. He had the bed tray set across his lap, ready for me. I set the food there.

"What? No chips?"

Dad loved Lays potato chips. "Sorry." I ran out to the kitchen and came back with a generous portion in a cereal bowl. "Here," I said, setting it on the tray. "Can I get you anything else?"

"Get me Bonnie back. How's that for a request?"

I sat on the chair nearby, my own grief too heavy to bear. "I would if I could, Dad. I miss her too."

"No you don't. You're going on with your life as if she didn't just die a month ago."

"If going on with my life means finishing school so I can graduate, then yes." I said, rehashing an almost daily argument we'd been having.

Dad thought that just because the world stopped for us when mom died, that everyone else's world should too.

"What's the purpose of school when Bonnie isn't here? Graduating from high school is overrated and you know it. You think you're better than me."

I'd heard it before. "But now school is over. The ceremony is tomorrow night. I made it, Dad."

He ate a chip noisily.

"Actually, I thought we could go out to dinner first to cele—"

Suddenly, Dad tossed his plate across the room. I flinched as bologna and cheese went flying. "I never had a high school graduation and you ain't gonna have one neither!"

His words did not compute. "It's important to me. And Mom. Before she died she made me promise I'd go. She said she was proud of me and—"

"Proud-schmoud. That was before she knew she'd die so close to the darn thing. Would she be proud you've forgotten her? You are not going. I forbid it."

The young me teared up, as did the older me. He was so incredibly unreasonable. And cruel.

The doorbell rang, giving me an escape. I hurried down the hall, the guilt, grief, and anger still raging inside. I tried to pull myself together. I pasted on a smile.

It was my friend Molly and her mom from next door. They handed me a plate of cookies. "I thought maybe you and your dad would like these," Mrs. Gardner said.

I was grateful. Many of Mom's friends had brought over food when she was sick and after she died, but Dad made me throw most of it out, as he claimed we didn't need charity.

He may not have needed it, but I did. "Thanks so much. They look yummy."

Molly looked at her Mom, who nodded at her, as if giving her permission to say something.

"Do you want to go to graduation with us tomorrow?" Molly asked. "First, we could give you a ride since you and I have to be there early, and then . . ." She looked at her mom.

Mrs. Gardner continued, "Then Earl and I could come back and pick up your dad."

Suddenly, the two of them glowed with a yellow light.

"What's that?" I asked the Room. Tony never mentioned anything glowing.

The younger me said, "That's awfully nice. But I don't think I'm going."

Their eyes grew large. "What do you mean you're not going?"

I didn't want them to know how unreasonable Dad was being, so I used Mom as an excuse. "We're grieving. It just doesn't seem right to celebrate."

Mrs. Gardner leaned close. "I miss your mom too. But I know she would want you to attend graduation with your friends, in your cap and gown. It's a big milestone."

I shrugged, my eyes threatening tears. I remembered thinking how they were right. I wanted to go. Mom would have wanted me to go. But with her gone, I had to keep Dad happy.

Dad rang his bell, bringing me back to reality. "I gotta go. Thanks for the cookies." I closed the door, and leaned against it. I slid down to the floor.

The scene ended.

Wesley came in. My heart hurt from the memory, the pain then making me hurt now. "That was hard to see," I said.

"How do you feel after seeing that scene?"

"I'm mad, hurt, and sad. Dad had no right to ask me to skip the ceremony."

"No, he didn't."

I was glad Wesley was on my side. "That was just the beginning of it," I said.

"Define *it.*"

Suddenly I was at a loss. I had never discussed my dad with anyone—except within the safety of my online family and the few times I'd mentioned him to Tony. "*It* was Dad. He was needy and demanding and I had to stay home to help him." I slowly shook my head back and forth. "If only eighteen-year-old Gracie knew what this thirty-two-year-old Gracie knows, she'd . . ."

"She'd what?"

"She'd go to graduation, that's for sure."

"You were offered a way."

"Mrs. Gardner and Molly?"

"Did you find anything unusual about them?"

"They glowed."

"Why do you think they were sent to your door at that very minute?"

"Who knows?"

"Who do you think sent them to you?"

"They were our neighbors. Nice people. Mom had a lot of good friends."

"She did," Wesley said. "But perhaps you should think bigger."

I knew what he wanted me to say. "God?"

"Very good."

"So you're saying God sent Molly and her mom to our door to get me to go to graduation?"

"Rephrase your question as a statement."

"God sent Molly and her mom to our door to get me to go to graduation."

"Indeed."

"You're saying I could have gone? I *should* have gone?"

"Both."

I rolled my eyes, feeling every teenage emotion from all those years past. "It wasn't that easy. Dad was stubborn and insistent, playing the martyr like he was the only one who missed Mom." Tears filled my eyes and I pegged a finger to my chest. "I missed her too! She and I were best friends. She was my confidante, my person. She was my mom!" I let the tears flow. "When she died she left a huge hole in my heart, and in my life."

"I am very sorry for your loss," Wesley said. He removed a tissue from his pocket and gave me a few moments to gather myself. "How long was your mother ill?"

"Fifteen months from her diagnosis to her death." I blotted away my tears. "She loved us so much. She did everything for my dad, waited on him like he was a king. In the last months when she was too sick, I took over not only taking care of her but Dad and the house as well."

Wesley put a hand on my shoulder. "That was a heavy burden for one so young."

It felt good to be understood. "I heard Mom tell Dad to take it easy on me. He promised her that we'd work together to take care of everything. And each other."

"Did he keep that promise?"

"Not at all." I fidgeted on the stool. "He lied." New tears came and were hot with anger. I stood and pointed at the wall in front of me. "He took care of me, all right! He ordered me around like he ordered her around. But I wasn't his wife, I was a kid. It wasn't fair!" My whole body shook with rage.

I looked at Wesley, embarrassed for him to see me this way. Yet all I saw was compassion in his eyes.

"If God cared so much, why did He take Mom and not him?" As

soon as the words were out I slapped my mouth and stepped back. "I'm sorry. I shouldn't have said that. I know I should've loved my dad, but I just didn't. I didn't serve him with a kind heart, I endured."

"You are allowed your anger and your questions. But I have no answer for you."

I threw my hands in the air. "Why not? You speak about God like you knew things, so why don't you know this?"

"Many speak God's truths, but there is only one God."

"That seems like a copout."

"It is a truth."

I flipped a hand at him. "Are we done here?"

"Do you want to be done? For there *is* more."

Of course there was more. I knew there was more from seeing Wesley go in and out of the Room many times for each client. "Fine. Show me another one."

"Have a seat and we'll proceed."

I took a deep breath, blew my nose, and collected myself. Now I understood why Tony had come out angry. Finding out what could-have-been hurt.

Wesley left and a new scene opened. There I was again in the same kitchen making dinner. My hair was up in a messy bun, so it had to be a year or so after high school. I'd always kept my hair styled for school, but being stuck at home, I'd lost the motivation. Who was I trying to impress anyway? There was no one in my life except Dad and he barely looked at me. I was a robot at his beck and call.

An episode of "Glee" was on in the living room. Cheery young people sang and danced in perfect unison while all their crises were wisely handled. If only the cast could have united to handle my crises—while teaching me a few dance moves along the way.

The young me took the meatloaf out of the oven. A bowl of boiled potatoes were ready to be mashed. I plugged in the hand mixer just as a commercial started.

I saw myself wince at the volume. "Why are commercials louder than the TV?" I asked nobody.

The TV blared: *Want to get a degree and don't have the time? You can get college credit with online classes. Registration is easy. Call Salisbury College at 800-363-5400.*

I put down the mixer. I'd been thinking about taking classes. I walked into the living room just as the next commercial started.

The TV began to glow. If what Wesley said was true . . . "I was supposed to take classes?" I asked the Room.

The twenty-year-old me heard the garage door go up. My young face looked panicked. I turned off the TV and rushed back to the kitchen. Dad came in the door a few moments later, wearing his navy logoed shirt from the water company. He tossed the mail on the counter. "I'm starved. When will it be ready?"

"A few minutes." I pointed at the meatloaf. "See? Your favorite."

"I hope it's done this time. I won't let you poison me with raw meat like you tried to do before."

I'd taken it out too early the first time I'd made it for him. He'd held it against me ever since.

I finished whipping the potatoes and added plenty of butter. A can of corn was heated on the stove. I got two dinner rolls out of a bag, ready for when he sat down to eat.

As soon as I heard his bedroom door open I watched my young self slice the meatloaf and give him two slices, then fill his plate with the rest of the food. He didn't like having serving dishes on the dining room table. He said they looked messy.

The adult me repeated a truth: "Dad liked to be served. And I was his servant."

As the young me scurried around to make everything to his liking, the older me remembered Mom's pointers for a happy home. Even when she'd been pale as death she'd told me, "Make sure you iron your father's work shirts. He doesn't like to look unkempt" and "Shine his shoes. You can tell a gentleman by the shine on his shoes."

Gentleman? Gentle-man? That was *not* my father.

I watched myself pour the iced tea. Then I noticed a color pamphlet on the top of the mail he'd brought in—a pamphlet that glowed: *Get your degree online with Salisbury College.*

Same as the TV. What a coincidence. I put the pamphlet under my arm and brought the glasses into the dining room.

Dad sat down. "What you got there? You know I don't allow reading at the table."

I took my seat and showed him the pamphlet. "This is from a college that will let me take classes online, from home."

He shook his head vigorously. "What do you need classes for? Trying to act all educated in front of me?"

"Since my friends went away to college and I didn't, I thought—"

"You thought you're better than me. So being here with me, as we both find our way without your mother, is an imposition to you?"

"Yes," the adult me whispered to the Room.

"It's just a few classes. Mom always stressed a good education."

"Hmph. Just because she had a year of college. She always lorded that over me."

I doubted that. *He* was her lord and master. She gave up everything for him.

Dad ate a bite of the potatoes, then pointed his fork at me. "Plus, you have things to do right here at home. You got that job stuffing envelopes for that marketing company."

"That's short-term and it's mindless. I want to do something to improve my mind."

"You want to be all hoity-toity?"

"I like to learn new things. I have free time so I'd like—"

He stopped chewing and looked at me over his glasses. "You have free time? Your mother never had free time."

"She had outside activities. She was involved with church and sang in two different groups."

"So, do that. As long as you keep up the house and are here for me in the evenings."

"We don't go to church anymore and I can't sing." And I doubted he'd truly let me go. "Even if I could, I don't have a car."

"That never bothered your mother."

"She got rides from friends. My friends aren't here anymore."

He picked at food in his teeth. "You want more to do, you could clean the basement. Your mother was a real hoarder. If it were up to me, you could give the lot of it away."

I remembered going through the family heirlooms with Mom many times. She loved to tell stories about when she was young. Each scrapbook, old doll, or vintage piece of clothing reminded her of the past. Now they would remind me of her. I would *not* toss them out.

I still hadn't.

He pointed at the pamphlet. "Get that outta here and get me more corn." He handed me his plate.

The scene stopped, the lights came on, and Wesley returned.

"My dad was incredibly stubborn," I said, shaking my head.

"So you didn't take any classes?"

"I didn't. I thought about doing it behind his back, but it hardly seemed worth it. He was right. There was no reason to learn something new when I was stuck there."

"You were only twenty," Wesley said. "You weren't doomed."

"Turns out I was. The following year he broke his ankle in two places and he decided he couldn't work, so he was home all day. And then he got sick with cancer and I became his nursemaid." I jabbed a finger toward the screen where his image had been. "If I would 've known then what I know now . . ." Apparently, this was my battle cry.

Wesley crossed his arms. "What would you have done differently?"

"Everything," I said flippantly. I remembered the glowing brochure. "At the very least, that scene means I was supposed to get a degree."

"It *was* Plan A."

"Whose Plan A?"

He pointed upward.

"So I ruined God's plan by taking care of Dad?"

"God gave you the option of taking classes. You made the choice."

"Apparently the wrong choice."

"*A* choice," he said. "You cannot foil the will of God. He *will* fulfill His purpose in you. Not *might*. Will."

I scoffed and looked around the Room. "So working for you is my life's purpose?"

"A part of it."

I shook my head. "No offense, Wesley, but I don't buy it. Most days my time here doesn't seem very purposeful." I stood, gesturing around the Room. "Unless you have something really amazing in store for me here, I think you've depressed me enough."

He pointed at the stool. "Sit." His voice had a hint of command to it.

I hesitated. Was he mad?

He took a breath and said it again, nicer. "Sit. Please."

I sat.

"Attitude is everything, Miss Sturgess."

I felt bad. I liked Wesley and I didn't want to disappoint him—or risk my job. "Sorry. Go ahead. Show me more. It can't get much worse."

But I knew it could. It had.

Chapter Twenty-Nine

Gracie

The Lord is my light and my salvation—
so why should I be afraid?
The Lord is my fortress,
protecting me from danger, so why should I tremble?
Psalm 27: 1

I braced myself for the next scene in the Room. I'd had so many negative moments in my life. I knew there was plenty of material to choose from.

The third scene showed a corridor in a courthouse. There were benches along the wall where people waited for their turn to testify.

I shuddered. I remembered this awful day.

And there I was, all dressed up in the black dress I'd worn to Mom's funeral. I was sitting on one of the benches, awkwardly shredding a Kleenex because soon it would be my turn to tell the truth or lie—that was the choice.

Unfortunately, I remembered which choice I had made.

I called out to the Room. "We can skip this one, Wesley. Turn it off, okay?"

But the scene continued. A twenty-something woman sat at the other end of the bench. We exchanged glances. "Do you go next?" she asked.

"So they tell me."

"They say I'm after you." We both looked straight ahead. Then she turned toward me. "Are you nervous?"

"Very."

"I've never done this before," she said.

"Me neither," I said. "I can tell you this, I don't want to ever do it again."

She chuckled. "My husband's lawyer said I only need to remember one thing."

"What's that?"

"Tell the truth."

I hesitated. "It's not that easy."

"Sure it is," she said. "You'll be taking an oath under God. You can't break an oath."

Suddenly the woman glowed.

She'd been placed there for a reason?

I stood up. "Please, Wesley, stop. I get the point. I don't want to relive it."

Surprisingly, the scene faded and he came in. I began to make my case before he stopped walking. "I wanted to tell the truth and say that Dad walked fine after the accident, that he easily could've gone back to work. I'd seen him tinkering with our car in the garage, which meant he could stand for a long time. But Dad insisted I tell them he was totally incapacitated, he needed help walking, and he couldn't stand for more than a minute. I was supposed to push the point that he was miserable because of the pain."

Wesley nodded once. "Why do you think that woman glowed?"

Seeing it now made it pretty obvious. "She reminded me to tell the truth. I would be under oath."

Wesley nodded.

The thought that God sent her was almost too much. "I wanted to tell the truth, I really did. But Dad said our future depended on him getting a big payoff from the insurance company. He said without that, we'd have to sell the house and move."

"You paid the bills. Did the house have a mortgage?"

I thought back. "No . . . Mom had been real proud that they'd paid that off before she died."

"So even without the payout you could've gotten by?"

I shook my head. "We still needed money to pay the other bills: the car, utilities, medical bills from Mom *and* from Dad's ankle. But overall Dad was healthy. The ankle ached a bit but he *could* work. And I would've worked if he'd let me."

"So why did you lie?"

My breathing quickened. "His eyes. I remember Dad sitting in the courtroom. He glared at me with his *do it* look." I shuddered at the memory. "I'd learned not to cross him."

Wesley's voice softened. "How did you learn that?"

I squeezed my eyes shut, hearing his voice, his screaming.

"Did he hurt you?" Wesley asked softly.

I opened my eyes. "Not physically. But I almost wish he would have hit me."

"You can't mean that."

"Yes, I can. A physical action would be done and over with." My hands tensed as vivid memories washed over me. "He hit me with his words, he slapped me with the names he called me, he punched me with his moody silence." I raised my chin. "After the screaming he wouldn't talk to me for days."

"Surely the silence was better than his screaming."

"Not better at all." Tears filled my eyes, but I shook my head, forcing them back. "When he screamed I would hide. I'd go to my room, crawl in my closet, and cover my ears. Sometimes I would even fall asleep in there, all curled up like a little kid."

Wesley's eyes met mine. "Gracie, I'm so sorry."

I needed to tell the full of it. "His silence was torture because I never knew where I stood. I never knew when it would be over or when the next explosion would go off. I walked on eggshells, trying to make amends: serving extra special food, or cleaning something that was already clean so he could see me doing it. I had no one to talk to. I was so isolated. Like it or not, he was my whole world." I sniffed and cleared my throat. "I think I would've liked being hit better than all that. Just get the pain over with."

Wesley stepped close but didn't touch me. "I am very sorry for your suffering."

I appreciated his sympathy, but it didn't change anything. "For all those reasons I had to lie for him in court. I couldn't risk an angry father."

"I understand. What happened with the settlement?"

"He got his big payout. Big enough that he didn't even try to get another job after that. Nope, he was around the house all day, every day. With me."

"Did you get a job?"

I scoffed. "Of course not. He'd play the guilt card whenever I mentioned it."

"That's totally unreasonable."

I snickered. "Acting reasonable was not Dad's forte. He lived for control and manipulation. Every bit of my time was accounted for and was considered necessary to serve him. Even when I had access to the car for errands, he kept tabs of the mileage and my time away. The grocery store was five miles round trip and should take forty-five minutes max. A minute more and I'd pay for it. For days."

"He *was* controlling. How did you cope with having him there all day?"

This memory brought with it a breath of relief. "I started to write."

"What kind of writing?"

I got up and strolled around the Room, needing movement to dislodge my words. "It was just personal essays at first. Long angry ramblings in my journal." I stopped. "But then one day when I was on the computer I saw an article about social media and how it was a way to build communities with like-minded people. That was the moment that changed everything."

Wesley nodded, and smiled knowingly. "There you go."

"What? You're not going to tell me that was God, are you?"

"Can you tell me it wasn't?"

I couldn't.

I put a fist to my mid-section. "When I read that article I felt this stirring inside and I suddenly knew that I wanted—I needed—a community, a place to tell my story. A place to connect with others. And I found that place through my social media accounts."

"You followed God's prompting. Well done." Wesley paused, letting that sink in. "What did you write about?"

"I named my page 'Moping, Coping, and Hoping.' I wrote about family dynamics, grief, anger, resentment. Coping mostly."

"I'm sure you helped a lot of people who were going through similar situations."

I nodded. "There's been a lot of nice comments and discussions. There's a lot of pain out there."

"Which you gave a voice."

His words made me feel good inside.

"What did your father think about your interactions?"

I snickered. "He never knew a thing about them. He was very anti-computer. Old school all the way. Since he was home all the time, I escaped to my room and wrote on a laptop. The posts became my outlet, my community, my outreach to the world. Writing helped keep me sane." I sighed. "Especially after Dad got really sick."

"The cancer?"

I nodded. "That was seven years ago. If he was needy before, that need paled in comparison to what he was like after the diagnosis. He milked *every* pain so I couldn't tell what was real and what was acting. Once in awhile a friend from his work stopped by. Dad could've won an Oscar for those performances. 'Best Martyr in a Starring Role' is Samuel K. Sturgess.'"

"That doesn't sound like a very fulfilling life."

"It's what he chose. Getting cancer and having to be in bed was like fate finally gave in and said, *You want to be lazy? You got it.*"

"At that point you fully became a caregiver."

I smiled for the first time since entering the Room. "It's weird to think of it. Yet having him confined to his room gave me a twisted sort of freedom. I was free to move around the house, not worrying if I was being too messy or if I ate my meals in front of the TV. When he needed to go out for treatments it got me out of the house for more than my allotted forty-five minutes. I loved those days. He would be tied up for a few hours which set me free. I'd let him off then run back to the car and drive around."

"Where to?"

"Everywhere. Anywhere. It didn't matter. I'd go sit in the park, or watch kids playing at recess, or stroll around Target." I chuckled. "You wouldn't believe how exciting Target can be."

"I'm sure I wouldn't."

My thoughts suddenly focused on my favorite part of Target. "I met a really nice guy working at the pharmacy there."

Wesley nodded once. "You mean Brody?"

I gasped. No one knew about Brody. "You know about him?"

"I do."

"If you say God sent *him*, I'd believe you. He was wonderful."

"Did you ever go out? Date?"

"He asked and I said yes. But no, we never dated."

"Why not?"

Wesley's question brought back another wave of regret, this one very different than the others. "One day when Dad was groggy from the meds, I told him I had a date. He didn't really hear. He dozed. I got all dressed up and was ready to leave. I expected Brody to show up any minute and went into Dad's room to check on him. Unfortunately he was more lucid and noticed my clothes. 'Where do you think you're going?' I told him I was going out to dinner with his pharmacist. He got all agitated and started getting up to meet the guy and tell him to leave me alone."

I closed my eyes against the memories. "I can still hear him ranting and fighting me. Totally out of control. During his rant he fell and I had to stay and take care of him. I called Brody and told him not to come—that night or any other night. I couldn't ever go out with him. He argued, saying we could work it out, but I insisted." I sighed. "He was such a nice man."

"I'm sorry."

I shrugged. "It is what it is. Brody's married now." I took a deep breath and let it out, hoping to expel the pain. "I never went out with anyone. Not until Tony and I had dinner the other night." I laughed. "It's pretty absurd that my first real date was at age thirty-two."

"Did you and Tony enjoy yourselves?"

"We did. Actually, he was instrumental in getting me to do all . . this." I spread my arms to encompass the Room.

"That's rather unexpected."

I wanted him to cut Tony some slack. "He's a good man, Wesley. He wants to do the right thing, but it's hard to change who you've always been." I took a fresh breath. "I would know."

"He's lucky to have your encouragement."

"As I said, he's a good man. He's helping an elderly neighbor, *and* he was thinking about making things right with his grandmother."

"Excellent on all accounts," Wesley said.

I felt nudged to ask a question. "Do you know something—about *us?*"

"I only know what I'm allowed to know. But personally, I like the idea of you two together."

I chuckled. "Wow. Matchmaker Wesley approves."

"You've met him before, you know."

"Tony?"

"Want to take a look?"

This movie excited me. "Absolutely."

Wesley turned on his heel and left the Room.

The scene began. It was the parking lot of Target. I spotted Dad's boat of a car in the lot. I heard his voice in my head and mockingly whispered what he'd said too many times: "Look at this beauty, a 1988 Buick LaSabre Coupe—Limited Edition, red with a white padded vinyl top. It's a classic, Gracie. And don't you dare get a ding on it."

A ding was the least of its problems as the vinyl top was peeling, and the engine sometimes made weird noises. Plus, it was enormous. Its size spurred me to park at the far end of the lot. I couldn't trust myself to maneuver in and out of parking spaces with other cars so close.

I searched the parking lot, looking for me. There I was, coming out of Target, carrying three bags. The scene before me melded with vague memories. This wasn't that long ago. Maybe last year?

I put the bags in the trunk and got in to head home.

But the car wouldn't start. It sort of sputtered. I tried it again and again until there was no sound but a click. Was the battery dead? I slammed my hands on the steering wheel. "I don't have time for this!"

I watched myself sit there and remembered wondering who to call. I didn't have any friends. I did a search on my phone for nearby gas stations. Yet would they have anyone available to come jump the battery?

Just watching the situation made me put a hand to my stomach in worry. But then the rest of the memory came back. I *was* saved that day by a nice man with jumper cables.

And there he was. Parked just a few cars away, a tall man with dark hair stepped out of his car. He walked toward me.

I stood up. "Tony?"

There was a yellow glow about him.

"Tony was sent by God?"

He went around to the driver's side. My window was down. "Need help? Sounds like your battery is dead."

The idea of getting help from a stranger had been unsettling, but I'd said yes. Tony took over, moving his car beside mine.

The scene faded. I rushed to meet Wesley when he came in. "Tony was the one who helped me!"

"It appears so."

"But when I saw him here in the office I didn't recognize him."

"That doesn't discount the fact he was brought into your life—twice."

I sat back down, overwhelmed by the implication. "Which means he's supposed to be a part of it."

"Is that a question or a statement?"

"You tell me."

Wesley shook his head. "Free will prevails."

I had to pace again. "If—*if*—God put Tony in my life in the parking lot, the fact is nothing came of it." I stopped and gasped. "Wait! He gave me his number. When he was through helping, he wrote his name and number on the back of a receipt and said, 'Call me.'"

"Did you?"

"No. Dad hadn't allowed me to see Brody, he certainly wouldn't allow me to see a stranger I met in a parking lot."

"Perhaps." Wesley hesitated a moment. "Are you up for one more?"

"If it's another good one, sure."

"No promises."

He left the Room and a scene appeared. It was at my accountant's office. I was bringing her the tax stuff—just a month ago—because it was too complicated for me to do taxes with Dad's death and the estate and medical expenses.

There I was in the waiting room, my receipts and information carefully organized in accordion file pockets. And then the door opened and Wesley walked in. Even as I watched, I remembered what happened next.

Before he reached his chair, he clumsily dumped a file full of papers and receipts all over the floor. The mess of papers glowed.

I watched as I helped pick them up.

"Sorry," he said. "I'm not very organized. It's such a mish-mash of stuff."

I'd seen receipts mixed in with papers that had numbers

scribbled on them. Knowing him now, the chaos was out of character. And the Wesley I knew would never say mish-mash.

I stepped up to the receptionist. "Could I have a dozen paperclips, please?"

I got the clips and proceeded to organize Wesley's papers.

"You don't have to do that," he said.

I realized I'd totally butted in. I started handing him back the papers. "Sorry I took over like that. If you want me to stop . . ."

"No. Please. I appreciate your organizational skills."

The scene faded and he came in.

"What came out of that meeting?" he asked me.

"This job. You said you needed someone who was efficient."

"And here we are."

I shook my head vigorously. "But this job requires zero organizational skills. You didn't need those traits at all."

"But I did need you to work here."

I blinked at him. The implication was clear. "You needed me to work here, so I'd go in the Room?"

"That's one reason."

There could only be one other. "To meet Tony again?"

He touched the tip of his nose.

"Wow."

He smiled. "Indeed."

I had a question for him. "What got *you* involved in all this, Wesley? What situations fell into place for you to take this job? You've seen my story, what's yours?"

"Mine is simple. I was asked and I said yes."

"That's it?"

He gave me his smirky smile. "That's all I'm going to tell you."

"That's not fair."

"Such is life."

"Argggh. You frustrate me."

His smile lingered. "We are here for *you*, Miss Sturgess, not me.

He was such a closed book, but there was no fighting him.

"Would you like to summarize your scenes?" he asked.

"I guess so. Maybe you can help me figure out why all of this is important."

He held up one finger. "The first choice you saw was when your neighbors offered to drive you to your graduation."

I shrugged. "If I'd gone, it would have been nice, but I lived without it."

"You accepted the absence of it. But you missed the memories it would have created."

I shrugged.

"What was the second choice?" Wesley asked.

It took me a moment. "I saw information about classes—more than once. But Dad said no."

"Knowing all that's happened since then, what do you think might have happened if you'd taken classes?"

"Probably not much. I have no use for a degree."

"We'll never know, will we?"

"That's hardly encouraging."

"Number three was . . ."

"Lying on the stand in court, which led to a big payout so Dad didn't work."

"Very true."

"But then he got cancer and had to stay home anyway."

"Yet what did you do while you were caring for him?"

With a jolt I saw where he was heading. "I shared with other caregivers online."

"Which enabled you to reach many people. Help many people."

It was an interesting notion. "Because of my posts, even if I was isolated, I wasn't."

"Exactly."

Things began to fit. "I actually thought of that this morning before work. I used to be alone, but I'm not anymore because of them, and you. And Tony."

Wesley clapped his hands. "The same wisdom from more than one source. That's excellent."

It did feel good.

"A question for you, Miss Sturgess. If you had been busy taking classes, if you had been occupied dating Brody, if you had not suffered being stuck at home with your father, would your online family exist?"

It was hard to fathom, but the truth was there. "Probably not."

Wesley spread his hands. "As usual, God brought good out of the bad. You discovered a talent you didn't know you had. And you've reached people far beyond the boundaries of your confinement. There is a wonderful verse: 'What I tell you in the dark, speak in the daylight; what is whispered in your ear, proclaim from the roofs.'"

"Meaning . . . ?"

"What you learn in hard times needs to be shared so others learn from *their* hard times."

Which is exactly what I'd done with my posts. I put a hand to my forehead, pressing the ideas into my mind. Yet I still had a big question. "So far I made three wrong choices. God making it good is great, but I still got it wrong."

"Wrong in the moment, good in the long run. God does not give up on anyone. He has a plan. If you turn left and were supposed to turn right, He will find a way to get you back on the correct road—if you let Him. Are you on the right road, Miss Sturgess?"

I felt a lump grow in my throat. "I think I am. Yet the notion that God would do all that for me, that there even *was* a plan—*is* a plan—it's mind-blowing."

"I couldn't have said it better myself. There may have been an easier way to get to where you are now, but God used the hard times to your advantage."

"So I didn't suffer in vain."

"Are you not stronger for the suffering? In spite of it?"

I drew in a deep breath and let it out. "I think I will be."

"Splendid." He nodded once. "Shall we talk about number four?"

"Tony helping me in the parking lot." Before Wesley could add more, I did it myself. "And me getting his number but not following through. I get it. My Bad."

"But God didn't—"

"Give up on me. I met Tony again."

"So you did." He smiled. "And finally we come to you getting this job. I gave you the opportunity—invited you to work here, as it were—and you said yes."

"It was the only choice I handled correctly."

Wesley shrugged. "Look at the full of it, Miss Sturgess. You've discovered all sorts of interesting things about your life."

I snickered. "I used to think my life was boring and worthless."

"It's far from it. You've gone through great stress and strain, great sorrow and pain—and you've come out in one piece. That's something to be proud of." His voice softened. "Your mother would be very proud of you."

My eyes welled up with tears. "I hope so."

Wesley handed me a tissue. "I know so."

I dabbed at my eyes and sniffed. "How do you know she's proud?"

He pointed upward. "God lets all of us know things in our hearts. Call it wisdom, peace, or just an inkling. He is always communicating with us. Give and take. And so . . . I know your mother is proud. And so do you."

I felt a calm come over me. I could imagine Mom looking down through some heavenly portal, seeing how things had turned out. Seeing I was okay and my future looked way better now than it had ever looked before. "You're right. I do know she's proud."

"And so it is," Wesley said. He took a fresh breath. "You have now completed your time in the Room, Miss Sturgess, and I declare it a success, don't you?"

"I do. It's turned this skeptic into a believer."

"Praise the Lord!" He turned toward the door.

"But what now, Wesley? What am I supposed to do with all this knowledge?"

He turned back to me. "Ponder it. Open your mind, your eyes, and your heart to whatever God has in store for you in the future. Recognize His ways and His work all around you. 'Trust in the Lord with all your heart; do not depend on your own understanding. Seek His will in all you do, and He will show you which path to take.'"

"Promise?"

"Absolutely." He held out his arms and drew me into a warm embrace. It may not have been proper, but it was necessary. And much appreciated.

Chapter Thirty

Lydia

If your gift is serving others,
serve them well.
Romans 12: 7

I sat on a bench outside my office building. It was a gorgeous spring day. I much preferred taking my lunch outside rather than sitting in the cafeteria where everyone was on their phones—which always had, and always would bother me. Out here, nothing bothered me. I had fresh air, blue skies, and purple tulips blooming nearby.

I unzipped the fancy lunch bag I'd bought and took out a container of fruit and another of lettuce. I had just stabbed a piece of cantaloupe when my phone rang. I thought about not answering it—wouldn't I be a hypocrite if I did? Yet when I saw who was calling, I took the call.

"Nova. Hi."

"Hi, Lydia." There was an odd pull in her voice.

"What's wrong?"

I heard Theo crying in the background. "Theo is sick."

I sat forward. "I'm so sorry. Is he throwing up sick or . . . ?"

"He keeps pointing at his throat, and he has a runny nose and a cough. I think he has a fever too."

I remembered JoJo being sick like that. "That's hard on both of you. What can I do to help?"

"The babysitter won't take him because she has other kids there."

"That's fine, I can help tonight."

"But there's more. She won't take him tomorrow either, or the next day if he's still sick. I asked other people in the building and no one will take a sick kid."

Babysitting for an evening was one thing, but during the day for two or three days?

"I know you have a job, and I wouldn't ask if I had another choice. I don't know what to do."

I wished I had a while to think about it, but I didn't.

Nova continued. "I asked my boss at the diner if I could have th days off, but they're short-staffed and he said they need me."

And *you* need *me*. "When do you work today?"

"Three. I could call and try to get it pushed a bit later . . ."

Lord, what should I do?

Just then I saw an ad posted on a truck going by: *Just do it!*

I put a hand to my chest and nodded at God's direction. "Okay. I'll figure out something here at work. I'll pick him up at two-thirty."

I heard her sigh of relief. "Oh, thank you, Lydia. I don't know what I'd do without you."

"Happy to help."

I hung up and put my food away. I'd lost my appetite.

My next step was talking to my boss.

**

I checked in with my supervisor's secretary. "I need to speak with Mrs. Smith, please."

"Regarding?"

I thought of a one-word answer. "Scheduling."

She took my name and got on the phone. There was some back and forth until she said, "Yes, ma'am" and hung up. To me she said, "She'll see you now."

I put on my best smile and entered the office. Since the Room, I knew she hadn't hired me on my merits but because my file was on top. I wasn't special to her in any way.

And now I was asking for a favor.

She looked up from her computer when I came in and took off her glasses. "Yes, Ms. Brogdon? How can I help you?"

She hadn't offered me a chair so I remained standing. "There's been an emergency and I need to leave early today and probably need the next two or three days off."

Her right eyebrow spoke its own language: she did not like what I'd said. "What's going on?"

"My friend's child is sick and the sitter won't take him until he's well."

"So you want time off to babysit?"

"Yes."

"And this isn't a family member?"

"No. But she's a close friend of the family. She has no one else to turn to but me. She can't stay home or else she'll lose her job."

Now I got both eyebrows. "And what about *your* job?"

"I . . . I would use my sick days, or personal days, or—"

"You haven't accrued any days yet."

Oh dear. "What if I take off for no pay?"

Mrs. Smith shook her head. "When you took this job, you made a commitment to do the job well and—"

"I believe I have been doing the job well."

She flipped a hand at my words. "You made a commitment to do the work. Here. In this office."

"I made a commitment to my friend too."

She sat back in her chair. "I would like to show compassion here, but if I give you special treatment, then I'll have a line out the door and down the hall of employees wanting such a favor. You know our backlog is huge and we need every body we can get."

"I know, and I'll work extra hours to make it up."

She shook her head. "If you're here, then I would have to be here. So that won't work."

"Can I do the work at home?"

"You cannot. There are security and confidentiality issues at play."

My breathing was heavy, like I'd been running. I *was* running—out of points to argue.

"Is there anything else, Mrs. Brogdon?" she said.

My mind had a thought which I discarded, then found myself saying out loud. "I'm sorry, but that means I have to quit."

"What?"

Though the words surprised me, as soon as they were out they felt right and good. I said them again with more certainty. "I quit. Family has to come first."

"But you said she's not family."

I took a fresh breath. "She is now."

With that, I walked out of her office.

I headed toward my cubicle. My entire body trembled and I felt on the verge of begging for my job back. To counter the impulse, I quickly stuffed a few personal items into my purse, grabbed my lunch bag and African violet, and made a beeline for the elevator.

"Hey, Lydia," someone called out. "Where you going?"

Now they paid attention to me?

"Home," I said.

**

I drove home, fueled with relief. And joy.

I'd never liked my job, but after meeting up with Nova and seeing how God had intervened to get me that job, I'd come to terms with it.

When I'd awakened that morning I'd never imagined I would be eating lunch at home.

I called Jeremy at work and didn't hedge. "I quit my job because Theo is sick and Nova can't find anyone to babysit."

There was a pause on the line. "Well then."

I continued. "Since I'm new, they wouldn't let me off so I quit. And . . . I'm sorry Jeremy but I feel awesome about it."

He chuckled. "I'm happy for you, Lyd."

I let out a breath. "You are?"

"Sure. You didn't like the job, but when you're with Theo you light up. God brought you and Nova together, so she and Theo have priority over any job."

I sank onto the couch and let the tears come.

"I hear you crying. Why are you crying?"

"Because you are the most wonderful, understanding, and supportive husband in the whole world."

"All that?"

"And more. I love you, Jeremy."

"I love you too."

As soon as we hung up I fell back on the cushions. There was someone else I needed to praise.

Dear Lord . . .

**

Nova and Theo were standing in front of their building. I pulled up, put my flashers on, and got the kid seat installed in the backseat.

I could tell Theo was sick because he was still. His head was nestled beneath Nova's chin, and his cheeks were flushed.

"There's Tylenol in his bag for bedtime, and a baby thermometer. He likes Jell-O because it's cool on his throat."

"Poor guy. I actually made some before I came, plus chocolate pudding."

Nova nodded. "You've had experience with this."

"I have." I touched his warm cheek. "We'll be just fine, won't we, Theo?"

Nova buckled him in and kissed him goodbye. We worked out the logistics for the next couple days. As I turned to get in the car, Nova surprised me by giving me a huge hug. "I don't know what we'd do without you, Lydia. Thank you."

"You're welcome."

Very welcome.

Chapter Thirty-One

Tony

But if we confess our sins to him,
he is faithful and just to forgive us our sins
and to cleanse us from all wickedness.
1 John 1: 9

Calling Nonna was going to be one of the most awkward phone calls I'd ever make.

I hadn't been a good grandson in the past few years. Actually, ever. After Papa died, I avoided her, my guilt eating at me every time I saw her. She was always nice and showed interest in me. But I quickly became the king of one-word answers. "Fine" and "Good" were my go-to words. Most of my family attributed my attitude to being a moody teenager. But after I hit my twenties, my parents talked to me about it. "Be nicer to Nonna. She's all alone."

Because of me.

In the past few years, I avoided family functions that involved seeing Nonna by saying I had to work late.

When I had a job.

Speaking of . . .

As I walked past the mailboxes in my apartment building's foyer, I saw a notice the landlord had posted announcing me as the new Maintenance Professional. I was hardly a professional, but the sign listed my number and encouraged people to call me with their concerns.

Which they had. I'd already replaced the innards of three toilets, repaired two garbage disposals, a few leaky sinks, and a sticky door. When I didn't know how to fix something, I found a video online. It really didn't take long, and people were nice. One woman gave me cookies. I'd even started keeping a list of names and apartment numbers so I could say hi when I saw them.

On the way to my car, I did just that. "Hey, Rhonda. Toilet working okay?"

"Just great, Tony. Have a good day."

"You too."

Me. Saying hi to neighbors. Never in a million.

I got in the car, took out my phone, and quit procrastinating. I called Nonna.

As it rang, my nerves started to flare. How was I going to do this?

She answered on the fifth ring. "Hey, Nonna. It's Tony." Why did I expect her to say, "Tony who?"

"Hello!" She sounded enthusiastic. "How are you, Antonio?"

I used my fallback answer. "Good. I'm doing good. How are you?"

"I'm as fine as an old woman can be. But I miss seeing my handsome grandson."

Her kindness was humbling. "Well . . . about that, I was wondering if I could come over and visit."

I heard her suck in a breath. "Of course you can. Anytime."

"Is now okay?"

"Now is perfect. You've made me very happy."

"See you soon."

That was way too easy. I'd expected her to throw in a few well-earned digs, but she hadn't. I glanced at the tin box on the passenger seat. Would she be as gracious when she found out what I'd done?

I passed a grocery store that had a window banner advertising flowers. I stopped and came out with a mixed bouquet in a vase. Yes, it was a bribe. I could use all the help I could get.

Five minutes later I pulled into Nonna's driveway. She lived in the same house they'd always lived in. Mom and Dad had tried to get her to move to a retirement place but she'd refused. Why stir things up by moving? I admired her spunk.

I sat in the car and tried to tap into my missing attributes like courage, honor, and humility. I'd always assumed those qualities were meant for someone else, not me. Never me. I'd given up all rights to even think of claiming them as my own.

Until the woods. Until the He-and-me moment. Until I stopped fighting against the good in my life.

Now it was time to put up or shut up. The past had to be finished, and confessing to Nonna was the final step.

"Okay then," I said to the car. "Here I go." I slipped the cookie tin under my jacket and carried the flowers to the door. I knocked.

"Come in," she called out.

The smell of the past roared back to me: the mustiness of dust and antique furniture, the smell of coffee, and a faint floral scent that was Nonna's perfume. I found her sitting in her pink, upholstered chair near the window. Nothing had changed. It was her spot.

"Hi, Nonna. These are for you." I held the vase close so she could smell them.

"They're lovely, Antonio. You didn't have to do that."

I kinda did.

"Set them on the coffee table so I can look at them all day."

I moved a few magazines aside and set them in the center. They *did* look nice.

"Now for a hug." She held out her arms to me.

I managed an awkward hug. Her cheek was soft against mine.

Then I sat on the couch and slipped the tin under a pillow. How should I begin?

"I'm ever so glad to see you, Antonio. How have you been?"

Oddly, I wasn't prepared for small talk. I was so focused on my goal that I'd forgotten the need to be polite. "I'm doing okay." I tried to think of positive things. "I got a new job, fixing things around my apartment complex. And I've been to a few of Zach's ball games."

"I miss seeing him. You should bring him over."

I'd never thought about the divorce affecting Nonna. "I'll see what I can do."

"It must be hard to live without him. And Penny. I bet you're lonely."

I had been. But then I thought of Gracie. "Actually, I met a real nice lady. Her name's Gracie."

Nonna clapped her hands together. "Good for you. I've been praying you find someone else."

"You have?"

She cocked her head. "Of course. I pray for my family every day."

I nodded, but looked at the carpet. I didn't pray for anyone. Except maybe myself.

"Now then," Nonna said. "What brings you here on this beautiful day?"

I glanced toward the stairs leading to the basement. I had to restrain myself from letting it all out in a rush, in a purging of the pain.

"Whatever it is . . . it's all right," Nonna said. Her eyebrows dipped with concern. "You can tell me anything and everything, Antonio. I'm a good listener."

I nodded and took a deep breath. "I have a confession to make."

She nodded once. "Are you in trouble?"

"I was. I mean, what happened was a long time ago. Twenty-five years ago."

She blinked a few times, looked up, then down. Then her eyes met mine. "When you stole my jewelry?"

The air went out of me. I fell back against the cushions. "What?" My voice was unsteady.

Nonna pushed against the doily-covered armrests and sat up straighter. "So it *was* you?"

She *hadn't* known, but now . . . "It was me. And two friends. I'm really sorry."

She started to nod, then stopped. "Don't you think that was something you should have said back then?"

"I was scared." I looked toward the hallway leading to the bedrooms—and the bathroom. "Especially after Papa died."

She closed her eyes and sighed. "That was a very, very bad day."

I hadn't planned on talking about Papa but since she already knew about the stealing . . . "If you only knew how bad it was. Oh, Nonna. I'm an awful person." Guilt burrowed deeper into my chest. "It wasn't just stealing. As we were leaving I heard a thud. I heard Papa call for help."

Her eyes grew wide.

I put a hand to my brow to partially cover my eyes so I couldn't see her, feeling like a little kid hiding in plain sight. "I thought he needed help with bathroom stuff and I didn't want to help like that. So . . . I just left him. And ran. I didn't know it was serious. I really didn't." Tears came and suddenly I was across the room, sitting on the ottoman in front of her chair, holding her hands. "I'm so sorry. I didn't mean for him to die. I should've helped him. If only I would've helped him."

She studied my face for a moment. Her eyes were deep brown, her lashes matching her silver hair.

She reached forward and cupped the side of my head. "Shush now. If only *I'd* been home to help him. If only he would have come with me to the church dinner he would have been around a lot of people when he collapsed. If only he'd gone to the doctor regularly. "

I sniffed and sat back. "So who's to blame?"

She touched my cheek. "No one, Antonio. We can acknowledge all the 'if not for this' moments, but we can't dwell on them. I miss him every day but the bottom line is, it happened. He died. And we grieved."

"I did. I really did."

She cocked her head, studying me. "Do you know how I guessed you were guilty of the theft?"

"How?"

"By *how* you grieved. You weren't just grieving Papa, you were grieving something else. You pulled away, grieving over what you'd done."

I remembered the feelings as if they were yesterday. "Everything changed that day. I felt guilty about Papa dying, guilty about lying to you, and guilty for letting two stupid friends goad me into stealing."

She gave me a grandma-look. "So it's their fault?"

With just that look, I was a kid again. "I mean, partly their fault. I wanted them to like me. They said they needed money."

"But *you* made the choice."

There was no getting around it. I drew in a deep breath. I needed to admit what I had been denying for over half my life. "Yes, I made the choice. I could've done something to stop it, but I didn't." Nonna sat in silence, letting my admission linger. "If you suspected, why didn't you say anything?"

She looked past me to the flowers. "The life lessons we remember most are best learned by living through them, not being hit over the head with them."

"I remember it all right."

"Plus, I didn't want to believe it. Not you. Not my Antonio."

Somehow her disappointment cut through me more than any imagined anger. "I wish I could take it back."

"But you can't. Regret is relentless. The trick is to stop yourself *before* you make the big mistakes. As well as the small ones."

I wasn't sure I'd learned that lesson either.

"The real question is what happened to the jewelry? Did you sell it?"

"The other two guys pawned their part of it."

"The other two . . . but not you?"

I retrieved the rusty tin and handed it to her.

Her breath caught as she set it on her lap and ran her fingers along the rusted poinsettias. "We used to store Christmas cookies in tins like this."

"This one was Mom's."

"It's certainly seen better days."

"That's because it's been buried in in the woods all this time."

"You buried it?"

"I didn't want the jewelry around the house where it would remind me of what I'd done. Open it."

Her eyes brightened. "My jewelry is really in here?"

"A few things."

Her fingers didn't work as good as they used to. I sat on the ottoman again and helped her pry the lid off. She gasped. "Oh. Oh my."

I'd taken the items out of the plastic bags, and had cleaned out the inside of the tin. She gently touched the velvet bag before delicately opening it. She spilled the pearls onto her lap, then picked them up lovingly. Her voice broke and tears welled in her eyes. "I'd resigned myself to never seeing these again." Her lip quivered. "Your Papa gave me this necklace as a wedding present." She held it to her neck. "Help me put it on." I fumbled with the clasp, but finally got it. "Now get me the hand mirror from my dresser." I got it for her and she looked at her reflection, touching the pearls, remembering . . .

"You look beautiful, Nonna."

"I look old. But they, *they,* are beautiful. The memory is beautiful." She turned her attention back to the tin, noticing the blue leather case. "Is this what I hope it is?"

"Open it."

The hinges of the case creaked as it was opened. She sighed when she saw the medal. "Your papa was so proud of this."

"He had a right to be. I remember him saying he was injured by bomb shrapnel."

"It's good you remember. That's what medals are for, to remember the sacrifice and bravery of the soldier." She gazed at the award.

I let her linger in her memories. I could tell it was much more than a medal to her, it represented Papa and their lives together.

Nonna finally closed the lid and held the case toward me. "Antonio, I want you to have this."

I shook my head adamantly. "No, no, no. I don't deserve to have it."

She paused a moment. "It's not about what you deserve. It's about what Papa deserved. And he deserved to have his family remember his sacrifice. If not you, then give it to your son. To Zach. Tell him about his great-grandfather's service."

I nodded, and a lump formed in my throat. It was a wonderful idea.

Nonna closed the tin and handed it back. "As a reminder of your folly."

I smiled. "I don't need a reminder. I've thought about it every day for twenty-five years."

She made a *tsk tsk* sound and pointed a finger at me. "Now that's a mighty waste of a life. How do you think those years would have been different if you'd owned up to it and returned these things right away?"

It was a powerful question. "I was so afraid you'd be mad and hate me. Plus I thought I caused Papa's death. I just couldn't do it."

She clasped her hands on her lap. "I wouldn't have been mad at you then, just like I'm not mad at you now—just sad and disappointed. And I would never hate you." She smiled her Nonna smile. "I love you, Antonio."

My throat tightened. "I love you too." I cleared my throat. "I didn't expect you to be so kind."

Nonna shook her head. "What point is there in being angry? Would anger change the facts of that night?"

"No."

"Did Papa suddenly *not* die?"

"No."

"Then you've wasted your adult life worrying about facts that couldn't be changed."

The truth hit me like a slug to my stomach. "I feel so stupid."

"Stupid is as stupid does." She scooted forward on her chair so she could put her hands on my knees. "You were a kid who should have known better—who *knew* better. You made a mistake. But you've spent the last twenty-five years lugging that mistake around like a fifty-pound pack."

"That's for sure."

"How did it make you feel?"

I tried to swallow, finally facing the emotions.

"Come now, *mio caro*. Recognize the truth and speak it."

"I felt guilty and . . . worthless. I didn't feel like I would ever amount to much. I've never thought I deserved to be happy."

"Or to feel loved?"

Her words hit me like hard slap. I remembered arguments I'd had with Penny and every other woman I'd ever dated. They'd often said, *Why won't you let me love you, Tony?*

"I pushed people away."

Nonna scoffed. "Because of some jewelry."

"Because of Papa."

Her voice grew harsh. "Enough of that. Papa had a bad heart. We knew it would probably kill him one day."

"He did? You did?"

She nodded once, as if that was that. "It wasn't your fault, Antonio."

I sighed, letting the words melt into my soul.

"Plus . . ." She took a fresh breath. "I'm far from perfect myself. I've made plenty of mistakes in my eighty-eight years, but one thing I've learned is that problems and mistakes are best taken care of sooner rather than later. 'Confess your sins to each other and pray for each other so that you may be healed.'"

"Healed? Forgiven?"

"*Certamente*. You can't get one without the other."

I focused on her wrinkled hands and took them in mine. "Will *you* forgive me?"

She squeezed my hands. "I will. I do. And so does Jesus."

I shrugged.

She chucked me under the chin hard, lifting it so I had to look at her eyes. "You act like His forgiveness is nothing. Or like you don't believe it."

"It's just hard to imagine."

Nonna shook her head back and forth, back and forth. "Jesus took the punishment *we* deserve. All of us. All the time. Past, present, and future." She leveled me with a look. "Or do you think you're special and are beyond the power of His sacrifice? Is that it?"

I pulled back. "No. No. I don't mean that. I did think that, but . . . I've changed." I remembered my special time in the woods and how I'd felt the new lightness and freedom coursing through my body. "I know I'm forgiven."

"You don't sound totally convinced." Suddenly Nonna slapped my knee and sat back. "Ah! *Magari!* I know what the problem is. You haven't forgiven *yourself*."

My first impulse was to deny it, and yet . . . her explanation seemed spot on. "Maybe . . ."

"Maybe nothing," she said. "Do it right now."

"Do what right now?"

"Thank Jesus for His forgiveness, and tell Him you forgive yourself."

I felt vulnerable and exposed. I didn't want to say such things in front of another person.

"Go on now. If you feel awkward, so be it. Call it restitution for your crime."

I sighed. "I'll do whatever I need to pay for it."

She shook a finger at me. "You have *been* paying for it, Antonio! Now's the time to break free of it." She pointed at the tin box. "Keeping things hidden in the woods kept the truth hidden, kept you a prisoner. But now you've dug up your past and filled in the hole. Soon grass will grow over the scar and no one will ever know what was there. Jesus will make your scar disappear in an instant so you can leave the past behind. Just say the words."

I felt my throat grow tight as I anticipated the words I had to say. I took a deep breath and bowed my head. "Jesus? I confess to the stealing, ignoring Papa, not telling people, and holding onto it for twenty-five years. But now . . . thank You for forgiving me. And help me forgive myself so I can move on." I thought of one more thing. "I really want to be a better person. Please help me do that. Amen." I looked up and saw Nonna smiling at me.

"*Bravissimo,* Antonio. Now give me another hug."

**

I rushed into Harvey's apartment. "Harvey?"

He wasn't in the kitchen or the living room—I could see both as soon as I opened the door. The TV was off. I didn't want to spook him, so I knocked on the opened front door and called out again. "Harvey? You here?"

No answer. I dashed into the hallway of the bedroom and bathroom but both doors were open. He wasn't there. He never went out anymore. Not without me.

His walker. He wouldn't go anywhere without his walker.

My heart began to beat wildly as I did another quick look and didn't see it anywhere.

Then I heard a tapping on glass.

I looked at the sliding glass door leading to the tiny balcony that he never used.

There he was!

I slid open the door and found him sitting on his walker's seat. There weren't any chairs out there so he'd created one.

"You worried me," I said. "What are you doing out here?"

"Breathing in. Breathing out. An hour ago I looked in this direction and saw a robin on the railing. He reminded me it was spring." He shrugged. "I got the notion to get some fresh air."

There was nothing wrong with what he'd done, it just surprised me. "Maybe we should put a chair out here."

He tapped the handles of his walker. "No room to maneuver with a chair *and* this. The walker works just fine." He studied me a moment. "How'd it go with Nonna?"

I couldn't help but smile. "Better than expected."

He pointed toward inside. "Help me back in and you can tell me everything."

With a lot of maneuvering we got him inside to his recliner. "So boy. How'd it go?"

"Nonna already knew."

Harvey nodded and smiled. "I'm not surprised."

I was shocked. "Why do you say that?"

"You don't have a poker face, Tony. Plus, it's hard for a teenage to hide their feelings, especially if they're feeling guilty. She had t have seen your pain." He shifted on his chair. "What did she sa when you gave the jewelry back?"

I remembered her face. The sad-happy face. "She was happy. I helped her put on the pearls."

"I bet she looked right pretty."

"She did. She told me to keep the Purple Heart to give to Zach."

Harvey slapped his thigh. "That's a grand idea."

I nodded. But then I ran a hand through my hair. "There's more."

He seemed surprised. "What else?"

"It turns out Papa had heart issues. She doesn't blame me for his death."

"She sounds like a very gracious lady."

"She forgives me, said God forgives me, and . . ."

"And?"

"She got me to forgive myself."

Harvey nodded and looked toward the balcony. "That's often the hardest part." He looked back to me. "How do you feel?"

A good question. "I feel . . . better. Free-er."

He touched my arm. "'If the Son sets you free, you are truly free.'"

It sounded so simple. "Even if that's true, it—"

"Even *if*?"

"Even *though* it's true, I think it's going to take practice for me to live differently."

"As expected."

Harvey made it seem possible. I was so lucky to have him to cheer me on.

"What now?" he asked.

I'd thought about this. "I need to give the medal to Zach soon."

"Then do it. Go over there today."

"It's not that easy. I missed his birthday and got him a present way late. Penny is mad at me." I added under my breath, "She's always mad at me."

"Rightfully so?"

I snickered. "Thanks, Harvey."

He shrugged. "Just asking." Then he said, "I'd like to meet Penny and Zach. And your Nonna. Can something be arranged?"

I loved the sounds of that. Harvey was on my side. Nonna was on my side. They would be good buffers between me, my ex, and my son. "I'll call Penny and see what I can do."

**

Penny sighed when she knew it was me on the phone. "Yes, Tony?"

There was a *what now?* inflection to her voice.

I almost said, *Don't sound so excited* but held it in. "I have a favor to ask you."

"I can hardly wait."

I deserved every snide comment. "I just talked to Nonna and—"

"*You* talked to Nonna?"

I deserved that too. "I'll tell you about it sometime. But the reason I called is because I have something I want to give to Zach, something real special."

"Another belated birthday present?"

The jibes just kept coming. "Something like that."

"I suppose it can be arranged."

"Good. And . . . I've got a new friend I'd like you both to meet. A nice old guy who lives in the apartment next to me."

"Because you have such a way with old people?"

"Stop it, okay? Everything you're saying is true, but give me a break, Pen. Please. I'm trying to do something good here."

There was a moment's pause, then she said. "Okay. You met an old guy . . ."

"His name is Harvey and he's amazing. He wants to meet Nonna, and I have something for Zach, so I was wondering if you could have one of your great dinners."

"You almost sound sentimental."

Actually . . . "So will you?"

"Sure. Sunday is Easter."

"It is?"

She laughed. "Do you even have a calendar, Tony? Zach and I are going to church and I was planning on picking up Nonna. We could all meet at the house after."

Although I couldn't believe I was saying it, I said, "Actually, can we go to church with you too?"

"You're kidding."

"I'm not." Suddenly I got another idea. "And can I bring someone else?"

"You have *two* friends?"

"As a matter of fact I do. Her name is Gracie."

She didn't say anything, but I guessed what she was thinking. "I know it's odd that you—my ex—would let a girlfriend of mine come to dinner, but—"

"It's beyond odd, but hey . . . why not? Church starts at ten, but get there early because there's usually a crowd for Easter."

"Will do. Thanks, Penny."

I hung up and fist-pumped the air.

I called Gracie next, but she didn't answer. I was about to leave a message when I decided it would be best to ask her in person.

Besides, I wanted to see her. Very, very much.

Chapter Thirty-Two

Gracie

I have swept away your sins like a cloud.
I have scattered your offenses like the morning mist.
Oh, return to me, for I have paid the price to set you free.
Isaiah 44: 22

On Saturday at noon, Wesley told me I could go home early. I was glad for the free time because I wanted to post some *good* news for a change. I wasn't going to share details of the Room, but the lessons I'd learned? That was something I could write about.

After I'd changed into my comfy clothes I sat on my bed and opened my laptop. I tried to get situated by adjusting the pillows behind me. But as I did so, my computer slipped off my lap and nearly toppled to the floor.

That was a close one.

As I got out of bed to get the pillows put into position, I thought—for the umpteenth time—about moving my office to somewhere more stable. Living alone with Dad had given my room additional functions. It had become an office, sanctuary, and hiding place. When he got sick, I'd also used it as a living room because being in close proximity to his room—and his frequent needs—was the logical thing to do. But now Dad was gone.

I looked around the bedroom. I had a regular kitchenette going on near the door. Online I'd bought a mini-fridge and an immersion water-heater for coffee—all because of Dad's acute hearing. Before then, if I snuck off to the kitchen to get something to eat or drink, he'd invariably hear and call me into his room for this or that. Soon after those additions, I added a basket of snacks, protein bars, and Reese's Pieces to appease my need for nutrition—or anti-nutrition. The bedroom fully evolved into a living room when I subscribed to online streaming services to watch on my laptop. Add a pair of earbuds and I was content in my quiet, self-contained girl-cave.

And yet . . . as I gave the space another look, had it also become a room of confinement? Other than going to the bathroom and the kitchen for Dad's meals, this one room had been my world.

I turned in a slow circle—twice—then had an epiphany: it was time to move out of my cave and claim the house. The whole of the house.

For it was *my* house now.

I left the laptop behind and did a walk-through, trying to see the other rooms with fresh eyes.

First stop was Mom and Dad's room. Since it was the biggest bedroom it was logical I should take it for myself. I stood in the doorway, letting the memories flood in. I ran my fingers across the 1950s walnut dresser. The wood was so smooth. As the person who did the laundry I knew what was in every drawer and closet. Mom's clothes were still there. Early on I'd asked Dad if he wanted me to move them out but he'd said no. I'd actually been relieved and had never asked again. But now . . .

I stood at the foot of the bed. How many times had I smoothed Grandma Sturgess' "Wedding Ring" quilt and tucked it around Mom, and then Dad?

Suddenly I couldn't stand the sight of it.

With a burst of emotion, I yanked the quilt off the bed, sending pillows flying. I wadded it up in my arms, strode through the house, and tossed it unceremoniously in the garage where it landed on the hood of the car.

I slammed the door shut and stood in the kitchen. My heart was racing. But as it calmed, my fresh eyes saw the kitchen for what it was: an outdated, broken down, rather sad space where meals had been made for a lovely dying mother and a bitter ungrateful father. It had ceased being a happy place ages ago.

I moved to the living room—where very little living had been done in over a decade. Dad's ugly recliner held the prime spot to view the ancient TV. There was a floral couch with tufted cushions where I'd been assigned to sit, and a glider-rocker where Mom crocheted while she and Dad watched "CSI" and "Survivor"—Dad's choices, not hers.

One time when he'd been invited to see a Chiefs game in person I'd found Mom sitting in his recliner watching "Gilmore Girls." As soon as I came in, she clicked the footrest down and shut the program off. I sat on the couch and asked her to turn it back on, which she did—hesitantly. I still remembered that special evening. We laughed at the rapid-fire dialogue and rooted for Lorelai to get with Luke. I never forgot Mom saying, "Wouldn't it be fun if you and I lived in Stars Hollow?" *Without Dad* wasn't said but was understood.

I sat in Mom's rocker and glided up and back a few times. There was a slight squeak in it, but I didn't mind. The sound had always been there. I created a rhythm, lulling myself into my memories.

I heard a car go by outside and realized Mom's chair faced th TV but also had a prime view out the living room window. B design? While Dad was watching what he wanted to watch, how many times had she stared outside wanting to be *away?* It was od that I didn't really know if she and Dad had been happy. remembered them arguing occasionally but as soon as I came in th room Mom always smiled like nothing was wrong. And probabl nothing was as long as she followed Dad's rules and anticipated h needs. I wasn't sure if I should admire her sacrifices or feel sorry fc her. Or angry.

It didn't matter anymore. Both of my parents had been silenced

On the floor next to Mom's chair was her sewing basket. In th evenings she crocheted or did other needlework.

Why hadn't I moved the basket? She'd died fourteen years ag It's like I'd let the house become her memorial, allowing all he possessions to sit as they'd always sat when she was alive.

I set the basket on my lap. There was a pincushion on the li filled with pins and needles with various colored thread hangin from them like happy streamers. Inside were an assortment of croch hooks and thicker thread. There was one item half done— snowflake. She'd always been the one to hang her snowflakes on th Christmas tree.

"If only I'd let you teach me how to crochet," I said to the emp room.

I noticed a piece of paper sticking out of a side pocket. I read silently, then read it aloud. There were verses from Ephesians: "'G rid of all bitterness, rage, anger, harsh words, and slander, as well a all types of evil behavior. Instead, be kind to each othe tenderhearted, forgiving one another, just as God through Christ ha forgiven you.'"

I was suddenly overcome with emotions rising out of th deepest part of me. Mom had lived this verse. She'd never spoke harsh words *to* Dad or *about* Dad. She'd been kind and tender-hearte to everyone, especially him. She'd forgiven him. Repeatedly.

But why?

I slapped a hand over my mouth as if I could keep the ang words of the past from coming out.

Yet it was too late. An awful truth hit me hard: I enjoyed beir bitter and angry. I liked playing the martyr, thinking bad though about Dad, letting him bully me into being his servant. I liked playir the victim: online, with Tony, and even with Wesley. Yet Mom's li had been a reflection of grace and kindness. She'd shown me how deal with Dad by her example. Why had I done the opposite?

I thought about the scenes I'd watched in the Room. Time after time God had offered me a way out of the house to get a reprieve from my prison. He'd sent a helpful friend, a chance to take classes, and a woman at the courthouse urging me to speak the truth. He'd sent me—not one but two— kind men I could have loved.

I'd ignored each chance, brushing them away like a pesky fly, choosing to marinate in my bitterness, blocking out anything good.

I checked the verses again, focusing on the last few lines. "'Forgiving one another, just as God through Christ has forgiven you.'"

Had I ignored God's interventions because I didn't want to forgive my father? Or forgive God for making my life so hard?

I closed my eyes and let my mind, heart, and soul whirl with regrets, misery, and squandered hope.

I let my hands fall into my lap and leaned my head back. "God? I'm so sorry for not seeing You. You were trying to help and I wouldn't let You. I was so mad at Dad—and at You." I took in a ragged breath. "Forgive me."

I was immediately jolted out of my thoughts when the doorbell rang.

God was at the door?

I shook my head against the stupid thought.

I ran my hands over my face and took a few deep breaths to get a hold of myself.

I walked to the door and opened it.

It was Tony. "Hi there," I said.

"Hi yourself." He had a sweet smile on his face—a smile I loved to see.

But then the dam of my emotions broke and I started to sob. He rushed inside and wrapped his arms around me. "What's wrong? Oh Gracie. What's going on?"

He hugged me so tight. I couldn't remember the last time someone had really held me as if they were willing to be my strength. I clung to him as though my life depended on it. I tucked my head against his shoulder.

He stroked my hair and rocked ever-so-slightly. "It'll be okay. I promise."

They were five trite words that people said when they didn't know what else to say. Yet they were five words that I clung to, hoping this time they were true.

His movements became slow and steady. Finally my tears waned. I took an unsteady breath and let go of him, giving both of us space to breathe. I swiped at my wet cheeks and took a deep breath.

"Let's start over. Hi, Tony."

He gave me a soft smile. "Hi yourself. Do you want to tell me what's going on?"

"Actually, I think I do. Come sit down."

I led him to the couch and angled toward him so I could see his face as I talked. His expression was patient, interested, and kind. I was so lucky to have him in my life.

Now, where to start?

Out of the blue I remembered a relevant scene from the Room. "Do you remember helping a woman jump-start her car in a Target parking lot?"

He blinked a few times. "Vaguely. I think that may have happened a few years ago? Yeah. I guess I do."

"Well, the woman you helped? That was me."

He blinked a couple times more. "No way."

I nodded. "I saw it in the Room. God sent you to me."

He chuckled nervously. "Wow."

"You gave me your phone number."

"I guess I did," he said. "You never called."

"I did not. But I should have." I leaned over and took his hand in mine. "I don't want there to be any pressure between us to do or be anything. But I like the idea that God wanted us to meet then, and now."

He winked. "I like that idea too."

Instead of shoving him away or turning my back on the idea of him, I found myself eager to let him in. I squeezed his hand, then stood.

He shook his head, pulling me down to the couch. "You don't get off that easy. Why were you so upset?"

If anyone would know about wasting years on a false notion it was Tony. "I just realized I've spent the last fourteen years playing the martyr. I've rejected every person and every thing God placed in my life to set me free." I looked down. "I chose to be miserable."

He lifted my chin gently. "From what you told me, it was your dad who *made* you miserable."

"I'm not saying I didn't have reasons to feel that way, but I think I wanted Dad to suffer by suffering myself."

"And did he?"

I snickered. "Not a bit. He didn't even notice I was suffering. He was in a world of his own making and he dragged me into it slamming the door behind me." I thought of something. "Or maybe—like a true martyr—I did the slamming." I got up to retrieve Mom's note from the sewing basket. "This is how I should have dealt with Dad."

Tony read the verses, his eyebrows rising. "Pretty powerful. That certainly has never been me."

"It wasn't me either." I took the note back. "But it was my mom. She was the kindest, most loving and generous person I've ever met."

"I wish I could've met her."

"Me too." I tucked the paper back where it belonged. "Her ability to forgive . . . it was unmatched. I have a long way to go to learn how to do that."

Tony scooted close and put an arm around my shoulders. "Your dad's only been gone a few months. Don't be so hard on yourself."

He was so kind. I kissed his cheek. "Thanks."

"Anytime."

We shared a look. I loved his chocolate eyes.

He touched my cheek. "If there's anything I can do to help . . ."

I smiled. "I'll remember that."

Then I snuggled against his chest and savored the moment.

**

The mantel clock struck the half-hour, breaking through the lovely time I'd spent in Tony's arms. I sat up.

"That was nice," he said.

I smiled and squeezed his knee. "It was." I looked around the living room, then glanced toward the kitchen. I remembered what I'd been doing before Tony had stopped by.

I stood. "You mentioned wanting to help?"

"I did."

"I may take you up on that offer sooner rather than later."

He stood beside me. "Tell me what you need."

"Follow me." I led him into the kitchen. "Before you came over I was doing an inventory of my life. I realized I've kept most of this house like it was when Mom was alive."

"How many years has it been?"

"Fourteen. Ridiculous, isn't it?"

He chuckled. "I'm not going to argue with you."

It felt good to laugh. I ran a hand over the mauve countertops. "I want to remodel the entire house. Make it mine."

"That's a great idea. But it's a big project."

"It is—but I'm ready for a big project. Plus, I know a certain handsome handyman who does great work."

"Me? You want me to fix up your house?" He looked a little shell-shocked.

I shrugged. I wasn't sure what construction talents Tony possessed. "At least help me figure out what to do and hire the right people to do it?"

He looked relieved. "*That,* I can do."

Suddenly I remembered he'd come over on his own. "I'm sorry I hijacked you as soon as you walked in. Did you have something you wanted to see me about?"

"I wanted to ask you to go to church with my family tomorrow and then go to Penny's house for Easter dinner. Harvey and Nonna are coming too. You'd get to meet all the important people in my life."

It was unusual to be invited to the ex's house for a holiday, but obviously Penny was okay with it. Actually, I was very touched. "I'd love to." When Tony beamed I felt something stir inside, a desire to be kind to him. Tenderhearted. And loving.

My mother would have been proud.

Chapter Thirty-Three

Minnie

Be on guard. Stand firm in the faith.
Be courageous. Be strong.
1 Corinthians 16: 13

It was Saturday. Museum day. Gabe day. A trifecta.

I got dressed—twice. I started with jeans, then spotted a pink T-shirt dress that Claudia had bought for me. Gabe always saw me in jeans, why not dress up a bit? To further show him—and me—that this was a real date, I left my hair down, spent more than fifteen-seconds on makeup, and wore hoop earrings rather than the silver studs I rarely changed. I even borrowed a pair of Claudia's sandals—she, Dad, and the twins weren't home, but I knew she wouldn't mind. I stood in front of her full-length mirror and swished the skirt of my dress back and forth. "Not bad, girl."

Ten minutes later I met Gabe at the door, ready to go. He gave me a full once-over. "Wow. You look beautiful."

I felt myself blush. "Why, thank you, sir. You look pretty nice yourself." He was always so put-together. Classic. He wore a blue tee-shirt under a blue check shirt he left open, jeans, and white leather sneakers. I was glad I'd dressed up a bit.

He bent down to give me a kiss on the cheek and whispered, "I'd like to meet your family."

"Sorry. Claudia's sister is in town and they all went to lunch."

He raised an eyebrow. "Another time then? Soon?"

"Absolutely." Whenever I spent time with Gabe, my nervousness about having my family meet him eased a little more. But Dad could be stubborn and over-protective. I didn't want them to ruin things just as our relationship was beginning.

We headed to the car and Gabe opened the door for me. When he got in, he said,. "You don't seem very excited to introduce me to your family."

"I am. Really. But it hasn't even been a week since Dad agreed to let me change majors. One change at a time."

He still didn't start the car. "Do they know about me at all?"

"Of course they do." I assured him, fidgeting with my purse.

"And they know we're going to the museum today."

"Well that's something. Do they know I'm an art major too?"

"They do . . ."

"Do they think I pressured you to change?"

I smiled sweetly and touched his face. "I don't know what they think, but *I* know I wouldn't be doing this without knowing you."

"Like I said—"

"I think you graduating in art is a huge bonus."

He smiled and kissed my hand. "Huge double bonus."

He finally started the car and we were off.

**

Nearing downtown Kansas City, I realized how seldom I'd been there. "I'm glad you're driving," I said. "I barely know where anything is."

"How is that possible when you've lived here your whole life?"

"Going downtown wasn't often on the agenda. I think Mom took me to 'Nutcracker' one time."

"You definitely need to get out more," he said. "There's a lot to do down here."

I touched his arm and smiled. "You'll have to show me."

"Gladly."

We drove to the museum's parking garage but there was a sign saying it was full. "No problem," Gabe said. "I know a place." He drove around the block and entered a gravel parking lot. "It's a bit of a walk," he said.

"I don't mind."

We walked hand-in-hand toward the museum. I liked people seeing us as a couple. I liked *being* a couple.

At the last corner we waited for the WALK light. A woman with a stroller came up next to me. I glanced at her, then did a double take.

"Nova?"

She studied me a minute. "Minnie?"

We laughed and hugged. "I haven't seen you in ages," I said. We both looked down at the toddler and I remembered why I hadn't seen her. The school grapevine had been brutal about Nova getting pregnant and dropping out her junior year.

She swept an arm toward the child in the stroller. "Put it this way… I've been a bit busy."

The four of us moved out of the way of the foot-traffic. I put my hand on Gabe's arm. "Gabe, this is Nova . . ." I wasn't sure about her last name. If she'd married . . .

"Wilson. It's still Wilson."

Raising a child alone. I couldn't imagine. "Nova, this is Gabe Morton."

"Nice to meet you," Gabe said. He leaned down to kid level, and shook the little boy's hand. "Glad to meet you, my man. And you are…?"

"His name's Theo." Nova smiled.

"He's adorable." Theo gave Gabe a toothy grin.

The light changed again but we stayed put. "We're going to the art museum. Are you going there too?"

Nova scoffed. "No. Theo and I live down here." She pointed north. "I just took him to the library." She looked across the street at the museum. "I've seen the banners for a painting exhibit. I still remember you and me painting backdrops for 'Fiddler on the Roof.' You had a real gift for it."

"You painted too."

"I filled in the outlines that you drew."

She was right.

"You had real talent," Nova said.

I wanted to tell her I was majoring in art, but since Nova never graduated from high school, I kept quiet.

Theo started to fuss so Nova squatted down to check on him.

Suddenly a man bumped into me. Turning, he grabbed Nova's purse from the handles of the stroller and ran.

"Hey!" Nova shouted.

Without thinking I ran after him. "Stop him!" I yelled.

The guy was fast, but there were a lot of people on the sidewalk so he had to bob and weave. Right before the next intersection a guy stepped in front of him, making him fall.

It gave me time to catch up. I snatched the purse out of his hands. "This isn't yours!" I yelled.

The man scrambled to his feet and ran away.

I looked down at the purse, completely out of breath. Gabe caught up to me. "Wow, Min. That was some sprint."

People started to clap. Everybody was looking at me. I nodded at the guy who'd help bring him down and he raised his arms like Rocky at the top of the steps. More applause. We fist bumped. "Way to go, girl," he said.

I clutched Nova's purse to my chest and Gabe and I walked back to her. Adrenaline, mixed with the physical exertion of running, was making my heart beat out of my chest.

I gave her the purse. "Here you go."

Nova gave me a hug. "You're my hero, Min. Thanks so much."

I was still out of breath. "I can't believe I did that."

Gabe smiled. "Hail Minerva! Slayer of bandits!"

Nova laughed. "I owe you one."

"I'm glad it turned out okay." I was still stunned that I had *run* after him. In a dress.

Nova adjusted her purse across her body. "I need to get going. I have to get Theo home and then go to work."

"Where do you work?"

"Nelly's Diner." Nova's face lit up. "Hey, after you two are through with the museum come over for a late lunch or pie. Whatever you want." She pointed up the street. "Two blocks on the right. It will be my treat for saving my purse."

I looked at Gabe. He nodded.

"Thanks Nova," I said. "It was real nice seeing you again."

"Thanks for being in the right place at the right time to save the day," Nova said. "I'll catch you later."

As she walked off I made a beeline toward a bench. "I need to sit." As Gabe sat beside me I said, "I don't know what I was thinking—even as I was running after him I couldn't believe what I was doing. That was so not me."

"Not the old you. But the new, more courageous, brave, and assertive Minnie . . ."

"Am I all that?"

"Like Nova said, God put you in the right place at the right time."

I rolled my eyes. "She didn't mention God."

"Her mistake. But you gotta admit, God gave you a chance to be courageous. And you took it."

"If that *is* true, I'd like to ask Him to let me rest before giving me another chance."

A lot of people walked past us, heading toward the museum. "You'll have plenty of time to rest later," Gabe said. "We should get in line." He offered his arm. "You up to it, Miss Heroine?"

I was. I absolutely was.

**

I sat on a bench in the museum, surrounded by all things Monet And Cassatt. And Renoir. And and and . . .

Gabe sat quietly beside me. I appreciated his ability to let us just be in the moment, to soak it in and let the beauty wrap around us like a lovely cocoon.

The vivid colors, the brush strokes, the light. The capturing of a single moment—an impression—overwhelmed me.

Suddenly, without meaning to speak aloud I said, "I want to do this."

Instead of saying something trite like, "You should" or "Then do it" Gabe surprised me by asking, "Why?"

How insightful. How empathetic. How astute he was.

His eyes caught mine and in a flash I knew that years from now I would say that *this* was the moment when I started to fall in love with him. And I would definitively be able to say that this was the moment when I understood why God wanted us to meet.

He was waiting for my answer. I drew in a long breath, hoping I could put words to my immense longing. "You asked why I want to paint like this?" I checked his expression. He was seriously interested. "I want to make people feel something when they look at my paintings."

"How do these paintings make *you* feel?"

"Calm. Yet excited. Like the whole world stopped at this exact moment. The artists captured time itself and they're sharing it with me. The beauty . . . I need to paint like this, share with others like this. It's overwhelming, yet the artists somehow make it feel possible." I looked right at him. "It's as though they're giving me permission to finally just . . . be me. "

He nodded, then said, "To finally be fulfilled."

Yes! He understood.

Of course he understood.

With the emotions came a new determination. "I need to learn everything, Gabe. Every skill they had, I want for myself." I touched his hand. "Going to art school is not just *right* for me, it's necessary."

He put his arm around my shoulders and squeezed. "Yes, it is."

**

I was flying high as Gabe and I drove to Nelly's Diner. I touched the roof of the car with both hands. "I wish this was a convertible. I want to raise my arms up and shout 'I'm going to be an artist!'"

He honked the horn twice. "Woo-hoo!" His smile mirrored mine.

It was so rewarding to have someone be happy for me—happy with me.

We found Nelly's Diner and Nova greeted us warmly, showing us to a quiet booth in the back. The menu highlighted home-cooking classics like chicken-fried chicken, burgers, cole slaw, and onion rings. We settled on pie and did not regret it—I had cherry and Gabe had lemon meringue.

Nova was very attentive and was constantly on the move. She was good at her job, chatting with guests, anticipating their needs. Always smiling.

She saw me looking at her and came to the table. "Can I tempt you with a piece to go? There's still apple-crumble, rhubarb, and French silk to try."

We both put a hand to our stomachs, "We couldn't eat another bite."

Gabe started to get out his wallet, but Nova stopped him. "Remember? It's on me."

"You don't have to do that," I said.

"And you didn't have to run after the thief. We're even now. It *was* nice seeing you again, Minnie. Come back sometime for a full meal."

"Maybe we will," I said.

She glanced to the side. Someone was holding up their coffee mug for a refill. "See you later," she said.

Gabe left a generous tip and we headed back to our corner of the world.

"You're quiet," Gabe said as we pulled into traffic.

"I keep thinking about Nova having a baby. I can't imagine having all that responsibility. I'm only one year older."

"All things considered, she's making a good go of it," Gabe said. "She's doing what needs to be done."

"I'm impressed with her even as I feel sorry for her." We accelerated onto the interstate. "Earlier, you called me courageous, but Nova, she's the brave one."

"Yes, she is. You both are."

I thought about the Room. "It's all about choices."

"Hard choices."

As we headed toward Dad's house, I made my own choice. "Don't just drop me off at Dad's. I want you to come in and meet everybody."

He grinned. "I thought you'd never ask."

**

When we pulled onto Dad's street, I heard the lawnmower before I saw him pushing it.

Claudia was planting begonias on either side of the sidewalk leading to the front door. Benny and Bryn were playing on the porch, a baby gate keeping them away from the front steps.

"Here we go," I said as Gabe pulled into the driveway.

He squeezed my hand and gave me an encouraging smile before we both got out.

The sound of the mower stopped. Claudia stood up from her planting.

I waved my hand awkwardly. "I'm back," I said—which had to be one of the stupidest lines I'd ever uttered.

"I see that." Dad walked toward us.

Gabe held out his hand for Dad to shake. "Hi, Mr. McLaughlin, I'm Gabe Morton."

Dad took off a garden glove and shook his hand. I quickly turned to my stepmother. "Claudia, this is Gabe. Gabe, this is Claudia." Benny hooted from the porch. "Come meet my siblings."

Claudia said, "Why don't we take a break and we can all visit on the porch."

As soon as we started up the steps, both babies raised their arms, wanting to be picked up. Claudia got Bryn and I took Benny. We sat around a small table. I let Benny sit on it, facing me. I introduced them to Gabe. He made silly faces and had them smiling within seconds.

"So . . . how was the museum?" Claudia asked, her gaze flitting between Gabe and me.

"It was wonderful," I said. "I kept walking through the rooms over and over. I couldn't get enough of the paintings."

"Tell them what you felt while you were there," Gabe said.

"Felt?" Dad asked.

Would Dad understand that art elicited feelings? "I was sitting in a room surrounded by Impressionist paintings and this feeling of excitement came over me. I just knew in my gut that I had to—had to—learn how to paint." Dad's expression was non-committal. "Art is a God-given talent," I said. "I have to use it."

Dad's right eyebrow rose. He'd used that look against me many times. "Have to?" he asked.

I swallowed. "Have to," I said.

Gabe nodded. "She means it. I saw a change in her. The paintings touched her deeply."

Dad fidgeted. "I like paintings—certain paintings. But—"

"I like Monet," Claudia said, coming to my rescue.

I appreciated her so much. "We should go see the exhibit," I said. "We could all go together."

"I am not going to an art exhibit," Dad said.

Claudia smiled at me. "Then Minnie and I will go. You can take care of the kids." As if his duties were starting now, she handed Bryn to him.

Bryn immediately wanted to stand on his lap.

Saved by the baby.

Dad looked away from me and his eyes narrowed in on Gabe. "Gabe, I have a question for you."

"Yes, sir?"

"The other day Minnie said you're graduating with a degree in art. Can a person actually make a living as an artist?"

Gabe took a moment to think. Then he said, "Artists are like the other creative types: singers, actors, dancers . . . everyone who strives to be the best in these fields is taking a chance. Only a very few make it big."

"That's what I thought."

Gabe continued. "But much of the satisfaction comes from the process, the act of creating something out of nothing."

"I suppose," Dad said.

Gabe raised a hand. He wasn't through. "Art is not altogether different from other careers, with highs and lows, and the occasional reward. Minnie told me about your recent sales award. Congratulations."

"Thanks."

"Not everyone who sells real estate achieves that level of success."

I smirked behind Benny's head. Ha! Good one, Gabe!

Dad sighed. "Point taken. I know there are successful people in every profession, and the corresponding unsuccessful people." He looked my way. "I just want you to be wise, Min."

"I know. And I believe I am being wise by taking this chance. If I don't try, I will always regret it."

Claudia took Bryn back on her lap. "Agreed," she said. "Go for it, Minnie!" She made Bryn clap. "Yayyyy!"

Dad just shook his head. Then he looked from me to Gabe and back again. "Is this thing between you two serious?"

Claudia chimed in. "She doesn't need our approval, Ben."

"I know, but . . . is it?"

I was glad Gabe answered for us. "Right now we're just getting to know each other." He smiled at me. "But so far, we like what w see."

"We do," I said.

Gabe continued. "We're excited for the chance to find out wher this is supposed to go."

There was that eyebrow again. "Supposed to go?"

It was my turn. "We truly believe God brought us together, Dad. He arranged for us to meet."

Dad scoffed. "And how do you know that?"

Gabe touched my leg. "If I may?"

Gladly. "Sure."

"Minnie and I met during college orientation two years ago. We went our separate ways and forgot about one another. Temporarily. "

I took over. "But then we kept running into each other this last month. We bumped into each other in class, at the art store, and the other day Gabe saw me sketching."

"I invited her to a party at my house."

"You did," I smiled at him. I looked back at Dad. "But I didn't go because I was babysitting the night of your award."

"That was *your* party she missed?" Dad shook his head. "That's all very nice, but coincidences like that happen all the time."

Here came the hard part. "I think God was responsible for all of those meetings."

Dad scoffed. "Since when do you believe . . . like that?"

"A friend helped me see the truth of it. He helped me get on the right track." Benny leaned toward Gabe, who took him onto his lap. "A lot of things had to fall into place for Gabe and me to meet. And since meeting . . ." I gazed at Gabe, smiling.

"I've never met anyone like your daughter, sir. We have a lot in common with our shared interests. And we talk so easily it's like we've known each other for years."

I nodded. "We click," I said.

"That sounds like you and me, Ben," Claudia said.

"You're not helping," he said.

Yes, she was.

We all looked at Dad. He was shaking his head, but I could tell it was a shake of resignation, not opposition. "Fine," he finally said.

I reached across the table to squeeze his hand. "Thank you for trusting me, Dad."

"Is that what I'm doing?"

"It is exactly what *we're* doing." Claudia stood. "I'm going to get some iced tea. And chocolate chip cookies."

Iced tea and cookies. Now that was a proper celebration.

**

Gabe stayed the rest of the evening. He edged the yard while Dad finished mowing, and Claudia and I planted the flowers.

Then we ordered Chinese food and ate on the porch. After the meal, my parents took the babies inside, leaving Gabe and I on the porch swing. We sat hand in hand, silently swinging as the evening breeze swept over us.

It was perfect. I wanted to stay in this moment forever.

But as the sun began to set, Gabe broke the spell. "I'd better be going."

"No . . . not yet . . ."

He squeezed my hand. "Yet." He got up and took a step toward the door. "I'm going to say goodbye to your family."

I followed him inside. Dad and Claudia were watching TV.

"I gotta get home," Gabe said. "I wanted to thank you for dinner."

"You're welcome." Dad stood up. "Thanks for the help on the yard, I really appreciate it."

"No problem. Working in the yard reminds me of home."

"Where is home?" Claudia asked.

"I grew up in Minnesota. My parents still live there. I moved here for school."

"I take it you won't be seeing them for Easter tomorrow," Claudia said.

"No. "

"Then you're invited to go to church with us, and to have Easter dinner here."

I wanted to hug her. I took Gabe's hand, and looked up at him eagerly. "Will you come?"

"I'd love to."

I walked Gabe to his car. "Quite the day," I said.

"Quite the big day," he said. "I'm so proud of you for remaining strong about school—and us."

I was proud of me too. "I couldn't have done any of it without your help." I smiled. "They really, really like you."

"I like them too." He leaned against the driver's door and intertwined my hands with his. "As I said, we're good for each other." With that he pulled me close and gave me a proper boyfriend-girlfriend kiss.

Which of course was another reason to celebrate.

Chapter Thirty-Four

Gracie

For this is how God loved the world:
He gave his one and only Son,
so that everyone who believes in him
will not perish but have eternal life.
John 3: 16

On Easter morning I woke up at five-thirty—ridiculously early, but no matter how hard I tried, I couldn't get back to sleep.

I finally gave in and made coffee. Through the kitchen window I saw a blaze of sun rising up behind the trees that lined the backyard. It drew me outside. I took a mug and a quilt to the back patio, snuggled up on the swing, tucking the quilt around my feet.

I couldn't remember the last time I'd sat outside—which was absurd when I considered being home-bound for years and years. Dad probably wouldn't have objected if I'd said, "I'm going out to the patio for a while." But I'd never said that. And worse than that, I'd never suggested to Dad that he go outside and get some fresh air.

"Why?" I asked the air.

Mom loved sitting out back. She and I would share the swing and talk for hours. We loved gardening and had planted the pink and yellow tulips that lined the patio. In fact, every flower or bush in the backyard was Mom's doing, imagined in her mind's eye, planted with her own hands, and nurtured by her green thumb.

Now the bushes were gangly and overgrown because I hadn't taken care of them. I hadn't gone outside to water, prune, weed, or fertilize them, much less enjoy them. I'd left them to fend for themselves. I'd hired a neighbor boy to mow, but left the rest to nature.

I'd left a lot to nature—my own skewed nature. I'd ignored the outside of the house just as I'd ignored the inside. I'd walked through each day on autopilot, doing the next thing, and then the next. My life swirled with logistics. Had I ever been fully awake and in the moment? I'd acted the part of the prisoner with the jailer being my dad.

I stopped the swing with a foot. Wait. That wasn't the way it was at all. I'd played a martyr and had created a prison of my *own* making. I had been both the prisoner *and* the jailer.

The rising sun spread light where moments before there'd been darkness. But it wasn't just what the sun was doing for me on the outside, it was what it was doing for me on the inside. I'd been blind, but now I could see. I could see the self-imposed darkness that I'd twisted around myself with big, knotted ropes. In the Room I'd seen times where God had offered me a way to be free. I'd blamed my refusals on Dad, but it wasn't all his fault. I'd gotten used to the ropes and had quit trying to escape. That was on me.

"I'm so sorry."

I was surprised to hear the words come out of my mouth. Was I telling Dad I was sorry? Or was I telling myself? I'd felt sorry for some time now, but had never let anyone hear. Had certainly never let God hear.

I sat still on the swing as a ray of sunlight burst through the upper branches of the trees. The sun's light.

My Son's light.

I sucked in a breath. Was that . . .?

It had to be.

I put a hand to my mouth and laughed aloud. My heart nearly burst with the awe of it, the joy, the gratitude that God was here, with me now.

I was truly, fully free! I knew I would never be the same.

It was a brand new world.

**

I hadn't meant to weed the flower beds, but just as God was giving me a new world, I felt the need to take care of the one in front of me. One weed turned into twenty. To fifty. By the time I stopped, the patio and grass were littered with a hundred weeds. *I'm sorry, Mom. I let you down. I'll do better from now on.*

I checked out the yard and was amazed at how much I'd gotten done. The sun was now fully up and—

Ooh no! The sun was up! It was Easter!

I rushed inside and saw that it was after eight. I took a quick shower and blew dry my hair. I put on makeup and even sprayed on Mom's White Shoulders perfume—regretting it almost instantly since it smelled a bit old. So be it.

Luckily, I'd figured out what I was going to wear the night before. I quickly slipped on one of Mom's vintage dresses from the Fifties. She always said they made her feel like a woman should feel.

I wasn't sure about that, but I'd chosen a navy and white polka dot dress with barely-there sleeves, a wide neckline, and a red bow belt. I remembered her wearing it on her last Easter—which ironically, had been the last time I'd been to a church service. It was rather soothing that the dress fit me as well as it had fit her.

I found her jewelry box and took out a pearl choker with matching pearl studs. I was ready to—

Shoes! I hadn't thought about shoes. The flip-flops and sandals I wore every day weren't nice enough for today. I found a shoebox in the closet labeled *Red Pumps.* They were classic with a two-inch heel that matched the belt. And they fit.

I stood at the full-length mirror and swished my skirt back and forth. My throat tightened as I remembered Mom doing the same thing. *A proper dress should have movement in it, Gracie. Men's clothes never move, so movement makes our clothes different.*

I was different all right. Fashion wasn't my thing. I dressed for comfort. After all, until Dad died I'd barely left the house. Since getting a job, Wesley had never complained about my attire—which I knew was out of style because it was taken from Mom's closet.

For good measure I found a navy clutch near the shoes and hurried downstairs to transfer a few things from my catch-all shoulder bag that I hadn't cleaned out in months. I snapped the clutch shut just as the doorbell rang.

When the door opened, Tony's eyes grew wide, and he smiled.

"Wow," he said. "You look gorgeous."

I grinned, feeling like a million bucks. "Thanks. It's my mom's dress."

"It's not just the dress . . ." he eyed me up and down. "You're glowing. Face it, Tinkerbell. You are a knockout." He whistled.

I felt myself redden. I liked his nickname for me. "You're quite handsome yourself."

He tugged on his navy sport coat. "You think? Harvey loaned it to me."

"It looks fantastic."

He smiled shyly and looked toward the street. "Speaking of . . . he's in the car. He can't wait to get to know you."

I peeked out the open door and waved at him. Harvey waved back. Then Tony offered me his arm and we walked toward the curb. His gallant gesture made me feel like a woman should feel.

Tony opened the passenger front door for me. Harvey was sitting in the backseat. As soon as I was in the car, I turned back to him. "Hi, Harvey. Nice to see you again."

He tipped an imaginary hat. "A pleasure to officially meet you,

Miss Gracie." He winked at me. "May I say you look lovely this morning."

I felt myself blush. "Thank you." A *gorgeous,* a *knockout,* and a *lovely.* I needed to dress up more often.

As Tony started to drive, he kept sneaking glances at me, smiling whenever I caught his eye. "What?" I asked.

"Nothing. I'm just happy."

The joy I felt from *that* was how a woman should feel.

The church wasn't far. Tony pulled in front and let Harvey and me out. I got the walker situated just-so for him, locking it in place.

"You've done this before, haven't you?"

It took me a moment to realize what "this" was. "You could say that. I took care of both of my parents when they were sick."

"We can be a bother, can't we?"

A month ago I might have agreed with him, or at the very least said a mental *'you sure are.'* Instead I said, "Getting older can be hard."

"On everyone involved."

"Agreed. I did what I had to do."

He nodded toward the parking lot. "That's what Tony's been doing for me." He pointed at his ears. "And look at this. Working hearing aids—thanks to him. He's a good man."

"He sure seems to be."

Harvey shook his head. "No 'seems' about it, Miss Gracie. I'm telling you—because you need to know—that Tony is a really good man."

"I'll take that into consideration."

Harvey turned his attention to the church building and gazed upward. "I love old churches with their spires pointing to heaven with a cross on top."

I looked up, seeing the cross. Tony joined us. "What are you two looking at?" he asked.

Harvey pointed to the spire. "A good reminder, that."

"What's *that*?" Tony asked.

"The cross, reminding us that Jesus died so all our sins are forgiven. That's life changing."

I was about to agree when I saw Tony turn white. "What's wrong?"

He was staring at Harvey. "I've heard those words before."

"I'm sure you have. It's the foundation of what we believe."

Tony shook his head. "No, I mean before-before." He looked at me. "In the Room."

Harvey's eyebrows rose. "Did someone say it to you?

Tony hesitated. "I think it was you, Harvey."

"Harvey was in one of your scenes?" I asked.

"I . . . I think he was."

Harvey leaned on his walker. "You didn't tell me we'd met before."

"I didn't know. I was in the Room before I even met you, but your words . . . a man said those words to me outside this church on the day of Papa's funeral. Was that you?"

"I don't rightly know," Harvey said. "But it could've been. I've been known to say those words when it's fitting."

"But what if—?"

I put a hand on Tony's arm. "There's no proof that man was Harvey, but there's also no proof he wasn't. And after all we've learned in the Room, don't you think we ought to give God the benefit of the doubt?"

Before he could answer, I heard my name called. "Gracie!"

A fifty-something woman waved at me. I remembered her as one of the early clients of the Room. What was her name?

She came close, bringing with her a large group of people. "Happy Easter, Gracie." I must have looked like I was searching for her name because she added, "I'm Lydia."

I smiled at her, relieved to put a name to a face. "Happy Easter to you, Lydia."

She was quick to introduce the people who were with her. "This is my husband, Jeremy, and our daughter JoJo. And this is Nova and her son, Theo."

The little boy was adorable and wore a bow tie. "Nice to meet all of you."

Harvey introduced himself and Tony.

Our heads turned as we heard someone behind us calling, "Nova!"

Another client—Minnie—came running over and gave Nova a hug. She introduced her dad, stepmom, and baby twins. And her very handsome boyfriend Gabe.

Minnie saw Lydia and said, "Mrs. Brogdon? What are you doing here? And JoJo?"

Lydia and the three young women began talking. It sounded like Lydia had briefly been Minnie's mentor in high school. What a small world it was.

Tony called out to another group. "Nonna!" He hurried to help his grandmother negotiate the curb. Walking with Nonna was a pretty brunette with a ten-year-old boy. That had to be Tony's ex and his son.

My stomach twinged with nerves.

They walked toward me and smiled.

"You must be Gracie," she said. "I'm Penny." She drew the boy close. "And this is Zach."

The boy glanced up at me through dark lashes. "Hi."

I could tell he felt awkward. As did I. "Nice to meet you, Zach."

As I met Nonna and everybody talked with everybody I marveled that this gaggle of people had connections before the Room and because of it.

If Wesley were here he would tell everyone that God had arranged all of it.

I, for one, believed it.

Chapter Thirty-Five

Lydia

Three things will last forever
—faith, hope, and love—
and the greatest of these is love.
1 Corinthians 13: 13

I glanced behind our pew and smiled at Minnie and her family. What a small world that she and I both had sessions in the Room, and were further connected through Nova and JoJo.

I glanced down my own row. Theo and Nova sat between me and JoJo. I loved seeing the girls chat and get reacquainted. Two girls who'd started out in Daisy Scouts but whose lives had diverged drastically.

Theo was so handsome in his big boy shirt and bow tie. He seemed to like the Jesus board book I'd gotten him. It was much better than the chicks and bunny book I'd ordered. I suspected the company sending the wrong one was a God-thing.

As the music started—which was always grand on Easter—I gazed toward the front of the church and saw the huge cross on the wall draped in white. Nova had said her mother was creeped out by it. While I could possibly see the cross being intimidating, I chose to view the draping for what it was - a symbol of purity, of Christ dying for our sins and wiping the slate clean.

As the service began I kept sneaking looks at Nova. Was she taking it all in? Was she understanding the celebration? Had she ever learned what Easter really was? If I had anything to do with it, both she and Theo would know.

After the sermon, as the choir sang a grand arrangement of "Jesus Christ is Risen Today," I saw Nova showing Theo the Easter book. The last page said, "We will all live forever because of Jesus!"

That was the bottom line.

I calmly pointed to the words and nodded. "It's true," I whispered.

Nova held my gaze a moment, then looked ahead to the cross and the choir as the alleluias swirled around us. *Jesus Christ is risen today...*

When she looked back at me her eyes were glistening. She

nodded slightly, then kissed Theo on the head.

Something had just happened. A God moment.

I could have bawled right there! Alleluia indeed.

**

Just as I put the hashbrown casserole in the oven, the doorbell rang. The Freemans—Glen's family—had arrived.

"I'll get it," Jeremy said. JoJo followed.

There was happy commotion as they came inside.

I motioned to Nova who was sitting at the island. "Come meet our friends." I snatched up Theo and moved to the living room. "Welcome," I said. I turned around to include Nova.

She smiled, but approached the group warily. I introduced Glen's sister Mandy, her husband Ross, and four-year-old Ellie. I set Theo on the floor and the two kids sized each other up.

Then I introduced Glen's parents. "Bob, Betty, this is Nova. Nova, this is Bob and Betty Freeman."

Nova shook their hands, but then her face turned pale. She took a step back and stared at them.

Something was wrong. "Nova? Are you okay?" I asked.

"Freeman? You're Glen's parents?"

"We are. You knew our son?"

Nova was frozen in the moment. Her forehead was furrowed. Suddenly she grabbed Theo and hunted frantically for the diaper bag.

I rushed over to her and whispered. "What's wrong? What are you doing?"

"We have to go." She rushed over to JoJo. "Would you take us home please?"

Jeremy stepped up. "Nova. Don't leave. Just tell us what's going on."

I put a hand on her shoulder, trying to calm her. "Talk to us."

Her face was flushed, her breathing heavy. Her eyes darted from Theo to the door, then to the others in the room. "I'm really sorry. I don't mean to ruin your Easter, but I really have to leave."

Bob put an arm around his wife, compassion in his eyes. "We didn't mean to upset you. Though I don't know *how* we upset you."

A groan escaped Nova's lips. Theo squirmed and she set him on the floor as if he were suddenly too heavy. She covered her face with her hands.

I had no idea what to do. "Why don't we go outside and talk, just you and me?"

She nodded yes. But as she let her hands fall, she shook her head tears in her eyes. She pointed at Theo. "Mr. and Mrs. Freeman? Meet your grandson."

"What?"

All eyes went to the boy who had started to sort plastic eggs with Ellie.

Everyone looked at Nova. "What are you talking about?" Betty asked.

Nova wrapped her arms around herself. "We didn't mean for it to happen."

Oh. My. Goodness.

"Why don't we sit down?" I led everyone to the living room as Mandy took the kids to the family room and turned on cartoons.

Betty and Bob sat on the loveseat and everyone else found seats nearby. Jeremy offered Nova a chair but she chose to stand by the fireplace.

"Nova, would you like to explain?" I made my voice calm and hoped she could hear the compassion I was feeling. There was no judgment here.

But before Nova could get her words together, Betty asked. "Were you and Glen dating? He never mentioned you or any other girlfriend. And he didn't go out much."

"Except to study with friends," Bob said.

Nova nodded, raising her hand low in the air. "That was me. I was the friend." Her eyes darted between Bob and Betty, pleading. "We were just really good friends at the beginning."

"At the beginning. And then . . . ?" Betty said.

"How long were you . . . together?" Bob asked.

"Why didn't he tell us about you?" Betty asked.

I wondered the same thing. I was Glen's mentor and knew nothing about any of this.

Nova put up her hands. "Can I just tell it my way? Please?"

With a quick look at Betty, I answered for everyone. "Sure you can. Go ahead."

She faced the fireplace and held the mantel for a moment, gathering her courage. Then she turned around. "First semester of our junior year, Glen and I had three classes together. We got paired up for a history project and he came over to my house to work on it. He was sweet and we both had the same sense of humor. We made each other laugh so hard."

She took a fresh breath. "But after the project was over, we ended up studying for our other classes too. At first it was just a friendship. Neither one of us had any experience with dating, but we understood each other. He got me and I got him."

Betty shook her head.

“The thing was, my mom wasn’t around much and—”

“That was convenient,” Bob said.

Nova kept on. “And then she wasn’t around at all. She and her boyfriend moved to Alaska right after Christmas—before I could even tell her about the baby. They left me alone to finish out the school year. I was pregnant and abandoned. All I had was Glen.” She wrapped her arms around herself again.

I couldn’t believe what I was hearing. “I’m so sorry, Nova. She shouldn’t have done that. You must have been so lonely.”

Nova shrugged. “I was lonely even before Mom left. But Glen made me feel *seen* like no one else ever had. We’d play video games and watch movies. We loved being together.“ Her face softened. “We loved each other. A lot.”

Betty spoke up. “What did he say when you told him you were pregnant?”

She looked at the floor, then met Betty’s eyes. “He was real happy. Excited. And scared. We both were.”

"Why didn’t he tell us?” Betty said.

“We talked about it, and he was going to tell you, but then . . .”

I drew in a breath. “He died?”

Nova’s eyebrows met in the middle. She nodded.

“Why didn’t *you* tell us?” Bob asked. “Why didn’t you come to us? We would have helped you and the boy.”

“The boy is Theo,” Nova said. “And I thought about telling you, but when I went to the funeral and saw how distraught everybody was—I was pretty messed up too—I didn’t want to intrude and make the situation worse.”

“Intrude?” Betty said. “It would have been a light in the middle of our darkness.”

Instead of being relieved, Nova seemed even more troubled.

“Is there something else bothering you?” I asked.

She bit her lip, clearly struggling. “It wasn’t just having a baby that would’ve made things worse. It was the other thing.” Her expression crumpled and she began to cry. “It was my fault Glen died.”

“What?” we all said in unison.

“What do you mean?” Bob asked.

Nova started sobbing and trembling. Jeremy led her to a chair and I gave her a tissue. She drew into herself, leaning forward, putting her head in her hands. “I’m so sorry, so sorry . . .“

We all looked at each other. How could Nova be responsible?

Betty knelt beside her chair and put a hand on her shoulder. “It’ be all right, Nova. I promise. Tell us what happened. We want to know."

"We need to know," Bob said.

Betty flashed him a look.

Nova tried to get control of herself as Betty comforted her. I was so impressed with Betty. She'd just heard a bombshell—two bombshells that could've blown her life apart—yet she'd found a way to be kind and gracious.

Finally Nova wiped her eyes a final time and took a deep breath. "Those oxycontin pills that killed him? He got them at my house. They weren't mine but we found them in the couch cushions—they belonged to Mom's boyfriend. We kidded each other that we should try some, but we both laughed it off." She shook her head. "He must have taken a few of them home, because the next thing I heard, he was dead." Her tears turned into racking sobs. "It's all my fault. I never meant to hurt him. I loved him so much. I'm so sorry."

Betty pulled her into a hug and held her. "It is not your fault. You couldn't have known what would happen."

Surprisingly, it was Glen's sister who spoke next. "It's not your fault, Nova. The autopsy said Glen didn't die from taking oxy, he died from the combination of oxy with his seizure medication." She shook her head. "Evidently, they can be deadly together. *He* didn't know."

"It truly was an accident," Bob conceded.

Betty and Nova let go of each other. "He's right," Betty said.

"Really?" Nova's eyes were eager.

Betty swept a strand of Nova's hair behind her ear. "Really. We all have felt guilty at one point or another. But our family is beyond that now. It was a tragedy on so many levels. Yet we know that no amount of guilt will bring Glen back. We have to move forward." Her eyes glistened as she caught Nova's gaze. "I am so sorry you had to deal with all of this alone."

My heart broke for everyone's pain. "You're not alone anymore, Nova."

Betty offered her a bittersweet smile. "I am so glad Glen found someone to love. And—"

Theo came running in the room full speed with Ellie chasing him. "I'm gonna get you!"

He grabbed onto Nova's legs and she drew him onto her lap. "Gotcha, Tiger." Then she smiled at Betty and told her son, "Theo? This is your grandma. Can you say hi?"

Theo put a pudgy hand on Betty's cheek. Betty took his hand and kissed it. "Nice to meet you, Theo."

**

The tensions continued to ease during dinner, where we all found stories to tell about Glen, high school, and mistakes we had made.

After dinner, Jeremy and I found ourselves alone in the kitchen, finishing the cleanup. I folded a dish towel and hung it on the humming dishwasher. I stared out the back window.

Both kids had loaded their baskets with candy-filled eggs, stuffed animals, stickers, and coloring books. Mandy, JoJo, and Ross sat in the grass with them, blowing bubbles.

Betty, Bob, and Nova sat on the patio, talking—and laughing.

Jeremy put his arm around my shoulders. "Well done, Lyd. A day full of surprises."

"Surprises indeed. I had no idea Nova and Glen . . ."

"He never told you he had a girlfriend?"

"Not a word. He seemed real happy that semester, but I thought it was because he was doing better in his classes. He seemed to have found himself."

"He had. He'd found Nova. It sounds like they helped each other." He put an arm around my shoulders. "Remember when Betty said they'd moved beyond the guilt. You have to do that too, Lyd. His death is not *your* fault either."

I took a deep breath and let it out slowly. "You're right. I need to let it go."

"Good for you." He pointed outside. "Focus on that. The Freeman family just grew by two. And Nova and Theo aren't alone anymore."

My next thought was selfish: *now they won't need me.*

As if reading my thoughts, Jeremy said, "You'll still be a part of their lives. People need people. Lots of people."

"I need *them* too. What a miracle it was that Nova and I even met. It's a good thing I listened to God's nudges."

"I agree."

"They changed everything."

Suddenly, he pointed at something over my shoulder. "Hey. Look at that."

I turned my head to look, but when I turned back he pulled me close. "My oh my. Look at how God just nudged you into my arms."

What a guy.

Chapter Thirty-Six

Gracie

Learn to do good. Seek justice. Help the oppressed.
Defend the cause of orphans.
Fight for the rights of widows.
Isaiah 1: 17

Tony and I left the living room where Harvey and Nonna were telling Zach stories about Easters in the olden days.

"They're really hitting it off," Tony said as he took a seat at the island.

Penny took rolls out of the oven. "Those two have a lot in common. And you know Zach has a soft spot for old people."

"Good for him," I said. He seemed like a very sweet kid. Polite, if not a bit quiet. I started to sit beside Tony then changed my mind. "Would you like me to take up the rolls, Penny?"

"That would be great. In that basket there." She glanced at Tony. "The ham's done. Would you slice it, please?" She checked the hashbrown casserole in the oven. "Just a few more minutes."

"I'm impressed," I said. "I admire how you time everything so perfectly. I've never had to cook for a crowd but you make it look easy."

She looked at me quizzically. "Thank you. But six is not a crowd around here. You should see it when my family and their brood come to town." She threw her hands in the air. "Utter chaos."

I laughed and pointed at the pickle and olive jars. Penny nodded at a divided dish.

"So tell me about yourself, Gracie," Penny asked. "You obviously know about *our* situation." She flashed a look at Tony.

Actually I didn't know much other than they were divorced. I found it remarkable they could celebrate holidays together. It spoke a lot about each of them.

"My story is rather boring," I said.

"Hardly." Tony flashed me a smile.

I shrugged. "My mom died after a long illness when I was eighteen. My dad took it hard and . . ."

"Kept you a prisoner," Tony said.

I was shocked to hear *him* said that. He must have seen the look on my face because he said, "Sorry. I shouldn't have said that. He wasn't my dad."

I appreciated the apology. And Tony didn't know about my patio revelation. "Dad held my reins a bit tight so I didn't go to college or have many friends. He got cancer and I had to take care of him. He died three months ago."

"Oh, Gracie, I'm so sorry for your loss." Penny said. "And your story is far from boring. You've had to deal with way more than most people."

"That's what I keep telling her," Tony said. "The fact she's come through it in one piece shows how strong she is."

"You are too kind," I caid. "I'm not there yet. Due to my father's fault—and my own—I've been isolated for fourteen years. Now I have to learn how to be social, and figure out what I should do with the rest of my life."

"I getcha," Penny said. "I've been doing that too."

"After the trauma of me," Tony said matter-of-factly.

She smiled at him. "You exaggerate. Plus, I know you're trying to find your way too."

He winked at me. "We'll see how *that* goes."

"In fact," Penny said, "I think most people are looking for clues to find their way." She unmolded a strawberry Jell-O mold on a plate by flipping it over.

I was in awe. "I've never seen anyone do that." Dad had banned Jell-O from our house because he hated the texture.

"It *is* tricky. I've spoiled more than my share." She put a serving spoon on the plate. "So Gracie, where do you work?"

I didn't know how much Tony had told her. "At the Discovery Room."

"That's where we met." Tony was halfway through cutting ham slices.

"Discovery . . . what does the company do? Or sell?"

Tony and I looked at each other. How should we put it?

He gave it a shot. "They help people see where they've gone wrong in their life."

"Or right," I added.

"Or right," he conceded.

"It sounds like therapy," Penny said.

I smiled. "That's exactly what it is—or turns out to be."

Penny transferred the ham slices onto a serving plate. "Whatever they do, it's helped. I see a change in you, Tony. You're . . . lighter."

He beamed. "Thanks. That means a lot."

I studied the two of them. Exes, coexisting and happy for one another. I was happy for them, that *they'd* come through their hard times in one piece.

And so had I.

Penny swept her gaze around the kitchen, then wiped her hands on a towel. "Well now . . . I think we did it. Dinner is served."

**

As we ate Easter dinner, I was reminded of a scene in one of my favorite movies, "While You Were Sleeping" when Sandra Bullock—a woman with no family—sat at a Christmas dinner table with an exuberant family. As the conversation was lobbed around the table she took it all in, amazed, entertained, and overwhelmed. That's how I felt at the Amato table.

I wasn't left out—they coaxed me into many a discussion—but I preferred listening. If it wouldn't have been seen as rude, I would have closed my eyes and let their words and laughter wrap around me like a tight hug.

Zach—who I'd misread as shy—was not shy at all. He talked about his baseball team, which led to Harvey talking about playing ball for Missouri, which led to a discussion of the Royals, which led to a discussion of our favorite stadium food, which led to . . .

It was heavenly.

When every plate was empty, there were contented moans all around. I helped Penny clear the dishes and everyone decided the lemon meringue pie would best be eaten later. Nonna suggested we play cards. The family tradition was to play Pitch. I had no idea how to play but they assured me I'd catch on.

As they were getting the cards out, I saw Tony whisper in his grandma's ear. Her face lit up and she drew his face close enough to kiss him. "You make me very happy, Antonio."

We sat around the table. Penny started shuffling the cards, but Tony stood behind his chair and put his hand out, stopping her.

"Before we get started I have a special gift I want to present to Zach."

The boy put a hand to his chest. "Me?"

"You, bud." Tony motioned for Zach to stand up. Then he pulled a lim box from his shirt pocket. "What I'm going to give you once elonged to your Great-Papa Amato."

Zach looked at Nonna. "I never met him, right?"

"That's right," Nonna said.

"You never met him, but I'm here to tell you he was a great man. I ope this makes you feel a connection to his history, to our history."

Tony handed him the navy box and Zach opened it.

The boy touched a finger to the medal and looked at Tony. "Wow. This is cool. What is it?"

Nonna answered. "It's your great-papa's Purple Heart, given to him when he was wounded in the Korean War. He sacrificed his own safety to protect us."

"It's quite an honor," Harvey said. "I fought in a war too, but I was never wounded. You should be proud of your papa."

Nonna's expression was wistful. "I was always very proud of him—for his service, but also because he was a very special man."

Zach studied it closer. "This dude has a ponytail."

Tony chuckled. "That *dude* is George Washington."

Zach's eyes brightened. "I've heard of him!" He wrapped his arms around his dad. "Thanks, Dad."

I saw Tony fighting back tears. "You're welcome, son." Then he took a quick breath and said, "Thank Nonna too."

Zach hugged his great-grandmother and they exchanged soft words. When they let go, Nonna wiped away a tear, which made Zach hug her again.

My heart felt so full. This family had shown me how much I'd missed, yet they'd also made me thankful that I was here with them, right now.

Speaking of *now* . . . I stood. "This moment deserves a picture. Everyone stand around Nonna."

One picture led to many combinations. I was even in a few. I could count on one-hand the pictures I'd taken since Mom died. That all changed today.

After pictures, we played cards. The game was lively. Zach helped me a few times, and I got the hang of it. We took a break mid-game to dive into the pie—which was delicious. When it was time to go I left reluctantly.

Hugs were given and received all around. Zach said he wanted t come to my house and help his dad fix whatever needed fixing. heard Nonna invite Harvey over for lunch and a game of Pinochle And I asked Penny to come over to give me ideas about how t decorate—because her house was gorgeous.

"Thank you, Penny," I said. "This is the best Easter I've ever had."

She cocked her head. "You're very welcome. I'm glad you had good time."

As she gave Tony a quick squeeze, I overheard her whisper, " approve." Then she smiled at me.

She approved of me? The happiness of her approval washed ov me like I'd won the lottery.

We walked to the car and Tony helped Harvey and Nonna into the backseat. He hurried around to open my door, but delayed by pulling me close. "So, how are you really? I know my family can be overwhelming."

It was an easy answer. "I feel better than I've felt in years."

"Really?"

I nodded. "I am totally and utterly content."

He winked at me. "Me too."

From inside the car Harvey called out, "Gracious sake-a-day, boy. Kiss her!"

Tony leaned down and saluted him through the window. "Yes, sir!"

And so he kissed me. And I kissed back.

**

"Wrench," Tony commanded from his position under the kitchen sink.

I handed it to him. "When I asked you to come in after Easter dinner I didn't expect you to work."

"I don't mind." He slid out and pointed to the faucet, "Turn it on."

I did. We both stared at the pipes. No leaks.

I clapped. "You did it!"

He got to his feet. "All in a day's work, ma'am."

"How did you know how to do that?"

"I watched a video online because Mrs. Osborn on the second floor had a leak, so she was my guinea pig. I've learned a lot of new skills being the maintenance man—the maintenance professional." He washed his hands and I handed him a towel.

"I know I could keep you busy here. "

He stopped wiping his hands and froze. "Wow."

"What *wow?*"

"Something just hit me. Do you think God arranged for me to get that job, so I'd learn stuff, so I could help you?"

I shivered. "I wouldn't put it past Him."

He chuckled and pulled me close. "Look at us talking about what God's doing in our lives."

"Wesley would be so proud." I gave him a short kiss. "God arranged for you to have the skills you'd need to help me. But I'm not sure what usable skills I've learned from being trapped in this house."

"That's easy," Tony said. "You made a community through your posts by sharing your struggles. You said your readers are like family. You help each other."

"We do."

"If not for your situation you wouldn't have helped all those people."

He made me feel better. "I suppose you're right."

He looked around the kitchen. "Where do you write? Do you have an office?"

"I write in my bedroom, sitting in bed."

He shook his head slowly. Then he stepped to the doorway of the kitchen. "Can I see the rest of the house?"

"Why?"

He shook his head. "Indulge me."

"Don't expect much," I said. I led him into each of the four bedrooms and he peeked into the one small bath. Then he backtracked and walked it all again, even opening up the closets. He was clearly in a zone.

"Tony, tell me what you're thinking."

He took me into my bedroom, the one closest to the master. "It might be a lot to visualize, but hear me out. What if we combined these two bedrooms? Take out the closets that back to each other and make a walk-through between both rooms. Then we could turn your room into a huge master bath with a walk-in closet." He finally stopped moving. "What do you think?"

My mind had trouble catching up with him. But then everything fell into place. "I love that idea."

He winked. "I'm not done yet." He grabbed my hand and pulled me into the hall. He pointed to the guest room. "This room is good as it is, but . . ." He stepped into the fourth bedroom. "This would make a great office."

The room was cluttered with old medical equipment I needed to sell. But I could see his vision. "I could buy a desk and write in here."

"It would be a proper space for someone who's the head of a very large online community."

I strolled toward the window and pulled back the pink floral curtain. The view of the backyard was nice. "The desk could be under this window . . ."

"Of course it could." He took my hand and faced me. "If we were in the Room, I'm betting this room would glow."

I laughed. "You've got it all figured out, don't you?"

"Not hardly, but figuring it out is the fun part."

"I believe you."

He put his arms around my waist. "No matter what the details

are, this room would make a great office. Yes?"
I held him close and nodded yes.
Yes. To so many things.

Chapter Thirty-Seven

Minnie

So be strong and courageous,
all you who put your hope in the Lord!
Psalm 31: 24

Gabe and I waved goodbye to Dad, Claudia, and the twins and drove away. Our Easter dinner had been a success. Gabe—may God bless him from head to toe—was a great conversationalist and fit in seamlessly. He asked Dad for his advice as a businessman regarding the purchase of Art's Art Shop, and charmed Claudia with just the right amount of flattery. It didn't hurt that Bryn quickly chose him as her favorite person and climbed on and off his lap too many times to count.

I'd enjoyed watching him. I hadn't had any real boyfriends, but I couldn't imagine any of the guys I knew being so at ease. Gabe had a good effect on me too, for I found myself talking to my parents like an adult.

He made me better.

He was helping me grow up.

Gabe drove us toward Mom's house for Easter Part 2. "I really like your dad."

I took his hand. "He likes you. The whole family does."

"Not all your family. I haven't met your mom yet."

I felt the slightest twinge. "About that . . . Mom doesn't know you're coming over with me. She just thinks I'm coming home after being at Dad's for Easter dinner."

He gave me a quick glance. "You didn't tell me that."

"Yeah. Well . . ."

"Maybe we should've invited her to go to church with us."

"I thought of that. But Mom can't be in the same room with Dad and Claudia. And as far as the babies . . . I can't even talk about them without upsetting her."

"How long has it been since the divorce?"

"Eight years."

"That's a long time to be bitter."

"Tell me about it. Mom kind of flounders when she isn't working on a craft project or is between boyfriends—like now. She gets stuck believing she doesn't have anything positive going on in her life."

"Except you."

"I guess. But change is hard for her."

"I get that," he said. "Yet she *was* supportive of you changing your major. That's huge."

"It is. Which is why she won't like the idea of me living away from home next year."

"Or you having a boyfriend who will eat up your mother-daughter time?"

"You got it."

"So what you're saying is, I'm heading into enemy territory?"

"It's not that bad." Though maybe it was. I needed them to like each other. "Just be yourself. It worked with Dad and Claudia."

"I'll do my best."

My phone rang. "It's my Grandpa McLaughlin. Do you mind?"

Gabe nodded toward the phone as I answered. "Happy Easter, Grandpa."

"Happy Easter to you too, honey. Are you at your father's for a meal?"

"We were. It was a good time. We're just driving to Mom's now."

"We?"

I glanced at Gabe. "My boyfriend and I."

"Good for you! What's his name?"

"Just a second. I'll put you on speaker." I motioned for Gabe to answer.

"Hi, sir. I'm Gabe Morton. I go to college with Minnie."

"He's an artist, Grandpa," I said. "He's graduating next month."

"Congratulations. Sounds like you make a good team."

"We do," Gabe said.

"We do." I grinned at Gabe. "Did you and Grandma have a big meal after church?"

"We hosted our neighbors. We are now stuffed and happy."

They were always happy.

He continued. "While we were together, another couple talked about their granddaughter who's in college, and one thing led to another, and—"

"We got an idea," Grandma said.

Grandpa spoke next. "Since you're on your way to your mom's I'll get to the point. Grandma and I have been talking about your studies next year. Art classes are very different from business classes. You're going to be busy with a lot of studio time where you have to stay on campus late."

Gabe nodded.

"I've heard that's true," I said.

"And so . . . we would like to pay for you to live on campus or your own apartment close by, so you don't have to drive the for minutes to and from school anymore."

I sucked in a breath. When I let it out my voice was warbl "Really?"

"Really, honey. I know you've stayed with your mom because sl needed you, but it's been two years since you graduated high scho It's time for both of you to let go."

Gabe nodded and put a hand on the back of my neck.

"I was going to talk to Mom about that this afternoon."

"Then it's good timing. Be strong," Grandpa said. "It's for t best—she knows that, but might need a little convincing."

"I know you're right," I said, "and I've been saving money to t and find a way."

"*We* are the way. We can't think of a better way to spend o money than to help our granddaughter fulfill her God-given purpo using her God-given gift."

I let the tears come, "Oh, Grandpa . . . Grandma . . ." My voice w shaky. "I don't know how to thank you for this—for everythi beyond this. I won't let you down."

"We know you won't, honey," Grandma said.

"Plus, now we'll be able to brag that we knew you wher Grandpa said. "We'll talk more soon. Say hi to your mom for us."

"And we look forward to meeting you in person, Gabe," Grandr said.

I hung up, stunned.

"You okay?" Gabe asked.

I took a few deep breaths as reality started to sink in. "I'm beyo okay. I'm in shock. I never expected them to . . . I never even thoug of asking them to . . ."

"They are very special people to think about what you need."

"And pay for it." I kept shaking my head back and forth. "Wow mean wow."

Gabe chuckled. "Happy Easter to you."

"It's an Easter I'll always remember, that's for sure."

Ten minutes later we pulled into Mom's driveway.

My stomach knotted.

Gabe took my hand. "Come on now. What's the worst that c happen?"

"She'll lock me in my room forever?"

"No, really. What's the worst?"

It was a good question. Introducing her to Gabe was the easy pa

But moving out? I was twenty—way past the age when most kids left home. "You're right."

Gabe paused a moment before getting out. He squeezed my hand and looked heavenward. "God? We're very thankful for the special gift from Minnie's grandparents. Now give Minnie the words she needs to talk to her mom."

"And somehow, make Mom not argue too much," I added.

Gabe smiled and shook his head. "Somehow?"

"You're right. There's no *somehow* to it. I *do* trust Him."

"Good. And remember how you want me to be myself with your mom like I was at your dad's? Then you be like you were at your dad's. You were strong, Minnie. Confident. A woman with a mission. Be that way now."

I took a deep breath, counting on the influx of air—and God—to give me the right words.

Gabe came around to open the car door for me. When we turned toward the front door, I saw Mom standing there, staring at us through the screen.

"Hi, Mom."

When we reached the door she didn't open it.

"Can we come in?"

"Who's this?" she asked.

"This is Gabe Morton."

"Happy Easter, Mrs. McLaughlin."

She moved aside so we could go in, then stood a few feet away with her arms crossed. "Was he at your dad's?"

"He was."

"Did you all go to church together?" She glared at me, as if daring me to say it.

"Yes, Mom, we did." This was ridiculous. "Can we maybe sit down?"

She hesitated, then swept an arm toward the couch. Gabe and I sat together. Mom sat in the comfy chair that was always hers—but she perched herself on the edge of its cushion as if she was ready to pounce at any moment. She was always testy after I spent part of a holiday with Dad.

"Are you two dating?" she asked.

"We are." I looked to Gabe.

He smiled back at me. "We are."

She nodded. "Why didn't I know about it?"

Ahh. So that was the problem. "You know about it now, Mom." A thought came to me, but I shoved it away, but then it came back. "The important part is that God brought us together."

Mom scoffed. "Yeah. Right."

"He did," I said.

"He did," Gabe said.

Mom looked from me to Gabe and back again. "It's not right to say such a thing, to be so . . . presumptuous."

"It's not presumptuous to tell the truth." My heart beat an extra beat. Had I just said that to my mother?

She sat back in her chair, which helped me relax a bit.

"I'm curious . . . why do you think that?" she asked.

I looked at Gabe but he nodded back at me for it wasn't his story to tell. Although I knew Mom believed in God and Jesus in general, I wasn't sure how she really felt about them. I'd heard her blame God for ruining her marriage. I didn't even know if she prayed. And I'd only told her a small portion about the Room. Knowing all this helped me figure out how to tell her without turning her off or frightening her away from Him.

"A lot of things fell into place that led to me and Gabe meeting. Too many things to write off as coincidence."

Gabe nodded. "There were nudges."

"Nudges?" Mom said the word like she was saying something inconsequential.

I felt a fluttering that led me to add, "God's nudges."

"I felt them too," Gabe said. "We've known each other for a while, but recently, when we kept seeing each other, we both felt a connection that went beyond friendship."

"We fit in a way that tells both of us this is special," I said. "Almost beyond *us*."

She didn't say anything and I braced myself for her shooting us down.

She studied us a few moments, but then she nodded once. "I will admit I am surprised. But you seem nice, Gabe, and Minnie, I've always wanted you to find a great guy. I'm glad you found each other—however you found each other. I'm afraid I haven't been a good role model in the dating department."

I wasn't sure what to say. "I've seen you suffer, Mom. From the divorce and . . . from the rest."

She scoffed. "I've taught you what *not* to do."

I shrugged. "Maybe. But I learned from that too." I took Gabe's hand in mine. "Don't worry about us. We'll be smart about it."

"We'll take things slow," Gabe said.

"Glad to hear it." Mom sighed deeply and I saw her face change from concern and guilt to acceptance and interest. "Are you still in school, Gabe?"

At that point I knew Gabe was in. I wanted to pop up and do a little happy dance, but stayed where I was.

Gabe told her about graduating, working at Art's, and maybe buying it.

Mom was impressed by that. "Is it a good business?"

"It is. Though I would like to expand its reach by offering classes."

Classes. School. Art school. I wasn't done standing up for myself.

I prayed a second prayer for the right words. I moved to the ottoman at her feet, then I dove in. "I just talked to Grandpa and Grandma. They told me to tell you happy Easter."

"Tell them thanks. They've always been kind to me, even after the divorce. They're good people."

"They are." Gabe nodded slightly. I could do this. "They had some amazing news for me."

"What's that?"

"Since art classes will include a lot of late night studio time, they're going to pay for me to live on campus."

Her smile faded. "That is extremely generous of them."

I nodded.

She cocked her head and looked past me. Then back. "But what will I do without you here, Min? "

I touched her knee. "You'll be fine. Good even. You're just used to *having* me here. But I think it's time both of us learned to be strong on our own. Don't you think? In some ways I think we've held each other back."

Mom contemplated this before reaching over and taking my hands. "You're right. We'll be fine."

I just sat there, blinking at her.

She laughed. "I agreed with you, Min. It's okay. Take a breath."

I fell into her arms and we hugged each other tight. "Thanks, Mom. Thanks so much."

"You're welcome, sweetie." She let me go. "I'm proud of you, Min. You're different today. Stronger."

I held back a laugh. "Knowing where I'm supposed to be and what I'm supposed to do *has* made me stronger. God's made me stronger."

"Well then. Amen to that," she said.

CHAPTER THIRTY-EIGHT

Lydia

November: 7 months later

God himself has taught you
to love one another.
1 Thessalonians 4: 9

Jeremy must have asked me something because he poked me. "Lydia? Yoo hoo. You in there?"

I blinked, forcing myself back to the present. "Sorry."

He held the coffee pot. "Want another cup?"

I pushed my mug forward. "Obviously I need it."

He filled my mug then sat beside me at the kitchen island. "Is one of your students making you worry about something?" he asked.

I put my thoughts into words. "Not just one, two. Belinda's parents are going through a divorce which is affecting her schoolwork, and David is acting out and I'm not sure why because he's usually a good kid."

"I'm sure you'll figure out how to help them." He spread strawberry preserves on a croissant. "So, was going back to mentoring worth it?"

I was surprised by his question. "Absolutely. My kids need me—and I need them."

He nodded once. "I know you do. Just checking."

"Actually, I just heard I'll be mentoring an additional student next semester."

"Starting from scratch with a new kid is always a challenge."

That was an understatement. "I like a challenge. But it does take a while to get them to trust me."

"*I* trust you."

I bumped shoulders with him. "I trust you too."

He leaned toward me for a kiss. Then he took a bite of the croissant and caught a stray crumb on his lip. "Are JoJo and Jonah coming to dinner tonight?"

"They are. I'm making lasagna." I swiveled my stool to look at him. "You like Jonah, don't you? Because they're serious."

Jeremy shuddered. "I do like him but it's hard for me to accept that I have a daughter who's getting serious about a boy."

"A man. He's a senior. And they aren't *getting* serious, they are serious."

"Like I said."

I turned toward the island again and recited, "'First comes love, then comes marriage, then comes a baby in a—'"

"Stop, Lyd! You're making me feel old. Having Theo, the king of the terrible twos running around here on Wednesdays makes me feel old enough."

"He's adorable and you know it."

"Too adorable for his own good." He took a sip of coffee. "Are Nova and Theo fully settled in at Betty and Bob's?"

"They are. Betty says the house feels complete again." It was happy news but it made me sad. I looked down at my coffee.

Jeremy stopped eating. "*You* don't seem thrilled."

I sighed. "You know me too well."

"So?"

I snitched a piece of his croissant. "Truth is, I'm jealous."

His eyebrows rose. "You want them to move in here?"

"No, no. I really don't want that. But Theo and I were just starting to get close and then his real grandma appears and takes over. Now she gets him all day Mondays and Fridays, not to mention every evening and weekend."

"They *are* his grandparents."

"I know."

"Plus, I'm sure this is a huge change for them."

Taking care of a toddler had been a huge change for us too.

"It's good he goes to preschool the other two days," Jeremy said.

"But that means I only get him one day a week. I know I'm missing out. He comes back every week knowing all sorts of new things." I thought of an example. "Do you know what a zebra sounds like?"

"Can't say as I do."

"Theo knows. Ask him next time you see him."

Jeremy chuckled. "Will do. But back to your jealousy. You have no reason to feel that way. Kids learn things from all over the place. Plus, without you, Nova would never have met Glen's parents. As Betty said, you helped their house feel complete again. All in all, everything has worked out great."

I knew he was right. "That reminds me, Nova really loves working in your office," I said. "But how's she doing? Honestly."

"Real good. She's a quick learner. And with her studying for her

GED in the evenings . . . she's in a good place."

"She is. She calls me for study help once in a while."

Jeremy stood to leave for work. "So stop feeling anything but good, Ms. Super Helper. You help kids at school, help with Theo, help Nova . . . and have a daughter who's supposedly in love. You are one busy lady."

"That I am."

"And you love it that way."

"That I do."

He kissed my cheek. "How about I come home early tonight and help the helper make dinner?"

I'd married a gem.

**

When I was twenty I would have been smitten with Jonah O'Neal. He was a witty, handsome redhead with an Irish accent. It was a no brainer.

JoJo had dated other guys, but for the most part they either tried too hard to impress us or didn't try hard enough. Jonah didn't have to try. He spoke easily, as if he was comfortable with who he was. That, in itself, was impressive. Plus, seeing how JoJo acted when she was with him . . .

It was clear our daughter was extremely happy and very much in love.

The four of us chatted through the lasagna dinner, and Jonah even helped clear the dishes.

He was a keeper.

When we were alone at the sink he said, "I have a question for you, Mrs. Brogdon."

"Lydia."

"Lydia. It's something I wanted to run by you first."

I panicked for a moment. Was he asking for JoJo's hand in marriage? Wasn't it tradition that he should ask Jeremy? But I said "Go ahead."

"My parents are having a big Thanksgiving dinner for my entire extended family and have invited JoJo to come along. They've met her but they haven't been able to spend much time with her yet. The catch is they live three hours west of here so that would mean JoJo wouldn't be here for your Thanksgiving."

My first reaction was relief that it wasn't the marriage question. But the second was gratitude that he'd even thought about us and our traditions.

I turned off the faucet and faced him. "I have a deal for you."

"What's that?"

"You can have JoJo at your family holiday if you come to our house Thanksgiving weekend to watch football."

Relief swept over his face. "Absolutely. I'd love to. We'd love to."

I gave him a little hug. "You're a good man, Jonah O'Neal."

I loved how his pale Irish skin turned a charming shade of red.

**

After the kids left I sat on the couch. The TV was on but I had no idea what was playing. My thoughts whirled around me, unable to land.

Jeremy came in the room, glanced at the TV, then me. "Since when do you like All Star wrestling?"

I had to laugh. I turned it off. "I'm not thinking real straight right now."

He sat next to me and pulled me under his arm. "What's wrong?"

I hadn't had a chance to tell him about the upcoming holiday. "JoJo is going to spend Thanksgiving with Jonah's family. They live three hours away."

I heard the breath go out of him. "Which means we'll be having our Thanksgiving alone?"

"It *is* inevitable," I said.

"But I'm not ready." He sounded so sad.

I sat up to look at him. "It'll be okay. I invited the two of them over that weekend to watch football and have a belated Thanksgiving. The Freemans are coming, and Nova and Theo. We'll have a belated houseful."

His face softened. "Our little family is expanding."

"God is amazing, isn't He?"

"Is that really a question?"

I snuggled against Jeremy's chest and rephrased it. "God *is* amazing."

CHAPTER THIRTY-NINE

Minnie

November

It is impossible to please God without faith.
Anyone who wants to come to him must believe that God exists
and that he rewards those who sincerely seek him.
Hebrews 11: 6

I went in the house and tossed my backpack on the couc "Mom? I'm home!"

When she didn't answer, I strolled through the rooms. She wasn anywhere. Maybe Hobby Lobby had called her in to work.

It wasn't a problem. With the extra free time I'd be able to har out with Gabe at the art store before I taught my kids' drawing class

I texted Mom, just so she'd know I'd stopped in. My phor immediately pinged and her return text surprised me: *We're outside.*

Sure enough, Mom was on the deck. And she wasn't alone.

"Hey there," she said.

"Hi, Minnie," John said.

"Hey, you two." John was Mom's boyfriend of three months. H was a nice guy who treated her well and made her happy. Tin would tell.

"See what we're making?" Mom asked.

The table was littered with artificial flowers, fruits, and sprigs this and that. "You're making a mess?"

She giggled. I always knew Mom was in love when she giggle "It's going to be a Christmas wreath," she said.

"She has orders for six more," John said.

"I've started a side business," Mom said. "Winsome Wreaths."

"When did this happen? I talked to you a few days ago and yc didn't mention it."

She smiled at John. "It was John's idea. I was making anoth wreath for a friend and he suggested I make it official and give m business a name. I got permission at work to post a flyer and . . ." Sh spread her hands over the mess. "Here we are."

John held up a wire-cutter. "My part is very important. I cut tl stems and bring her coffee." He winked at Mom.

"Oh you," Mom said. "If you hadn't encouraged me I never would have thought of it."

"Glad to be of service." He checked his watch and set the tool aside. "However . . . *I* have to get to work." He kissed her cheek. "I'll take you to dinner after I get off."

"That would be lovely."

After he left, I sat at the table. "I don't know what to comment on first, your flourishing business or your flourishing relationship with John."

Mom's sigh was one of deep contentment. "Both are pretty wonderful, aren't they?"

"They seem to be, but go slow. I don't want you to get hurt again."

"I don't want to get hurt either." Mom removed some unneeded leaves from a sprig of white flowers, then stopped working. "But this time . . . I really don't think I will be."

"What makes this time different?"

"You."

"Me? I've only met John a few times. He seems nice, and I like that he's supportive of you, but—" I thought of something awful. "He's not moving in, is he?"

"No, he's not." She smiled as she said it. "That's why I credit you for making this time different. Watching how you and Gabe are together has made me want that kind of love."

"What kind is—?"

She stopped my words with a hand. "I've been thinking about this a lot. When your father walked out I was lost and desperate to fill the hole he'd left in me. So I latched on to all sorts of men—pretty much any sort of man—hoping they'd fix me."

I gave her a look. "And we both know how that turned out."

Mom shook her head. "We do. I went all-in way too fast, hoping I could make them love me."

"But they didn't."

"And I didn't love them." Her face turned sad. "And I never should have married Roberto."

I remembered the scene I'd watched in the Room prior to their wedding. I'd wanted to talk to Mom about it, but never had.

"I need to confess something to you, Mom."

"What could *you* have to confess?"

I shoved a few flowers aside so I could lean my arms on the table. "Remember after the divorce, when Dad was taking me to the beach?"

"Oh I remember. He loved rubbing in how much he could give you that I couldn't. He wanted to hurt me more than he already had. He—"

I put my hand up before she said more. "That's not the point right now. The point is, before Dad and I left, you called his apartment wanting to talk to me."

"Did I? I don't remember talking to you." She took a seat across from me and her face lit up with a memory. "Actually, I didn't talk to you because you didn't answer. We didn't talk until . . ." she faltered.

"Until it was too late and you were married to Roberto."

"Which was one of the worst decisions I ever made." She stared at the wreaths, her thoughts lost in the past. "Do you want to know why I called that day?"

"You didn't like Dad taking me—"

She shook her head. "I called because I wanted you to talk me out of marrying him."

And there it was. "I should have been there for you, Mom." I smoothed a stray leaf against the table. "The truth is, when I saw your name on the ID I *chose* not to talk to you."

"Why?"

"Because I was young and stupid. And hurting. The divorce tore my whole life apart. You and Dad were always fighting and I was stuck in the middle. And then you let Roberto move in . . . the guy gave me the creeps."

"I'm sorry about that."

"Him living with us made everything more complicated. I didn't want to talk about it anymore. I just wanted to escape."

"With your father, who had a fancy apartment, and spoiled you with everything you ever wanted. He bribed you."

I shrugged. "It's not that hard to bribe a twelve-year-old."

"That's probably true."

"I bring this up because that phone call was a turning point. Maybe if I would've answered or even called you back, you wouldn't have married him." I wound a stray leaf around a finger. "Because I was a selfish kid, you suffered. You were going through bad times, but I only thought about myself." My voice broke. "I'm so sorry."

Mom came to my side of the table, pulling me up into a hug. "You don't have a selfish bone in your body, Minnie McLaughlin. Don't ever blame yourself for my mistakes. As far as the drama I had with Roberto? *I* made the choice to live with him and marry him. It was right that I suffered for my stupidity."

I held onto her, leaning my head against hers. My breath steadied as I went from feeling very young and vulnerable to feeling strong and capable. It was as if we gave each other strength.

She let go first. "Plus I learned something very important from that whole thing. After Roberto I never let a boyfriend move in. I still got involved with the wrong men, but I never let it get as far as it had with Roberto."

Very true. "So how do you feel about John?" I asked.

"How do *you* feel about John?"

"I don't know him, Mom, but he seems caring. And nice. Nicer than a lot of the others."

Mom snickered. "I hate that there were a lot of others."

I looked at her with different eyes. "You've changed since I moved out. You seem happier in your own skin. Lighter."

"Again, I give you the credit, Min. Seeing you follow your dreams and tapping into your creativity has been amazing. Plus I've seen you and Gabe go slow and easy with great results. I want that for myself." She smiled. "You've inspired me, sweetie. And me having to do things for myself . . . you challenged me." She hooked a thumb in her shirt. "I am now an independent businesswoman."

I laughed. "I'm glad."

Mom grinned. "And you know what else?"

She was like a young girl with a surprise. "What?"

"John and I have been going to church." She put a hand to her chest. "I know! Me? At church? It's a miracle."

It wasn't the only one.

**

I helped Mom finish a wreath then went to Art's to have lunch with Gabe before I taught my class. When I went in, he and the other clerk were both helping customers. The owner was straightening some chairs and tables in the corner of the store that we'd taken over for art lessons. "How are things going today?" I asked Art.

"Things are pretty perfect, Miss Minnie." He beamed.

"Perfect? I'll take some of that."

He waved a hand over the area. "*This* is perfect. Gabe kept bugging me to offer classes but I never got around to it. Truth is, I'm an old man who was tired and stuck in my ways."

"But now you like it?"

"There's nothing that makes me happier than seeing people take an interest in art."

"It helps sales too," I said.

He shook his head. "A secondary perk." He turned away from the tables and chairs. "How are *your* art classes going, Miss Minnie?

Are you learning a lot?"

I used his own words. "They're pretty perfect."

He beamed. "That's what happens when you find the place you belong."

Another customer came in, so Art excused himself to help.

Gabe finished checking out his customer while the other clerk was showing a woman acrylic paints.

"Whew," Gabe said when the customer left. "It's been a crazy morning." He gave me a quick kiss. "All ready for your class later?"

"I am. Art told me he really likes that we're teaching classes."

"He told that to me too."

Another customer came in. The chance that we'd be able to go out for lunch faded. "Do you want me to grab sandwiches and bring them back here?"

"That would be fabulous," he said as he went to help the customer.

I walked to a sandwich shop a block away and came back with lunch. Luckily, there was a lull.

"Quick! Let's eat." Gabe pulled me into the back room. We sat at a tiny break table and unwrapped our sandwiches. He took a bite. "Yum. Thanks for this."

"You're welcome."

He smiled and swept an arm to take in our surroundings. "You see how I've spared no expense to impress you. Not everyone gets to eat takeout in a storeroom next to boxes and cleaning supplies."

"I don't mind a bit." I leaned toward him and we kissed. "In fact, I think Art had the right words for the day."

"What'd he say?"

"He said things were pretty perfect." I waved a hand around the room. "Storeroom or not, this is pretty perfect because of your excellent company."

He smiled broadly and gave me another kiss. "I was going to tel you something at a better time and in a more suitable setting, but can't wait."

"What is it?"

"Like you said, Art is happy about the art classes. More tha happy. He told me they've convinced him that the store would be i good hands. And so—"

I gasped. "He's selling?"

He nodded. "He's selling me the store."

I popped out of my chair and leaned down to hug him. "That marvelous! I'm so happy for you!"

He stood and pulled me into his arms. "I'm happy for us."

I touched his cheek. "I love when you talk like that." I finally got a proper kiss. Kisses. Reluctantly, we let each other go.

"We are a pair, you and I," Gabe said, with his hands around my waist.

I nodded. "So many things fell into place to bring us together. God certainly knew what He was doing."

"And now we know what *we* are doing." He beamed. "We're buying the store!"

He picked me up and whirled me around in a perfect circle.

Perfect indeed.

Chapter Forty

Tony

So now I am giving you a new commandment: Love each other.
Just as I have loved you, you should love each other.
Your love for one another will prove to the world
that you are my disciples.
John 13: 34-35

I poured coffee in a mug, put in a hefty splash of milk, plus two sweeteners. I often kidded Gracie that she really wasn't drinking coffee with all that sweet in it. In turn, she thought my black coffee was disgusting and bitter. To each his own. I'd heard a hundred times that marriage was all about compromise. Funny how giving Gracie what *she* wanted came easy. I wanted to please her as much as she pleased me.

I set the mug on a breakfast tray that already contained a glass of orange juice and a plate of peanut butter toast—broiled to perfection. If it hadn't been November I would've cut a flower from the backyard.

Man, I was turning into a softie.

I took the tray into the bedroom where I'd left my Gracie sleeping. I cleared my throat.

She opened her eyes.

"Surprise, Tinkerbell!"

She blinked a few times and pushed herself to sitting. "Wow. Breakfast. You're so sweet."

I set the tray over her lap.

She grinned. "Broiled peanut butter?"

"In honor of our first meal together."

She motioned for me to come close and we kissed. "Morning, husband," she said.

"Morning, wife."

I still couldn't believe it.

"Aren't you eating?" she asked.

I sat on the side of the bed, being careful not to make the drink spill. "I'm too nervous."

"Zach will love his room. I know it."

I shrugged. "I know it too. But I'm nervous because this will b the first time he's got to spend the weekend with us. Here. At our home."

She laughed. "This is our first weekend together in the house too, my love. We just got back from our honeymoon last night."

I stood and leaned over the bed to kiss her again. "So we did. But I promise you, Mrs. Amato, our honeymoon is far from over."

**

Zach had helped a lot with the house remodel, but he hadn't seen it since it was done—and he hadn't seen his room since way before that because we'd wanted to surprise him.

The three of us stood at the closed bedroom door. I put my hands on his shoulders. "If you like it, it's my doing. If you don't, it's all Gracie's fault."

"Hey!" Gracie said.

Zach rolled his eyes, then smiled at his new stepmom. "Don't worry, Gracie. I know you're the one who picks out colors and furniture. Dad doesn't do good with stuff like that."

"Hey!" I said. But he was right. If it was up to me all the walls would have been painted white and the furniture would have been whatever was on sale.

"Can I go in now?" he asked.

"Go for it."

Zach opened the door, stepped in, and immediately stopped. "Whoa . . . this is so cool."

Yes!

He ran his hand along the gray metal bed frame, then bounced on the red comforter. "This bed is huge. At Mom's I have a small one."

Gracie adjusted a plaid pillow. "This is a queen because you're going to be tall like your Dad." She pointed at the bulletin board above the bed where she'd pinned some Royals posters. "I started you out with baseball stuff, but you can put whatever you want up there."

He grinned. "Baseball is good." He spotted the beanbag chair in the corner and fell onto it. "I can play video games from here."

I moved to the desk. "And over here you can do homework or draw or put Legos together. Speaking of . . . open the closet."

He slid the door open and took out the new Lego set I'd picked out. "No way!"

"To get you started," I said.

He turned the box all around to see the pictures. "It's the

Mandalorian Imperial Armored Marauder. I've been wanting this."

I chuckled. "I'm glad you like it."

He wrapped his arms around me. "Thanks, Dad. This is really amazing."

I pressed his always-messy hair against my chest. "You're welcome, bud."

Gracie got her own hug. Just seeing them together made me happy.

Just being together made me happy.

**

We left Zach alone so he could properly break in his room. He eventually came into the kitchen, "So? How's the room working for you?" I asked.

He slid onto a stool, eyeing the chocolate cake Gracie was frosting. "It's awesome. Can I have my friend Cody sleep over sometime?"

I was shocked—and pleased. "Sure. This is your house too."

"Tonight?"

I looked to Gracie, who handed each of us a beater to lick. "Not tonight, Zach," she said. "We're about to go pick up Nonna and Harvey to play cards. How about next Friday night?"

"That'll work. Can I call Cody right now though?" He slid off the stool.

"Of course," Gracie said.

Zach picked up the kitchen phone, but didn't dial. "Dad? The basement . . . did you finish it without me?"

"You know I wouldn't do that. I need you to help figure out our man cave."

He beamed. I beamed.

I could get used to this.

CHAPTER FORTY-ONE

Gracie

November

I pray that the eyes of your heart
may be enlightened
in order that you may know the hope
to which he has called you.
Ephesians 1: 18

We gave Nonna and Harvey a tour of the house. In return they gave us exactly the reaction we were looking for. Back in the living room Nonna turned in a slow circle. "Lovely, simply lovely. It's right out of a magazine."

"You have good taste, Gracie," Harvey said.

Tony pretended to take offense. "What about me?"

Harvey peered at him over his glasses. "I saw your apartment. This has to be Gracie's doing."

I slipped my hand around Tony's arm. "Actually, Penny helped with the ideas, and Tony was the one who got the work done."

Harvey flipped a hand at us. "I'm just joshing ya, Tony. You've turned into a fix-it man of the highest degree. Maybe you can remodel my apartment." He shook his head. "But maybe not. Then everybody will want you to do it."

"They'll have to get in line," Tony said. "Amato Remodeling is open for business."

Nonna raised her eyebrows. "Your own business?"

"Yup," he said.

I swear Tony stood taller.

"While remodeling this house, I met a lot of the neighbors. Then I started getting requests to work on their houses—including the remodel of a full basement and a kitchen. I have enough work for months."

"What about our man cave?" Zach asked.

"Don't worry. That's on the schedule too."

Zach looked relieved.

Tony motioned to me. "Your turn. Tell them about your business idea."

It was not as clearly thought out as Tony's.

Harvey shifted his weight from one leg to the other. I gestured toward the other room. "Let's sit in the dining room and I'll tell you about it."

"Can we have the chocolate cake?" Zach asked.

"Oooh," Nonna said. "My favorite."

"Everybody's favorite," Harvey said.

"Hold your horses, bud," Tony said.

I waited until everyone got settled. If the conversation moved on to something else, I was okay with that.

But my husband didn't let it go. "Come on, Gracie. Tell them about your business." He gave me an encouraging nod.

"Okay. You asked for it . . . My idea is a little out-there, and not totally formed yet."

"As are most ideas," Harvey said.

I wasn't sure where to start.

Once again Tony came to my rescue. "As you all know, Gracie was a caregiver to her parents for fourteen years. She was virtually stuck in this house with no relief."

It was the perfect opening. "While I was stuck here, I started posting online, venting and asking questions. It ended up reaching a lot of people who were in the same situation."

"And it's really taken off," Tony said.

I nodded. "The point is, amid all the shared frustrations there is a common need: everyone longs for a break. Which got me thinking . . . Maybe I could do more than just talk about it, I could offer local caregivers a break—some relief—by going on errands for them, or taking care of their family member so *they* could go on errands or even go for a cup of coffee or to see a movie."

Zach's eyes lit up. "Like a relief pitcher in baseball."

I smiled. "Very much like that. We have a lot of details to work out, and I'm still working full time at the Discovery Room, but I really want to help people who feel trapped like I did."

"Gracie's Break Time," Harvey said.

It wasn't a bad name.

Nonna reached across the table and put her hand on mine. "It's wonderful idea, Gracie. You're a natural."

"All your suffering was not in vain," Harvey said. "Your da took advantage of your serving spirit, but God intended all of it fo good. He brought you to this point so you could save the lives many people."

"I'm not going to *save* anybody, but—"

"You don't know that," Harvey said. "You just might."

I shivered.

Tony clapped his hands together once and pointed at me. "See that, Harvey? She shivered. Tell her what you told me."

I had no idea what they were talking about.

But Harvey answered. "God sometimes talks in shivers when we're on the same page as He is."

"Oooh," Nonna said. "I like that. And I believe it."

I shivered again.

"See? Look at that!" Tony said.

"Two times!" Zach said.

"God's definitely talking to you," Nonna said.

I pressed a hand against my chest and felt my heart swell. "I . . . I hope that's true."

Nonna squeezed my hand. "Of course it is," she said. "God likes your idea as much as we do."

My throat tightened. I was overcome by their constant support. This give and take, this bonding and encouragement was everything I'd ever wanted. I cleared my throat to speak. "I need to tell all of you that . . . I haven't felt so loved since my mother was alive."

Zach made the moment perfect by giving me a hug.

**

After playing cards at our house, the five of us got in the car to take everybody home. It did my heart good to see Zach and Tony helping Nonna into her house, and soon after, getting Harvey to his apartment. I waved each one goodbye.

The guys came back to the car. "Next stop, Zach's house," Tony said.

"I wish I could stay longer with you guys," Zach said. "I love my new room."

"I'm so glad, bud. But we'll see you and Cody next Friday."

"Can Cody help plan the man cave?"

Tony chuckled. "We can use all the help we can get."

As soon as we pulled away from the curb I asked for a detour. "Before we let Zach off, I'd like to stop by the office on the chance Wesley is there. I want to tell him we're back from our honeymoon. And I'd like to let him see Zach again."

"And see how happy we are?" Zach said.

"Absolutely."

"Can't you wait until tomorrow when you work?" Tony asked.

"I could, but . . ." A weird feeling washed over me. Since Tony and I had lived through a lot of weird I just said it. "I have a gut feeling we should go there now."

"Whatever you say." He turned in that direction. "I still can't believe you don't have a phone number for him."

"Wesley's tight with the personal info. I have no idea where he lives either." I started second-guessing myself. "Actually, we don't have to go. It's Sunday. He's probably not even there."

"Is he the guy from the wedding that kinda looks like Star Wars' Obi-Wan Kenobi without a beard?" Zach asked. "The one who always looks like he has a secret."

I laughed. "Yes, on both accounts."

"I want to see him again," Zach said. "He's cool."

We headed to the Discovery Room. I'd been gone a whole week while we were honeymooning in Colorado. I'd offered to set up a temp for Wesley, but he'd told me not to worry about it.

As soon as we pulled into the parking lot, I noticed something was very wrong. The sign on the windows was gone. We parked and I jumped out of the car and ran to the front door. It was locked, but I could see through the windows that something big had happened. The desk and chairs were gone. The coffee bar table was in the middle of the room with a box of mugs and supplies on top of it. The landscape picture from my house leaned against the table. And my plant was there with its long tendrils carefully wound together in a pile.

"Use your key," Tony said.

We went inside and found an empty shell, drywall gone—the walls stripped down to the studs. I ran into the Room, but all the curves were gone. It was just a square room. Generic. Blah. Nothing to hint at the amazing things that had happened under its dome.

"Where did it all go?" Tony asked.

"Why did it all go?" I asked.

Tony strolled around the perimeter. "Did Wesley give you any hint he was closing up shop?"

"Nothing." I felt hurt. "Why wouldn't he tell me? I've been with him since the beginning."

"That's pretty rude," Tony said.

It was. "I thought we were close, but I guess not."

Tony put an arm around my shoulders. "You were close. He came to our wedding."

He was. We were close.

Tony walked toward the door. "Maybe someone bought the entire strip mall. I'll go next door to the liquor store and see—"

"Liquor store?" I said. "There's no liquor store around here."

"Sure there is. Right next door. With a sports shop on the other side."

Now he was being ridiculous. "I don't know what you're talking about. There's a vitamin store and a pet supply store."

He shook his head. "Gracie, are you blind?"

He was the one who was blind—and I'd show him. We went outside and walked to the right where the vitamin store was—or used to be. It was empty.

Tony pulled up short. He ran past our office to the other side and said, "Here too! Everything is completely cleared out."

I felt faint and leaned against the car. "Where did it all go? Where is Wesley? Why didn't he tell me anything?"

"Maybe his work here was done."

I didn't buy that. I swiped a hand toward the street and beyond. "We had a lot of people come in, but there are tons more that needed to be invited."

"Tons more?" Tony smiled.

I didn't feel like smiling. "I liked my job. And I really, really liked Wesley."

"Maybe he'll contact you and explain," Tony said.

"Wesley explain? That's never been his style. Obviously he doesn't feel the need this time either. He just left." I felt betrayed and more than a little sad.

Tony pulled me upright. "Let's get your stuff. You can worry about this tomorrow."

We went inside and between Tony and Zach they got the table, picture, and box put into the back of the SUV. I picked up the plant—

An envelope fell to the floor.

I held it up, examining it. "Guys. Look at this."

"It has your name on it," Tony said. "It's probably your paycheck."

I hoped it was far more than that.

I opened the envelope. Inside was a check, but also a letter. I read aloud: "'My good Gracie. Forgive my sudden departure, but do not be afraid. All is well. You are well and God approves of your good work at the Discovery Room and with Gracie's Break Time." I stopped. "How did he know the name of my business?"

"Harvey just thought of it tonight," Zach said.

"What else does he say?" Tony asked.

I returned to where I'd left off. "'Be assured that you and Tony *have* discovered your unique purposes. Now you have the pleasure of living them out together. Do not worry after me, for having completed my assigned task, I am in the presence of our Lord.'"

"He's dead?" Tony asked.

"Really?" Zach said.

I shook my head. "Surely it can't mean that."

"Does he say anything else?"

I silently read ahead, then clapped a hand to my mouth.

"What's wrong?" Zach asked.

I handed the letter to Tony. He skimmed what I'd read, his face lighting up as he got to the words that surprised me. "Whoa. Do you really think he means what I think he means?"

I nodded and smiled. "I think he means exactly what we think it means."

"What's it say?" Zach asked again.

Tony read the words out loud. "It's a Bible verse. Hebrews thirteen-two. It says, 'Don't forget to show hospitality to strangers, for some who have done this have entertained angels without realizing it.'" He looked up. "Wesley is telling us he's an angel?"

"He's an angel?" Zach repeated.

"Of course he is," I said with a laugh. "I'd thought it was possible, but I never let myself fully believe it. Yet think back to the many times Wesley seemed *more* than human."

"Like knowing things he couldn't have known," Tony said.

"He knew about Gracie's Break Time," Zach said.

"He did," I said. "Wesley being an angel would explain how he could come and go at just the right times, and how he could say things like he was speaking for God."

Tony paced in front of the windows. "It would explain how he could appear as a clerk at Home Depot—complete with the orange apron and a nametag, yet never work there."

My heart beat double-time with the wonder of it all. "Everything about the Room was beyond real. It was supernatural. Everyone wondered how the movies had been made, and how things of importance glowed, but Wesley always skirted the question."

"It was God," Tony said simply.

"God? God-god?" Zach asked.

"You got it, bud."

I took the letter from Tony and read it again, to myself. The cursive writing was perfect as if it were penned by a calligrapher. I smiled at the thought of Wesley the angel, writing the words. "This—all of this—is God's doing. Wesley is God's doing."

"Did he have wings?" Zach asked.

"Not that we could see." I smiled. "Humanly speaking, all this is impossible."

"Wesley would say nothing is impossible for God."

"Nothing." I felt full to overflowing. And then I had another thought that added to the blessing. "I was worried about working full time while I tried to start up my new business. But now — "

"Now, you don't have to," Tony said. "You're free."

I drew in a deep breath. "What a wonderful word, *free.*"

"God arranged all of it, didn't He?" Tony said.

"Every single thing," I said.

I gazed at the two men in my life — two good men I wouldn't have met if not for this. We were a new family created from three bruised souls.

"Come here, you two." I pulled them into a three-way hug. "Thank You, Jesus," I said.

"I second that," Tony said.

"I third it," Zach said.

I smiled as I imagined Wesley's one-word response to our prayers.

Indeed.

THE END

**

I am convinced that nothing
can ever separate us from God's love.
Neither death nor life, neither angels nor demons,
neither our fears for today
nor our worries about tomorrow —
not even the powers of hell can separate us from God's love.
Romans 8: 38

Letter to the Reader

This book has been in on my mind since September 1997—for 25 years! It started with me being forgetful. I was going on errands to look at curtain fabric. When I realized I'd forgotten my wallpaper samples I had to turn around. I was annoyed at myself but suddenly thought *what if God got me to turn around to save me from an accident?* Of course, I would never know. I couldn't prove He'd saved me, but the notion of His intervention was strong and lasting.

The intervention idea repeated itself a lot during the next twenty-five years. My eyes were opened to other possible God-interventions:

- In the early 2000s I happened to sit next to a woman named Carolyn in chorus. We hit it off immediately and the sound of our combined voices was yummy. Soon she started going to my church and we were in choir together. Then she was invited to join an octet I sang with (Seeds of Faith) and later we both joined in the creation of another singing group (Vocalease.) All because we *happened* to si next to each other one Tuesday. Chance? I think not.
- My brother-in-law Jim was called up during the Vietnam War Advanced Infantry Training the sergeant said, "Form two lines.' One line went to Vietnam. Jim's line went to Germany. Chance? think not.
- My husband Mark and I would not have married if not for the fac that his best friend didn't get accepted into an out-of-state universit they planned to attend. Instead they both went to a loca university—where I was going. Mark and I were both workin toward an architecture degree. We married after our sophomor year. It's been 47 years now. Chance? I think not.
- In 2015 the publishing world went through turbulent times as th introduction of eBooks changed everything. One of my publishe who'd given me a 3-book contract suddenly went out-of-business. was without a contract for the first time in 19 years! It was hea wrenching. Yet in my panic and pain I got the idea to learn how

publish my own books and eBooks. After clawing my way up and over a huge learning curve, Mustard Seed Press was born. Since then I've published 14 new books, and reissued 29 old titles—books that would be dead if not for the reissue. In retrospect I see that losing that 3-book contract was one of the best things to ever happen to my career. God needed to take everything away in order for me to broaden my path. Chance? I think not.

I could go on and on. I'm sure *you* could think of many of your own non-coincidences. It's said that a coincidence is when God works a miracle and decides to remain anonymous. He does often remain anonymous, but I believe He wants us to know it's Him—and gives us hints, if only we open our eyes. It's so special when those *aha!* moments of revelation happen, when we see the puzzle pieces fit together. *If not for this* moments are precious and extremely meaningful. If only they would glow!

Although many of our moments have big consequences and outcomes, many are more subtle. But it's often not the big events that shape us as much as the connections and the relationships that come out of the smaller, daily events. They are the threads that weave together to become our lives, weave together into the most important relationship of our lives—our relationship with our Heavenly Father.

My biggest desire for you, dear reader, is to open your eyes to what God is doing in your life right now, ponder what He has already done, and be ready for what He might do in your tomorrows! Look for the signs of His presence—the crosses in the sky (like the picture above, like Tony sees in Chapter 27.) Above all be aware of our Lord! Look for His hand. I guarantee you will find it. And find Him.

And the peace of God, which transcends all understanding,
will guard your hearts and your minds in Christ Jesus.
Finally, brothers and sisters, whatever is true, whatever is noble,
whatever is right, whatever is pure,
whatever is lovely, whatever is admirable
—if anything is excellent or praiseworthy—think about such things.
Whatever you have learned or received or heard from me,
or seen in me—put it into practice.
And the God of peace will be with you.
Philippians 4: 7-9

Blessings to you on your journey,

Nancy Moser

VERSES IN *IF NOT FOR THIS*

All verses NLT except as noted
Verses marked (P) are paraphrased

Dedication:	Blessings	Psalm 31: 19
Prologue	Possibilities	Matthew 21: 21
Chapter 1	Good people	Proverbs 14: 14
Chapter 2	God's direction	Psalm 37: 23
	Opportunities	Matthew 7: 7
Chapter 3	Endurance	James 1: 2-8
Chapter 4	Good work	Galatians 6: 4
Chapter 5	Fearing the Lord	Psalm 111: 10
Chapter 6	Mercy	Psalm 103: 8-9
Chapter 7	Getting help	Psalm 102: 17
Chapter 8	Giving	2 Corinthians 9: 7
Chapter 9	God's watching	Proverbs 5: 21
Chapter 10	Giving up fear	Isaiah 41: 10
	Mind of God	1 Corinthians 2: 11
(P) Chapter 11	Doing God's will	Psalm 143: 10
Chapter 12	Mercy	Proverbs 28: 13
Chapter 13	God hears	Psalm 10: 17
Chapter 14	God knows us	Jeremiah 17: 10
Chapter 15	Comfort	Psalm 34: 18
	The right road	Matthew 7: 14
Chapter 16	Doing good	Galatians 6: 9
Chapter 17	Helping the poor	Proverbs 14: 21
	Praying all the time	1 Thess. 5:17 (ESV)
Chapter 18	Praising God	Psalm 73: 24-26
Chapter 19	Finding strength	2 Corinthians 16: 13
Chapter 20	Gifts	Romans 12: 6
	Asking God	James 4: 2 (NIV)
	Plans	Proverbs 16: 9
	Who needs God?	Luke 5: 31
	Lukewarm	Revelation 3: 15-16
	Seek and find	Matthew 7: 7
Chapter 21	Gaining Wisdom	Proverbs 1: 23
Chapter 22	God's help	Psalm 61: 1-2
Chapter 23	God's promises	2 Peter 1: 4
	Created with purpose	Jeremiah 1: 5
Chapter 24:	Using our blessings	Matthew 25: 29
	Truth	John 8: 32
Chapter 25:	Seek God	Matthew 6: 33

Chapter 26:	Running the race	Hebrews 12: 1-2
Chapter 27	Mysteries of God	Isaiah 45: 15
Chapter 28:	Working	Colossians 3: 23-24
	Purpose	Psalm 138: 8 (P)
Chapter 29:	Being afraid	Psalm 27: 1
	Sharing lessons	Matthew 10: 27
(NIV)		
	Trust	Proverbs 3: 5-6
Chapter 30:	Serving	Romans 12: 7
Chapter 31:	Forgiveness	1 John 1: 9
	Confession	James 5: 16
	Freedom	John 8: 36
Chapter 32:	Being Forgiven	Isaiah 44: 22
	Forgiveness	Ephesians 4: 31-32
Chapter 33:	Being strong	1 Corinthians 16: 13
Chapter 34:	Jesus	John 3: 16
Chapter 35:	Love	1 Corinthians 13: 13
Chapter 36:	Help each other	Isaiah 1: 17
Chapter 37:	Courage	Psalm 31: 24
Chapter 38:	Love	1 Thessalonians 4: 9
Chapter 39:	Faith and rewards	Hebrews 11: 6
Chapter 40:	Love	John 13: 34-35
Chapter 41:	Open your eyes	Ephesians 1: 18
(NIV)		
	Good from bad	Genesis 50: 20 (P)
	Angels	Hebrews 13: 2
	Miracles	Matthew 19: 26 (P)
	God with us	Romans 8: 38

Discussion Questions

1. Why do you think the invitations to the Discovery Room didn't specify a time?

2. Each character sees the stores on either side of the Discovery Room differently. Tony sees a liquor store and a sports shop. Lydia sees a quilt store and a beauty parlor. Minnie sees a bead shop and book store. And Gracie sees a vitamin store and a pet supply store. Why do you think that's so?

3. Chapter 9: Lydia is relieved that she can talk openly about God to Wesley. "I was so used to watching my words while out in the world. To be able to speak freely about God was a relief." Have you ever felt this way? Do you find it difficult to speak about God in our secular world? Why?

4. Chapter 9 and 10: While she's in the Room Lydia embraces what she sees, eager to learn. As such, Wesley shows her a "bonus" scene that shows how she got her job. God often gives more to those who are faithful. Matthew 11: 29 says, "To those who use well what they are given, even more will be given, and they will have an abundance. But from those who do nothing, even what little they have will be taken away." Discuss how this verse plays out in real life.

5. Chapter 15: Gracie asks Wesley if there's one client he's looking forward to having in the Room. He says Minnie: "She may not need the Room more than anyone else, yet I feel a soft spot for her." Why do you think he feels this way?

6. Chapter 19: When Minnie talks about her family, Wesley says, "Intellect plus emotion equals intuition." What do you think this means? Do you agree?

7. Chapter 20: Wesley asks Minnie where she sees herself in ten years if the sky's the limit, no restrictions. How would you answer this question?

8. Chapter 20: Minnie didn't ask her parents about entering an art contest, assuming they would say no. She finds out different. Have you ever *not* asked for something and later found out you could've had it? James 4: 2 says, "You do not have because you do not ask God." Is there something you should ask God for?

9. Chapter 23: Harvey's life lessons: people matter, everybody has God-given gifts, time is short, and God *is*. Which life lesson is hardest for you to embrace?

10. Chapter 26: Minnie has told her Dad, Claudia (and later in Chapter 37, her mom) a little about the Room. But when her dad asks *how* she knows things, she realizes he won't understand the mystical workings of the Room. So she adjusts her explanation to reach her family where they are. Jesus and His disciples did the same thing, adjusting God's message to their audience. If you'd spent time in the Room, how much would you tell your spouse or best friend?

11. Chapter 28: Wesley invited Gracie to the Room many times. And in Chapter 15 he'd even told her not to wait too long or she might miss her chance. "It's like an unseen clock was ticking down the minutes." How is this an analogy for believing in Jesus?

12. Chapter 29: Wesley helped Gracie realize what she learned during her hard times gave her skills she wouldn't have gotten any other way. What skills have you learned in your hard times?

13. Chapter 31: Nonna says, "The life lessons we remember most are best learned by living through them, not being hit over the head with them." Do you think she's right? What life lesson did you learn the hard way?

14. Chapter 35: Lydia believes that the company sending a Jesus board-book instead of the bunny-one she'd ordered for Theo was a God-thing. What do you think about her belief?

15. Share one or two "if not for this" situations from your own life. Keep thinking about this and start a list.

About the Author

NANCY MOSER is the best-selling author of over 40 novels, novellas, and children's books, including Christy Award winner *Time Lottery* and Christy finalist *Washington's Lady.* She's written nineteen historical books including *Love of the Summerfields, Masquerade, Where Time Will Take Me*, and *Just Jane. An Unlikely Suitor* was named to Booklist's "Top 100 Romance Novels of the Decade." *The Pattern Artist* was a finalist in the Romantic Times Reviewers Choice award. Some of her contemporary novels are: *An Undiscovered Life, The Invitation, Solemnly Swear, The Good Nearby, If Not for This, Crossroads, The Seat Beside Me*, and the Sister Circle series. *Eyes of Our Heart* was a finalist in the Faith, Hope, and Love Readers' Choice Awards. Nancy has been married for over 47 years—to the same man. She and her husband have three grown children, eight grandchildren, and live in the Midwest. She's been blessed with a varied life. She's earned a degree in architecture, run a business with her husband, traveled extensively in Europe, and has performed in various theaters, symphonies, and choirs. She knits voraciously, kills all her houseplants, and can wire an electrical fixture without getting shocked. She is a fan of anything antique—humans included.

Website: www.nancymoser.com
Blogs: Author blog: www.authornancymoser.blogspot.com
History blog: www.footnotesfromhistory.blogspot.com
Facebook: www.facebook.com/nancymoser.author
Bookbub: www.bookbub.com/authors/nancy-moser?list=author_ books
Goodreads:
www.goodreads.com/author/show/117288.Nancy_Moser
Pinterest: www.pinterest.com/nancymoser1/_saved/
Instagram: www.instagram.com/nmoser33/

Want more "Magical Realism" books?

EXCERPT FROM *THE INVITATION*

JULIA CARSON STARED out the window of the bus and smiled at the children waiting for her.

"Stop here, Murray," she told the driver of the Book Bus.

Murray stopped the vehicle in front of the Minneapolis Magnet summer school. Two dozen children ages six through fourteen waved at their ex-governor.

"Is it always like this?" Murray asked. He was new on the job.

"Word is definitely getting around." Julia waved at the children through the window. "Some of these kids have never owned a book, so getting a free one every time I come makes it feel like Christmas—for all of us."

"Ho, ho, ho," Murray said.

Julia put a hand on his shoulder. "Hey, I'll take one happy kid over a dozen grumpy politicians any day."

Murray opened the door, and Julia stepped out amid cheers and hugs. She found the open adulation satisfying but also embarrassing. All this gratitude for a few books, for something that was a basic need in every child's development. She vowed as long as she and Edward had money to fund the Book Bus, it would continue.

"Mrs. Carson, Mrs. Carson, I read my last book two times already," said a little boy whose oversized T-shirt skimmed his knees.

She put a hand on top of his head. "I'm proud of you, David. Are you ready for another one?" He nodded, looking up at her with dark eyes. She leaned close and whispered. "Do you want to go first?"

He smiled like he'd won the lottery.

"Me, too!" said ten-year-old Telisha. "I finished *Little House in the Big Woods* all by myself."

Julia tugged her hair affectionately. "Then you shall be second."

David and Telisha's good fortune spurred the other children to all talk at once as they vied for Julia's approval. She was relieved when the director of the summer school clapped her hands, quieting them.

"Get in line, kids. You know the rules. Six at a time. No dawdling when it's your turn. Mrs. Carson will help if you have questions."

The children got in line with a minimum of commotion. There was another cheer as Murray exited the bus carrying a crate of juice boxes and three packages of cookies.

Julia eased her way past the children and entered the bus. She stood in the door. "David, Telisha, come on in. And then you, Sarah? Is that your name? You and Gaylord and Grant, and we'll end the first group with the handsome young man with the gorgeous smile . . . yes, that's you, kiddo. Come, children."

The children scrambled in, shoulders bumping shoulders as they jockeyed for position near their favorite bookshelf. Julia loved this part. She delighted in helping each child pick out a special book they could take home forever. Books had been such an important part of her childhood. One of her most precious memories was her family's evening ritual: after the dinner dishes were cleared, her father had read to them around the walnut dining table with the tatted lace tablecloth. It was there that Julia had been introduced to Oliver Twist, D'Artagnan, and Anna Karenina.

If only she could do the same for all the children who searched the limited shelves of the Book Bus. With a hot meal warming their stomachs, she'd gather them close and safe and read aloud to them. She'd marvel as their faces glowed while they absorbed the ageless stories.

Julia's attention was brought back to the crowded bus by the sound of a book falling to the floor. "Don't grab, Sarah. There are plenty of books for all of you." She retrieved the book. *"Christy,"* Julia said, reading the title as she handed it to the girl. "A very good choice." Sarah beamed and held the book to her chest as she headed for the door.

Julia watched the little girl step out of the way so a middle-aged woman could enter the bus. *Probably someone's mother or grandmother,* she thought. The woman's clothes were rumpled, and a wisp of black hair pointed left when it should have pointed right. Her eyes studied the titles of some young-adult books. She seemed to be looking for something.

"May I help you, ma'am?" Julia asked.

When the woman turned to look at her, Julia felt an odd jolt pass through her. She had the kindest eyes. They were the eyes of an old friend, yet Julia was certain they'd never met.

"Do you know anything about Haven?"

The woman's question pulled Julia out of her thoughts. "Haven? I don't think I've heard of it. I'm afraid we don't have adult books." She looked around at the children, trying to match one of them with the woman. Then she thought of something, "Haven? Perhaps you mean *The Raven?* The poem by Edgar Allan Poe?"

The woman smiled. "No, Julia. I mean Haven." She held out a creamy white envelope.

Julia took it, then looked at the woman. "What's this?"

"You've been chosen, Julia. You have things to do." With that she moved toward the door.

Julia frowned, confused. "Things to do? What are you talking about?"

As the woman stepped onto the pavement, she turned back and pointed to the envelope, then gave Julia a wink.

"Mrs. Carson? Mrs. Carson?" A child tugged at Julia's skirt. "David took *The Dawn Treader* and I wanted that one. Do you have another copy?"

Julia watched the woman walk away from the Book Bus.

"Mrs. Carson? Do you?"

Julia let her attention return to the immediate needs of the little girl. "I'll bring a copy for you next time, Telisha. I'll even put your name on it. Why don't you pick another book for today."

Telisha nodded and wove her way down the aisle to find another book.

Julia looked down at the envelope in her hand. Her name was written in an elegant cursive across the front. She slid a finger under the flap, breaking the seal. She removed an ivory card. Along the side was a botanical drawing of a broad-leafed plant bearing a cluster of small flowers.

"Mrs. Carson, can you help me find a book about spaceships?"

Julia held up a hand, her eyes scanning the contents of the card. "I'll be right with . . ." She trailed off.

Julia Eugenia Carson is invited to Haven, Nebraska.
Please arrive August 1.
"If you have faith as small as a *mustard seed,*
you can say to this mountain,
'Move from here to there' and it will move.
Nothing will be impossible for you."

"Haven?" Julia mumbled. (continued . . .)

BUY *The Invitation* on AMAZON: Book 1 of the Mustard Seed Series

Made in the USA
Monee, IL
28 December 2022

23654232R00177